Praise for

AURIEL RISING

"A fast-paced historical thriller that intertwines alchemy with political and sexual intrigue and religious hatred with unbridled violence . . . vivid characterizations and colorful descriptions of a squalid London." —*Library Journal*

"Intelligent." —*The New York Times*

"Richly atmospheric . . . Redfern's strength is in re-creating a morally corrupt world obsessed with the letter's mystical-sounding abstractions." —*Publishers Weekly*

"Bring[s] another era of British history vividly to life . . . Redfern makes a complicated web of allegiances and betrayals accessible and interesting, adding just the right dose of violence and romance to her well-researched tale." —*Booklist*

"[A] smashing climax." —*Kirkus Reviews* (starred)

"[A] superb historical . . . Elizabeth Redfern captures the mood of England less than a decade after the death of Elizabeth I, adding background depth to a one-of-a-kind fascinating reading experience." —*BookBrowser*

Praise for

THE MUSIC OF THE SPHERES

A *USA Today* Bestseller

"A period brainteaser reminiscent of Caleb Carr's *The Alienist*." —*People*

"An enthralling story of espionage and murder, madness and obsession . . . Redfern's story is as spooky as a Jack the Ripper tale, but with its multiple layers of plots, more intellectually engaging." —*Chicago Tribune*

continued . . .

"Quite wonderful . . . For readers who like atmosphere, history, a few corpses, dissolute French aristocrats, and a moving reconciliation . . . It is Redfern's ability to bring each scene, each character alive that makes this such toothsome reading."
—*USA Today*

"Intricately plotted, beautifully paced, *The Music of the Spheres* is an elegant historical novel, rich in detail, at times Dickensian in its depiction of London. Elizabeth Redfern has made an exciting debut."
—Martha Grimes

"Unputdownable . . . [a] remarkable debut . . . a glittering tale of London in 1795, full of science, intrigue, war, revolution, and obsessive passion."
—*The Guardian* (London)

"Ambitious and challenging . . . rich in astronomical lore and historical detail."
—*The Times-Picayune*

"As if John Le Carré has gone Age of Enlightenment on us . . . As if *Silence of the Lambs* has been reset in the Napoleonic Era . . . seamlessly incorporates the diverse elements of historical fiction, romance novels, and spy thrillers."
—*Booklist*

"A worthy companion to such successful literary historical fiction as Iain Pears's *An Instance of the Fingerpost* . . . its multiple harmonies enchant and satisfy the senses."
—*Kirkus Reviews* (starred)

"The author has a gift for creating vivid images of eighteenth-century London."
—*Fort Worth Star-Telegram*

"The whole universe is grist for Redfern's story."
—*Arkansas Democrat-Gazette*

"Astronomical and political intrigue, a complex Jacques the Ripper subplot, and dissident French aristocrats on the run from the Terror . . . gripping."   —*Time Out* (London)

"A masterful piece of period suspense fiction . . . set against the aftermath of the French Revolution . . . Like Patrick Suskind's *Perfume* and David Liss's *A Conspiracy of Paper*, this intensely atmospheric historical suspense novel is alive with the sights and sounds of the day . . . Solidly grounded in the history of a perilous time, the novel's imagery and characterization bring eighteenth-century London to life with its contrasts of wealth and squalor, poverty and power, and people it with a compelling cast of finely drawn characters acting out an intricate and powerful human drama."   —*BookPage*

"I found this novel unputdownable. The complex narrative is brilliantly handled to keep the reader guessing right to the end, [with] some ingenious surprises along the way. The colourful background is an atmospheric and evocative re-creation of London in the 1790s, with all the complex political and diplomatic intrigues of that wartime era."
—Charles Palliser

"*The Music of the Spheres* has everything! An outstanding, guilty pleasure."   —Sarah Smith

AURIEL
RISING

ELIZABETH REDFERN

JOVE BOOKS, NEW YORK

THE BERKLEY PUBLISHING GROUP
Published by the Penguin Group
Penguin Group (USA) Inc.
375 Hudson Street, New York, New York 10014, USA
Penguin Group (Canada), 10 Alcorn Avenue, Toronto, Ontario M4V 3B2, Canada
(a division of Pearson Penguin Canada Inc.)
Penguin Books Ltd., 80 Strand, London WC2R 0RL, England
Penguin Group Ireland, 25 St. Stephen's Green, Dublin 2, Ireland (a division of Penguin Books Ltd.)
Penguin Group (Australia), 250 Camberwell Road, Camberwell, Victoria 3124, Australia
(a division of Pearson Australia Group Pty. Ltd.)
Penguin Books India Pvt. Ltd., 11 Community Centre, Panchsheel Park, New Delhi—110 017, India
Penguin Group (NZ), Cnr. Airborne and Rosedale Roads, Albany, Auckland 1310, New Zealand
(a division of Pearson New Zealand Ltd.)
Penguin Books (South Africa) (Pty.) Ltd., 24 Sturdee Avenue, Rosebank, Johannesburg 2196,
South Africa

Penguin Books Ltd., Registered Offices: 80 Strand, London WC2R 0RL, England

This is a work of fiction. Names, characters, places, and incidents either are the product of the author's imagination or are used fictitiously, and any resemblance to actual persons, living or dead, business establishments, events, or locales is entirely coincidental.

AURIEL RISING

A Jove Book / published by arrangement with the author

PRINTING HISTORY
G. P. Putnam's Sons hardcover edition / March 2004
Jove mass-market edition / May 2005

Copyright © 2004 by Elizabeth Redfern.

All rights reserved.
No part of this book may be reproduced, scanned, or distributed in any printed or electronic form without permission. Please do not participate in or encourage piracy of copyrighted materials in violation of the author's rights. Purchase only authorized editions.
For information address: The Berkley Publishing Group,
a division of Penguin Group (USA) Inc.,
375 Hudson Street, New York, New York 10014.

ISBN: 0-515-13942-4

JOVE®
Jove Books are published by The Berkley Publishing Group,
a division of Penguin Group (USA) Inc.,
375 Hudson Street, New York, New York 10014.
JOVE is a registered trademark of Penguin Group (USA) Inc.
The "J" design is a trademark belonging to Penguin Group (USA) Inc.

PRINTED IN THE UNITED STATES OF AMERICA

10 9 8 7 6 5 4 3 2 1

If you purchased this book without a cover, you should be aware that this book is stolen property. It was reported as "unsold and destroyed" to the publisher, and neither the author nor the publisher has received any payment for this "stripped book."

PROLOGUE

To Auriel, I will give the gift of gold.

After the night of long and false captivity, the golden SUN is about to rise, and all this by the power of the Stone, *lapis ex caelis;* for be sure that as Auriel rises the LION shall fall.

Qui non intelligit aut discat aut taceat.

Calcination

In *spiritus vini* is the base material first engulfed, then nurtured in a sealed vessel on the consecrated athanor, bearing the sign that also nurtures many pilgrims. Let the earthly part be well calcined.

Separation

And INSTRUMENTS OF FIRE will be kindled close to the lair of the Scorpion. Be sure that when the NOBLE PRINCE is laid low in spirit through the threat of union with that same Scorpion, then must the actuated mercury be added, in the fashion of *navicularius*, in judicious incitement to princely war.

Digestion

Next cast the native birds of righteousness into a prison with the alien beast—*cinis et lixivium.* Add scrupulous antimony in this manner; so that the ingredients may be incensed to fight by the sulfurous vapour arising from doleful *planities*. But beware, for if the concoction manifests too early a disposition for ignition, the Scorpion will devour both Prince and Lion.

Putrefaction

Now, from the putrefaction of the dead carcass of hope, a fruitful CROW will be generated, base at first, but which little by little stretching out his wings will begin to fly with his precious seeds, aided by ATTRAMENTUM; and when the emblem of MORUS is strewn throughout the land, then is the time for the rebirth.

Albedo

Increase the fire till the glorious rainbow of the East appears, which is the CAUDA PAVONIS. Behold, MERCATOR grows to full size with great fanfares and explosions. Accordingly you must heat and ripen the princely white tincture. At the spectacle of SILVER LUNA, raised to bestow libation, the Noble Prince will be elevated, and the Lion shall fall. By the names of the Seven are the impurities purged away, but mark that silver luna must rule or all is in vain.

Rubedo

Now increase your fire in the vessel of *orichalcum* until it shows a redness like blood taken from a sound person.

THE SCORPION WILL BE BLOWN FROM HIS LAIR. AURIEL SHALL RISE AGAIN.

A new Age of Gold will rise from the ashes; which is the Philosopher's Stone of all men's desiring.

1.

The alchemist should avoid having anything to do with princes and noblemen.

ALBERTUS MAGNUS (C. 1193–1280)
"LIBELLUS DE ALCHIMIA"

LONDON. 5TH NOVEMBER 1609

It was two hours past midnight, and at London Bridge the gaunt wooden piers exposed to the moonlight showed that the tidal river, having duly ebbed, was about to turn. And indeed within moments the black waters began to swirl in, setting all the moored ships by Botolph's Wharf rocking gently; but then there was a stillness, a silence, and for a moment the currents of the Thames churned uncertainly round the great pillars of the bridge, then began to fall away again, to retreat seaward past Deptford and Chatham to the lonely salt marshes by Gravesend, as if the pull of the ocean would not be denied.

The drinkers emerging in stupor from the low riverside taverns blinked at this vagary of the tide, shaking their heads as their breath misted in the November cold, and vowing sobriety come morning. Others felt a touch of fear like the finger of the devil on their skin as they paused to watch and wonder.

As if sensing some change in the midnight air—remembering some half-forgotten scent, perhaps, of distant oceans, distant lands—Master Phineas Pett, the King's shipbuilder, who knew the tides as well as any man in London, awoke from his dreams. Nightshirted, nightcapped, shivering in the cold air of his chamber, he rose heavy-eyed from his bed in his Thames-side house and tiptoed over to the window so as not to wake his wife. He noted the turbulence of the murky waters glistening beneath the November moon; he checked his timepiece and looked again, and still the tide ebbed as it should not, revealing the weed-blackened timbers of the river-stairs by Oystergate.

He opened the window and gazed out, as though following, in his mind's eye, the progress of those turbulent waters downriver to Deptford, where the hulls of the two new East Indiamen, to be launched before the end of the year, dominated the royal dockyard.

A breath of wind rattled the casement. His wife, stirring, called him sleepily back to bed; so he closed the window and went to join her, still calculating rope yardage and beam-to-keel ratios until at last he sank into a dreamless sleep.

DOWNSTREAM THE SURLY THAMES MENACED THE ramparts of the Tower, where the lonely prisoner Ralegh, whom sleep so often evaded, limped to and fro within the stone walls of his prison yard, and remembered distant voyages, and gold. When a night bird called from the marshes to the east, Ralegh stopped his pacing to draw his patched cloak around himself as the chill salt breeze stole up from the sea. He listened a moment longer, then he went back inside. But the breeze continued its journey across the sleeping roofs of the city, and the turrets of Whitehall, then out to the silent countryside to circle the palace of St. James, where more people were astir in the dead of night; where candles flickered and men talked in grave voices. For in their charge was the fifteen-year-old heir to the throne, Prince Henry, oldest son of King James of England and Scotland: a youth brave and manly in all ways—except when his dreams unmanned him, as they did now. His face was pale in the candlelight, his hands clenched at his sides. "I saw it again. I saw my death in my dreams," he said to the older men who were his advisers, his guardians. "My enemies are gathering; the stars foretell it; there is nothing to be done."

They reassured him, reminding him of the armed men who surrounded him at all times; of themselves, ready to lay down their lives for him. But the young Prince, still shaken by night fears, whispered, "What of poison? I saw it, I tell you; I foresaw my end."

The fire in the great stone hearth had died long ago, and servants were summoned to rekindle it. Someone was sent, at a murmured order, to check that the guards were vigilant at their stations around the palace.

The Prince feared secret enemies. His Protestant soul saw Catholic assassins in every dark dream. Last month he had arranged for charts of divination to be drawn up in dread of his death, though this was against the urgings of his spiritual mentors, who suspected that the blood of his dead grandmother Mary, doomed Queen of the Scots, ran too thickly in his veins.

As the Prince shivered in the ensuing silence, a boy in a palace of ghosts, as bolts were drawn and doors closed on empty corridors, they said to him again, "We have told you that we will guard you from all those who would harm you."

"Yes," he said. "Yes."

ACROSS THE CITY CANDLES WERE EXTINGUISHED ONE by one. The tide had forgotten its transgression and was surging upriver once more, causing the watermen who rowed secret sinners homeward from the brothels of Bankside to grab their oars and curse as their lamps were set wildly rocking in the blackness.

Prince Henry slept at last, soothed by a sleeping draught. Old Ralegh, once the favorite of Queen Elizabeth, stood by his window, breathing in fiercely the chill salt air from the river, as if to prepare himself.

Ralegh had endured disgrace and imprisonment since the death of the Queen six years ago and the succession of Scottish James. But he had reason to hope again. He had been told that by the end of this year his enemies would fall, and his star would rise once more. He had been promised that a letter was to be sent, telling him of a plan to set him free.

But the year was drawing to its close. The letter, if sent, had not arrived. And he knew, none better, that in the wrong hands such a document would bring death, both to himself and to those around him.

2.

*It was in my mishaps, as hitherward
I lately travelled, that unawares I strayed
Out of my way, through perils strange and hard.*

EDMUND SPENSER (C. 1552–1599)
THE FAERIE QUEENE, BOOK I: CANTO XII: V. 31

IN THE SHADOW OF ST. PAUL'S, BETWEEN CARTER
Lane and Knightrider Street, was a tavern known as the
Three Tuns, which was notorious for the roughness of its ale
and its company. That night, though midnight had come and
gone, the tavern's ragged patrons drank on or gambled in
desultory fashion by the light of the stinking tallow candles;
and amongst these regulars was a burly ex-sailor with a red-
veined nose called Tom Barclay, who since being flogged
from the navy now made a living of sorts as a housebreaker.

He should have gone home long ago, to the room he shared
in nearby Oystergate with a shrewish fishwife who had too
many relatives. But tonight he had stayed on at the Three
Tuns, because someone had come in who interested him.

A shabby stranger, with a pack strapped over his shoulder
and a big tawny-gold dog at his heels, had arrived at the Three
Tuns shortly before midnight. A traveler, from the looks of

him, come in perhaps on one of the timber boats that unloaded by night downriver at Billingsgate. This newcomer took off his cloak and feathered hat and sat in the coldest corner of the Three Tuns—the fire was commandeered by regulars—with a tankard of ale in front of him, and a dishful of the landlord's greasy mutton broth, which he spooned up in desultory fashion, while his long-haired dog gnawed a bone at his feet.

He was most likely, thought Tom Barclay, a musician, to judge by the lute strapped to his pack; and not a successful one either. His suit of old russet was worn and patched; his dark hair was unkempt; and his lean cheeks and jaw were shadowed by a week-old beard. Only his boots, recognizably of fine Spanish leather even though covered with the dust and mud of his journey, looked to be of any worth. Not much to rob there. And the dog was a deterrent, indeed.

Yet Barclay continued to watch the man, partly because he seemed to be sober—unusual enough for this place—and partly because, judging by the way he kept glancing across at the door each time it opened, he was expecting someone to join him. So at last Tom Barclay, his curiosity tickled, went to sit beside him and beckoned to the landlord for more ale for them both.

"You're waiting for someone, friend? For some news?"

The man turned to look at him. He was younger than Barclay had first surmised: twenty-five, twenty-six, perhaps, though his eyes, a cold shade of blue, seemed old enough, above those sharp cheekbones.

He said, "Perhaps. But I think I've made a mistake."

"In thinking your friend would be here?"

The man picked up his ale. "In coming back to England."

Barclay looked at him quizzically, and pressed him to play his lute, and sing them a song; but the man declined, saying he was out of practice. So Barclay turned to his drinking companions and told them that he would call the stranger Orpheus, an Orpheus with no voice. He roared at his own wit, then suggested to the stranger that the time might pass the better for a friendly game of dice. Barclay fancied himself as a dice player, though it was rarely that he could find someone foolish or drunk enough to play with him. But tonight he appeared to be in luck, for the lute player said, "Why not?"

Any regular of the alehouse could have told him why not, but they chose not to; and so the two of them, Barclay and his new friend Orpheus, sat at the wine-stained table and took it in turns to play at pass-dice. Barclay's friends, who looked born to hang, all of them, with their leering faces and filthy clothes, abandoned their own places and gathered closer, like carrion birds, in the smoky circle of candlelight. Barclay did well, casting frequent tens and twelves. The stranger appeared heedless of how many pence he was losing, appeared scarcely to care, while his big dog lay on the straw at his feet and watched his master constantly. Just as his master watched the door every time it swung open. Barclay, of course, didn't mind his opponent's lack of concentration; it meant the fellow was losing money all the faster.

"Will you double the stakes?" suggested Barclay.

The lute player nodded. "If you like." He gathered the ivory dice in his hand, beckoned to the landlord for more ale for them both, and played on with a resolute carelessness that took even these hardened gamblers aback. At last he spread out his empty hands and said, "I'm out of coins. But I'll play you for my lute."

There wasn't much of a market for lutes in the circles Barclay frequented. "I'd sooner have those Spanish boots you're wearing," suggested Barclay.

"Oh, no." The lute player smiled for the first time, a smile that made Barclay somehow uneasy. "The lute, or nothing."

"So be it." Barclay rubbed his big hands together. "The lute. Against a quarter angel."

"Half an angel," said his opponent calmly.

Barclay opened his mouth to argue him down, but then he thought, What is the point? His dice were weighted, so he knew he could be certain of casting as many high doubles as he needed. He sipped his ale with relish, then threw. Two threes. Not good enough.

Sometimes in the past he had lost deliberately—just for a while—to lull a suspicious opponent. But this time he never meant to lose anything. Meanwhile the lute player, blue-eyed Orpheus, who'd cast double after double, most of them high enough to win, took up the half angel he'd pulled toward him and said, "I'll wager the lute and this half one for a full angel."

Barclay wiped the back of his mouth with his hand. He wanted his half angel back, and he wanted to see that cool expression smashed from the lute player's face. He gathered the dice up and threw with the concentration of a man who knows he has drunk too much. A four and a three.

Orpheus said, "You owe me an angel now."

Barclay gripped the edge of the table. He realized that quite a crowd had gathered round the players, their faces avid, their clay pipes clamped between toothy grins. They were enjoying his humiliation. "I'll pay you tomorrow," he muttered.

His opponent said softly, "No. Now."

There was a long pause, as the stranger was reassessed with interest by the circle of onlookers. Someone said to him, "You said you'd traveled, stranger. Did you see anything of the warfare in the Low Countries?"

"Enough."

"Were you a soldier there?"

The stranger nodded, and the men gathered around him, exchanging meaningful glances. The warfare in the Low Countries between the Spanish and the Dutch had been bloody and brutal, attracting foreign mercenaries—many of them English—to both sides. This man's lute, and his feathered hat, were clearly deceptive. The onlookers turned to look at Barclay with even more interest.

"I've not got enough in coins," Barclay muttered, digging in the pocket of his ragged jerkin. "You'll have to take something else." Amongst the things he pulled out were some pilfered brass trinkets, a kerchief or two, a pretty little silver candlestick, and a couple of small books that he'd stolen from a bookstall in St. Paul's for their fine leather bindings. They were in Latin, which meant as little to him as English, because he could read neither.

"Here." He thrust the books grudgingly toward his opponent. "You can have these." He hadn't noticed that two loose sheets of paper covered with handwriting had slipped from one of the books and fluttered to the floor. An old sailor who'd learned a little reading on his travels bent to gather them up, and looked at the first few lines quizzically as he knelt on the rushes. *"To Auriel,"* he read out laboriously under his breath.

The long-haired dog, whose space he had invaded, joined him in friendly fashion and nudged his face. "Get away, you great brute. *To Auriel, I will give the gift of gold...*" He could manage no more. He stood up and pushed the sheets of paper back between the leaves of the uppermost of the small volumes, which Barclay had slapped down on the table.

But papers or no papers, the lute player didn't even bother to pick the books up. "You really think," he said to Barclay, "those are worth an angel?"

The onlookers chewed on the stems of their pipes and muttered their agreement. They liked to see justice done. Barclay, hot and cursing, delved once more inside his jerkin and pulled out the little silver candlestick he'd been keeping as a gift for his woman, the fishwife with too many kinfolk.

"I've nothing else," he declared. "You'll have to wait till tomorrow if you want money."

His opponent was examining the candlestick with a practiced eye, when the door was flung open and one of Barclay's friends came in from relieving himself at the jakes.

"There's a man out in the lane," he announced as he straightened his clothes, "looking for someone called Warriner. *W-w-w Warriner...*" He mocked the searcher's stammer and guffawed.

The lute player had gone very still, though the golden dog at his feet stirred and growled softly. He soothed his dog, then looked up at the man who'd spoken and said, "Is he still there?"

The man grinned. "I doubt it. I told him this wasn't the place for the likes of him. Are you going to give Barclay another game?"

The lute player was already standing, pushing the books and candlestick into the pack from which his lute protruded.

"I'll quit while I'm winning," he said. He whistled to his dog and made his way out into the night. The door slammed shut behind him. Disappointed, Barclay's fellow drinkers started to disperse. Barclay scowled bitterly. Then he slapped his pockets and scrabbled amongst the tankards on the table, lifting them up one by one in some vain search.

"My dice. The bastard. He's stolen my dice..."

But one of Barclay's drinking companions had spotted something half hidden by an empty plate. He pushed the plate aside, then held up his hand triumphantly. "No he hasn't. Look what I've got here."

He held out a pair of dice. Barclay, red-faced, reached out to pluck them from the man's hand. He felt them all over and whispered, "Yes, these are mine. Damn it, that smooth-tongued son of a whore; he slipped my dice under his plate and used his own. And his must have been crooked..."

"Like yours, Barclay?" The onlookers roared with laughter, then stood back as Barclay went rushing out into the street to catch the villain. But although he ran up and down several times, the street was empty. A steady rain was falling. "Damn him," he swore again. "The thieving crook. Damn him..."

Still cursing, he made his way back inside. "Orpheus," his companions mocked, shaking pretend dice in their fists. "Orpheus!"

IT WAS IN DEAN'S LANE, CLOSE BY THE OLD CHURCH of St. Martin, that blue-eyed, black-haired Orpheus, whose real name was Ned Warriner, finally caught up with the man who had been asking for him at the Three Tuns. The man was hurrying toward Paternoster Row, his head down against the rain. His boots were mired with the filth of the London alleys, and his fine black livery spattered with mud. The livery of the Earl of Northampton.

"Simon," called Ned. "Simon."

The man sped on, out of sight again. Ned Warriner, with an oath of exasperation, took a shortcut through the burial ground of St. Paul's. As a boy, he'd explored every inch of this part of the city, knew every low dwelling to the north of the riverbank, knew where the beggars lived, and the whores. You had to grow up quickly, when your father died a bankrupt.

"Simon!"

The man jumped when Ned appeared in front of him. The light from a cresset burning in a holder on the wall showed the fearful face of a thin man in his late twenties, with a pock-marked complexion and pale hair.

"So you were in that hellhole after all," he breathed. "I c-couldn't believe you would ever come back to England, let alone to such a filthy place."

Ned wearily pushed his feathered hat back from his un-shaven face and gestured to his dog, Barnabas, to stay at his side.

"I sent word to you to meet me at the Three Tuns at mid-night," he said. "Instead of which you turn up at four, proclaim-ing my name to every rogue in the vicinity, and dressed in the Earl of Northampton's livery. Was that wise, do you think?"

Simon Thurstan had been Northampton's courtier for more than ten years. He had always regarded Ned's rather more flamboyant career with a kind of fascination. Now he looked as if he was regretting the connection wholeheartedly.

"I didn't get your message till late. And then I couldn't find the d-damned alehouse."

Ned looked quickly round and guided him into the shad-ows, away from the light. "Don't tell me," he said. "The whores of Cheapside diverted you."

Simon colored indignantly. "No! And then, I wasn't sure if your message was a trap. It's been over two years, Ned. How was I to know it was really you?"

"If anyone's likely to have a trap laid for them, then it's me. Look, Simon. I need your help. Will you speak, in confi-dence, to Northampton, and ask him if he will see me?"

A couple of drunkards staggered past the end of the lane, singing, in defiance of the Watch that patrolled the city after curfew. Ned backed farther into the darkness, taking Simon with him.

Simon wiped the perspiration from his brow. "I think I can t-tell you the answer now. From the occasional—very occa-sional—reference to your name, I think the answer will be no."

Ned was silent a moment. Then he said, "I've been risking my neck for him for the last two years. He wanted news of the Netherlands war. He got it, firsthand."

"I heard you'd joined the fighting there," said Simon, not without sympathy. "Was it hard, Ned?"

"The soldiering? You get used to it. But I never bargained for permanent exile."

"Some would have counted themselves lucky with that. There were rumors, you know, after you'd gone." Simon looked at him carefully. "Rumors that you'd helped a Catholic prisoner to escape."

"There are rumors about all sorts of things wherever any poor bloody Catholics are concerned."

"Nevertheless, a man doesn't g-go into exile on rumors only. He's best to stand and refute them. You once told me that yourself. People whispered that the Catholic prisoner, Ashworth, was a good friend of yours."

"There were no actual charges, were there, over Ashworth's escape? No evidence to link it to me?"

"No. Oh, no . . ." Simon looked round, as if every wall had ears. "But p-people *remember*."

"I want to see Northampton. Will you help me, or not?"

"I only wish I could. Ned, if you are determined to see him, it might be best if you throw yourself on his mercy, as a supplicant—"

Ned put his head on one side. *"Down on your knees, And thank heaven, fasting, for a good man's love,"* he quoted. "Where will the noble Earl be tomorrow?"

"He'll be at the service at Whitehall in the morning. The Thanksgiving."

"Thanksgiving for what?"

"Our King's deliverance from the Powder Treason, of course. Four years ago. November the fifth. Surely you haven't forgotten?"

Ned rubbed his forehead. "No. No, of course not. Where will he be later?"

"He plans on going to the theater—the Swan. You c-could approach him there."

Ned nodded slowly. "So you'll do no more for me?"

Simon held up his hands in a gesture of helplessness. "What can I do? I have little influence. And—a word of warning—neither do you. He has new favorites now. Ned, I must go—I have so much to do—"

"And it's not safe to be seen here with me. Very well. I'm grateful to you for coming here, Simon."

"For old times." Simon turned to go, but Ned called, suddenly, "Wait. One more thing. Have you heard any news lately of Sir Thomas Revill's daughter?"

Simon turned back, his reluctance ill concealed. "She's still living at her father's house. In the Strand. But did you know she is m-married now, to Francis Pelham, the recusant hunter? It was soon after the Ashworth affair. Soon after you left the country."

"I heard rumors."

"They have a child. A little boy."

"So the marriage was fruitful. Well, well. A son, for Francis Pelham." Ned pulled his cloak around his shoulders. "My thanks, Simon. Ever my trusty bearer of tidings. You'd better go, before I think up more illuminating questions."

Simon nodded and hurried off with evident relief.

N ED REACHED THE CITY'S BOUNDARY BY WAY OF Carter Lane, where he avoided the watchman at the gate by scrambling over the part-ruined wall at Amen Corner, an area of dereliction that had awaited repair by the city authorities since the days of Queen Elizabeth. In the darkness he crossed over the Fleet Bridge, his cloak slung over his shabby russet suit, his feathered hat pulled low against the rain, and Barnabas at his heels. The great midden, a mound of human excrement, still marked the no-man's-land between the boundaries of the city and Westminster. Nothing had changed in the two years of his absence. Not even the vile weather.

Some would have counted themselves lucky with exile, Simon had told him. But Ned had never been one to accept the vagaries of fate without protest. He'd learned, early on, that good fortune never lasted. For the first fourteen years of his life, he'd enjoyed a relatively prosperous and fortunate upbringing, with private tutors of whom Ned, an intelligent and ambitious boy, took full advantage. But his father's sudden bankruptcy, disgrace, and death meant that Ned and his older brother had to face the harsh reality of poverty.

Ned had been reckoned lucky to find an apprenticeship with a joiner in Dowgate. He labored and endured. The only remnant of his old life that survived was his weekly visit to his kind old music tutor, Evan Ashworth, who on learning of his misfortune insisted on giving his talented pupil lessons, without payment.

And Ned's music gave him his freedom from the drudgery of the joiner's yard, for through Ashworth's encouragement, he was introduced, when he was seventeen, to the Master of the King's Music, who exclaimed at the damage the manual work had done to Ned's hands, and offered him employment as one of the court's musicians.

It was not long after that that Ned was espied by the elderly Earl of Northampton, a generous but jealous employer, who required Ned's services—as a lute player and messenger, he explained—in his own household.

When Northampton, known for his fondness for young men, made it clear what else he required from time to time and what might happen if Ned did not comply, Ned only had to remember the grinding poverty he had suffered, to endure the aging Northampton's occasional attentions, if at the same time resolving that he would soon move on. Unlike Simon, he vowed he would not wear the Earl's livery forever.

What marked the end of his career with Northampton, one night in May two and a half years ago, was the news that his old friend and tutor, Evan Ashworth, had been arrested for giving shelter to a traveling priest.

Ned, who had always known Ashworth was a secret Catholic—as were so many others in London—went straight to Northampton to plead for the old man, but Northampton, angry, told him there was nothing he could do.

On the night that Ashworth was due to be transported from Newgate prison to the Tower, Ned gathered together some colleagues—he had not lost touch with the tough friends of his prentice days, and he offered good money—and together they ambushed the convoy escorting Ashworth, scattered his guards, seized the keys to free him from his chains, and hurried the frail, overwhelmed old man down to the waiting boat at St. Botolph's Wharf that would take him to a ship bound for France, and freedom.

All the rumors Simon had heard were true.

Immediately after Ashworth's embarkation, Ned, too, prepared for exile. He was summoned to one last meeting with Northampton. No one else had yet connected Ned with the old man's escape, but Northampton did.

"You are a fool, Warriner. Someone, sooner or later, will work it out. And perhaps I will be tainted by your crime. You know, of course, that you will have to leave the country."

"Are you sending me into permanent exile?"

Northampton tapped his jeweled fingers on the arm of his chair. "Not perhaps permanent. Work for me. Send me news from abroad, from the armies in the Netherlands; and I will see what I can do, to ensure that someday it might be safe for you to return."

Early the next morning, in May 1607, Ned had taken a wherry to Gravesend, where a ship took him to join the Dutch army of Prince Maurice, to fight alongside many other Protestant mercenaries against the might of Catholic Spain in the ravaged battlefields of the Netherlands. Many of those mercenaries were, like him, English; disillusioned, sickened, by King James's retreat from the Dutch alliance; by his pandering to the old enemy, Spain.

Ned sent dispatches, by the usual tortuous routes, to Northampton. After the fighting he traveled, visiting other places, other cities. He waited to hear from his old master that the furor over Ashworth's escape had died down.

He heard nothing from the Earl. But then other information reached him, which meant he could postpone his return no longer; the news that Simon had just confirmed. The news that Kate Pelham had a son.

Two hours to go before dawn and still the rain fell steadily. He heaved his lute and pack higher, called Barnabas to heel, and headed westward, to the broad and muddy thoroughfare of the Strand.

Close by the turning into Chancellor's Lane was a modest house separated from its neighbors by a high-walled garden. Ned knew that in summer, peach-colored roses scrambled over these walls and honeysuckle filled the air with fragrance, but now the autumn-withered foliage made skeletal shapes in the dark. The house was in blackness, except for one first-floor window where a candle burned.

There was a secret door set in the wall, scarcely high enough for children to pass through without stooping. It was half hidden now by brambles and overhanging apple boughs; he pushed some aside and saw, carved into the archway over the door, the coat of arms of the Revill family.

If what Simon said was true, this house would belong to Francis Pelham now.

Francis Pelham was a recusant hunter, paid to hunt out and report secret Catholics to the government. Ned had first met him four years ago, when he saw him escorting a sick and frightened old woman to the Tower. When Ned had challenged him over his treatment of the woman, Pelham had scornfully produced his letters of authority from William Waad himself, the governor of the Tower.

Ned let the apple boughs fall back over the carvings, and ran his fingers round the edge of the half-hidden door.

Atop of Paul's steeple there did I see
A delicate, dainty, fine Apple-Tree.
The apples were ripe, and ready to fall,
And kill'd seven hundred men on a stall . . .

He turned the handle and found it, as he expected, locked.

To the east he could see the first gray fingers of dawn, but it was raining more heavily now. He turned away from the house and walked to the river's edge, where he sat in the lee of an old fisherman's hut and found a crust of bread he'd saved for Barnabas, who shifted closer, smelling of wet dog hair. The rain swept across the gray water, and in the distance he heard the creaking wheels of an early coal cart being hauled through the mud of the Strand.

He leaned back and closed his eyes, remembering the sound of distant armies traversing war-swept plains.

3.

They found that he was of the Jesuit breed,
And one that had been a great rascal indeed;
Now therefore they sent him to Newgate with speed.

TRAD. BALLAD
"THE FRYAR"

BACK AT THE HOUSE NEAR CHANCELLOR'S LANE that Ned Warriner had so briefly surveyed, there was an early-morning bustle of servants, and a hurried lighting of candles; for the household had been woken by the sound of someone knocking urgently at the front door.

The master of the house, Francis Pelham, employed as a Catholic hunter by William Waad, governor of the Tower of London, was instantly awake. His steward would answer the call; but even so, Pelham, who preferred to know for himself everything that was going on, had risen swiftly from his bed, dressed himself as ever in black (the severity of which suited his Puritan conscience and made him look older than his thirty-two years), taken a candle, and gone quickly to the head of the dark-paneled staircase, pausing only as he passed the closed door of his wife's bedchamber, the room she had slept in ever since she was a child.

He had made this house his home on his marriage to Katherine Revill two years ago. But her closed door still made him feel like an intruder, and he was always afraid to try to open it, in case he found it locked against him.

He made his way quickly down the stairs, in spite of the marked limp that marred his stride; and he found, as he expected, a messenger from the Fleet prison, his hair and clothes wet from the steadily falling rain, who doffed his cap and said, "There is a new suspect for you, sir."

Pelham was already buckling on the sword his servant had handed to him. Another servant was lighting more candles around the dark-paneled hall. "Is he a Catholic?"

"They think so, sir. Master Waad's men paid a night visit to the man's lodgings by the Temple, where they found a rosary and a silver crucifix. But he will not talk."

Pelham fastened on his cloak. "He will."

Francis Pelham saw it as his personal, Protestant duty to hunt down and eliminate every Catholic enemy of King James. Today, the fifth of November, the anniversary of the Powder Treason, was for Pelham and his associates a time not for rejoicing, but for offering humble thanks to God for the capture four years ago of Guy Fawkes and his fellow plotters, who would have blown the King and his Parliament sky high.

It was also a time for extra vigilance. He said to the messenger, "Tell them I am on my way."

The man, who had come on horseback, offered to ride to the prison with him as escort through the still-dark streets; but Pelham refused his company, and limped to the stable that adjoined the house.

As soon as his manservant had made his horse ready, he set off through the driving rain, past Temple Bar, and northward toward St. Bartholomew's and the Fleet prison. It was a route he knew well. In the shadow of the ruined city wall were clusters of half-built hovels where beggars and thieves lurked. He felt their eyes on him as he rode by, but Pelham feared none of them. He had his sword, and besides, there was something formidable about his black clothes, his stern, ascetic features, his cropped pale hair. It was as if his journey was his preparation for the task ahead, a purging of his mind and soul.

By the time he reached the Fleet prison, a cold dawn was breaking. The keepers at the gate let him in quickly. In he marched, through the heavy iron-studded door, reentering darkness. Letting the turnkey who escorted him follow behind, he turned right then left down dank stairwells, along passageways lit by flickering rushlights, until he came to the cell where the prisoner was hanging by chains at his wrists.

Pelham saw, without emotion, that the agony of the old man's suspension had caused the sweat to bead his forehead. Although he was silent, Pelham could smell his fear.

Earlier that month all of William Waad's investigators had been warned of a suspected plot against King James and his ministers. "We must be on our guard against Catholic spies in our midst," Waad had told his trusted servant Pelham. "And we must watch for traitors of all kinds."

As if Pelham needed anyone to remind him of his duty.

Now he told the turnkey to go. Then he closed the door of the cell and turned to his manacled prisoner.

KATE, WIFE OF FRANCIS PELHAM, HEARD THE AWAKening of the city as dawn broke, and carts full of produce began to wend their way to the markets from the adjoining countryside. She pulled on a shawl over her lawn nightdress and stood by the window of her bedchamber, where a candle had been burning since midnight. Her brown hair tumbled loosely round her shoulders, making her look younger than her twenty-two years.

She pressed her forehead to the glass of the diamond-paned window, remembering how she had risen in the night, plagued by an inability to sleep. And how she had imagined she saw someone she had not thought to see again, out there in the darkness beyond the gate, gazing up at her window.

She could see no one now. It was still raining. The gray November daylight was creeping reluctantly across the fields and houses to the east of the city; and in the distance she could see the river, which she knew in all its vagaries, for she had always lived here, as had her mother, who was related to the Earl of Shrewsbury and could claim noble blood.

Kate could scarcely remember her mother, for she had died when Kate was three, in giving birth to a much-longed-for son who died also. Kate's father, the bluff seafarer Sir Thomas Revill, had never married again but cherished his only daughter fiercely. Before he set sail three years ago on that last expedition from which he did not return, he had taken her in his arms and held her close, and told her that he had once wished that she had been a boy. But not for long, he said. Not for long. No one could wish, he'd told her, for a braver or a dearer child.

Kate had laughed, and told him that he'd brought her up as roughly as any boy, which he'd tried to deny, but only faintly.

"What about the Warriners?" she had reminded him. "Ned and his brother came to the house nearly every day when I was small. I hardly ever saw any girls my own age."

"I thought the boys would make your lessons less lonely. I thought they would be like brothers for you. Before his misfortune, their father was a good friend of mine."

Brothers? Yes, indeed. To be emulated, and secretly worshiped.

Kate was seven when Ned and Matthew started to join her at this house for her daily lessons; and from the start she had loved Ned, two years older than she, for his ability to make her laugh, and his skills at all things athletic, somersaults, and archery with homemade bows, and tree-climbing; which skills he did his best to impart to Kate, to the despair of her tutor. And Matthew, Ned's older brother—well, she loved him because he was just Matthew, big and kindly and not over-bright. He couldn't even think up excuses as to why he'd missed lessons, as Ned did for himself and Kate, so he got beatings, regularly.

The Warriner brothers came almost every day from their home nearby in Faitour Lane. It had lasted for nearly four years, this time of childhood bliss, of companionship—until something happened, some kind of ruin befell their father, and their daily visits stopped.

Kate, her heart broken at eleven, had said, "I miss them. I want to see them."

"Their father is dead, dear Kate," her father told her. "And they have no money now."

"We must help them, then!"

He hesitated. "Their mother is proud. They are proud."

Kate had fewer and less vivid memories of the ensuing years. She found out afterward that William Warriner, the boys' father, had become involved in some fraudulent business venture and killed himself. His widow, in her shame, had hauled the boys away, and Ned, her musical, mischievous Ned, became a joiner's apprentice. She thought of his hands, so skillful with the lute, roughened by manual work. Her father appointed a governess whom Kate could not abide, and he spent less time with his daughter. Perhaps he was regretting the freedom he'd allowed her, and was trying to compensate for it. Perhaps it was a natural distancing, between father and daughter.

She hated growing up. It was as if a part of her had died.

When her father was lost at sea, she was nineteen. Now she was truly alone, and nothing seemed to matter anymore.

At a time when no other option seemed open to her, she married Francis Pelham, whom she had met when she was presented at court because he was a friend of her father's. His courtship had been passionate and steadfast.

That was over two years ago. Now she found it harder and harder to let her husband touch her. She took to sleeping in another room, or in the bedchamber of her small son, who was often not well.

And she had not thought, no, she had not believed that Ned Warriner would ever come back.

In a nearby room, her child called out in his dreams. Turning from the window, mocked by childhood memories of the summer mornings spent outside in the garden, Francis Pelham's young wife hurried along the passageway to her little son's room, and held him tightly to her breast until he slept again.

MORNING FOUND THE THREE TUNS ALMOST EMPTY OF clients, save for two hungover gamesters who argued in some confusion over a pack of cards, and a few early carters who'd brought poultry in from Holborn for Stocks Market, and were now breakfasting on ale and day-old bread. Barclay and his companions had long gone.

The old sailor who'd picked up the fallen papers from the floor and put them back with the two books Ned had won from Barclay—Samuel Turner by name—was snoring open-mouthed at a table in a corner when the landlord shook him awake. He staggered out of the tavern and cursed the rain.

Turner had once sailed with Ralegh to garner the treasures of the Orinoco for Queen Elizabeth. Now he was a casual laborer at the wharves, when drink or inclination allowed, and as he set off down to the river he found himself thinking about those papers that had fallen out of the books. *"To Auriel,"* he whispered to himself as he walked down Thames Street. That was what it said. *"To Auriel, I will give the gift of gold."*

The phrase expanded in his mind. Sam Turner was not a man given much to philosophical speculation, being normally too inebriated or too busy scavenging a living for such indulgences, but he liked this phrase *the gift of gold,* and the name Auriel.

A passing coal cart splashed him. He pulled up and cursed again. Why hadn't he just kept that letter? No one would have missed it. By the time he had tramped down King's Lane toward the wharf, where he had heard there might be work that morning, he had spread a fine story to all the acquaintances he'd met on his way about how he'd seen a letter that contained some secret about gold, and how it was addressed to someone called Auriel.

When he was almost at the wharf, he was hailed by three men he'd never met before, who said they might have work for him, better-paid work than that he'd been promised. They invited him to come for a drink in a tavern nearby. They were good company at first, but then they wanted to know about the letter to Auriel, and gradually their voices changed. They kept questioning him about the damned letter, and about the dice-playing stranger—the man Barclay had jokingly called Orpheus—who'd tricked Barclay and gone off into the night with that letter in his pocket.

Sam Turner remembered little enough about the man, in truth. He had a golden, long-haired dog, he kept saying, and had a lute in his pack. He wasn't old, he wasn't a beggar, but he wasn't rich. He had blue eyes and black hair, and he hadn't shaved for days, so his face was half hidden by stubble; but Sam could tell them no more, nor any more as to what was in the letter.

He was getting tired of their questions. He told them so, and got up and left them there in the tavern; but they followed him, and caught up with him in a back street. There they twisted his arm behind his back until he screamed for mercy and vomited into the gutter. This time someone else had come with them, a man with a quiet, odd voice, who would not let him see his face, but who asked him more questions he could not answer. "He had a lute," he told this man, again. "And a dog. That's all. I swear..."

They turned briefly away from him, to confer. Dizzy with pain, Sam Turner lurched away in an attempt to escape them. But they quickly caught him again.

And then, one of them produced a knife.

4.

If thou beest borne to strange sights,
Things invisible to see,
Ride ten thousand daies and nights,
Till age snow white haires on thee,
Thou, when thou retorn'st, wilt tell mee
All strange wonders that befell thee,
And sweare
No where
Lives a woman true, and faire.

JOHN DONNE (1572–1631)
"SONG"

B y NOON THAT SAME DAY, A LIGHT WIND HAD DRIVEN
away the last of the rain clouds. To the west of the city, the
pale November sunshine glittered on the myriad roofs and
windows of the riverside palace of Whitehall, appropriated in
the last century by King Henry VIII from a begrudging Archbishop of York. Pennants adorned with heraldic lions flew
over the royal suites and state rooms to show that King James
was in residence. Courtiers and servants hurried about their
duties through the maze of lanes and passages that formed the
palace's thoroughfares.

Since morning a winding queue had increased in length
and noise with every boat that arrived at the riverside stairs: a
queue that stretched up through the first entry port, past the
Banqueting Hall, and along dark-paneled corridors to the state
room where the members of the Privy Council were that day

holding audience. The customary delay was longer than usual because of the morning service of thanksgiving for deliverance from the Powder Treason, which the councillors had attended at Westminster. Men and women stood in line, some with petitions clutched in their hands, others with great sheaves of papers to document their woes. All had come to beg for succor or for patronage, or for other, more private services.

"Move along, now. Holy saints above, is there no end to this rabble?" Thus alternately cajoled and complained the distracted servants who pressed to and fro in the gaudy liveries of their various masters: Cecil and Northampton, Suffolk and Shrewsbury, Sussex and Arundel. In an attempt at order they sent those with property petitions to queue at one doorway, and those with judicial at another. The delays for both seemed interminable. "Leave your letters," commanded the harassed servants, "give them to us if you do not wish to wait. My lord Cecil is in the presence of His Highness the King; he will not be available for at least an hour."

The queue continued to grow, and the supplicants waxed noisier in their impatience. But one man waited quietly in the shadows by the first doorway; a man in a feathered hat, and a cloak of faded russet, with a tawny-colored dog at his heels and a lute strapped over his back.

He stepped forward as a thin-featured clerk came hurrying out, peering at the faces in the crowd.

"There you are," the clerk said, in a voice that scarcely concealed his exasperation. "It took me long enough to find what you wanted."

Ned Warriner said, "I told you I would make it worth your while. Now tell me what you found."

"I looked in the records of court proceedings. And then in the recusant register, as you suggested." The clerk peered with some suspicion up at Ned, who was taller than he was. "You seem to have some familiarity with such things. Well, I checked through, and copied out the names of all Catholics listed for prosecution in the spring and summer of 1607. Here they are."

Ned took the paper he offered and spread it open, holding it steady in the breeze.

Nothing. Nothing at all relating to the man called Evan Ashworth. Yet Ashworth had been arrested, and charges laid, in the May of that year. Even though he escaped so soon afterward, his name should still have been on record.

He said, "You're quite sure you checked every list?"

"As sure as anyone can be. I've worked there for ten years." The clerk held out his hand for the list and pushed it in his pocket, then, looking round quickly to make sure they weren't being watched, he held out his hand again.

Ned gave him the coin he'd promised him—one gold angel. The clerk hurried off. And Ned knew he was, technically at least, a free man. Northampton must have kept his promise and eradicated all evidence of the matter that had driven Ned into exile. Though whether Ned remained free, once Northampton learned of his return, was another matter.

HE WHISTLED TO BARNABAS AND HEADED EASTWARD through Charing village to the Strand. It was now well past noon, and the sun turned the autumn trees that lined this rural way between Westminster and London to bronze and crimson. To his right, with their large gardens sloping down to the river's edge, were great mansions that had once been the palaces of prelates, but were now taken over by the new potentates of the realm: Durham House, Arundel House, and the largest of them all, Salisbury House, which was Cecil's London home. To the north, the fields and hedges of the countryside had been pushed back by the newer dwellings of the gentry, overspilling from the city. Some laundry maids, laying out sheets on hedges to dry, saw him coming with his dog and his lute and called out teasingly for a tune, but Ned walked on, shaking his head and smiling.

When he got to the house he had gazed at that morning, he stopped by the little door, over which was inscribed the emblem of Sir Thomas Revill. Then he hunched down beneath the overhanging apple boughs and, drawing out a scrap of paper from his pocket, wrote on it quickly, with a stub of pencil.

Leaving Barnabas to guard his lute and pack, he vaulted over the wall at a place where there was an old pear tree, its limbs tangled now with ivy. He remembered climbing it once to pick fruit for Kate, but a branch had given way, and he'd fallen and broken his wrist. Kate had brought him some stolen cakes from the kitchen to console him as he lay fighting the pain on the bed in her father's chamber. She had wept and said it was her fault.

She was nearly ten and he was twelve. It was almost the only time he had seen her crying.

Now, to him, the garden seemed smaller, and not as well cared for as it used to be. He edged carefully along the path that adjoined the wall, hidden from the house by a line of yew trees, his footsteps muffled by moss and fallen leaves, until he came to a secret place, a trellised arbor, almost overgrown now by climbing roses run wild, where he stepped inside and took out his folded paper.

He whirled round when he heard the footsteps.

Kate stood there with her hands clasped to her mouth, as if to suppress a cry of disbelief, of fear even. She was not as tall as he remembered. She looked slender, fragile even, in her gray woolen gown. Her silky brown hair was pinned to the nape of her neck; her green eyes burned in her pale face.

"Ned," she breathed at last, "I can only think you must have taken leave of your senses, to come here, like this, unannounced, unexpected. Please go. Now."

"We were once friends," he said.

"Once. A long time ago. Now you are the last person on earth . . . You left, without a word of explanation. I did not understand. I still do not understand."

"I left," he said, "because if I stayed I would have gone on trial for my life. I was the man who set Evan Ashworth free; and anyone I saw afterwards, anyone I contacted, would have been implicated also, especially you."

"Evan *Ashworth*?" She shook her head in disbelief. "But he was set free on his way to the Tower. An armed band attacked his guard . . . So it was you. Oh, if only you'd told me. If only you'd written."

"I could not do anything—*anything*—to put you at risk. Your father had been Ashworth's good friend. You, too, might have been under suspicion over his escape. I was going to let you know. To explain. I thought, in my folly, I had a little time."

She was shaking her head. Tears welled in her eyes. "Time? What was time, to me, that spring two years ago?"

Ned folded his arms. "It was a time of some jubilation, I imagine, seeing as you married Francis Pelham almost as soon as I'd gone. *'A fickle thing and changeful is a woman always...'*"

"Go," she whispered. "Just go. It is over. Do you understand?"

She turned and hurried back toward the house. Ned stood there. A drowsy bee, beguiled into the open by the deceptive autumn sunshine, blundered past him, searching for flowers that had long since died.

He thought he could still smell the perfume of her hair.

How long he stood there, by the arbor, he did not know. But he came to his senses quickly enough when he heard footsteps and voices, coming from the side of the house. He spun round to see two manservants in livery moving in on him, their cudgels raised. One of them barked a challenge. "State your business. Quickly."

"I have something," he said, "for Mistress Revill—"

The name was a stupid error, made in his haste.

"There is no Mistress Revill here," snarled the man. "This is the house of Francis Pelham. How did you get in here, when the gate was locked?"

Ned hesitated. They moved closer. "Try and break in, would you?" one challenged. "We'll show you how we deal with your kind round here."

The other one lunged at him with his cudgel, catching him across the cheekbone. Ned sprang back, looking round swiftly for escape, feeling the blood trickling down his cheek. The first man was shouting for reinforcements from the house. Ned was already running, crashing through bushes as thorns and rose briars tore at his clothes. He could hear them pounding after him as he heaved himself back over the wall to where Barnabas waited. He fell in the mud as he landed, covering his clothes with filth, but almost immediately hauled himself up and pulled Barnabas into a blackthorn thicket across the way. There he waited, breathing hard.

Francis Pelham's men had emerged from the gate and were coming closer, scouring the roadside, beating at the undergrowth with their sticks. But salvation was at hand, of a sort. Ned heard the noise first, the shrill cacophony of pipes and tabors, together with the sound of tramping feet coming along the muddy road from Westminster toward the city. From his hiding place he saw a line of marchers approaching: men carrying torches that blazed against the gray November sky; women in tattered rags, with small children laughing and chasing between their skirts.

Some of the men led packhorses, or pulled carts laden with firewood. It was the anniversary of the Powder Treason, and these people were going to the city, to light the great fires that celebrated the capture of the Catholic plotters.

It would not be safe to be a Catholic on the streets of London tonight. Ned, seeing that his cudgel-bearing pursuers were temporarily blocked from his view, slipped quickly out from his hiding place with Barnabas, and joined the marchers where they were at their thickest.

So, as the pipes squealed and the tabors rattled, he proceeded with his new companions toward their destination: the great bonfire by Lincoln's Inn Fields, where the students of the Inns of Court, and the outlaws from the vagabonds' den of Whitefriars, and all the various citizenry of London and its environs, some law-abiding, others not so, would be gathering, in celebration of the capture of Guy Fawkes and the other traitors, who died screaming in agony as their entrails were torn from them and thrown on the fire.

So perish all the King's enemies.

Someone gave him a bundle of firewood to carry. The children, shy of Barnabas at first, began to play with him, throwing sticks for him. Ned wondered, as he marched, if Kate had set those men on him. He had told her once not to believe all the things she might hear about him. But with Pelham as her informer, it was no wonder that she wanted him beaten from her door. He wondered what else Pelham had told her.

• • •

WHEN NED HAD TURNED HIS BACK ON ALL THE joinery trade had to offer and sought instead the excitement of the court, the chance of entering the service of the Earl of Northampton had seemed to offer all for which he was hungry. He was nineteen when Northampton spotted him as he ran an errand for the Master of the King's Music and hired him as his own musician, and also as his spy. Northampton taught him much. He encouraged his new, sharp-witted employee to mix with the great people of the court, to pass on the gossip and intrigue to his elderly master. Ned quickly became popular with the ladies of Whitehall, whose morals were as loose as those of their husbands.

Ned already knew that Northampton's tastes, like those of the King, ran not to women but to younger men. After a while the Earl made it plain he required more personal services from his young informer; and that he could make trouble for Ned, perhaps amongst those cuckolded husbands, if he didn't agree.

Ned was already drinking too much, and the wine made everything else bearable, including that first touch late one night of Northampton's bone-dry fingers on his skin, the whisper of his cracked old voice in his ear, the murmured invitation and underlying threat. The dark purple hangings of the old man's bedchamber, the scent of the incense burners set in the walls, the heavily embroidered robe the Earl wore in private, and the rattle and sigh of his breathing as Ned did what he was ordered: all these were memories that Ned had since striven to obliterate, but had failed.

Then he met Kate again. His childhood friend. They encountered each other at the court, for Kate had just been appointed as lady-in-waiting to the King's wife, Queen Anne. Now that her father had died, Kate Revill was a young woman of property: self-contained, dignified. And, Ned saw with wretchedness, beautiful.

They spoke to each other like civil strangers. He was tongue-tied, full of self-loathing in case she had heard about his relationship with Northampton.

She asked him to visit her at the house in the Strand, where he'd spent so much of his childhood, but he did not go. After three weeks had passed, she came to him one night at his lodgings by the Temple. He'd been out with friends, drinking. When he saw her at his door, cloaked and alone at past midnight, he was instantly sober, and filled with a kind of despair.

"You have not been to visit me," she said. "I worried about you."

"You shouldn't," he said bitterly. The wine fumes were filling his head. "No one should worry about me. I don't."

His friends had already left. Ned looked out into the darkened street. "You should never have come out at this time of night," he said. "You can't go back alone."

"Then I shall have to stay," she said. She pushed past him into his hallway. "Have you some wine left?"

He showed her into his untidy parlor and hid his surprise as she sat down and swallowed all the wine he offered her. He drank no more himself. They talked of the old days: of the garden, and the river, and of her father, who had died on a voyage to Guiana a year previously, and his endless courage.

After a while she stood to take off her cloak. Ned, standing, too, as she handed it to him, saw that beneath it she was wearing a beautiful gauze gown, of the kind he had seen worn by the promiscuous women of the court, but never by her. The fabric, cut tightly to her figure, outlined her breasts and her tiny waist. He could see the veins at her throat, and a pulse beating there. Her cheeks were flushed, her beautiful green eyes bright with the wine she'd drunk. Her silky brown hair rippled loosely to her shoulders, gleaming in the candlelight.

He stood there, not knowing what to say, what to do.

Kate said, in a low voice, "I heard them talking about you at court the other day. The Queen's women. Lady Boughton, Mary Waltor, and others. They said they enjoyed your company, Ned. And that you could be bought. They paint their faces, and wear gowns like this. They drink too much wine. And they give you presents. Is that what I must do, to make you notice me?"

"Kate," he said, taking her by the shoulders, "Kate, dear God, I will take you back to your home, now . . ."

She pushed him away. "Men think I am cold," she said. "I am not beautiful, like Lady Boughton. I am expected to sit and do *embroidery*."

He took hold of her again, and shook her. "Those women are whores. They are nothing compared to you."

"But they are why you do not visit me. They are why you want me to go home now."

"Oh, Kate. You are beautiful. Too beautiful, for me . . ."

"I will go to court tomorrow," she said. "I will offer myself to the first man to approach me. I will go out on the streets, at night, to learn what it is men want."

"No . . ."

"Unless you show me, Ned. Tell me what they like. This? Or this? I know, Ned, I am not stupid." She was pulling at her gown, parting the bodice, in a fever. Her nipples were dark-crested, her small breasts white and smooth. He stopped her by holding her, by kissing her, and she responded to his kiss as if her body was on fire.

They did not sleep that night. He found her passion almost overwhelming, her beauty luminous, as if a flame burned at her core.

She told him, as dawn came, that she had never loved anyone else, and never would.

After that he visited her almost every day at her house in the Strand. The few servants there who still remembered Ned knew him as their mistress's childhood companion. If it was thought that they spent too much time together, nothing was said.

It was a glorious spring. The sun blazed down. And at night, she was everything to him. That burning dark flame at her core.

"No one else," she whispered, as she held him to her. "No one else, ever . . ." She took him in her arms, almost fiercely. "I wish we had sailed away together, as children. I wish we had gone away forever."

But then he heard that Ashworth was being taken to the Tower, and everything was over.

• • •

AFTER A WHILE NED HANDED OVER THE FIREWOOD
he'd carried, detached Barnabas from his new friends,
and left the procession to head south to the Temple Stairs. He
bought food for himself and Barnabas in a riverside tavern,
and while he was searching in his pocket for coins he found,
deep inside the lining of his doublet where he'd pushed them
for safekeeping, the two little books he'd acquired in the
Three Tuns.

He pulled them out. The books were in Latin. One was a
treatise on the gospels, and the other was a collection of sermons.

He was just about to push the books back in his pocket,
when he noticed the two sheets of paper folded inside one of
them.

He opened them out, and gazed at the close-written handwriting.

"To Auriel," he read, *"I will give the gift of gold. After the
night of long and false captivity, the golden Sun is about to
rise, and all this by the power of the Stone, lapis ex caelis..."*

Lapis ex caelis. The stone from the heavens. Just for a moment Ned was far away from London and back in the city of
Prague, where he had gone when his soldiering was over. He
remembered the Street of Gold and the crooked little houses
that lay in the shadow of the castle wall, where the alchemists
worked over their low furnaces behind shuttered windows, laboring night and day to create the Philosopher's Stone that
would convert all base metals to gold.

He settled back on his bench and read more. It was a set of
instructions, couched in the bizarre language of the alchemists.

*"In spiritus vini is the base material first engulfed, then
nurtured in a sealed vessel... Qui non intelligit aut discat aut
taceat."*

Who does not understand should either learn or be
silent...

He put the papers away and tramped down to Temple Stairs
to call a boat to take him across the river. In the distance he
could see showers of sparks flying up from the great bonfires

around the city wall. At the Swan theater he waited and watched in the growing darkness; and just when he was thinking that Simon must have been wrong, he saw a torch-lit sedan chair being carried through the throng by black-liveried servants who cleared the way imperiously. The sedan came to a halt by the theater's entrance, and a familiar figure dressed all in black alighted with the careful dignity of a sixty-nine-year-old man into the street.

Ned drew in his breath sharply, stepped forward to the edge of the torchlight, and swept a low bow. "My lord," he said.

The Earl turned, frowning. Then his hooded eyes lifted a little in surprise. "Warriner. I thought you were abroad." He gestured his men away and said to Ned in a low voice, "You would have been well advised to remain there."

"I thought to claim some reward, my lord, for the services I have rendered you—the information I have sent."

"Information? Warriner, you are no longer any use as a spy abroad, now that the treaty has been signed between Spain and the Dutch rebels. In fact your services for the last six months have been quite redundant. According to His Highness the King, the Spaniards are now our friends."

Ned drew a sharp breath. "Then I will work for you here. In London."

"So eager to enter my service again ... You realize, of course, that your safety lies in my hands?"

"I realize that you ensured no charges were laid against me over the escape of the Catholic prisoner."

"But those charges could be resurrected at any time. And yet you have returned. I will not ask you why. I will not flatter myself that it is to seek my company. Instead I must assume that your return is the act of a desperate man. And that you are, accordingly, willing to do anything in order to prolong your sojourn in London. Well, well." He stroked his chin. His entourage waited, restlessly, at a distance. "I will be at Deptford tomorrow morning," said Northampton suddenly. "See me there. I might, perhaps, have work for you."

The Earl moved on, and was escorted by all his attendants through the open doors of the theater, leaving a drift of expensive perfume on the air that reminded Ned of the stench of the court. Northampton had guessed, correctly, that he was a desperate man, and out of his senses also, because he'd nurtured some dream of taking Kate away, when she wanted nothing more to do with him.

5.

Freeze, freeze, thou bitter sky,
Thou dost not bite so nigh
As benefits forgot:
Though thou the waters warp,
Thy sting is not so sharp
As friend remember'd not.

WILLIAM SHAKESPEARE (1564–1616)
AS YOU LIKE IT II.VII.174

IT WAS PAST NINE O'CLOCK IN THE EVENING BY THE time Francis Pelham left the Fleet prison. The man he had been interrogating all day was not, it turned out, a secret priest or Jesuit, not even a Catholic, but an elderly, frightened moneylender who had the incriminating rosary and crucifix in his possession simply because they had been offered to him in payment of a debt.

Pelham, angry because his whole day had been wasted and he'd learned nothing about Catholic plots from his prisoner, questioned him a little longer without success about the identity of the previous owner of the idolatrous objects. Then he told the warders to keep the man there one more night by way of revenge and set off home along Ludgate past St. Martin's church. All around him the bonfires were burning in defiance of the intermittent rain, and the bells of London pealed through the damp, dark night. Pelham reflected bitterly that the Catholics who still practiced their faith in the city should be burning on those pyres, for they were all traitors, like those who protected them.

He urged on his horse. He preferred to ride rather than walk because of his lame leg, shattered twelve years ago by a Spanish cannonball when he sailed under Essex and Ralegh on the failed venture to capture the Spanish treasure fleet off the Azores. The ship's surgeon had told him he would lose the limb, but Pelham refused to believe him. Then, as he lay weak and fevered in the stinking hold during the long voyage home, but with his leg healing at last, he was told that he would never walk again. Pelham defied that prediction also, helped by an older man on board the ship, a colleague of Ralegh's called Sir Thomas Revill, who inspired him with his unfailing solicitude for the younger man's welfare, and with his stories of his voyages to the Americas—one of them with Ralegh himself—and of the wonderful things he had seen there. Pelham listened to Revill, and was helped by him up onto the deck, where he walked up and down, up and down, leaning on Revill's arm. Slowly he grew well again. And he had remembered everything Revill had told him, including his description of his much-loved only daughter, Kate.

B Y THE TIME HE GOT HOME THAT NIGHT AFTER IN-terviewing his prisoner, Pelham expected his domestic staff—his two manservants, the housekeeper, and his wife's maid—to be absent, for he had instructed them to attend the evening service at St. Dunstan's church nearby. But as he unlocked the door and stepped into the oak-raftered hallway in which a lone candle burned, he became aware of his housekeeper standing in the shadows. A spinster of indeterminate age, she had served him for many years before his marriage. As he started to remove his cloak, she stepped forward, holding out a piece of paper.

"There was an intruder in the garden today, sir," she said. "The manservants beat him away, thinking he was a thief. But he dropped this." She handed him the folded paper. "It is addressed to your wife. But I thought you should have it."

Pelham smoothed it out. It was a poem. He read it silently.

They flee from me, that sometime did me seek
With naked foot stalking in my chamber.
I have seen them gentle, tame and meek
That now are wild and do not remember
That sometime they put themself in danger
To take bread at my hand...

Pelham turned the sheet over. On the other side was written his wife's name. Her maiden name.

I DO NOT KNOW WHO WOULD WRITE SUCH A THING," said Kate, standing in her bedchamber. She was clad in her silk dressing gown; she met his gaze directly. "It is a trivial matter, surely."

"Trivial?" said Pelham. "A poem about love?"

She walked to the window, from where she turned and faced him once more. "It's nothing but nonsense," she reiterated. "The kind of verse that travels for a day or so around the court. People recite it everywhere for a while, and then it is forgotten."

Pelham held the poem out, like an accusation. "Why would someone write it out for you? Using your unmarried name?"

"I do not know. I have no explanation. But I do not invite such attentions. Someone has made a mistake."

Still gazing at her, he tore up the poem into tiny pieces, then went over to the fire to scatter them on the flames. He stood with his back to the fire and said, "One more thing. I went to the Virginia Office today, to ask if there was any news of the *Rose*."

She sat down on the edge of the bed waiting, her hands twisting in her lap.

"One of the ships that sailed with her," he went on, "reached Bristol a week ago. But the *Rose* was badly damaged in a storm and apparently had to make for the American mainland, in the direction of the Spanish coast. There are fears that her cargo might have been impounded. If these rumors prove true, then the shares that I hold in the *Rose* could prove worthless, and I will have unpaid debts."

"Debts you incurred long before you married me."

"Is it my fault I was not born into wealth and privilege? I am telling you this because we might need to make economies. We might even need to sell this house."

She stood up slowly and looked around. "This house was my mother's. This is where I have spent all of my life..."

Pelham cut in, "You were brought up to expect too much. It was your father who reduced your inheritance, with his foolish foreign adventures."

"At least his occupations were something of which I could be proud."

He paled, catching his breath. "You wish you had not married me," he said, "you have always been cold to me, always; and in God's name, I sometimes wish I had never seen you."

She made for the door, but he reached out and spun her round.

"Let go of me," she said. But as she tried to push him away he seized her gown by the neck and ripped it, all the way down so that her breasts, high and blue-veined, were exposed to the chill air. "You are my wife," he said. "My wife."

He pushed her back against the bed, so hard that she lost her balance and fell back onto the counterpane, her legs splayed. Pelham crouched over her, forcing himself on her. "Do not cry out," he warned.

She closed her eyes and heard the church bells outside, and the rain beating against her windowpane. He took her swiftly, panting with the effort, hurting her. He shuddered as he reached his climax, then pushed her aside and strode from the room, slamming the door behind him.

She did not cry. She went to wash herself fiercely, using the ewer of water that stood on the chest, scrubbing herself with her washcloth. She pulled her torn and crumpled gown across her breasts and paced the room, to and fro, to and fro, with her arms folded and her chin tilted high, just as she had done when she heard the news of her father's death three years ago. Then she went to unlock a drawer in the chest by her bed, and drew out her father's old books and papers: maps and diaries, letters adorned with sketches of his travels to the Orinoco with Ralegh, fourteen years ago, when she was a child.

She looked at them, then put them down and went over to the dying fire, where Pelham had scattered the torn pieces of the poem. They had all turned to ashes, but she knew the words by heart.

It was no dream; I lay broad waking.
But all is turned thorough my gentleness
Into a strange fashion of forsaking . . .

Oh, Ned. How had it happened? How had her life come to this?

6.

⟜⟜⟜⟜⟜⟜ ⟜⟜⟜⟜⟜⟜⟜⟜⟜⟜⟜⟜⟜⟜⟜⟜

London, thou art the flower of Cities all.
Gem of all joy, jasper of jocundity.

WILLIAM DUNBAR (1465–1530)
"LONDON" l.16

ON THE WEST BANK OF THE FLEET RIVER, TO THE
south of Golden Lane, was a neighborhood of houses that
had been built for the rich merchants of the city in the heady
days of Queen Elizabeth's reign. The merchants found these
houses spacious, their rooms light and airy. The merchants'
wives and children enjoyed the flower-filled gardens that
stretched down to the sparkling waters of the River Fleet as it
hurried to meet the mighty Thames. These riverside mansions
had been prized dwellings, less than thirty years ago. But
times had changed.

The rich had moved on to more fashionable abodes. The
mansions had one by one been divided into tenements and allowed to sink into squalor. Rough shacks and hovels had been
built adjacent to their walls, and some of the empty buildings
had been pilfered for stone and brick. Now, only six years after Queen Elizabeth's death, the area was inhabited by the

feckless and the criminal. Ragged urchins played barefoot amongst the debris that was strewn over the once cherished gardens. A few late roses bloomed even now, but no one noticed them.

The River Fleet, fed by the springs of rural Hampstead, had become an open sewer. Rafts of waste rode downstream, surrounded by scum. Sometimes the children would point out to each other the swollen body of a dead rat or dog, bobbing in the sludge. Occasionally they spied a human corpse, the victim of an unheeded crime.

When the plague struck here, as it did most summers, the justices would set men to burn great bonfires strewn with pitch to fumigate the air. Workers were paid to gather up the bodies and take them to the lime pits in the fields out beyond Holborn. They even, at the height of the summer's pestilence the year before, attempted to clear the great mound of excrement and rubbish piled up by the tannery works to the north of Fleet Street.

But the river still stank, and few came to live here who could live anywhere else.

At the heart of this unappetizing neighborhood lay Rose Alley, which ran westward from the Fleet toward Shoe Lane and Holborn. It once boasted several spacious timbered houses owned by grain merchants who kept warehouses down by the Thames; but now beggars clustered in permanent residence round a fire at a corner of the street, and the only business done around here—apart from a rough tavern called the Crown just up Shoe Lane, and a coal merchant's dilapidated premises at the northern end of Rose Alley—was carried out by a dealer in stolen goods called Matthew, whose house was larger than the others, and had not been divided into tenements.

Matthew's front door was substantial, of necessity, with good bolts and locks, and his windows were stoutly barred and shuttered at night. But tonight, at ten o'clock, a lamp shone from one of those windows, indicating that Matthew was at home, counting up the profits of the evening's work. It had been a successful night, too, since so many citizens were out either dancing round the Powder Treason bonfires or listening to sermons in church. Since dusk, when all the city's bells had pealed in jubilation, his colleagues in crime had come to him through the rain, either alone or in pairs; some with sacks, others with their pockets full. One even came with a cart, borrowed from the coal man, at the end of the lane, Black Petrie, with several stout coalmen of Petrie's to guard it. But successful nights like this were becoming rarer.

Matthew and his men, as was customary, had a clearly defined boundary in which they worked. Matthew's assistants brought him the goods they'd stolen, so that he could sell them on, and give them a share of the profits. Neighboring villains kept to their own patch, and the local constables left Matthew alone because he made it well worth their while to do so. Besides, he was a peaceable sort of fellow, whose gang of thieves did not resort to bloodshed unless hard pressed, unlike some of their more vicious rivals on the streets.

Lately, though, it was as if all Matthew's plans were anticipated by some secret enemy. For example, forewarned the other night of a lightly guarded consignment of silks just arrived by river at a warehouse down by the Thames, Matthew had sent some of his best men—Brogger Davey, little Pentinck, Pat the big Irishman, and four of Pat's fellow countrymen—down to remove it. But they were foiled—indeed, they only just escaped arrest—because there turned out to be twelve armed watchmen at the warehouse, hiding in ambush.

There were other incidents: local businesses suddenly refusing to pay his men the usual protection fee; neighboring gangs causing trouble at the taverns where his men drank. And the local constables were demanding more and more money to let Matthew get on with his business in peace, despite the hard work of Scrivener Steen, the smooth-spoken, struck-off lawyer who lived next door and acted as Matthew's legal adviser, clerk, and expert forger of all the various licenses needed to practice any sort of trade at all in London.

So it was not with an entirely trouble-free mind that Matthew, in his old fur cap with ear flaps to protect him from the November cold that crept up from the river, completed a final tally of the night's acquisitions. At least tonight there had been no ambushes. At the moment he was all on his own except for his cook in the kitchen; but soon his comrades in crime would be calling, and he was just anticipating a few pints of ale at the Crown, when he heard the front door opening slowly.

Matthew, a burly and formidable black-bearded figure, strode out into the hall to see a man there, shaking the rain from his cloak. The man was dressed in tattered russet clothing and had a pack slung over his shoulder. He had a dog with him, a big, shaggy creature, as wet and bedraggled as his master; puddles of water were gathering on the floor where they both stood. But Matthew opened his arms wide in joyful greeting.

"Ned," he exclaimed. "Well, damn me. My little brother . . ."

Old Tew the cook, who was half-deaf, had heard vague noises in the distance and came through from the kitchen to investigate, bringing whiffs of smoke from something burning; but Matthew gestured him away, then took Ned Warriner in a squeezing, bear-like embrace and thumped him on the back.

"Come in," he urged. "Come in. It's good to see you, even if you do still owe me rent from your last visit." He had taken Ned's arm and was leading him through to the inner room, where he swept his tally sheets aside and poured wine from a leather bottle into two beakers.

Ned took the wine and raised it in greeting. "Three guineas. I've not forgotten. I had to leave in a hurry."

"So I heard. I always told you those fancy friends of yours at the court would bring you trouble."

Ned said quietly, "Believe me, I have no friends at the court."

Matthew snorted, with just the hint of a rebuke. "You spent enough time there. But we've both made mistakes. We had a poor start, you and I, Ned. Trying to be something we weren't, at old Revill's house. Tutors. Music. Latin . . ."

"Revill wanted to help us," said Ned. "And anyway, you missed most of the lessons."

"I ran off most days because I was bored. Holy Jesus, what use was Latin or fancy poetry to me?"

"I see the mathematics came in useful." Ned pointed to Matthew's tally sheets and Matthew laughed.

"So I've not done too badly for myself. But for people like you and me, Ned, the only way out of stinking poverty is to break the damned rules." He leaned back in his chair, assessing his younger brother. "Do you still write ballads?"

"Yes." Ned was surprised. "Yes, as a matter of fact, I do."

"Good." Matthew reached across the table and pulled a pile of grubby papers toward him. "Lots of people want ballads. If you're back here for a while, can you write some for me?"

"Embracing culture at last, Matthew? Do you want these ballads in Latin, or French? Or just English?"

Matthew waved his hand in his smiling brother's face. "Jesus, Ned, I'm serious. Listen to this. This one's about Lord Cecil and his friends in the Privy Council. Where is it, damn it?" He leafed through the sheets. "Here. It sold brilliantly the other week.

"Little Cecil trips up and down
For he rules both court and crown
In his fancy fox furred gown..."

He stabbed at the printed sheet with his finger. "There's more, about all of Cecil's mistresses, and how he's plagued with the French pox. They say he's even richer now than the King himself. Can you write stuff like that? Gossip, scandal? I've got shares in a printing press in Ludgate; we're selling this sort of thing by the dozen out on the streets, at sixpence a time. It's a private press, of course..."

"Unlicensed, you mean."

"I do things properly!" protested Matthew. "Scrivener Steen has made me a license good enough to fool even a judge. It's a gold mine, Ned."

"Sounds worth a try. Better than your efforts at selling that quack cure for the plague last time I was here. How many ballads do you need?"

"As many as you can write. Will you do it?"

"I will. As long as you can you fix me up with somewhere to stay for a week or two."

Matthew pondered. "There's the little attic bedroom. But the roof leaks worse than ever. I know! You can stay at the end of the lane, in that room over the stables. Do you remember it?"

"What happened to the two whores who used to live there? Or will I be sharing?"

Matthew rubbed his nose. "They moved on. It's a roof, boy, a roof." He hunted in his pocket for the key.

"Indeed," said Ned. "Thanks, Matthew. How's business? Apart from the ballads?"

"Oh, thriving, Ned, thriving." Matthew drained the rest of his wine and poured out more for both of them. "My little brother," he chuckled. "Back home again. Who would have believed it? Now tell me everything you've been up to."

SEVEN YEARS BEFORE, WHEN NED BROKE OFF HIS AP-prenticeship to seek his fortune at the court, Matthew was happy to stay on in his own chosen field, working as a laborer in a timber yard at Queenhithe. He'd had no regrets about lost learning, or musicianship. But he profited well from those years in the rough world of the London riverside. He learned the tricks of minor felony, and made useful friends amongst the gangs of thieving, hard-drinking ruffians who inhabited the wharves. When he fell out with his crooked employer, he graduated from working for one of those gangs to running his own business in passing on stolen goods, based here in Rose Alley.

Though Matthew disapproved of Ned's life at court, he had always remained fiercely loyal to his younger brother, and he listened now, shaking his head, to Ned's brief account of his travels, and his experiences in the Netherlands war.

"And now the Dutch have been forced to make peace," he muttered. "Peace with the bloody Spaniards. Who would have believed it? It would have been a different matter if our King and his councillors hadn't abandoned the poor Dutch five years ago, Ned."

They were presented with dishes of broth that Matthew's cook, John Tew, had concocted in the kitchen. Tew, an old and half-deaf comrade of Matthew's from the days of the timber yard, was good at picking locks, on doors and safes, and Ned had always assumed this was why Matthew kept him on. It certainly wasn't for his culinary skills. After eating a little, Ned promised to meet his brother later at the Crown, where he also quietly resolved to purchase a decent meal. Then he set off to his new abode.

It was still raining, and the water pooled in the lane, forming puddles in which the rubbish thrown out by the locals made unsavory islands. Ned climbed up the rickety outside stairs above the stable where Petrie the coalman kept his nags, unlocked the door, and struck tinder and flint. The room was furnished with an assortment of broken furniture that looked as if it had been pushed up there because nobody else wanted it.

At least he could lock the door. He lit a candle stump above the fireplace and put his pack and his lute on the box bed. While Barnabas sniffed around he went over to the window, which was bare to the elements except for a wooden shutter that dangled from one hinge. From it he could see to the far end of the street. He settled the candle in the empty grate and felt the straw-stuffed mattress, which was mildewed. There were no blankets. The whole place smelled of damp, and seemed colder than outside.

Some wood and coals had been left in the grate, and he was crouching over them, preparing a fire to warm this desolate place, when the door began to open slowly. He sprang to his feet, alert. Then he relaxed. A girl of around eighteen with curling fair hair stood there, holding some blankets over her arm. "Alice," he said.

She grinned at Ned and threw them on the bed. "I told Matthew you'd be needing these. How are you, Ned? I couldn't believe it when I heard you were back. Thought you'd escaped for good. Jesus, I know I would."

She ran her fingers through her long hair and gave him a sidelong glance. Beneath her half-open cloak she wore a gaudy print gown with a low-cut bodice that did little to conceal her full breasts. Alice belonged to Matthew. Once, when Ned had taken refuge for a short while at his brother's house during one of his frequent arguments with Northampton, she had made it clear that she was prepared to transfer her favors to him. He had resisted, but guessed that she wasn't one to give up lightly.

Now she moved farther into the room and prodded the wall where the plaster crumbled.

"I'll just be staying here for a week or so," he said.

"Not made your fortune, then?"

"Not yet, no." He walked past her to the door and held it open. "It's good to see you again, Alice. But I have things to do. And won't Matthew be wondering where you are?"

He noted a quick spark of disappointment, of resentment even, in her heavy-lidded dark eyes; but she shrugged and said, "Matthew can wait. You. Back in Rose Alley. Who'd have believed it? After all, you've always despised your brother."

"That is not true," he said quickly. "I'm very grateful to him. He knows that. Thanks for bringing the blankets." He held the candle out over the steps to light her on her way.

She started to go, then turned back, her sloe eyes glinting with malice. "Oh. By the way. With you being away and everything, you might not have heard, about that girl you and Matthew once knew. The girl who gave herself fancy airs. Kate, she was called. Kate Revill."

Ned said, "What about her?"

"She's married," she said. "And has a child. A little boy called Sebastian."

"I know."

"Her child is sick," went on Alice. "Her little boy. Born in the spring of last year, he was. Not yet two years old. The doctors are always at the house."

"I am sorry to hear it." He still had his hand on the door.

"And Pelham, he's strict with the little boy, he tells Mistress Kate off, for spoiling him; he makes her cry. I know because I've a friend who sometimes helps with the laundry there. She hears all the news."

"True or false, it's none of my business." He held the door open wider. She scowled and went off down the stairs at last.

Ned shut the door and leaned back against it. He thought, Alchemy is not as strange as real life, real people. How men—and women—are transformed by their fate. Times change, and we change with them. *The putrefaction of the dead carcass of hope...*

The bells of St. Bride's church down on Fleet Street told him it was ten. He unpacked his meager possessions, then went off whistling in the darkness, with Barnabas at his heels, to meet his brother at the Crown.

Around London, the bonfires burned on damply, and all the church bells of the city rang to celebrate Powder Treason night.

RAIN POURED DOWN ALSO ON A NARROW ALLEY OFF King's Lane, between Thames Street and the river. There in a pool of darkness in the shadow of a great hemp warehouse lay the body of Sam Turner, ex-regular of the Three Tuns, half-hidden in a heap of moldering canvas where rats crawled. After he had told his assailants as much as he could about the Auriel letter and the lute player—had screamed it out, in fact, again and again, if only to make them leave him alone—his suffering had at last ended. Apart from a little bruising to his arms and face, there was no mark on him to indicate the violent manner of his death; except that the little finger of his right hand was missing, hewn off with a sharp implement. And yet there seemed to be no blood, unless perhaps the rain had washed it all away.

7.

♪

Spies, you are lights in state, but of base stuffe,
Who, when you have burnt your selves downe to the snuffe,
Stinke and are throwne away.

BEN JONSON (1572–1637)
EPIGRAM LIX

UNTIL TUDOR TIMES THE VILLAGE OF DEPTFORD, three miles downriver of the City of London, was an isolated country hamlet set between the marshes and the river, where boys hunted for snipe or went fishing along the reedy banks of the Thames. But now the busy offices of the East India Company jostled for space with the expanding storehouses for timber and hemp. Docks and slipways for the construction of great seafaring vessels lined the riverside. Sawpits and masthouses covered the former pastureland, and the air was filled with the clamor of coopers and shipbuilders.

Only the lonely cries of the seabirds, and the emptiness of the distant horizon where the broad river flowed between the salt marshes on its way to the sea, kindled memories of Deptford's vanished past.

The tide was racing in, and the river was a mass of gray and white swirling peaks as Ned alighted from the hired boat that had brought him there and walked to the place where he guessed Northampton would be.

Northampton, like his arch-rival Cecil and other wealthy magnates, including Henry, Prince of Wales, kept a well-guarded warehouse here at Deptford, where the valuable goods he imported from the Continent—Italian paintings, marble sculptures, costly silk fabrics—could be stored in safety for a brief while prior to their transportation to his great mansion at Greenwich. Ned's assumption was correct: he saw the Earl's barge, gilded and adorned with his standard, moored by the river stairs. The Earl's bodyguards, standing impassive in their black livery outside the warehouse, saw him approaching. One of them beckoned wordlessly, and Ned followed him into the warehouse, knowing full well he could be walking into a trap.

He had cleaned himself up as best he could. Out in the cold November dawn, he had stripped and washed himself under the pump in his brother's yard. He had shaved off his ragged beard also, then borrowed a suit of clothing from Matthew's store of stolen goods, and left Barnabas with old Tew the cook.

He missed Barnabas at his side now. It took him a moment to adjust his eyes to the darkness. A single cresset burned on the wall, unevenly illuminating the life-size statues and oil portraits that were stacked against the wall. Ned was checked for weapons, and the guards retreated. The big doors slammed shut behind him.

Ned whirled round as the Earl himself stepped out of the shadows. In his hands he held a fragile porcelain bowl—Chinese, Ned guessed, and of considerable value.

"So, Warriner. You haven't changed your mind. About wanting to work for me again."

"My lord, I never stopped working for you during my exile."

Ned broke off, the skin on the back of his neck prickling as he became aware of more men moving up behind him, from the shadows by the great doors. Northampton raised his hand in a sharp gesture, ordering them to stand back. Then he put the porcelain bowl back into a straw-packed crate that stood open against the wall and said softly to Ned, "Your letters were certainly interesting, Warriner. You spent a busy two years in the army of Prince Maurice. But your efforts, as I said, became redundant with the recent peace treaty. A pity you failed to realize it. And I never, ever suggested that you return home."

"My lord, I had not anticipated two years ago that my exile would be permanent—"

"That was, I think, your decision. You imposed exile on yourself." He smiled, a lupine smile. "Yet you planned it all so well. Until then, I had no idea you were a secret Catholic lover."

The single cresset spurted in its socket, illuminating the details of a somber portrait nearby. Ned said, "Ashworth was not a spy. Not a traitor."

"And you hoped the affair was well and truly forgotten by now, no doubt. But people still talk of those guards who were ambushed and injured as they escorted their prisoner to the Tower. They remember the convicted Catholic set free, whisked away into thin air. People mutter that it was the work of traitors, in Spanish pay."

"My lord, you know I am no traitor. And I am tired of exile. I will earn your protection, I swear it."

Northampton raised his hooded eyelids. "I wonder what you are planning now? What can you possibly offer me, to earn my protection? You are an unemployed soldier, Warriner, in need of new clothes and a barber; you are no adornment. You have a dubious reputation, so you are no use as a spy. Someone, somewhere, if you stay in London, will sooner or later connect you with Ashworth's escape." His lip curled. "You could hire yourself to the ladies of the court, perhaps, as you did before. They would like to hear that you had killed men in battle. But you are a little old now, a little too scarred by life, to claw your way up into favor by appealing to men of certain tastes. Though the Master of the King's Music, as I remember, always harbored a certain penchant for you."

Ned braced himself. His face was pale with anger.

"Now, if you had returned with money," Northampton went on, "or with news of some newly discovered gold mine in America or the Indies, such as the ones old Ralegh still boasts of in his prison room, then, indeed, people might have listened to you. The greed of the court is endless. King James wants gold for all his pretty youths. The Queen wants money for her idle fripperies. My lord Cecil—why, little Cecil wants gold, to build his great mansion at Hatfield and buy presents for his mistresses." He was softly stroking his pointed beard. "They say he has even set his men to look for the Philosopher's Stone, but that, I cannot believe." He snapped his jeweled fingers dismissively. "And Prince Henry, our illustrious young heir to the throne, has spread his wings since you left. Have you heard? He is setting up his own household in the palace of St. James, and Cecil is watching him most carefully. Henry hates his father, and his father's craven attempts to keep peace with the Catholic powers. He longs for a fresh war against the old enemy, the Scorpion Spain. He consults with astrologers, herbalists, and other such charlatans to ascertain the best time for attack. And across Europe the armies are gathering. You will have seen this for yourself."

"I saw, my lord, that peace treaties have been signed. But the armies have not been disbanded."

"A good point. Soon there could be a war, in which our Prince would join, oh, so gladly. So young. So misguided. So ill advised . . ." He stroked his chin again, then looked at Ned sharply. "You wish to stay in London. You are willing, you say, to undertake any job for me if I ensure that the Ashworth business is kept secret. Do you still mean what you say?"

"I do."

"Here, then, is my proposition. You were a mercenary, for two years. You have killed to order. Very well. I want you to kill someone for me."

Ned could see the Earl's guards, fully armed, standing by the closed door to the warehouse. The darkness, away from the pool of light cast by the cresset, was impenetrable. If he refused, it was unlikely that he would leave this place alive. "Who is this man?"

"Ah, Ned, Ned. How I would love to know why you are so

desperate to come back.... The man is called John Lovett. He works for Prince Henry. And he has maligned my name. You must kill him quietly and quickly, and it must look like an accident, a robbery, or illness, perhaps. No one must suspect intrigue of any kind. Do you understand? Achieve his death, without causing alarm in the Prince's household, and I will guarantee your safety."

"It seems a drastic revenge, my lord."

"Indeed. And nothing else will do. That is your task, Ned. Do you accept?"

Ned bowed his head. "I do."

Northampton nodded thoughtfully. "Good. But I want the business concluded swiftly. I do hope you understand."

Northampton walked back to his attendants, who swung the great doors open and escorted him out. Then one of them turned, lifted the cresset from its holder, and closed the doors in Ned's face.

The darkness and the silence enveloped him. He whirled round. He could hear nothing but the thud of his own heart in that vaulted, echoing space. The faces of the three life-size marble statues peered at him dimly through the gloom. Something moved in a dusty corner. He spun round again, his hand reaching for the sword he didn't have, his breath coming sharply.

He thought, They could kill me here, and no one would know.

He went to try the doors. They were barred shut on the outside.

And then he heard the rattling of a latch and another, smaller door opened to the side. One of Northampton's guards stood there, outlined against the daylight.

"You," he said. "Come out this way. The Earl prefers not to be seen in public with his supplicants."

Slowly Ned's pulse stopped racing. He followed the man outside and saw that Northampton and his attendants were already on board the waiting barge, canopied against the rain. The Earl's standard flew from the prow.

He was alone, and free to go. As long as he killed a man called John Lovett.

• • •

LOVETT?" MATTHEW FROWNED. "YES, I REMEMBER HIM. A smooth customer. There was always talk that he was in the thick of the corruption at the docks."

Ned ordered a fresh tankard of ale for his brother. They were at the Crown. Some of Matthew's companions had joined them earlier—Brogger Davey, Matthew's deputy, who was ginger-haired, thickset, and fierce; Scrivener Steen the ex-lawyer, who told Ned some of the latest rude ballads about the court; and Tew the cook, who'd formed a bond of friendship already with Barnabas by feeding him scraps from the kitchen.

But now Davey and the others had moved on to another tavern, where there was rumored to be a good card game going, and Matthew and Ned were alone.

Ned said, "I've heard that now Lovett is secretary to Prince Henry. At St. James's Palace."

"So he is. Now. But he started his career as a clerk, with the East India Company. It would be just after you began working for Northampton, a few years ago. They say he's still involved in the pilfering there. But unlike some, he has the damned brains to cover his tracks."

"In what way?"

Matthew drank some of his ale. "Earlier this year, in May, there was a big inquiry into the corruption at the docks. The Earl of Northampton demanded it. He's been protesting for years to the King about Pett and the shipyards."

Ned said, *"Go on."*

"Well, Northampton and his cronies set up all the accusations, and got together enough evidence to ensure that Pett and Mansell and the rest of the dock masters had to be hauled up to answer questions. They were sweating with fright, I'll tell you. The whole town was talking of it. Then Prince Henry arrived, with that smooth, clever secretary of his, John Lovett. The Prince declared the whole inquiry a sham, defended his friend Phineas Pett to the hilt, and got Lovett to present facts, figures, and so on to show that everything was totally aboveboard at the King's shipyard."

He paused for another drink, but his tankard was empty. Ned summoned the potboy and said, "Who was telling the truth?"

"For once, I think the Earl was. You've spent a lot of time at court, Ned. You can picture it, and how Northampton must have felt. This hearing was in front of the King himself, and Northampton was made to look an utter, bloody fool. He'd got just a few minor facts wrong, and Lovett—very civilly, very deferentially—called him a liar, while Prince Henry made some pompous speech about the wickedness of false accusations. The news of it was all around the city the next day, in rude rhymes, ballads in the taverns—you know the sort of thing. I heard that Northampton stormed out with his lecherous old face as black as thunder. I think he would have liked to kill someone. Lovett's been going round ever since with a bodyguard nearly as good as Prince Henry's. Of course, Northampton is quite right. There certainly is corruption at the docks. It all stinks to high bloody heaven."

Ned paid for Matthew's fresh tankard of ale. "Is Prince Henry involved in the corruption, do you think?"

"I doubt it." Matthew took a swig of his drink. "He's fresh-faced and innocent, and that's no doubt how his wily advisers want him to stay. Though they say he's had peculiar dealings now and then with men whose advice borders on the occult. All hocus-pocus; but some men like to be guided by the stars. Perhaps he's putting a curse on his father—they say there's no love lost between them." He grinned and downed the rest of his ale appreciatively.

"Matthew," Ned said, leaning forward, "do you know any alchemists?"

Matthew let out a bellow of laughter. "That desperate, are you, lad? Davey was talking a week or two back about an old alchemist, down by Billingsgate, who was rumored to have the secret of gold. Davey was thinking of robbing the place, but it turned out just to be full of crucibles and stinking sulfur. No Philosopher's Stone there. Nor ever likely to be, if you ask me." He chuckled again, and just then someone else came up to Matthew, wanting to talk business, so Ned got up and left.

He looked up at the heavy skies. The charred remnants of

last night's bonfires had made the air sour with the stench of smoke. He remembered the sparks flying up into the blackness above London and showering down again like streams of molten gold. *"The golden Sun is about to rise, and all this by the power of the Stone, lapis ex caelis..."*

The gift of gold. What had Northampton said? "The greed of the court is endless. King James wants gold for all his pretty youths. The Queen wants money for her idle fripperies." Even Cecil, Northampton had said, had set his men to look for the Philosopher's Stone. He wondered why Northampton, who had so many spies, so many secret servants capable of murder, had decided to make Ned the instrument of his revenge on John Lovett. Probably because he considered that Ned was expendable.

It was up to Ned to prove otherwise.

8.

Son, be not hasty. I exalt our med'cine
By hanging him in balneo vaporoso,
And giving him solution; then congeal him,
And then dissolve him; then again congeal him;
For look, how oft I iterate the work,
So many times I add unto his virtue.

BEN JONSON (1572–1637)
THE ALCHEMIST

BY THE NEXT MORNING, THE RAIN CLOUDS HAD DIS-persed. A fresh breeze blew up from the river, teasing at the plumes of smoke which rose from the stacks of the foundry by the Ropery and leaving the odors of fish, brine, and tar in its wake as it tested the windows and doors of all the houses between East Cheap and Billingsgate.

The old man in his lair at the back of Crooked Lane was sitting on a stool by his workbench, but his eyes were closed. He had nodded off, as he often did these days, to dream of Ficino, who had tramped the world with his dog at his side seeking the secret of gold. He dreamed that the great alchemist had arrived here and was imparting his knowledge; but just as Ficino was about to announce the vital ingredient for the making of the Philosopher's Stone, there was a sudden rattling at the door, and the old man almost fell off his stool.

He jumped to his feet, muttering. The door shook again.

Was it just the wind? Anxiously he turned to his workbench, where retorts and crucibles bubbled and steamed, and called to his young assistant to leave the bellows and look to see what the disturbance was; but the boy had scarcely reached the door when the alchemist, who called himself Albertus—his real name he had discarded so long ago that he could hardly now remember it—called him back to tend the fire.

It was only the wind, surely, disturbing the old building. Old Albertus was as fearful of losing heat for his cherished crucibles as a mother bird of letting her nestlings grow cold; for in the oldest and most precious of his vessels—how old? he did not know, it was many years old, perhaps, for this was a business in which hours, days, weeks were not counted—his long-nurtured mixture of philosopher's mercury and sulfur, bathed in alchemical dew, was evaporating and crystallizing again and again as it endured the long path to perfection. With trembling hands he went to lift up the heat-blackened crucible from the fire and gazed at its mysterious contents.

Calcination. Distillation. Cohobation.

He was almost daring to hope that with this crucible he was close to attaining the Sixth Stage of which philosophers dreamed: the White Tincture, which would be followed by the final fruition. All the old philosophers, Paracelsus, Pico, Agrippa, and Ficino himself, described different pathways to reaching the pinnacle of the Philosopher's Stone, that miraculous substance which would transform everything to gold; and Albertus had, for many long years, tried all of them. His hair and beard had grown white as he read his books, and distilled his mixtures, and calcined and purified again and again; the boys he had employed to run his errands and keep his braziers had come and gone so often that he had given up with their names, as he had with his own.

At night, ever fearful of robbers after his secrets, he scarcely slept, but continued to read of the hermetic mysteries in the Picatrix, and the Emerald Tablet. He studied also the wanderings of the planets, which preordained not only the lives of men but the growth of all things, including gold. When he did sleep, Albertus dreamed of gold. He yearned with his whole being to discover the secret recipe for the

Stone that the magus John Dee was believed to have learned from an angelic messenger just before his death, the knowledge of which was said to have died with him. Sometimes Albertus feared that he, too, would die before the secret was his.

The boy had returned to laboring over the bellows, for Albertus had told him again and again that constant heat was needed to nurture his concoction. Then outside in the street a dog barked, and there was a fresh rattling at the door. Albertus, muttering, went himself to secure the catch against the troublesome November wind that was sending plumes of smoke back down his chimney. But as he was checking the bolts, he heard a man's voice calling,

"Master Albertus. Master Albertus. Are you there?"

Albertus pulled back the bolts and opened the door a few inches. He blinked shortsightedly in the morning sunlight, and screwed up his wrinkled face. There was a man standing there, a young man, in a shabby suit of russet, with his dark hair blowing in the wind and stubble shadowing his jaw. A long-haired, golden dog stood at his side, plumed tail wagging.

"Master Albertus?"

"Yes. What is it?" snapped Albertus.

"I have heard," said the stranger, "that you are a learned man—"

Oh, no. Oh, no. Not someone else after his precious secrets. Albertus was about to slam the door again, but the man had his booted foot in the way. "Go away," quavered Albertus, aware of his boy peering out from his perch by the bellows. "Leave me alone."

"In a moment. I just wanted to ask you some questions," said the man. "About this." And he held out a sheet of paper, folded up, so that Albertus could read only part of it.

"To Auriel, I will give the gift of gold..."

Albertus looked up at him sharply. "Where did you get this?"

"Does it matter?"

"Are you a student of the Great Art? Are you an adept?"

"I know nothing about it at all," said the man. "I just wanted to know what some of the words mean. And who Auriel is."

Albertus made a gesture of contempt. This was the fourth time in as many days that he had been interrupted by rogues pretending to be students of alchemy. They usually either asked for his help or tried to sell him some quack recipe. He suspected that often their real motive was robbery. "Auriel," he said, with heat, "was God's angel, who wrestled with Jacob on the stairway to heaven, just as we genuine practitioners have to struggle daily with charlatans."

"Is the letter of any value?"

"Your ignorance is the answer to your own question, sir! What you have there must be worthless; your very possession of it proves it to be so! The pursuit of the Philosopher's Stone is a preparing of the spirit, a calling to the highest degree; now go, with your so-called recipe, and leave me to my work—"

He tried to shut the door but the man was young and strong. His foot was still wedged there, his shoulder too.

"Very well," the young man said. "Unworthy as I am, just tell me this. Are they all like this, these recipes for gold? Do they all talk of Noble Princes, and Scorpions?"

Albertus said, "Be off with you, before I call the constables..."

But the man, thrusting the letter in the pocket of his jerkin, had pushed his way inside the room. He looked round quickly and picked up a warm glass crucible, the one containing the oldest and most precious of Albertus's concoctions. He held it above the stone-flagged floor and let it swing. "No," cried Albertus hoarsely, "no..."

"Then answer my question, old man. What is the significance of the Noble Prince in alchemy?"

Albertus looked at the suspended crucible with horror. His boy cowered, open-mouthed.

"Many of the philosophers have talked of the Noble Prince," quavered Albertus. "Take care, I beg you! He is a symbol of the rebirth of new life after sacrifice, the flowering of the precious mixture after calcination."

"What is calcination?"

The man held the crucible higher, by its neck. Albertus stammered out, "All the philosophers begin their work with the process of calcination. The base material must be heated in a sealed vessel, with *spiritus vini*—please—my crucible—"

"A sealed vessel." The man nodded, still dangling the crucible. "What is base material?"

"It's dung," gasped Albertus desperately. "Dung from the streets."

The stranger snorted. "And the *spiritus vini*?"

"Spirit of wine, distilled liquor, whatever you please—I implore you, be careful—that phial is precious ..."

"Just tell me what the Scorpion is."

"Scorpion? Is that in your letter? It is not an alchemical term I am familiar with."

The man put the crucible down. Albertus let out a great sigh. The man scanned his paper once more; then he gazed at Albertus's crucibles, taking in the stark poverty of his abode, his clothing. He said, "How long have you been attempting to discover the Philosopher's Stone?"

"All my life."

The man said, almost wonderingly, "All your life. For this. Well. *Qui non intelligit aut discat aut taceat.*" He folded up his paper and started toward the door, where his great golden dog was patiently waiting.

And here was a transformation, for old Albertus was leaping after him: not to slam the door and bolt it after him, but to call out to him, in entreaty, "Sir. Please. What did you just say?"

The man, already out in the lane with his dog at his heels, turned back in some surprise. "The Latin? It's just something in the letter." He marched on.

Albertus was trembling. He reached out his gnarled old fingers in entreaty. He called out, "Perhaps I might be able to help you with your letter after all. Please. If you would like to show me more ..."

But the stranger did not even hear him, for he and his dog were already disappearing swiftly into the labyrinth of alleys that lay behind Crooked Lane. Albertus hobbled forlornly after them, but soon they were out of sight. Albertus went back inside, where he clouted the boy, who had come to the door to watch, and shouted to him angrily to get back to his bellows. Then he paced to and fro, muttering, *"Qui non intelligit aut discat aut taceat..."*

For the intruder had quoted the motto, the inscription that was equivalent to a signature, of none other than Dr. John Dee, the great astrologer, scientist, and magician, who was respected by Europe's monarchs and who summoned angels to do his bidding; but who died in penury without the Philosopher's Stone he had been promised, having been reduced to selling all his books and possessions to buy food.

"THE MAN QUOTED DEE'S MOTTO TO ME, YET HE didn't seem to realize what he had!" whispered Albertus excitedly to his friend Godwin Phillips the draper, whom he had met by chance amidst the bustle of West Cheap later that day. "In his letter I even saw Dr. Dee's sign of the Sun. The fool will most likely sell it for a few coins, when he could have there the secret of the Philosopher's Stone."

Phillips shared Albertus's obsession with the business of alchemy in his reading, if not in practice. Now they walked together along West Cheap in the fresh morning air, surrounded by the clamor of street traders and housewives at their shopping. "He would only let me see the first sentence," Albertus went on. "And he seemed not to understand a word of it. But he asked me questions which indicated its content. Oh, the waste, the waste..."

At the crossroads they had to stop, because of the crowds pressing so heavily around them. Phillips shook his head in sympathy. "For whom do you think this letter was intended?"

Albertus was suddenly aware that he might have been wiser perhaps to keep the stranger's visit to himself, but he quickly dismissed his doubts. His old friend Phillips was as trustworthy as anyone he knew. Indeed, he had to be, for the gentle old draper was a secret Catholic, and so appreciated the necessity of silence. Therefore Albertus drew closer, and confided, "It was addressed to Auriel. The angel in whom Dee placed most trust. *To Auriel, I will give the gift of gold...*"

He broke off as someone pushed and almost fell against him. It was impossible to speak properly in this noisy throng. So the two friends bade farewell, promising to meet very soon. Godwin Phillips set off to cover the short distance to his shop, while Albertus hurried home with his packages, the antimony, arsenic, and red sulfur he had bought for his experiments. The boy, surprisingly, was still awake.

But Albertus could not concentrate on his work. He sent the boy home and knelt again, not praying as he should have done, but thinking with longing of the stranger's letter. Then he pulled on his old cloak and hat, and checked his purse. He had a few coins in there, which he dropped and picked up again; his agitation made him clumsy.

Old, rheumaticky Albertus had a secret of which he was too ashamed to tell anyone. He dreamed that the Philosopher's Stone would bring him not only gold, but also the elixir that would restore him to health, and would make the wrinkles of age vanish like the sloughed skin of a snake. Secretly he yearned to enjoy again the sweet pleasures of his far-distant youth; but he could tell no one of his longing, for an adept was supposed to be pure in thought, word, and deed. Albertus tried so hard, but he dreamed, often, of soft sweet skin and youthful maidens' breasts . . .

He left his house, having carefully locked all behind him. He hurried along St. Michael's Lane, turning the corner by the church of All Hallows, and the rooms where the dyers worked; then he went up a narrow alley to a place where the work was mostly by night. He knocked at the sturdy door, and trembled as with an ague as they let him in.

They laughed at him, and asked first to see his silver, but they were kind. He had been there before many times. Three of them led him down a passageway into a small room where they sat him in a chair; and there one of them, a slim girl with raven hair and pale skin, perched lightly on his skinny knee and said, "Have you come to watch again, old man?"

There was a spying hole where he and other ancients like himself could see the younger men taking their pleasure with these girls. "Yes," he breathed. "I have the money to watch. But soon I will want more . . ."

"Well. Old man." The three girls teased him gently. "We can expect some action next time, can we?"

"Yes," he said, urgently. "Yes."

"And which one of us will you choose?" They were laughing now. He touched the shoulder of the girl who had sat on his knee, the one with lustrous black hair. He thought of the words of the alchemist Ficino: *"For the crow is of all birds, most rich in hue and texture..."*

"I will choose you," he said earnestly.

He thought that John Dee's beautiful spirit Madimi must have looked like this girl. Old Albertus summoned her often in his dreams, and adored her with his body, waking enervated from his dreaming. As if she guessed his secret, the girl smiled and pocketed his silver, then went from the room. He was led to the door with the grille, where he watched in an agony of longing as his Madimi was violated by a young, brutal man who did not realize the worth of the precious vessel on which he coarsely spilled his seed. Madimi was pretending, he knew; she let her long dark hair fall in twisting coils over her white breasts, crying out as she feigned enjoyment of this man's vile attentions, his brute strength as he took her. Albertus was thinking, Soon, when the Philosopher's Stone is mine, I will have the elixir of life. Soon I will be young and strong again...

He felt a hand on his shoulder. "It's over, old man. It's time to go."

He set off for home in the fast-fading daylight, already regretting the silver he had spent so recklessly. He should have stayed in his laboratory, laboring over his life's work, just in case the stranger came back—the stranger with John Dee's letter to Auriel...

Oh, he was unworthy.

He began to unlock the door to his workshop, then realized with a jolt that it was not locked. His breath came short and fast. Perhaps he had forgotten, in his haste, to make all secure. He went inside, and saw, by the gentle glow of the oven, that there was someone else in there. A stranger. The shadows made the intruder's face indistinct. Was it the man who'd called here earlier? He stepped forward, and his old voice shook in challenge. "Who is it?"

Then he realized that it was not the man who had been there earlier, and that there were others in the room, too; four, no, five of them altogether, filling him with a fear that chilled his already cold limbs.

He would have tried to flee, but two of them stepped forward to seize him by the arms, though he was so weak with fright it would have taken only one of them. As they held him, they began to ask him questions, moving around him in the darkness so he could not see which of them asked, nor which of them hurt him. And hurt him they did, because they wanted to know who the stranger was with the letter, and why he had come to Albertus of all people.

"I do not know," he whispered, "I do not know who he was."

"And what was in this letter?"

He told them all he could remember. He felt the tears in his eyes, for himself, and for his lost dream of Madimi. He told them of Dr. Dee's sign of the sun, and of what the letter said—*"To Auriel, I will give the gift of gold."* He told them all he could remember of the man; they wanted to know what he looked like, they wanted to know if he had a dog; they even wanted to know if he had a lute slung over his back.

"I have told you everything, everything. Please leave me alone."

It was then that someone blew out the last of the candles, and they closed around him.

9.

The alchemist should be sufficiently rich to bear the expenses of his art.

ALBERTUS MAGNUS (C. 1193–1280)
"LIBELLUS DE ALCHIMIA"

AFTER HIS VISIT TO ALBERTUS, NED WARRINER HAD gone to St. Paul's and wandered up and down the many stalls that filled the aisles of the half-derelict cathedral. He'd stopped at a bookseller and haggled over several volumes; then he'd walked off with a little book called *Agrippa's Elixir: The Mystery of the Stone* hidden under his jerkin. He'd also obtained a glass crucible from an apothecary, but he'd had to pay for that. Afterward he went round the city asking more questions, hour after hour; and by the time he set off home darkness had fallen.

He'd been aware for some time that he was being followed. Whoever it might be was making no effort, though, to catch up with him, so he pressed on past the tannery yards of Bowyer Row and across the Fleet bridge to Rose Alley.

Then Ned turned and glimpsed his pursuer, some way behind him still, darting into the shadows. At the same time another figure came hurtling out of nowhere and threw himself upon the fleeing man.

The two of them struggled, rolling to and fro in the mud, but eventually the second man was the victor, holding down the first man bodily and pressing a knife at his throat.

Ned, who had drawn close, called out, "Don't kill him, Pat."

The dark-haired man with the knife looked up at him, still panting, his swarthy, hook-nosed face the picture of disbelief. "Why ever not? The bastard was going to kill you."

"Were you?" Ned asked the man on the ground, who was spread-eagled beneath Irish Pat's fierce grip.

"No," he whispered. "I swear I wasn't."

Ned had already recognized him as one of the men who'd been guarding Northampton at the warehouse. He said to Pat, "Let him go."

"You're jesting, Ned."

"Let him go. He was only watching me. And if you kill him, there'll be more of them."

Pat stood up, shaking his shaggy head in despair. He was tall, much taller than Ned, and powerfully built beneath his loose, threadbare coat. The man he'd fought to the ground glanced up at him with fear, then ran off into the darkness.

"Well, Ned. I heard you'd grown tired of exile. They didn't tell me you'd grown tired of life."

"I told you. He was just watching me. Checking on where I'm staying, at a guess."

"You've been back—what?—three days? Someone is watching you. And you say there are more. Are you sure it was a good idea to return?"

"I'm giving myself a week or two to decide."

"That gives them, then, a week or two to kill you."

Pat was an old friend of Matthew's, and of Ned's. He lived out at Bride's Fields, site of the ruined lazar house, with his fellow Irish exiles, but he often went thieving with Matthew's gang, taking particular delight in robbing the town houses of the rich when their owners fled from the city to hide from the plague. He played the fiddle like one possessed, making magic out of the haunting tunes of his native country. He had taught Ned a little, but Ned knew he could never play as well as Pat did.

"The music would break your heart if you let it," Pat had once told him. "Like life."

Pat's woman had died four years ago. Stricken with grief, he had left others to look after their three children, and had tried to drink himself to death. Ned had found him when he was almost unconscious, and stopped him drinking more, and talked to him all through the long night. He made him talk back to him, about the home in Ireland he'd left when he was a child, about his music, his children. After that, Pat had always said that he owed Ned his life.

Now, as they stood together on Rose Alley, Pat said, "If your idea of lying low is to let spying bloody scoundrels creep round after you and live, then so be it. Let me buy you a pint of ale so we can discuss your logic. And let me tell you about your brother. I'm worried about him."

"I'd noticed business doesn't seem good," Ned observed, following him in the direction of the Crown.

"Business for Matthew Warriner is very bad," said Pat emphatically. "People daren't bring him their goods to sell on anymore. The constables—though he still pays them, damn it—are clearly being paid a lot more by someone else. I've told him to watch his back, but he's a stubborn Englishman, like you, and will not listen. Your brother needs help, Ned."

"Then I'm glad to be back."

"Even if only for a little while?"

"Indeed."

"And if I see any more of those black-coated, whey-faced spies creeping around after you, I'm to let them live?"

Ned grinned. "Until I say otherwise, yes."

They had reached the tavern. It wasn't long before someone brought Pat a violin to play, and people got up to dance and sing. Two of Pat's Irish comrades joined him with a bodrun and penny whistle, and Ned sat back and let the wild Gaelic music flood his senses.

The big Irishman always calmly justified his way of life, the thievery.

"It's a way of making things on this earth a little fairer," he had once told Ned. "The rich bastards can afford to lose something of their wealth. And quite a lot of needy people are made much happier, if only because they can fill their families' bellies. Thus is the rich man's gold transformed into food and clothing for hungry children. It's a kind of Philosopher's Stone, in reverse."

"Do you believe in it?" Ned had asked.

"In what? The Philosopher's Stone? Dear God, I hope not. If it really existed, surely it would be the ruin of us all," Pat had replied.

Ned remembered his words as he listened to Pat's playing, but his contemplation didn't last much longer, for after a while Pat put down his fiddle and asked Ned to sing. After his excuses had all been turned down, Ned obliged the crowded tavern with ditties from the alehouses of Kraków, about the whores there, and the trouble they had with the Polish knights back from fighting the Turks. At last he decided it was time to go. "Good to have you home," Pat said quietly. "Keep an eye on your brother's friends. Some of them are a good deal cleverer than he is."

Ned looked at him sharply. But Pat had been called to play again, and Ned had other business.

JUST DOWN THE LANE FROM MATTHEW'S HOUSE STOOD a single-story stone building with a tiled roof and a sturdy chimney. It had once been a bakehouse, but the bakery had closed years ago, along with the other shops around there. Instead of the sweet scent of loaves baking, the smell that pervaded the alley now was of animal dung from Petrie's horses, and the faint, foul miasma from the Fleet ditch.

The bakehouse was where Ned headed, after leaving Pat. The place belonged to Matthew; Ned had obtained the key from him earlier. He let himself in and lit the old baker's oven, in which some coals were heaped, to fend off the bitter cold; he also lit a tallow candle that sent shadows flickering around the peeling lime-washed walls. Cobwebs floated from the old oak rafters and from the stone shelves that ran along each wall. When the oven was warm enough, he put some lumps of horse dung from Black Petrie's stable into the crucible he'd bought that afternoon. Then he poured in some wine borrowed from Matthew's cellar, sealed it with a cork, and placed it on top of the oven. To ripen, just as his Auriel letter said.

"In spiritus vini is the base material first engulfed, then nurtured in a sealed vessel..."

He wondered what Pat would have said. He would surely have questioned Ned's sanity as smells, pungent and alien, filled the room. He sat on the low stone bench by the oven and started to read *Agrippa's Elixir,* without much understanding. After a while he gently dozed in the warmth with Barnabas resting at his feet, only to jump awake to the sound of a great bang, and of glass shattering.

Cursing under his breath, he saw that his crucible had exploded with the heat, splattering the old bread oven and the floor around it with charred dung.

He sat back on his heels, assailed by the stink of burned manure. Barnabas, curious, came over and licked his hand.

Ned fondled his ear absently and drew himself up. He pulled his Auriel letter from his inner pocket and looked at it again, by the light of the single candle. Then he opened up the book he'd stolen and read on.

"In contemplating our First Matter, wherein the Seed is contained, remember that the key to this consists in a right dissolution of the ores into a water, which the Philosophers call their Mercury, or water of life..."

No mention of Princes or Scorpions. Just horse manure in wine. If people everywhere were trying to make the Philosopher's Stone, then they were fools, all of them, himself most of all. There were no answers here.

He drank the rest of Matthew's wine and slammed the oven door shut on the evil-smelling wreckage. He put his Auriel letter in his pocket, along with the little book, and left the bakehouse, locking the door behind him. He realized that he had drunk too much, when he went out into the night and saw that the stars were spinning overhead. Though the stars stopped spinning as he breathed in the cold air, and remembered Kate, and his son whom he had not yet seen.

• • •

WHEN NED DREW NEAR TO THE COALMAN'S STABLE where his room was, for a moment his heart raced, because there was someone clad in black standing in the shadows at the foot of the stairway. He knew that there would be no escape from Northampton's watchers, but he had expected subtlety.

Then he saw it was Alice, in a black cloak, with a woolen hood covering her fair hair. She let the hood fall and gazed up at him with her dark eyes.

"You looked as if you were expecting someone else," she said. "Someone you didn't want to see. But I hope you are pleased to see me."

"Alice," he said, "I'm tired, and it's late."

"You've been drinking, with Pat." She was watching him assessingly. "Pat needs watching. He is a rough and violent man."

"Only when he needs to be, I think."

She frowned. "Oh yes? One night, when Matt was away, Pat tried to force himself on me."

Ned recoiled. "I do not believe it—"

"It's true. I called out for help, and he backed off before Matthew's other friends should see what was happening. Pat has borne me a grudge ever since, damn him."

"I am surprised," he said. "He is a good man."

She laughed. "All right. He is your very, very good friend, for drinking with, and making music with, when you have had too much ale . . ."

"Alice—"

She took his arm. "I think there are things you want to forget," she said softly. "Let me help you." She began to lead him up the stairs, to his room.

Once they were inside, she found his tinder and flint, and lit a candle. Then she reached up on tiptoe to kiss him, to insert her tongue between his teeth. He made a last effort to detach himself, but she was insistent, and he was weary. And he had forgotten how pretty she was when she smiled at him. She stepped away a moment to unfasten the lacings of her gown, and he saw that beneath it her shift was of white lawn, embroidered with cream-colored flowers. He touched the fine work wonderingly. She fastened her hand over his.

"My mother made this," she said. "She slaved over such things. A penny a flower. That was all she earned. A penny a flower . . . My mother hoped for a better life for me. She taught me to read and write. She hoped to make me a lady, but I soon found there were other ways to live. That men weren't interested in embroidery, or books."

"Alice. My brother loves you—"

"Your brother," she said softly, "is a bloody fool. He is throwing his business away. Ned, my mother died in poverty and pain. I watched her. I will not end the same way. I swear I will not."

She was pulling her bodice down. The flowers on the linen were creased under the weight of her full breasts, which she cupped to ease them out of her clothes. Her nipples were dark and taut in the shadows of the candlelight.

"Alice," he said urgently, "this is not right, you should go back, now, to Matthew's house." But she was reaching to touch his groin with her cool, small hand.

"Matthew is away till the morning." She was kissing him, her tongue in his mouth again; she drew away just a little and went on, "You must forget your Kate. She won't leave her husband. You know she won't. Even though she is unhappy. He is the father of her child, he feeds and clothes them both, he provides a respectable life for her, which you could never do, ever—"

Ned was shaking her. "How do you know all this? How do you know she will not leave him?"

"I told you, servants' gossip." She shrugged. "Nothing is secret in a house with servants. Kate Pelham will put up with anything, to keep her child safe, to have the doctors' bills paid . . ."

"Stop," said Ned. "No more."

"Indeed," she said softly, and her lips were on his, her hands fondling him. "No more talk." And he was lost.

Calcination was the first stage of alchemy, he suddenly remembered. Utter blackness.

So he completed the degradation of his return. She was lascivious, and kept thinking of new ways to rouse him; the scent of their lust enveloped him. And after the pleasure, which was intense, as she intended, all was blackness. Especially when he remembered in the dark hours of the early morning that he had orders to kill a man.

10.

I have a newe gardyn,
And newe is begunne;
Swych another gardyn
Know I not under sunne.

TRAD. RHYME (SLOANE MS 2593) C.1440

THE NOVEMBER MIST HUNG ALL THE NEXT DAY OVER the park and gardens of St. James, where the outline of the redbrick Tudor palace stood gaunt against the gloom. In the Friary Garden, to the south of the cloistered yard, the last leaves of the sycamore trees drifted to the ground. Rooks called from bare branches, and the damp air was filled with the scent of leaf mold. The smoke from the gardeners' bonfires traced a slow path upward.

By four o'clock the light was fading fast, but workmen were still raking up the autumn debris and pushing it on the embers. Others were turning over the earth with spades. In charge of the work of these industrious laborers, moving amongst them in his light-colored cloak, was Stephen Humphreys, who was thirty years old, though his stooped shoulders and air of weariness made him appear older. He wore an old felt hat, pulled low over his protuberant forehead;

and on drawing close to him it was possible to discern, above the linen of his shirt, a livid scar that encircled his neck.

Humphreys had fought in the Low Countries, long before Ned's sojourn there, on the side of the Dutch rebels against their Spanish oppressors. Five years ago, at the siege of Ostend, the Spaniards had captured and tortured him. He survived, but as if he could not yet face the prospect of return to his native country, he had traveled the continent for some years, a quiet, solitary wanderer, whose unprepossessing appearance attracted few friends. It was in this time that he reverted to an original love of his, the study of herbs and garden plants; and in his travels he met many famous plantsmen and saw rare specimens of flowers and fruit trees. He returned at last to find work as assistant gardener to the Earl of Shrewsbury at Shrewsbury's fine house in Coleman Street in the city; and then in the summer of 1609 he was recommended to Prince Henry.

At four o'clock each day, whenever Henry was in residence, the Prince came to talk to his gardener. It was time for his visit now; and Humphreys, seeing the young heir to the throne approaching with his retainers following behind, waited for him in the fast-dwindling light.

The Prince looked round at the working men, at the bonfires of leaves and the newly turned earth beds. He talked to Humphreys for a while about the weather, and the progress of the plantings; then he drew his gardener a little apart and said quietly, so no one else could hear, "They say that herbs, like all living things, are related to the stars. Do you believe it is true?"

Humphreys's pale eyes, beneath that low forehead, were sharp with intelligence. "Your Royal Highness," he replied, "you will agree with me that some plants and herbs are found only in certain places." He spoke in a curious whistling voice that people found as odd as his unattractive appearance, for in his time of captivity the Spaniards had half-strangled him, and his vocal cords were damaged irreparably.

"Why, yes," answered the Prince, looking around at the mosses in the shade, at the lonicera that struggled up to the light. "They grow in the places that suit them. It is a matter of light and shade, of warmth and moisture..."

"Exactly, my lord. And as soon as these plants are transplanted into soil foreign to their nature, they fail to thrive. They lose—as any herbalist will tell you—all or most of their curative virtues."

Henry listened, while in the distance his entourage waited: chief of whom were the old ex-soldier Spenser, the smooth attorney Lovett, and Henry's young chaplain Mapperley, who in truth could not have wished for a worthier master; for the Prince attended church twice on Sundays, held daily services in his private chapel, and forbade swearing in his puritanical household, on pain of heavy fines. It had often been said that the ascent of this Prince to the throne would not be relished by any of England's Papist enemies, of whom there were many, both within and without the realm.

Humphreys pressed on. "My lord. What causes growth, change, and decay in plants? Why, the minerals they absorb through their roots, and the moisture from the earth and atmosphere. By night their leaves absorb the rays of the wandering planets, by day the rays of the sun. Some thrive in the light, some in the shade; this we all know. But there are some things we cannot understand.

"How does the pimpernel know to close its tiny flowers long before night draws near? Why does the trefoil contract its leaves when thunder is expected? All plants draw their nourishment from the soil and air, but also from the ruling planets. For example, the celandine and marigold are governed by the sun; chickweed and loosestrife by the moon. Venus commands the cowslip and featherfew, while Mercury—your own ruling planet, my noble lord—rules marjoram and valerian, amongst others."

Prince Henry nodded. "Is it the same for men? Are they, too, governed by the stars?"

"I believe so, my lord."

"Then just as you can read the fortunes of plants in the stars, Master Humphreys, so you can surely see a man's fortunes! Tell me this. Can you protect a man from his fate?"

"I can sometimes foresee danger, my noble lord. That is perhaps protection of a kind."

"But it is no answer..." The Prince broke off, looked round distractedly. "Enough. This is, perhaps, not the time, or the place...Tell me, Master Humphreys, what you plan for this part of the garden."

He had noticed that his attendants were drawing closer. Humphreys glanced at them also, then rubbed the raised scar on his neck and answered, "With pleasure, Your Highness. Here along this walkway will be adder's tongue and arrach, to draw away the maleficent rays of the moon; over there, ground ivy and burdock, to ward off jealous Venus. But to enhance the influence of your chief ruler, Mercury, I will, in the springtime, establish a garden here, facing westwards, of sweet basil and marjoram beds, hedged by may..."

On hearing Humphreys's words, Edward Spenser, the Prince's fifty-year-old military adviser, gave a snort of impatience and turned away, his hand rubbing the hilt of the sword at his waist. Prince Henry turned his intent gaze on him. "Sir Edward. You do not seem happy."

"Oh, my lord." Spenser spread out his sword-calloused hands and shook his grizzled head. "If this talk of stars and moonshine keeps you happy, then I am content. But herbs, planets, horoscopes—why, give me action, and a trusty sword, anytime!"

John Lovett, fifteen years younger than he, suave and urbane in the costume of a courtier, not a soldier, put a warning hand on Spenser's shoulder. "Leave him," said Lovett quietly, as the Prince wandered on with Humphreys. "I want a word with our gardener friend."

All around them the spotted yellow leaves fell silently to earth, and the rain began to fall also. The Prince talked to Humphreys for a little while longer. Then Henry turned and walked toward the newly built riding school at the west side of the palace, to rejoin his friends who were training the fine horses that had been sent that summer as a gift by the King of France. Prince Henry was followed by a dozen men-at-arms—his constant guard—and by Mapperley, who was anxious to ensure that the rigors of the Protestant church were not about to be displaced by talk of plants and astrologers. Edward Spenser returned to the house while Humphreys and his gardeners continued with their labors. And Lovett waited nearby, until the Prince's party had disappeared from sight.

John Lovett was the Prince's chief clerk, and had rooms in the palace in keeping with his high station. He was an attorney by profession, and had worked as a secretary at the Royal Dockyards before entering the Prince's service two years ago. He was a handsome, slim courtier of thirty-five, clean-shaven and well groomed; he shared the Prince's love of Italian art, attending to the goods that were imported for him frequently from the continent; and he supervised the staff of St. James's Palace with unobtrusive yet precise efficiency.

Now Lovett walked up to Humphreys and said, "You and I need to talk."

"Do we?" Humphreys's manner was too vague to convey outright insolence; but he took long enough, to give some final orders to his gardeners, before returning to Lovett and saying, almost companionably, "I see that even before my arrival here, the Prince was eager to have more mulberry trees planted—both in his garden and further afield." He pointed to some rows of saplings nearby, barely four feet tall, heeled in trenches by their root-balls until the time was right for their permanent planting. "I understand," Humphreys went on, "that some of these young trees are to be established in the walkway that leads to the house—a wise choice indeed, my lord."

Lovett glanced impatiently to where he was pointing. It was cold and he was ready to go in. "A wise choice? Why?"

"Because the mulberry tree is ruled by the Prince's own planet, which is Mercury," explained Humphreys benignly. "And I wonder—is that why the Prince wants the remaining trees sent further afield?"

"It is the Prince's idea, yes." Lovett was looking back at the palace with longing. "He wishes to promote a native silk industry."

"Silk? An enterprising notion. And ambitious. Whose idea was that, I wonder?"

"The Prince's, of course. He knows that if silkworms can

be nurtured throughout the south of the realm—which would, of course, necessitate plantings of mulberries to feed them— then the country could avoid the vast sums spent on imports, and create a native source of wealth and employment."

"The Prince always has the welfare of his people close to his heart," said Humphreys with admiration.

Lovett said, "Indeed. As I said, we need to talk. Will you be much longer?"

"Perhaps an hour or so."

"Then when you have finished your work here, you will report to me. The Prince's men will tell you where to find me."

EXACTLY AN HOUR LATER, WHEN DARKNESS HAD fallen, and the gardeners had finished their work and dispersed, the guards escorted Humphreys to Lovett. They did so with caution. There were whispered rumors that the Prince relied on his gardener to protect him against poison, though Humphreys had been in Henry's employment scarcely two months. They weren't the only rumors. All the soldiers of the palace mistrusted Humphreys, with his unearthly countenance and unnaturally pale hair, and that hideous scar on his neck. They didn't like his pale eyes, or his strange talk of stars and planets, and of baleful rays from above. To them his presence reeked of sorcery. Those among them who had been brought up in the old faith, secretly crossed themselves whenever he was near.

Neither did they like the men who worked for him, the four gardeners who had come with Humphreys from his previous employment, and who abjured the camaraderie of the servants' quarters. At first there had been fights, until it became apparent that Humphreys's gardeners could defend themselves against anyone. The Prince's guards hoped, as they escorted him into the palace that evening, that Humphreys was about to be dismissed.

As ordered, they led him to the long, candle-lit gallery on the first floor, where was displayed the Prince's burgeoning collection of European art. Spenser was there, still in his soldier's leather jerkin, smelling of the stables. John Lovett stood beside him beneath the heavy oil paintings, watching Humphreys's shambling approach. Lovett, in his black velvet suit, was as languid as any of the painted courtiers in the portraits, but Spenser was clearly uncomfortable here, with his sweat-stained armpits and muddy boots, and his big sword at his belt, for he was a man of action, not a courtier. They both watched and waited as Humphreys approached, hat in hand.

The guards were ordered to wait outside. Lovett and Spenser took seats at a big table in the window alcove, and gestured to Humphreys to sit also. Spread out on the table were some well-used maps of the Low Countries and of the Holy Roman Empire.

Spenser pushed the maps aside. He said to the gardener, "We think there are things that you have not told us."

"My lords," replied Humphreys, arranging the skirts of his coat as he sat, "I have told you everything you asked. What more would you know?"

Lovett leaned forward. The light from the branched candelabra glittered on his ruby ring, and on the tiny silver fleur-de-lis emblems that were embroidered on his green silk doublet. He said, "How about telling us the truth about your past?"

"The truth is always elusive, my lords," replied Humphreys gently. "But if you would expand your question a little more, I will endeavor to answer it. Perhaps you will explain which aspect of the truth you require; for as Pontius Pilate so memorably said, 'What is truth?' "

Spenser said, "Ah, shut up, you foolish man; stop all your nonsense and just tell us this: *Why did you not inform us from the beginning that you were born and raised a Catholic?*"

"Because, my lord," said Humphreys with patience, "you did not ask me—no, no"—he moved nimbly aside as Edward Spenser reared heavily from his chair and lunged toward him—"because, my lord, I no longer practice that faith."

Spenser lowered himself into his chair again, his face still dark with anger. "Why should we believe you? You come here, filling the Prince's mind with magic and with superstitious fancies—"

"Hush," said Lovett at his side, putting a restraining hand on Spenser's arm. "Hear him out."

Spenser put his hand over his face. Humphreys bowed his head in acknowledgment to Lovett, then looked up again, his pale eyes bright beneath his prominent forehead. "My lords. I was born into a Catholic family. It was my misfortune. I was accordingly raised in that faith, but as soon as I could, I renounced it."

"When exactly?" put in Lovett softly.

"As soon, my lords, as I was old enough to be able to exercise choice. You will know, I am sure, that when I was younger I joined the Protestant army in the Netherlands under Sir Francis Vere."

"We know," said Spenser gruffly. "It was in 1602. And Vere was a good man. So by then you had put your Catholic upbringing entirely behind you? You must understand: we have to be on our guard all the time, against Papist spies."

"I was captured by the Spaniards in 1604, my lord." Humphreys's eyes were expressionless. "I was with a raiding party, sent out for supplies from within the beleaguered town of Ostend. I was interrogated by Parma's men."

"Is that how you got the mark on your neck?" put in Lovett.

"Indeed. I have not always talked like this. The Spaniards half-strangle their prisoners, my lord, to make them betray their comrades."

"And did you betray yours?" rapped out Spenser.

"I am wounded, my lord, that you should even ask."

Spenser, tapping his fingers on the table, said sharply, "I have lately been talking to some survivors of the Ostend siege. They say that out of those captured by the Spanish, the only ones who got away were those who talked. The traitors."

"Parma's men thought I was dead," replied Humphreys. "I was thrown out, and left on a rubbish heap where dogs scavenged. Some kindly local folk found me there and helped me to recover. Shortly afterwards the peace treaty was signed between England and Spain. Bereft of English help, Ostend, as you know, fell to the Spaniards."

"It was a base betrayal of our brave Dutch allies," growled Spenser.

Lovett leaned forward again. "You must forgive us our questions, Humphreys. We know you were interviewed for this post by Prince Henry himself. You were recommended by the Earl of Shrewsbury. But you have to understand that we need to know everything about everyone who has any access whatsoever to the Prince."

"Do you believe there is danger still?" asked Humphreys, meeting his gaze.

Lovett hesitated, then nodded. "You will have realized," he said, "that our noble Prince, though valiant in every respect, fears secret enemies. He has every confidence in those who serve him. But he has been raised to believe in the malign capabilities of the stars. You will be aware of this, of course, because he has already requested that you should plant the palace gardens in a manner that is conducive to his safety and well-being."

"The mulberries. Of course. I am here to serve his Royal Highness in every way I can."

"You are here to supervise the plantings, yes," replied Lovett. "You are also here to reassure the Prince, and to calm his mind, for he foresees his death in his dreams. But you are to say nothing of these fears to anyone else, master gardener; and nothing at all of his conversations with you regarding herbs and stars. Do you understand?"

"My lords," said Humphreys quietly, "my lords, do you think I would ever betray the Prince's trust?"

THEY TOLD HIM HE COULD GO, AND WATCHED HIS stoop-shouldered figure in silence as he walked back along the gallery, his pale cloak trailing behind him, his hair almost white in the candlelight. Then, as he disappeared through the big main doors, Spenser angrily slapped his hands together and said, "I cannot believe that man was a soldier. He is nothing but a soothsayer, a charlatan."

Lovett turned to face him. "His experiences will have altered him. We must remind ourselves that he will set the Prince's mind at rest. Henry has to be reassured, for a sickness of the mind is as fatal as that of the body."

"And you think this business of star-ruled plantings will reassure him? This trickery, this necromancy? Ah, but I forget: your wife favors such things, does she not?"

"She is interested in herbs and astrology," said Lovett shortly. "But all women gossip of these matters. They mean nothing."

Spenser still looked belligerent. Lovett went on, "You know as well as I that our Prince is haunted by fears. He cannot sleep. His dread of secret enemies fills his mind. He sees foreign assassins at every turn."

Spenser looked round at the sea of Italianate and Spanish faces that regarded him from the heavy oil portraits. "It does not surprise me," he said with irony. "Are you are quite sure this gardener is to be trusted?"

"If the gardener's obsession with plants calms the Prince, then let us make use of him. And I hope you remember that the distribution of the mulberries is intended to serve quite another purpose—"

"Hush!" interrupted Spenser. He put his hand on Lovett's arm to silence him. Then he pointed to the half-open door at the far end of the gallery and said in a low voice, "I thought I heard someone. Over there, behind the door."

Lovett was already on his feet, pushing back his chair. He went swiftly to the doorway.

A woman was retreating down the corridor, her footsteps pattering on the wooden floor. Lovett strode after her and caught up with her as she sought refuge in an empty chamber. He swung her round to face him.

"You were spying on us, madam," he said softly, "you were trying to listen. What, I wonder, did you learn?"

She tried to pull herself free, but his grip on her tightened. She was younger than he, by a few years; she was slender, with black hair bound up in ribbons, and burning dark eyes. She wore a green silk dress bedecked with lace at the sleeves and throat. She carried herself as if she had once been beautiful.

She said scornfully, "What did I learn? I actually heard nothing; but I can guess from your present behavior, and from the secret messengers bearing money for you who have been coming here lately, that you are up to your usual sort of trickery: something that will make you richer and someone else poorer—"

He drew back his hand and hit her. He hit her again, to silence her; then he went to lock the door so he could continue his chastisement of her in private, though no one else would have interfered with what he did, for she was his wife.

Afterwards Lovett went to his office, where he settled at his desk and started to study certain papers which related to the royal docks, for he had worked at the shipyards under the navy treasurer Sir Robert Mansell for several years before his appointment to the young Prince's household, and he still, to his content, had lucrative interests there. After a while he prepared to go out, adjusting beneath his cloak the bombast-padded jerkin he wore always to protect himself against assassins' knives.

HUMPHREYS HAD GONE OUTSIDE AGAIN, TO WHERE, by the light of a lantern, the youngest of his gardeners, the tall, strongly built youngster perhaps seventeen or eighteen years of age, was putting away his tools for the night, in the storehouse allotted for Humphreys's use. Humphreys praised the youth for what he had done, and showed him how to sharpen the blades of the scythes and axes with sandstone. Then he dismissed the young gardener, who lodged in the palace, and left the garden by the northern gate. As the guards dragged the bolts home after his departure and the November mist rolled up once more to obliterate the moon, he walked at a steady pace along the wooded country lanes to Holborn village, and the home he shared there with his invalid mother.

They lived in a small cottage of lath and timber that looked out over the fields toward Clerkenwell. There had once been heathland all around, but the shacks which the brick workers and the vagrant Irish built outside the city walls to evade taxes and the surveillance of the city fathers had crept up close, as had their taverns and noisy gaming places. The little garden that encircled Humphreys's home was a last bastion of the countryside.

There was a candle burning in the window of the cottage. His mother sat by the fire. She rarely went out, because her rheumatism almost crippled her. Now she looked up querulously. "You should not leave me for so long by myself,

Stephen. So long." He took off his coat. "It's not right that I should be here," she went on, "in the dark, by myself . . ."

He paid a neighbor, a kindly woman, to come in often during the day to check that his mother lacked for nothing, that her candles were lit, her fire well stocked. But he apologized nevertheless, and soothed her. After washing his hands he went to cut her some bread and cold meat, and ate with her. Then, as she sat in her chair watching the flames of the fire he'd built up against the chill November night, he sat down at the desk in the corner and wrote in his notebook, as he did every evening, about the work he had completed in the gardens of St. James's Palace: the plantings, the prunings, the state of the moon and the stars, to which all true gardeners were subject. And he worked, too, on the notebook he was compiling of gardeners' lore.

The planet Mercury rules the mulberry tree, therefore are its effects as variable as Mercury's are. The mulberry is of different parts: the ripe berries, by reason of their sweetness and moisture, open the body, and the unripe bind it. The juice of the leaves is a remedy against the biting of serpents, and for those that have taken aconite. A twig of the tree taken when the moon is at the full, and bound to the wrist, is said to stay bleeding in a short space.

When he had finished, he helped his mother to prepare herself for bed, taking her outside to the little washhouse for her ablutions. He was a devoted son, and sometimes she was grateful.

He damped down the fire, blew out the candles, locked the door securely, and went to his own bedchamber.

11.

I will not ask why Caesar bids me do this;
But joy that he bids me.
It is the bliss
Of courts to be employed.

BEN JONSON (1572–1637)
"SEJANUS"

THERE WAS MORE AGONY DELIBERATELY INFLICTED
late that same night in the prison called the Counter, on
Wood Street close by West Cheap; for Godwin Phillips, the
old friend to whom Albertus had spoken of the miraculous letter to Auriel bearing Dee's inscription, had other secrets besides alchemical ones to keep. He was a Catholic, a timid,
secret one at that, and his worst fears had just come true, for
here he was in a foul prison cell whose walls ran with damp,
being held under suspicion of knowing about dire plots. As
was the way of things, he was questioned while his poor thin
body dangled from the wall, for his wrists were locked in iron
manacles driven deep into the cold stone.

A necessary cruelty, this, declared the authorities. Were
not all Catholics, timid and secret or otherwise, sworn servants of the Pope, and allies of England's old enemy Spain?
Were not all Catholics traitors to the realm and the people?

Phillips the prisoner moaned. The sweat poured from him. The tendons of his skinny old arms, visible from elbow to wrist where the sleeves of his doublet had fallen back, were stretched with the weight of his body. The humble draper looked too cowardly by far to be part of some infernal plot; but they were often in some sort of disguise, like witches' familiars, these servants of Satan who infected the realm of England with their dark poison. Such was the opinion of Francis Pelham, the old man's inquisitor, who waited as the prisoner sobbed softly in his chains, and the damp trickled steadily down the green-stained walls, and rats scuttled in the corners where the light of the single candle could not reach. Phillips did not seem likely to last long without talking. He claimed to know nothing, but all Catholics had secrets to reveal, if only the names of fellow recusants, of priests and priest-hiders.

Pelham leaned back in his chair, which, together with the table, was the only furnishing in the bare room. The floor was scattered with filthy straw. A man of fastidious as well as puritan nature, Pelham lifted a scented kerchief to his nose from time to time. The old man dangling from the wall stank from his suffering; but then, as Pelham reminded him, only he could end it.

Pelham cleared his throat and prepared to start his questions anew.

"You were seen," said Pelham, "in West Cheap. You were observed talking to a fellow conspirator called Albertus. You whispered. You looked at some papers together."

Phillips's eyes watered with pain and terror. He must know that the next stage, after this, was Waad and the threat of the rack, in the grim Tower.

"Albertus is no conspirator. The notes were only about some experiments—"

"Experiments?" Pelham drew closer. "What do you mean?" The prisoner, even more terrified, licked his cracked lips. Perhaps he was thinking that what he was about to say would draw down another kind of punishment on his head, for it was a crime to practice alchemy unlicensed, or to associate with anyone who did so.

"My companion Albertus was trying to make gold," whispered Phillips. "The notes he showed me contained some guidance, some instructions merely..."

Pelham snorted impatiently. Charlatans and wizards abounded in London; man's gullibility and greed seemed to him endless. And he was reluctant to abandon his suspicion of a Papist plot.

Pelham was Protestant through and through, raised from birth to honor Queen Elizabeth, defender of her country, and her country's faith. The names of the heroes Drake and Ralegh, who had saved England from the Spanish Armada, had been etched on his mind from an early age, though how different were their fates: Drake was long dead of a fever at sea, while Ralegh, perhaps the noblest of them all, languished in the Tower, having been accused—falsely, surely—of plotting with Spain against King James.

Pelham's life was a long battle against the treachery of the Spaniards and their Catholic henchmen, even though England had made peace with Spain five years ago: a treachery in itself, Pelham thought, and so did many others. But Governor Waad would not permit talk of such a kind, because his master in turn, Robert Cecil, who was the most powerful and cunning man in the kingdom, was the person responsible for that peace. He had drafted word by word the 1604 treaty that had betrayed their brave Dutch allies, who had continued to fight on gallantly against the Spanish on their own; until the struggle, even for the courageous Dutch, had proved too much. A final treaty—a surrender, thought Pelham—had been signed earlier that very year, between the Dutch and Spain. King James had sent his lackeys to the Hague to take part in the peace talks, when it was the opinion of countless honest Englishmen he should instead have sent an army to support the Netherlanders in their fight against Spanish supremacy.

And now the shadow of war was spreading across Europe once more, cast by the dispute over the Cleves-Julich succession; but once more King James held back. He equivocated, and half-promised soldiers to help the Protestant powers, but did nothing to muster them. He wanted a Spanish marriage for his son and heir, Prince Henry. He wanted the Spanish gold that was offered as dowry. Catholic gold.

Pelham detested such consorting with the enemy—an enemy which still, he was convinced, plotted England's downfall through methods far more subtle and dangerous than open war. He said sharply to his agonized prisoner, "Where does this Albertus live?"

"In Crooked Lane, by the Fish Wharf. Next to the chandler's shop. Everyone knows him there. *God help me...*" Phillips groaned anew, and Pelham frowned. The man was no use to him dead. He called a gaoler to release him, and Phillips, semiconscious, had to be carried by two men back to his place of imprisonment. For a while after he'd gone, Pelham paced the cell, deep in thought.

Alchemists, sorcerers, magi; they were charlatans all of them, preying on the superstition of stupid folk, and their greed for the Philosopher's Stone, that would make gold. Everyone wanted gold, of course, Francis Pelham as much as anyone, because before he was twenty-five he had accumulated heavy debts. He came from a respectable but impoverished family. His father, a clerk, had died when he was young; and Pelham had borrowed the money necessary to complete his own education at the Inns of Court and to travel on the ill-fated Azores expedition. Since his marriage, he had the expenses of the household to bear, and the financial rewards of his job had dwindled since the peace with Spain.

He had hoped for prosperity from another, less predictable source. Three years ago, before he married Kate, he had bought from her some shares in a ship—the *Rose*—that had sailed for the New World: shares that Kate had inherited from her father, and wished to sell.

He had bought them in a kind of madness, firstly because he felt he owed Thomas Revill his life, and secondly because he had fallen in love with Revill's orphaned daughter. Love? he thought bitterly. It was more like some enchantment. He had longed to have Kate Revill's gratitude, to such an extent that his normally sound judgment had become awry. In the same calamitous way—as if, he thought, the stars that ruled him were that season in chaos—he had been stirred, as many others had been, by tales of the success of other, similar ventures to the New World; he had heard that there were furs and dyes, silver and timber to be found in abundance in its forests; fortunes to be made. He had borrowed, on the strength of his hopes in the ship, a large sum of money with which to pay off his previous debts. But although one of the ships with which the *Rose* had sailed had already returned to England, it brought only bad news of the *Rose,* feared lost in Spanish territory.

And Kate? She had accepted his hand, but never loved him.

For many years now, Francis Pelham had watched others with far less intelligence, far less dedication than he—had he not been lamed in the service of his country?—living off the fat of the land. Either they secured patronage, or they had some petty talent for music or poetry; or sometimes—and this seemed to Pelham the vilest way of all—a man would capture the eye of the King, and become his favorite; but for that, one had to lie, and flatter, at the very least.

Pelham could not lie, he could not dissemble; his career, like his marriage, was failing.

Angry because he'd learned nothing about Catholic plots from the old draper, he made his way to the gaol's portal; and there was more bad news to come, for there, as he handed in his keys and listened to the gossip of the gaolers, he heard the news that Ned Warriner was back in town.

Pelham felt the blood rush to his face at this news. This could not be, this could not be. The authorities could not be aware of Warriner's return. It was Pelham's job to remedy their ignorance; for Pelham, despite attempts at the time to silence him, to convince him he was mistaken, suspected that Warriner— who had once dared to challenge Pelham over his treatment of Catholic prisoners—could well have been responsible for the escape of the Catholic traitor Ashworth two years ago.

Warriner's hasty flight into exile so soon after Ashworth's escape had confirmed Pelham's suspicions. His accusations were dismissed by the authorities. But Pelham remained convinced that someone was protecting Warriner. And now he was back.

He went straightaway to report Warriner's return to his

master, Waad, at the Tower; but he was told that Waad was busy and could not see him. He asked for pen and paper and wrote a swift letter. He handed it over and reiterated the fact that his message was urgent.

He walked purposefully back toward the city, no stranger to the nighttime streets. His resolute air, in defiance of his limp, protected him as well as his sturdy sword from lurking vagrants and thieves. He passed St. Peter's church, where a cold wind blew, dispelling the mist that had hung all day, and bearing the odors of stale meat and vegetables from the market. But as he came to Candlewick Street, he hesitated.

Looking all around, he walked up to a house in the shadow of the church, entering through a side door that was used by late-night visitors. There, he paid as he had often done before for the services of a woman who was neither young nor beautiful, for her thin, dark face was marked by a scar on her forehead. When he had first seen her, he had felt that she, in her imperfection, shared the same torment as he. Certainly she knew what he wanted, which was degradation and oblivion; for Francis Pelham found that whenever he struggled manfully against the demons of Popery in the Counter prison, the demons at his own loins roared for release, in ways that shamed him.

So Pelham felt the thin, hard face of the woman watching him as she bestrode his tortured body. He was purged, and bitterly ashamed. But he knew, and she knew, that he would visit again; and so with the aftermath of expelled lust enervating his soul, he limped at last on his way home, past the muttering beggars in the shadow of the city wall, past the thieves lurking there, who watched him warily.

Warriner was free. But not for long, he vowed. Wherever he was, whatever he was up to, Pelham would put an end to his trickery.

12.

The wise ancients did not in vain use musical sounds and singings as to confirm the health of the body and restore it until they make a man suitable to the celestial harmony, and make him wholly celestial. Moreover, there is nothing more efficacious to drive away evil spirits than musical harmony.

HENRY CORNELIUS AGRIPPA (1486–1535)
"THREE BOOKS OF OCCULT PHILOSOPHY" II.XXVIII

"YOU MUST PLAY AGAIN FOR ME. YOU MUST. I INSIST."
Thus spoke Prince Henry, in the first-floor music room of St. James's Palace, where the mid-November sunlight filtered through the windows. The Prince, pale, ardent, in black as ever, was surrounded by his advisers and protectors: by Edward Spenser, by Lovett and the chaplain Mapperley, and by his Master of Horse, the Scotsman Duncan. And he was addressing Ned Warriner, who was seated close to the harpsichord beneath a magnificent candelabra that hung from a ceiling painted with cherubic musicians. Carrying his lute on his knee, Ned had just finished playing some slow pavanes from the French court. Ned's audience with the Prince had begun with prayers, and he had been careful to maintain the tone accordingly.

He had discovered that to gain entry to the well-guarded palace of Prince Henry was easy enough if you came unarmed and bearing a lute, and also hinted at news from foreign battlefields, especially if you claimed devotion to Saint Martin of Tours, patron of Christian soldiers.

They had poured him wine, but only one glass. Life under this Prince, Ned thought to himself, when he comes to the throne, will be a serious business indeed.

He bowed his head to the Prince's request for more music, but explained that first he must retune his lute. Spenser, the old warhorse, shifted uncomfortably, clearly bored. As Ned adjusted his instrument's pegs, Henry leaned forward and asked him questions about his time spent as a soldier in the Netherlands; about Maurice's innovative tactics against the might of Spain; about Parma's use of siege warfare, and his weaponry. Gruff old Spenser also questioned him about his soldiering, interrogating him about places, and commanders, questions that Ned guessed were intended to trap him. But Spenser did not succeed.

Spenser would be responsible for security, Ned surmised, and Henry was certainly well guarded here. His companions all wore weapons, and there were discreet but fully armed guards at every doorway. Ned himself had been thoroughly searched before entering the building. He had come unarmed, and had dressed with care, in a sober doublet made of black broadcloth, complemented by his freshly polished Spanish boots, which were perhaps too polished, for he saw old Spenser gazing at them disapprovingly.

Spenser was suspicious of him; a wise fellow, thought Ned; but John Lovett, whom Northampton wanted dead, was the most civil of them all. Lovett turned out to know more than the others about music, and had traveled more widely, having visited the court of the Emperor Rudolph. Now he drew closer and asked Ned if he had communed with any of the famed musicians from eastern Europe with whom the Emperor Rudolph notoriously surrounded himself. Ned picked up his lute and thought a moment. Then he sang,

> *"The dragon devours himself,*
> *And the black raven is dead;*
> *Metal yet liquid,*

Matter yet spirit,
Cold yet engulfed in flames;
Poison yet healing draught."

Lovett, who wore an embroidered waistcoat covered with the Prince's insignia, and had a large ruby ring on his right hand, frowned as Ned reached the end. "It's a song about alchemy. An interesting conceit. But nonsensical, surely?" He added, more quietly, "And hardly suitable."

Spenser's scowl showed plainly enough what he thought of it.

But Prince Henry leaned forward, his eyes burning, and said, "Do you know any more about gold-making? About alchemy?"

Ned was aware, immediately, of a frisson of alarm that passed between the Prince's attendants. Lovett broke in, before he could reply, "Our visitor has already claimed expertise in music and warfare. I doubt that he has had time to absorb any such esoteric knowledge on his wanderings." He glanced at his watch. "It is time, now, my lord, for your appointment with your Master of Ceremonies. May I escort you there?"

The Prince stood up. "If you must." He turned to Ned. "Come again soon. I have enjoyed listening to your music, and to your account of the warfare in the Low Countries. My servants will see that you are given refreshment before you leave."

After the Prince had gone with Lovett, Spenser turned belligerently to Ned. "Watch yourself, lad. We don't like troublemakers here. Come this way." Spenser led him to the kitchens and left him there, looking as if he hoped the food would choke him. A servant brought him a dish of cold meats and a loaf of bread. Ned asked for ale, and as soon as the servant set off to fetch it, Ned hurried from the kitchens and turned down a long, deserted corridor, in the opposite direction to the way he had come.

The palace had, he knew, been empty since the reign of Mary Tudor, and was now being renovated by the Prince for his own occupation. Some of the building work was completed. The Royal apartments, the gallery, and the various chambers adjoining the chapel were already refurbished. But the rest was in a state of abandonment, almost of decay, for

Queen Elizabeth had had no desire to occupy a palace where her older sister and enemy Queen Mary had regularly celebrated mass with her husband, Philip of Spain.

Another servant, not the one who had served him, was hurrying toward him. Ned did not look at him, but walked on steadily, purposefully, as if he knew where he was going. The servant passed by, intent on his errand.

Many of the chambers Ned looked into were deserted. Piles of timber lay in some of the rooms, unused furniture in others. He entered one of the empty rooms, where from the window he could see the courtyard and the doorway to the stables; then he heard a slight sound behind him and quickly turned.

In the doorway was a woman. She was dressed simply but expensively in a gown of green silk adorned with lace. Her dark hair was bound up but uncovered, and she wore a necklet of pearls. She was perhaps a little over thirty, and Ned thought that the beauty of her face was overshadowed by bitterness.

She was regarding him quizzically, almost with amusement. "Are you lost, master musician? I heard you playing, earlier."

He bowed and said, "I was looking for the way out, madam. They pointed me in this direction, but I seem to have taken the wrong turning."

She smiled, disbelievingly. "I cannot imagine," she said, "that they would let you roam this place alone. A word of warning: It's not a good idea to get lost here. You might never get out. Like me." He could not conceal his surprise. "Oh," she went on, lifting her hand to her brow, "the boredom of this place drives me to distraction. Church daily, and twice on Sundays. Often it seems that every day here is a Sunday. Here, you are fined if you blaspheme—even a little bit, master musician—and whipped if you fornicate. Do you ever fornicate?"

She drew closer. Ned realized, from her slightly swaying gait and the smell of wine on her breath, that she was drunk.

He backed farther into the room, but she followed him.

"There is no chance for fornication here," she continued, gazing out the window. "No chance for any kind of pleasure. I wander in the parts of the palace which are ruined, because they are the only places where I can get away from the Prince's guards. Spies, all of them." She turned back to him swiftly. "Are you a spy, master musician?"

He tried to laugh. "Oh, no. Simply a poor lute player."

"Why, then, are you roaming the palace?"

"Because I have an even poorer sense of direction. As I said, I was trying to find my way out. I don't suppose any spy would ever get inside this place."

"True. As you'll have seen, Prince Henry is surrounded by his soldier friends—Spenser, Duncan, and the rest. My God, how I hate Spenser. He makes me think of dead bodies on battlefields every time I look at him. And as for all the others, they pretend to be as brave as brave as can be ..."

"And you don't think they are?"

"Prince Henry is brave, when it comes to riding, and tilting, and swordplay. But he has a dread of poison. He once had his horoscope cast. It said that he would never be king; that poison would shorten his life. Poison and plotting ..." Her voice faded away; she seemed distracted.

Ned said, "I am sure that all necessary precautions are taken."

"Precautions?" She was drawing nearer again. "What can anyone, even a prince, do against a determined enemy? To be sure, various people are hired, to minister to him, to ensure his safety, whether that safety is real or supernatural. At the moment our noble prince is obsessed with the planting of his garden. He believes that the appropriate trees and flowers will make him safer. Especially mulberries—they are everywhere around us. His advisers secretly mock him for it. But my husband makes gold out of his obsessions."

She had picked up Ned's hand and turned it palm upward, stroking the fingers that were callused from his sword.

Gold. Ned withdrew his hand. "Is it true that the Prince is interested in alchemy?"

"Indeed, yes—they all are; but my husband knows there are much surer ways to make a fortune. You see, he once worked at the King's dockyard at Deptford, which is a veritable gold mine to those who know how to dig out its treasures. Paintings, for one. He makes a fortune in gold out of imported art, supposedly for the Prince, which I don't think Henry ever sees."

"What happens, then, to this imported art?"

"God alone knows. It's stored, in great secrecy, in the Prince's warehouse at Deptford. I doubt if it really exists. But the gold does. I've seen my husband counting it."

"Where is this gold from?"

"From the Prince's loyal friends. But I do not believe they would contribute, in secret, so much money just to buy paintings for Henry—"

She broke off at the sound of footsteps coming along the corridor and turned to the doorway, where a figure had appeared. John Lovett, Henry's chief clerk, stood there. He looked at his wife; then he and Ned gazed at each other. After a moment's silence he said to Ned, "If you had wished for a guided tour of the palace, Warriner, you should have asked. My wife"—he came forward and took the woman lightly by the wrist—"has not been well. She should be resting."

Lovett's wife laughed, a brittle sound. Then she coughed. "It's not your poor lute player's fault that he's strayed so far. He was on his way out, but I waylaid him, and brought him up here."

"May I ask why?"

"To show him the ghosts that haunt this hateful place," she said. "My God, one day soon I shall be one."

Lovett smiled tightly. "Sarah, you should not, you really should not tire yourself so." He said to Ned, "Stay here. I will get someone to show you out. I must take my wife to her room."

Ned bowed his head. Lovett led his wife away. Ned waited, then went quietly to the doorway and looked after them.

He saw, in the faint candlelight, that Lovett had stopped. He took his wife by the shoulders and pushed her back against the wall. Then he shook her. He appeared to be questioning her; she turned her head and at last said something, closing her eyes in denial; he shook her again. After that he lifted his hand and struck her hard across the cheek.

Sarah Lovett cried out once and sagged in his grip. He

dragged her away, out of sight. After a while a servant appeared at the end of the corridor to lead Ned outside.

By the time they left the building, the sky was growing dark. Ned set off after his escort across the half-finished garden, which, like the palace, was a mixture of decayed ruin and fresh beginnings. Parts of the garden were being re-dug and replanted. Walls and pathways were being built. Only the old trees, arching overhead, were a reminder of the uncultivated woodland that this once was; they and the rooks, raucous as they roosted in the bare, leafless branches.

The servant, striding on ahead toward the distant gate, was already disappearing into the gloom. Ned stopped a moment to look back again at the house. It was well chosen, this place, to keep the Prince safe, with its stout Tudor walls, its high windows that gave views over the surrounding grounds, and strong walls to separate it from the rough pasture of St. James's Fields.

When he turned round again, he could not see his guide, and his way was blocked. A group of men, garden laborers to judge by their garb, gathered round someone on the ground. Ned drew closer and saw that their attention was focused on a youth who was in the throes of an epileptic fit. Two of them guarded him from himself as he thrashed on the soft earth. Ned had seen epileptics living rough on the streets. Often they were goaded into fits by mischievous children, or by fellow beggars who hoped to make money from their wretchedness.

Suddenly he realized that a man was standing at his side, dressed in a long, pale coat, with a wide-brimmed hat pulled low over his prominent forehead. His shoulders were stooped, which made him appear older than he was; his eyes were pale and watchful. A livid scar, like a cord around his neck, added to his unprepossessing appearance.

"I prepare the medicines myself," this man said to Ned, as if he had asked a question. "Henbane and rue are efficacious in soothing an overagitated brain. Careful, careful!" He was calling out to the youth's helpers, who were lifting him up now that his fit had ended. "I am a plantsman, sir," he went on to Ned, "and Prince Henry's chief gardener. My name is

Stephen Humphreys. And you are a musician." He indicated Ned's lute. "I heard you; I was working for a while beneath the open window of the music room. I, too, was once a soldier in the Netherlands."

That explained the scar. But before Ned could reply, or ask him more, the gardener nodded toward the gate. "I mustn't detain you. Your escort is waiting."

Ned made his way to the big gate, which the guard had unlocked for him. He passed through, noting the ornate stonework carved with pilgrims' staffs and scallop shells; and all the time, until he heard the final slam of that gate, he thought he felt the pale eyes of the plantsman, with that terrible scar round his neck, watching him.

HE GOT BACK TO ROSE ALLEY TO FIND THAT HIS brother had been injured in a brawl.

"We gave them a good fight though, Ned," said Matthew from his bed, winking at his friends who had gathered round. "Didn't we, lads?"

It took a while for Ned to extract the full story. It seemed that Matthew had gone to raid an apparently empty house down by Baynard's Castle, accompanied by several of his men and Petrie's two coal carts, but just as they were preparing to break in, they were ambushed. Matthew was cheerful about it, but his face was pale beneath his bristly black beard, and there was an ugly cut on his brow.

His friends stood around his sickbed protectively. Petrie the coalman was there, and ginger-haired Davey, looking belligerent. Scrivener Steen hovered close by also, looking more than ever like some disreputable lawyer with his lank brown hair and scholarly dark garb. Alice was seated at Matthew's side. She avoided meeting Ned's eyes.

It was a relief to Ned to see plump old Dr. Luke come into the room with a bowl of some herbal concoction in his hand. Luke, who must be almost sixty now, often told people that he held a Cambridge degree and had been licensed by the Royal College of Physicians, though of the occasion when the College took his license away from him, he was somewhat less open. He had traveled—escaped, some said—abroad, and served as a doctor for a while with the English forces in the Low Countries, some years before Ned served there. Now he contrived, between bouts of crippling drunkenness, to minister with kindness and not a little skill to the local population. Ned trusted him as much as any doctor he'd known. As long as he was sober.

Matthew took the medicine Luke proffered and drank it, grimacing at the taste. Then he turned again to his brother.

"I've been telling them, Ned, about your ballads," he said. "Especially the ones about Scrope, and the King's pretty little Scotsman Carr, and Lord Cecil and his mistresses—" He broke off, coughing. "Luke, this medicine is foul."

Ned promised, "I've written more ballads for you, Matthew. I'll take them up to the printer's tomorrow."

Matthew smiled and leaned back, only to scowl once more as Luke, with his wispy gray hair sticking out like a halo round his balding pate, bent to pour him out more medicine. "Listen"—Matthew beckoned Ned closer—"listen, Ned, I've got an idea. Find me a profitable way to get rid of fifty pairs of shin plumpers, and I'll split the proceeds with you."

"Shin plumpers," repeated Ned. "You'll have to tell me what they are first."

"They're calf fatteners made of cork, to put inside a skinny man's stocking and give him a fine leg. Davey stole them by mistake. And who the devil wants them," went on Matthew, pointing to his own sturdy limbs, "except the fops at court?"

Ned grinned. "If they're cork, you could sell them for fishing floats. Or export them to the Muscovite company. I've heard there's a demand for English fashions in Moscow."

Matthew frowned, not sure if his brother was in earnest. "Send them to Moscow? No. It would take me too long to get my money back. Luke, you old butcher, leave my arm alone."

Luke, who had been examining a cut on Matthew's arm, turned back to his bag to fetch out a fresh roll of bandaging. Matthew pulled Ned closer. He lowered his voice, so no one else could hear, and whispered, "Something else. The Revill girl came today, the one we had lessons with."

"Kate? She came *here*?"

"Yes. She'd tracked me down—asked around, I suppose. She wanted you, and when I said you weren't here, she said, 'Please tell him there must be no more poetry.' Do you understand that, Ned? *No more poetry,* she said...Ouch, damn you!" He winced as Luke finished with his bandage and pressed some pungent ointment to the cut on his forehead.

"He needs to rest," Dr. Luke told them all. "Give him a little peace. He'll be much better by morning."

"No visit to the Crown?" grumbled Matthew.

"Perhaps tomorrow."

Ned pressed his brother's hand in farewell and went downstairs. In the kitchen he saw Pat, who drew him to one side.

"What happened today was not right," Pat said to Ned in a low voice. "Those men who attacked us at the house we raided were the Whitefriars gang. They're moving into your brother's patch, Ned. I think they've got the constables paid up. And—worst of all—I reckon they knew we were coming."

Ned, still reeling from the news about Kate, said, "So you still think that someone's betraying Matthew?"

"More than ever. But I don't know who. You must speak to him, Ned, when you get the chance."

NED WENT TO THE BAKEHOUSE, WITH BARNABAS following, and lit the coals in the old oven to warm the room, sweeping aside the debris of the exploded crucible. By the light of a candle he gazed at the Auriel letter again. He wondered how long it took to become a mad old alchemist like Albertus.

"After the night of long and false captivity, the golden Sun is about to rise, and all this by the power of the Stone, lapis ex caelis; for be sure that as Auriel rises the Lion shall fall..."

There was a tiny drawing of a lion with its mane like the rays of the sun. The creature's expression was unhappy. Alchemy was full, Ned knew, of beasts both real and mythical: of pelicans and phoenixes, of basilisks and peacocks.

He stepped over Barnabas's sprawled warm body and sat on the stone bench. It was raining again, beating on the roof of the little bakehouse. The oven glowed, winking at him. He reached out for his book, the one he'd stolen, and read:

"Alchemy is at the root of much of the metalworker's art. And the Lion emblem has been sacred since ancient times. The priests of Heliopolis described the Lion as guardian of the gates of the underworld. More recently the Lion, in alchemy, has been used as the symbol of the fallen King, whose destruction is necessary for the rebirth of his nation."

He thought how Kate would have read his letter aloud, in her beautiful, serious voice. She would have made it sound like poetry. Then she would have looked up at him and smiled. "Another riddle for you, Ned. How long will it take for you to solve this one?"

Ned realized that he was getting cold in here, in spite of the heat from the oven. The athanor, he corrected himself. *The consecrated athanor, bearing the sign that also nurtures many pilgrims...*

He closed his eyes and saw again the carved shells that were used everywhere as decorations in St. James's Palace. Scallop shells, universally recognized as the emblem of pilgrims traveling to the shrine of St. James in Compostella.

He folded his letter away impatiently and paced the tiny room. Alchemy. Plotting. Corruption... When Kate told him she wanted nothing more to do with him, he had almost resolved to go back into exile. But now, even though she had reiterated her message, he had changed his mind.

Now he wanted to know what was going on at St. James's Palace. Not only that, but his brother needed him. Matthew, like Ned, had enemies.

THE NEXT MORNING NED SET OFF TO TAKE THE BALlads to the printer, as he had promised Matthew, but first he went back to the lair of the old alchemist Albertus, determined to try again there with his letter, since the old man knew more about alchemy than anyone else he'd talked to. But when he knocked on Albertus's door in Crooked Lane, next to the chandler's, there was no answer. He opened the door and went in.

He stepped back in shock. Everything had been wrecked. The oven was cold. Bowls and vessels lay scattered about the floor. He picked up a glass crucible which had somehow survived the carnage. Pushing it under his coat, he called at the chandler's shop next door, to find out what had happened.

"You're out of luck if you want Albertus," said the chandler, looking up from the bundles of tallow candles that he was checking against an inventory. "He thought he'd found the secret of making gold. But much good did it do him. He's dead."

"But he was well only a few days ago. How did he die?"

"He was murdered. Stopping someone trying to rob the place, most likely; you'll have seen the mess it's in. He put up a fight. Hacked about, he was; he'd even lost one of his fingers. Perhaps someone thought he'd got gold hidden somewhere, and tortured him for it. But I think he had nothing. Poor as a church mouse, he was, for all he was supposed to be an alchemist."

Ned turned away, running his hand through his hair in perplexity.

He was aware, yet again, of a profound feeling of disquiet.

HE WENT ON TO THE PRINTER'S SHOP. CHEAPSIDE was crowded in the noonday sun, and Ned let the throng carry him along. Then he sidestepped down an alley, in the shadow of St. Paul's, because he had realized for some time that he was being followed. Again. As his pursuer cast around for him in the busy street, Ned stepped out. He said levelly to the man's back, "You should have announced yourself, Simon. Instead of just following me."

Simon Thurstan let out an exclamation and spun round. "Jesus, Ned. You g-gave me a fright. I was only trying to catch up with you!"

"Why?"

"I've got bad news, I'm afraid. I've been looking all over for you."

"Well?"

"Francis P-p-pelham has heard that you're back in town,

and he's trying to stir up trouble for you, over the escape of that man Ashworth two years ago."

Ned frowned. "Will anyone listen to him?"

"Probably not. But I reckon he's after some sort of reward. He's pretty desperate for money, to pay off his debts."

Ned absorbed this slowly. "Pelham is in debt?"

"Oh yes. He's in deep with one of the usurers in Lombard Street. Duprais is his name. But who hasn't got money problems these days? What's that you've got under your coat?"

"A crucible," said Ned, pulling the glass vessel out and turning it as the sun winked on its curves. "Everyone seems to be after the secret of the Philosopher's Stone. I thought I might join them."

Simon glared. "You've got Pelham trying to get you arrested for treason, and you talk of alchemy."

Ned patted Simon's shoulder. "I've been writing some ballads about it, that's all." He indicated his sheets of paper destined for the printer. "Everyone knows it's nonsense."

"Perhaps. Though you'd be surprised by how many people are taken in by it. Your crucible's no good, by the way. It's got a crack in it."

Ned lifted it slowly. "So it has. How useful you are, Simon." He lobbed the glass vessel aside, into the rubbish-strewn gutter.

"Ned, Northampton asked me to deliver a message to you. He has unexpected b-business out of town; he'll be away for the next few days. But he wants to see you at Whitehall on the thirtieth. He says there's to be a rehearsal for the Queen's new masque in the Banqueting Hall, so with all the crowds and noise, you should be able to get in unnoticed. He said to remind you to concentrate on what you are supposed to do. Even in his absence."

"And do you know what I'm supposed to do, Simon?"

"Of course not. I'm just his messenger."

"Do you know anything about the dockyards, Simon? Anything about the corruption there?"

"I know that Northampton pressed hard for an inquiry earlier this year. But his allegations came to nothing."

"Do you think he'd welcome some fresh evidence about corruption?"

"I'm q-quite sure he would. Why, have you found some?"

"Perhaps. I'll see you at Whitehall. Thanks for the warning about Pelham."

Simon nodded and went on his way. Ned watched him go. So he had a little—just a little—more time to find out what was going on, if Francis Pelham didn't get in his way.

But first, he had to find out more about making gold: a hazardous pursuit, it seemed.

13.

Some thought to raise themselves to high degree,
By riches and unrighteous reward,
Some by close shouldring, some by flatteree;
Others through friends, others for base regard;
And all by wrong wayes for themselves prepared.
Those that were up themselves, kept others low,
Those that were low themselves, held others hard,
Ne suffred them to rise or greater grow,
But every one did strive his fellow downe to throw.

EDMUND SPENSER (C.1552–1599)
THE FAERIE QUEENE, BOOK 2: CANTO VII: V.47

ARBELLA STUART WAS COUSIN TO KING JAMES, BUT
although the royal blood ran as strongly in her veins as in
those of the King, she was an outcast amongst the court's
beauteous peacocks. In her childhood, she had been the un-
knowing focus of much of the plotting that filled the last years
of the aging Queen Elizabeth; but now there was no rivalry between the great men of the kingdom for the favors of this
plain, learned noblewoman. Rather, she was pitied; either that,
or she was gossiped about as a witch, the fate of many a spinster. And she was more prone to the gossip than most, for her
grandmother Bess of Hardwick was said to have strange powers drawn from the devil, and to have dabbled in herbal medicine; a skill which she taught, perhaps unwisely, to Arbella in
the girl's youth.

Arbella knew what the gossips said. And she found their

pity harder to bear than their malice. For she was a Stuart, and unlike James, of English birth. She believed she should have been queen.

Arbella lived in a humble house in Blackfriars, where she and her servants managed to survive with some difficulty on the pittance James allowed her. She knew she would never be allowed to marry, for marriage meant children, who would be rivals to the throne alongside James's brood.

At least lately in her loneliness Arbella had found a friend, who was with her today at Arbella's invitation. Her new companion was Mistress Kate Pelham, wife to one of Sir William Waad's recusant hunters, and related, like Arbella, to the Earl of Shrewsbury. Arbella found Kate Pelham quiet, intelligent, and modest; and so she was not jealous of her, even though she was young and beautiful. Though she did envy her in one matter. Kate was married, and she had a beautiful little son who made Arbella dream even more desperately for marriage and children.

That afternoon, little Sebastian, not yet two years old, played with his toy soldiers in Arbella's sheltered courtyard garden under the watchful eye of his nurse while Arbella sat with Kate in an upstairs parlor with the window open so that they could hear Sebastian's laughter.

"I have news for you, Kate: news to make you so happy!" said Arbella. "The Queen is rehearsing a new entertainment, a masque, for the Christmas festival. She has given permission for you to be my attendant. You will have to come to Whitehall, to play your part in the preparations. There will be beautiful costumes, and music, and dancing!"

Kate recoiled, her cheeks quite pale. "A masque? But that will mean time spent at the court, day after day. Sebastian is often not well; I cannot leave him for so long."

Arbella was always eager to be of assistance where medical matters were concerned. "The poor child. Does his breathing still trouble him?"

"He has a lung sickness, yes."

"You should try giving him wine in which woodlice have been steeped overnight, in the light of the full moon. It was a cure my grandmother prepared, for one of her Derbyshire servants; it was most effective."

Kate shivered. "Perhaps. Meanwhile, I prefer to tend my son myself."

"You have a nursemaid," pointed out Arbella, frowning. "The other ladies of the court do not let their children hinder them. You will enjoy participating in the masque."

Kate said quietly, "I really would rather not."

"I am afraid, dear friend, that you must." Arbella's voice had grown harder. "I have already told the Queen that you will attend. She is delighted. Perhaps, too, it will be an opportunity for you to meet up again with your great-uncle, the Earl of Shrewsbury, and his wife. I gather your family and his are somewhat estranged."

"We have drifted apart a little. But there has been no estrangement between us."

Arbella said briskly, "Whatever, it would do you good, and the boy, to take advantage of your connections, Kate."

"Perhaps." Kate, still pale, got to her feet and said that she had to take Sebastian home now. Arbella kissed her farewell, assuring her that she would surely enjoy taking part in the masque. "You must not be too wrapped up, you know, in your love for your husband and his precious child."

Outside, a mist had rolled up from the river. Kate made sure that Sebastian, rosy-cheeked and happy from playing with his soldiers in the Lady Arbella's courtyard, was warmly clad. Then, with the nurse and the manservant who attended them on Pelham's orders, she set out to walk home.

The manservant lifted the child up on his shoulders. "Come, little man. We'll soon have you home again." Kate walked behind, turning up the collar of her cloak against the cold.

Wrapped up, Arbella had said, in her love for her husband and child...

Oh, she loved Sebastian. No one could ever doubt that. The fierce love of a mother for her only child; like a lioness she had seen once in the King's menagerie below the Tower, being baited cruelly by the keepers with their dogs—another court entertainment, like the masques, that she hated. She would not have gone to the baiting. But Pelham, invited by his master William Waad, had insisted.

The lioness had young ones. At first she refused to leave them, refused to be baited, so the keepers—rough, cruel men—hurt her cubs with long pointed sticks. The mother lion came forward then with bared fangs and fierce eyes, and tore into the mastiffs the keepers let loose on her, ripping open the belly of one, breaking the back of another, all to defend her cubs; and Kate, sickened, had thought, I would do that. I would do anything, for my child.

But the hardest thing she had ever had to do was to say, *"No more poetry."*

FRANCIS PELHAM WAS GROWING IMPATIENT TO HEAR the news that his old enemy Warriner, whom he suspected of freeing a Catholic traitor two years ago, had been hauled in for questioning, now that Pelham had alerted the authorities about his return to England. Pelham was waiting to be summoned to give evidence against him. But he also had other matters on his mind.

Pelham's debts—incurred before his marriage—were becoming an increasing burden to him. It cost money to run a household, to keep up appearances, as a servant of Waad. He had to attend at court and to entertain when necessary, even though he despised ostentation. "I am waiting for the ship in which I invested to return," he told his creditors whenever they tried to press him.

Debts even larger than his were commonplace in London, but he hated owing anybody anything, and his detestation of his debts drove him, on this dreary late-November day, while his wife was visiting the Lady Arbella Stuart, to go back to the Wood Street Counter to interview the craven old draper Godwin Phillips once more. As he limped along West Cheap that afternoon to the Wood Street prison, with the mist from the river curling up between the lamplit shops and cottages, clinging to his cropped fair hair and chilling his bones where the old wound still ached, he was hoping that the man

Phillips, who had been arrested twelve days ago, might be persuaded to give him more names: the names of recusant friends, or of lurking priests, or even, most lucrative of all, of those most deadly of enemies of the state, the Jesuits.

But as he entered the grim gates, and the dank prison smell of sour humanity rose to greet him, he was told, "I'm afraid he's dead, sir."

Pelham stepped back. He shook his head. No, no; he had been cautious in what he did. He had suspended the prisoner in manacles; but unlike other investigators, Pelham had never ordered the punishment for so long that the prisoner suffered dislocated shoulders or ruptured stomach muscles. He remembered with disgust how only last month a Papist's belly had split open as he was questioned by one of Pelham's colleagues.

Pelham had been careful. Phillips had been living when he left him . . .

"How did he die?" he rapped out.

"He must have been taken ill in the night, sir. The physician said that most likely his heart gave out. After you'd gone the other day, we took him back to his cell and left him with bread and water, as you ordered. He seemed comfortable enough; ate well, slept well, even talked to us a little. But when we went to him this morning he was dead."

Pelham was shaken, and angry. No further names, then. No prosecution, to bring small but vital rewards his way. Just the threat, now, of a possible investigation into his methods, into one foolish old man's untimely death.

He walked to the Tower to seek out Governor Waad to forestall any complaints about the old draper's death and to ask at the same time for more work, more lists of suspected recusants to pursue, but he was told that Waad was absent, had gone to a meeting with Robert Cecil. He asked the man he spoke with, Waad's clerk, if the traitor Warriner had been brought in yet; the clerk looked evasive and said he knew nothing.

So Pelham, distracted with worry, walked down to the river in the fast-fading November light. He limped along the wharves, past the dockworkers and sailors, and the bales of hemp and timber, to the office of the Virginia Company, to ask if there was any news yet of the *Rose*.

One of the clerks, when he eventually caught his attention, looked up his records and replied that nearly all of the ships that had sailed on that expedition had returned now. But the *Rose,* he said, leafing through various reports, had been badly damaged in a storm off the American coast.

"I know," put in Pelham. "I heard that she had had to head to the mainland for repairs."

"Yes." The clerk examined his papers. "She made for the coast of Terra Florida, and was expected to catch up with the fleet as they passed the Bahama islands. But she did not keep to the rendezvous, so the others sailed without her."

"Then what can have happened? Where is she?"

The clerk shrugged. The general opinion, he said, was that the *Rose* had sunk, or been taken by privateers.

Pelham turned and made his way out. If the *Rose* really was lost, then he was ruined.

AS DARKNESS GATHERED HE TOOK A BOAT UPRIVER, to the stairs at Charing village. From there he limped along the Strand to his house and went to his study, and counted up all the outstanding bills, and the interest he owed the moneylender, Duprais. From a locked drawer he took out the papers that represented his shares in the *Rose*. They were carefully written, punctilious documents.

He remembered the long voyage home from the Azores when he was young, and how Thomas Revill's face had lit up as he talked to the injured Pelham about the riches to be found in the New World: the fabulous fruits and minerals, the gold mines there.

He wasn't sure when he realized that Kate was standing behind him in the doorway. He turned round slowly.

"There is to be a masque at the court," she said. "The Queen has asked me to take part in it. I do not wish to do so."

"Do you have a choice?"

She spread her hands. "I thought—rather, I assumed—that

you would prefer me to be here. It would mean many attendances at court. I thought that my duties lay rather in our home, with our son."

He said, "You will offend the Queen if you refuse."

"Are you saying that I must go?"

"I am telling you, as you surely already know, that you have no option."

She bowed her head briefly, her lips tight, and turned to leave the room.

He sat there alone as the candles guttered, until a manservant came to tell him that there were two men at the door who wished to speak with him.

He stirred himself and rose heavily, expecting that it would concern his work: a newly arrested recusant, perhaps, to interrogate. But when he got to the door, the men who stood there were strangers to him. They were well dressed, in sober livery of dark green adorned with silver fleurs-de-lis.

They told Pelham they were servants to Prince Henry. They asked him if he could spare the time, very soon, to come to the palace of St. James, where the Prince was most anxious to talk with him.

14.

$\cdot\cdot\cdot$

Mercury and Sulphur, Sun and Moon, matter and form, these are the opposites. When the feminine earth is thoroughly purged and purified from all superfluity, then you must give it a male meet for its ripening.

EDWARD KELLEY, ASSISTANT TO JOHN DEE (1555–1595)

IT WAS THE NEXT DAY, ALMOST DUSK, AND NED WAR-riner was wandering along East Cheap with Barnabas at his heels. Lamps were being lit in windows, and the rain was falling steadily. At last he pulled up at a house with a carving over the doorway of a Turk's head with a gilded pill on his outstretched tongue, beneath which was a notice:

Jacob Underwood. Licensed to practice as apothecary in the city of London, by the Royal College of Physicians...

He opened the door and a bell tinkled. Inside, candles had been lit, but the shop was filled with shadows, and the air was strongly scented with rosemary against the plague, with camphor and cinnamon, and other, more sinister odors issuing from the jars and phials ranged on the shelves around the walls. On the counter was a human skull—an unpromising omen for the apothecary's customers. Ned could not at first see the apothecary himself, as he was dressed in black and was bending, in the far corner of the room, over a mortar and pestle, in which he was grinding some pungent substance.

Then the apothecary looked up, sharp-nosed, pestle in hand, and said, "Take that dog out."

"I only—"

"Out, I say. Dogs are not allowed."

Ned took Barnabas outside and told him to wait. Then he went back in and asked for some oil of lavender. Jacob Underwood pursed his lips and went to hunt amongst the lozenges and pills, the bottles of fumitory water and the jars of Elsham ginger that lined his shelves.

He was just a little older than Ned, and to judge by the quality of his black garb, and his neatly groomed hair and hands, he was plumply prosperous. He assessed Ned's rain-soaked, threadbare coat and his mud-spattered boots with something approaching scorn. "That will be two shillings," he said, pouring the oil into a small glass bottle and stoppering it.

"How much are those crucibles?" Ned pointed at the empty vessels ranged along a shelf.

"Five shillings apiece."

"Then I'll take one."

Underwood raised his eyebrows a little in surprise as he put one on the counter. "Interested in alchemy, are you?"

Ned was pulling out some coins. "Not especially. A friend of mine, a herbalist, asked me to get one for him. Do you get a lot of customers who claim to be alchemists?"

"I certainly do," said Underwood with some asperity, taking his coins and holding them up to the light. "Almost every day I get people coming in here asking for crucibles, hoping to brew up some hellish mess which they think will make their fortunes. You'd be amazed how many people imagine they can make the Philosopher's Stone. They even bring me letters they say they've found—forgeries, all of them—written to Agrippa, by Flamel, even Hermes Trismegistus himself."

Just then the door of the shop opened, setting the bell tinkling again. A thin youth, drenched from the rain, came in and stood waiting his turn in the shadows.

Ned said to the apothecary, "What do they want to purchase from you? Apart from the crucibles?"

"Oh, it's often a phial of Egyptian sulfur they ask for, or some philosopher's mercury. Fools, all of them. If the ingredients for the Stone do exist, then they are not to be bought. Philosopher's mercury? Philosopher's salt and sulfur? I don't sell such things. But people never cease in their delusions."

He beckoned to Ned to come closer. Ned was aware of the boy who'd come in standing in absolute silence by the door.

Underwood said, confidingly, "Sometimes—just sometimes—I'm visited by customers who, I think, know a little more than the usual charlatans. People who, I think, might just have some secret, some ancient knowledge. They only ask for simple ingredients, like arsenic and antimony, but I wonder if they have some esoteric recipe."

"Has anyone ever spoken to you," asked Ned, "about a recipe for gold that was addressed to someone called Auriel?"

"That's a new one," said Underwood. He was grinning again. "A letter to an angel. Why not? Why not?" He wagged his finger admonishingly. "Now, you're not going to try to *sell* this Auriel letter to me, are you, sir? That's another trick that's been tried on me once too often, I tell you."

Ned picked up his crucible. "I wouldn't dream of it," he said, "even if I had it. Thank you for your help."

He went out and saw that Barnabas, sheltering under the overhanging eaves of the shop from the rain, was finishing off a morsel of bread or cake that someone had given him. Was it the boy in the shop? Barnabas had a talent for making friends.

Barnabas cocked his leg against Jacob Underwood's door. Ned didn't stop him. When he'd finished he whistled to him and set off down the crowded street, with the crucible tucked under his jerkin.

JACOB KNEW THE LAD WHO WAITED TO BE SERVED. HIS name was Robin Green, apprentice to a silversmith, and he had come to buy arsenic for his master, to be used in the plating of silverware. The lad always looked half starved and was normally reluctant to say much, so Jacob was surprised when Robin drew a deep breath and said, in a rush, "Master Underwood. That man was talking about a letter to Auriel. Didn't you know that Auriel was one of the angels with whom Dr. John Dee was said to have talked about the making of gold?"

Jacob heaved a weary sigh. Not another lunatic after the secret of gold! Then he remembered that Robin's master, Tobias Jebb, was interested in such things—though privately he would have thought Master Jebb made riches enough from overcharging for his fancy wares.

He patted Robin on the shoulder and said, "It's all trickery and nonsense, dear boy. Remember it. Trickery and nonsense."

NED WENT ON HIS WAY, HIS MOOD IN NO WAY LIGHT-ened by the fact that his route to Rose Alley was blocked at Paternoster Row by a full-blown street riot. Apparently the trouble had started an hour ago, when some prentice lads had spotted three drunken Scotsmen jeering at a portrait of St. George which hung outside a tavern of that name. The prentices had promptly abandoned their duties to set upon the Scots; at which the Scots had summoned reinforcements, the apprentices likewise, and now all the muddy lanes between Paternoster Row and the Shambles were filled with warfare as the various factions surged up and down in a manner to which they were well accustomed, oblivious to the heavy rain which poured down upon them.

Ned, guarding his crucible, tried to take an alternative route down by Old Change, but on seeing a crowd of roaring youths trying to tear down the shutters of a shopkeeper whom they cried out was a Catholic—for, in the absence of any Scots in this vicinity, who had sensibly hidden, they were quite happy to turn on anyone at all who looked as if he deserved a sound beating—Ned retraced his steps to take refuge in a tavern close to the apothecary's he had just left. There, by the tavern door, he found the young lad who'd waited in the shop to be served, cowering from the din of the approaching rioters who surged eastward like a spring tide. The boy was trying to enter the inn for safety, but the innkeeper barred his way and growled that he wouldn't have prentices skulking round here and letting their friends in as soon as his back was turned.

The boy almost shook with fear. "But I have a package for Master Tobias the silversmith. If they find me with it, they'll steal it. I must keep it safe."

Ned turned to the innkeeper. "It's all right. He's with me." He steered the lad inside, just in time, for the landlord then warned his customers they were about to be locked in and set off to bolt and bar the doors and shutters. He had only just finished securing the place when there was the sound of yelling outside, and the thundering of feet, and a fresh wave of noise crested and broke in the street.

Most of the inn's customers had settled resignedly to drinking or dicing. The lad whispered, "Thank you, sir."

Ned ordered them both ale, and a bowl of broth for the boy. He said, abstractedly as he listened to the sounds of riot outside, "That's all right. What's your name?"

The lad put down his spoon. "Robin, sir. Robin Green. Sir, I couldn't help hearing your conversation with the apothecary. Master Jacob can be arrogant, he did not treat your inquiry with the respect it deserves."

Robin Green was well spoken, deferential. Ned turned to him, his eyebrows lifting slightly. "Really? You think, then, that the business of alchemy is worthy of respect?"

"Of course," said Robin eagerly. "Alchemy is the very essence of things. It was known even by the ancient sages, Enoch and Idris, that everything in this world is made of the three sacred ingredients, the precious mercury, sulfur, and salt which the philosophers seek. Of course they are not mercury, sulfur, and salt as we know them, but represent transmuted substances, after the grosser physical properties have been removed."

"Good God," said Ned. "How do you *know* all this?"

"I have listened for years to my master, Tobias Jebb, and his friends. I borrow my master's books and study them through the night." Robin blushed. "Though Master Jebb would be very angry if he knew. He is a silversmith, and he thinks such matters are too lofty for mere apprentices."

Ned nodded slowly. "I think, Robin Green, that you prove him very wrong. What do they consist of, then, these sacred ingredients?"

Robin took a deep breath. "Some say air and water make up the sacred mercury, while fire and earth make sulfur. The residue of the process is called the salt. Paracelsus, who was perhaps the greatest alchemist and philosopher of them all, said that heaven and earth have been created out of these three holy elements, but he warned also that the only possible means of transforming base matter into the higher substance—in other words, gold—lay within men's hearts. Those three elements are what the alchemist tries to grow for himself. From the prime material."

Ned rubbed his forehead. "I know what the prime material is. It's dung."

"Indeed! And did you know that the best kind to use is horse dung, dried out in tiny pellets in the alchemist's athanor?"

"No. I must confess," said Ned, "that I didn't."

"Afterwards you must dissolve the pellets in wine, and warm them gently, then distill some of the liquid and burn the solid residue until it becomes black."

"Calcination. I know. When I tried it, it blew up."

Robin glanced at him, uncertain whether he was serious or not. "But you did it. You can do it again. The burnt residue—'non-flammable and fixed'—that is the philosopher's salt. Master Bacon said so—I was studying his book late last night. The distilled liquid is philosopher's mercury, renowned for its volatile, feminine properties; and within it is captured the philosopher's sulfur, which consists of all that is fiery and masculine."

"Well, damn it," said Ned, rubbing his forehead. "It sounds easy."

"Yes," replied Robin earnestly, "the first stage is straightforward! But for the next stage, you must warm the mercury and salt together, in a special crucible—like *this*." He pulled a stub of pencil from deep within his jerkin and scribbled a diagram on the corner of the package he carried. "You must use a warming dish to even out the heat, like so, and for the next stage you need glass tubing, to draw the condensation into a separate vessel, a cold vessel, like *this*." He scribbled again. "But you must make sure that the fumes do not ignite. For a truly steady heat, Paracelsus recommended the use of peat as fuel, though others have argued for the use of oil, wax, pitch, hair, bones, and even camel dung."

"Not sea coal?"

"No. Sea coal is too full of smoke, and produces sparks if bellows are used. Above all, you see, you must make sure that the sulfurous fumes do not ignite."

"You are knowledgeable indeed, Robin Green. I thought only crusty old magi in their laboratories knew about all this."

"Whatever I read, I remember," said Robin. "I don't know why. I don't usually tell anyone about it. I recited one of Master Jebb's silver recipes to him once, and he beat me for it. He said I was planning to steal his knowledge: but I wasn't, I wasn't—"

"You are wasted on Master Jebb, I think."

Robin gazed at him as if making a decision. He took a deep breath. "Sir, I think you, too, have some valuable knowledge. I heard you telling Master Underwood the apothecary that you once heard of a recipe for gold that was addressed to someone called Auriel. Did you know that Auriel was one of Dr. Dee's angels?"

Ned, who was listening with half an ear to the noises outside, turned back to the boy. "I had heard something to that effect, yes."

"Did you know," went on Robin eagerly, "that before Dr. Dee died last year, he told people that he had actually found the secret of making the Philosopher's Stone? But he died before he could pass it on to anyone."

Outside the din had receded. The landlord was opening the shutters warily. Ned put his hand on the boy's shoulder and stood up. "Isn't it always the way? Thank you for everything you've told me, Robin. But if I were you, I wouldn't place too much store on all this nonsense about man's spirit, and the sacred mercury. Perhaps all that counts, in this rather difficult and nasty world in which we find ourselves, is money; money and survival. I have found, incidentally, that the one helps the other quite considerably. Take my advice, and use that prodigious memory of yours to find yourself a better career than being a drudge to a silversmith."

He nodded to the boy, summoned Barnabas, and went off into the gathering dusk, and the rain that still poured down.

Robin waited until he had gone a little way. Then, his eyes alight with hero worship, he left the tavern and followed him doggedly through the rain-swept streets to Rose Alley, thus ascertaining for himself exactly where the man with the Auriel letter lived before returning to his duties and his secret studies at the shop of the stern Master Tobias Jebb the silversmith.

O N REACHING ROSE ALLEY, NED WENT TO THE bakehouse, which was still warm from the old oven. Barnabas shook his shaggy coat, spraying the stone floor with raindrops, while Ned lit a tallow candle and put in some more coals. He unstoppered one of the leather bottles of wine that Matthew had pressed on him earlier and poured some of it into his new crucible. He sat it experimentally on top of the oven.

After a while it glowed redly. Encouragingly. The scent of warming wine began to fill the room. *Spiritus vini...*

He took the pieces of dried horse dung he'd left earlier on a rack above the coals—small, black, odorless pellets, just as Robin had described—and dropped them one by one into the wine.

He paced to and fro distractedly in the near-darkness. Watching, wondering. So Auriel was an angel—one of Dr. Dee's angels. But what if Auriel was a person, a friend of John Dee's? *"To Auriel, I will give the gift of gold..."*

And what if Dee—once favored by Queen Elizabeth herself, rumored to be her secret intelligencer, but scorned by King James and his entourage—was writing to this friend Auriel not about gold, but about some even more vital secret he had learned?

He gazed at the crucible as if the answer lay there. A vapor rose from the surface of the dark liquid, only to cool and trickle back down the sides of the vessel to rejoin the original mixture.

"As Auriel rises, the Lion shall fall..."

He opened another bottle of Matthew's wine and drank

it, despising himself. As if any of the answers to his questions could possibly be hidden in the ramblings of a dead conjuror.

The door of the bakehouse began to open very slowly. He leaped round with his back to the oven, to hide the crucible. Barnabas growled gently as the door opened wider, and Alice came in.

She closed the door behind her.

"Secrets, Ned?" She let her cloak and hood fall away. Her long fair curls tumbled round her shoulders. "Now, I wonder why you are hiding away in here?"

"It's warm," he said. "Warmer than my room."

His Auriel letter lay open on the bench. He cursed himself for leaving the door unlocked.

She leaned back provocatively against the wall so he could see her full breasts rising and falling. She pointed at the crucible. "How long will it take you to make gold?"

"What makes you think that's what I'm doing?"

She shrugged. "I'm not stupid. I've seen it all before. Heard about it. Though I thought it was only mad old magicians who did this sort of thing, buried away in cellars. I never thought you'd go in for it. Got the taste for it abroad, did you?"

"It's nothing. Just a foolish experiment to pass the time."

She gave him a pitying glance, then wandered to the stone bench by the wall and picked up his Auriel letter. He snatched it from her.

"You're so damned secretive," she mocked. "Is it because you've not got a license?"

"Yes," he said quickly, "yes, that's it. I've no money for such things."

"Steen would forge one for you."

He said nothing, and she continued to study him. Her skin was clear and pale. Her eyes, like dark amber, seemed to burn into him. "We're like each other, Ned, you and I," she said. "We both want what we can't have. Both want to be something we can't be. Want to change ourselves. Like that crucible of yours." She looked round. "You've got enemies, haven't you? What's it worth not to tell anyone what you're up to?"

She was sidling toward him. She put her hand on his chest and let her fingers trail downward.

He tried to hold her away. "Alice. My brother is very fond of you. He has been good to you, as he has to me."

She frowned. "Your brother will get fat and die either in a drunken brawl or of drinking too much. I want something better. You want something better. You and I both. Come away with me, Ned. Let's go somewhere far away, together."

He said, "I think you had better leave."

"You are still thinking of your Kate, aren't you?" she said scornfully. "Mistress Kate Pelham. But I wonder if she would do *this,* or *this,* as I would, for you."

He was tired, and dispirited, and the movement of her lips over his distracted him. Her fingers were skillful as they dealt with the points of his breeches. Then the heat and moisture of her mouth engulfed him completely as she pushed him back onto the bench and knelt over him. Her tongue was warm and sweet and insistent. Wearily he gave in.

The crucible glowed in the corner, casting strange lights on her skin, her breasts, her lips as she moved; and she never closed her eyes, but watched him, watched him all the time as the fierce pleasure consumed his being.

By the time Alice left him, in quiet triumph, the oven was dying. Ned tiredly got up and went to the crucible, which still glowed gently. The residue had gathered in the base, but shifted from time to time, as if driven by an unseen current. The liquid itself was a red jewel color. He gazed at it, feeling as if it were drawing in his soul.

He thought of dead Albertus, of Underwood's mockery and Robin's ardent belief; of Alice, gazing first at the crucible, then at him: "We both want what we can't have."

"YOU CAN EAT LATER," SAID PAT, "IF YOU'VE THE AP-petite for it. I was looking for you earlier, but then I saw that you had company in that bakehouse of yours."

Ned had gone to the Crown to get some food when Pat found him. The big Irishman's expression told Ned that he knew about Alice, even before he spoke.

"Why were you looking for me?" he said, pushing his plate aside. "Is there some news about the men who attacked my brother?"

"I'm more concerned about the men who are after you," replied Pat grimly. "I've got you a prisoner. Another of those black-coated bastards you wouldn't let me kill. Come on. I'll show you."

He led Ned to the cellar of Matthew's house, which was used as a strong room for stolen goods. Two of Pat's companions were keeping guard on a man who sat on one of the empty crates down there. He looked up quickly when Ned and Pat came down the steps. He smelled of fear. Ned recognized him as one of Northampton's bodyguards.

Ned turned to Pat and said wearily, "I told you. These men just appear from time to time to keep an eye on me."

"Why?"

Ned shrugged. "To make sure I don't leave the country. Or start spying for Cecil. If you get rid of one, there'll only be others. They mean me no harm."

"Now, are you quite sure about that?" Pat told his two men to leave the cellar, then went and stood over the man. "Tell him, you bugger. Tell him what you told me earlier."

The prisoner looked up. Pat put his fist an inch from the man's face. "What were your instructions again?"

The man cleared his throat. "We were told to watch the man Warriner."

"And?"

"He is supposed to be finding someone, for the Earl of Northampton. Finding him and killing him."

Pat looked at Ned. "I assume it's true," he said quietly. "I hope you had good reason to agree to this." He turned back to the prisoner. "Go on. What else did you tell me? What else, damn you?"

"As soon as Warriner has done what he is supposed to do, we are to kill him."

"Well," said Pat, "and it's a bloodthirsty world we live in, to be sure."

Ned was silent. Pat drew him away from the man, then

turned on him and hissed, "Why did you agree to kill this man for Northampton? I thought you'd left his service long ago."

"It was to buy time," said Ned quietly. "For myself, and for someone who needs my help."

"Why didn't Northampton set his own black-coated ruffians to do the job?"

"I've been wondering that myself. I think it's because I'm dispensable, Pat. I think the Earl feels he might as well make use of me before he gets rid of me for good—"

Pat whirled round at a sudden movement from behind. The prisoner was on his feet and reaching beneath his coat. Almost in the same instant he was pulling out a wheel-lock pistol and was taking aim.

Ned had already thrown himself at him, had grabbed him by the wrists, and was trying to thrust his gun hand upward.

"Be careful," cried out Pat, "it's ready cocked . . ."

Ned kicked Northampton's man hard on the shin, then kneed him in the groin. The man let out a howl, and his fingers tightened on the trigger as Ned knocked his gun hand backward so the barrel was twisted away.

The gun went off. There was a sulfurous stink of gunpowder. The man collapsed, his jaw a mass of pulped bone and blood.

Ned stood back, breathing heavily. Pat said, "Jesus, man. I'm glad you learned something in your soldiering."

Ned looked at him. "The first lesson in warfare, Pat, is to search all prisoners." He gazed down at Northampton's man. "If he's not dead yet, he will be soon. Can you get rid of him?"

"A weighted sack in the Fleet should do the trick."

Ned said, "See to it."

THE PLUMP APOTHECARY JACOB UNDERWOOD, WHO made most of his money from selling love philters to bored housewives, and protectives against the French pox to their husbands, continued to find amusement in the visit of the shabby stranger who came into his shop, bought a glass crucible, then asked him about recipes for the Philosopher's

Stone. In fact he found it so amusing that he had to tell his friends, some fellow apothecaries, as they all met up that evening in an eating house in Bread Street, if only to demonstrate his own vastly superior knowledge of the business of alchemy. He told them how the young fool was asking about the ingredients for making the Philosopher's Stone, as if they could be bought; and then had gone on to talk about some secret recipe, a letter written to someone called Auriel.

Well, they decided, still laughing, the name of poor Auriel—one of John Dee's angels—had been falsely used indeed, and this young man, if not a charlatan, was a gullible fool. A letter to Auriel, indeed. They laughed and laughed.

Later that night, Jacob Underwood, alone in his back room, counting out the money he had made that day, heard a muffled knocking at his door.

He closed up his money chest and went to the barred door, and called sharply, "Who is it?"

He heard an indistinct voice. It could be one of the wealthy women who came secretly for a love potion, or to ask him to get rid of an unwanted babe. He unbolted the door and saw four men standing there in the darkness; four men whose silence was as sinister as the way they gazed at him.

One of them said, "Are you Jacob Underwood?"

"And what if I am? State your business or be off with you, before I call the Watch!"

The first of them stepped forward and shoved him backward so he almost lost his balance. Then the others pressed into the room with him, and the last one bolted the door.

Underwood looked round wildly, but there was no point in calling for help, because he had sent his manservant home hours ago. He did not like having servants or prentices sleeping here; he did not trust them with his valuables.

He backed away. "I have no money here. Leave me alone."

The first man tipped over the big money chest on his desk. All the coins spilled noisily out and rattled on the floor. Another said, "We don't want your money, Underwood. We just want to know why you've been going around talking about a letter to someone called Auriel."

"Auriel?" He was stupefied; he could not believe they were here over so trivial a matter.

"Auriel." Two of them moved closer, while the last one in guarded the door. Jacob thought he saw the gleam of a knife in one man's hand, and his teeth chattered in terror.

He said, "A stranger came into the shop today, talking about a letter, but he was a rogue, a simpleton, he didn't know what he was talking about—"

They looked at one another. One of them said at last, "What was the name of this man who claimed to have the letter to Auriel?"

"I don't know. I swear I don't."

"Describe him to us."

"He was young—younger than me—perhaps twenty-five, twenty-six," stammered Jacob. "He had dark hair and a clean-shaven face. He was soaked by the rain; his clothes were worn out and shabby. He had a dog . . ."

"Was he an alchemist?"

"I would say he knew nothing, nothing at all about the business of the Philosopher's Stone!"

Unfortunately for Jacob Underwood, his interrogators thought otherwise. There in that room they asked him more questions, and they knew how to make him tell them more. Dear God, he would have told them anything, anything at all, if only the pain would stop. Two of them dealt with him excruciatingly, while another ransacked the papers on his desk, throwing them one by one to the floor.

Another inquisitor, who seemed familiar with all Underwood's tormentors, arrived and began to ask him questions anew, about Auriel, about alchemy. His knowledge clearly exceeded that of his companions, but he was no more successful than they in extracting information from his victim.

They let Underwood go at last. He subsided in a semiconscious, bloodstained heap to the floor. His interrogators stood back in distaste from the stink of him.

"It is no good," said one at last. "He really has told us everything he knows."

"Then let us end it," said another.

15.

All my good turns are forgotten; all my errors revived and expounded, to all extremity of ill. All my services, hazards and expenses, for my country—plantings, discoveries, fights, councils and whatsoever else—malice hath now covered over. I am now made an enemy and a traitor.

LETTER, RALEGH TO LADY RALEGH, 1604

IT WAS ALMOST THE END OF NOVEMBER, AND KATE PELham was out in her garden at dawn, standing in the shrubbery where the holly bushes were rimed with the first hard frost of winter. She watched the fiery sun rise in the east and she grew cold in her thin woolen gown and light shoes, but that in itself gave her a sense of freedom: the freedom she had known as a child, to roam this garden and all the riverbank, her hair flying loose, her clothes muddy and torn, as she had hunted for adventure with Ned Warriner.

This morning she also felt a sense of freedom, because her husband had left the house early for work, though she knew his servants would still be watching her.

Her liberty did not last long. Soon the nurse came out to find her, to tell her that Sebastian was calling for his mother; so she went inside, and she held him to her fiercely and stroked back his curling dark hair. For the last two days her little son had suffered from the tightness of the chest which left him choking for breath, and made her cold with fear for him. She and Pelham had visited many medical practitioners, tried many cures, but when this lung sickness was upon him, it seemed there was little to be done.

She sat him on her lap, and she sang songs to him, of the kind she liked to think that her mother used to sing to her. Songs of distant times, distant journeys. Kate had been so young when she died that she could not remember her; but from a miniature Kate could see that she had delicate features and silky brown hair, just like Kate's, only since her marriage Kate kept hers covered in a veil. Her mother's powerful relative, her great-uncle the Earl of Shrewsbury, had told Kate that she also had her mother's clear green eyes, and her mother's spirit; though Pelham had done his best to quell it.

Pelham was the reason she no longer saw Shrewsbury. She had lied to Arbella. The families had not drifted apart; they had always maintained contact, if only once or twice a year, at the festivals of Christmas or Easter. Until Kate married Pelham.

Shrewsbury was known to have secret sympathy with those of the Catholic faith. His wife, Mary, was reputed to attend Mass herself, in secret. So Shrewsbury expressed his disapproval, his regret, at Kate's betrothal to a recusant hunter; and yet he had not entirely cut her off. He told her she was welcome, whenever she wished, to bring her little son to his house. Indeed, a letter had arrived, as ever, this year, inviting her to attend the Christmas festivities in Shrewsbury's town house in Coleman Street, with Sebastian. But Pelham's name was not on it, and her husband forbade her to go.

Now she kissed Sebastian, and wrapped him up warmly and led him by the hand out into the garden, in the sunshine. Fresh air and exercise, her doctor had told her, would do the child as much good as any medicines. She knelt at his side to point to the distant boats on the river, and told him of his grandfather's travels, though the ship he had sailed on, she told Sebastian, was bigger, so much bigger, than any of the river vessels. After an hour or so the nurse came out to gently take him from her, saying that it was time for his morning rest. Kate kissed him, holding him tightly, as if she would not let him go.

She went to her room and unlocked a chest to take out some papers. Going to the kitchen, she collected three jars of apricot preserve which she had made in the summer from the fruit trees that grew against the south wall. Placing the jars and the papers in a basket, she covered them all with a cloth. Then she put on her cloak and went to find her maid.

She should not venture beyond the house, Pelham had told her, without a manservant. But the men were all his, and she knew they reported everything back to him. So she took Bess with her, who had served her for many years. Together, they hired a boat downriver. The waterman looked at her curiously, for it was not often that women of quality traveled like this, with only a maid for company. But Kate, though young, had a demeanor that discouraged any liberties. She sat straight and silent, her maid beside her, as the boat carried them downstream, past the riverside palaces of the old bishops that now belonged to King James's chief courtiers; past the wharfs and under London Bridge, where it was safe to pass between the great piers because the tide was low. The waterman slowed as he came to the Tower, to those low and blackened curtain walls where cannon and sentinels kept guard. The boat pulled up close to the broad steps, against which the river was lapping. The waterman watched with even more curiosity as Kate went on ahead of her maid to the visitors' gate, with its dark arch, where a warder nodded to her and let her in through a grated wicket.

She had come, as she did often, in spite of her husband forbidding it, to visit Sir Walter Ralegh.

Kate was known here simply as her father's daughter. As Kate Revill. If the warders thought of her at all, other than as the quiet, self-contained young woman who was among the great man's many visitors, they thought of her as her father's daughter, for Sir Thomas Revill used to visit Ralegh regularly, sometimes bringing his daughter with him. She had been as bright and as spirited as any lad, they used to say admiringly, though now she was quiet enough.

Like all visitors, she was questioned and searched before gaining access to the famous prisoner. All the noise and activity of the Tower surrounded her as she was escorted through more locked gates to inner courtyards that were dark beneath the soaring stone walls, and up cold stairways; for here were the headquarters of the King's Ordnance, where cannon were forged for the nation's ships and armies. Here gunpowder was stored, below the foundries; here also was the King's Mint, where the coins of the realm were cast in constant heat and clangor. The noise and smells of the metalworkers' craft filled the air.

Kate was led to Ralegh's chamber in the damp and thick-walled Bloody Tower, where he was sitting at his desk, writing. But he turned round, and his face lit up as he saw her. He was fifty-five years old now, this Elizabethan hero who led the English fleet against the Armada and captured Cadiz from the Spanish. Bowed with ill fortune and illness, he had been laid low by scheming courtiers, and imprisoned here these last five years, but there was still a quality about him, a nobility, to catch the eye, and to stop the heart.

No wonder, thought Kate quickly, no wonder they said Robert Cecil was still afraid of him.

"My dear Kate," he said, coming forward to take both her hands.

He limped like her husband as a result of a Spanish gun-shot wound. His was received at Cadiz, thirteen years ago. After the sacking of the Spanish town he had returned to a hero's welcome. It was then, her father had told her, that Robert Cecil, an unsoldierly and jealous hunchback, marked him as a man to be destroyed.

Kate let his gnarled old hands enfold hers and smiled up at him. "I have brought you a delicacy, Sir Walter," she said. "Some of my apricot preserve. The harvest was wonderful this year."

He took the little golden jars she offered, and held them up to the light of the window. "You are very good to me, Kate. I cannot think why you humor an old man so."

She took off her cloak and turned to him quickly. "The goodness is in you, Sir Walter, rather than in me. Sometimes I feel that seeing you is all I have left of my father; that seeing you is all I have left of myself."

"You have your son."

"Yes. I am so lucky; I have my son."

"How is Sebastian? Is his breathing any easier?"

"There is a new medicine that the doctor wants to try: a tincture of chervil and rue. We are hopeful that it will ease the tightness in his lungs. The lady Arbella told me earnestly of some cure her grandmother swore by, a concoction of wine in which powdered woodlice had been steeped."

"Her grandmother was held by many to be a witch. This potion was to be mixed beneath the light of the full moon, no doubt." He raised his eyebrows, to show what he thought of such remedies.

"No doubt," replied Kate, smiling back. "I thanked her, and said I would consider it." She reached once more into her basket to fetch the papers, and held them out to him. "Look, Sir Walter. I have been going through more of my father's writings. On his last journey to Virginia, he made these drawings of the plants he found there. I thought you might like to see them."

He spread them out on his table and gazed at the beautifully drawn pictures. His eyes lit up. "Ah! This is the sassafras; the natives use its leaves in a cordial." He pointed eagerly. "And this one is a type of plantain; it grows so freely, and in the autumn has bright berries which draw the birds from miles around—how this brings it all back!"

He studied them for a few moments more, then turned to her. "You must miss your father so much. He was a brave and honorable man. I was proud to call him my friend."

"Thank you," she whispered. "You do not know how much those words mean to me at this time..." Her voice trembled a little, but then she lifted her face squarely to his. "Enough, enough; I have brought you something else. Look. It's a map that my father brought back. Someone drew it for him, a settler he met at Jamestown, who had traveled south the year before to Guiana. He said the natives there had told him—do you see?—that if he followed this tributary of the Orinoco up into the mountains, beyond this canyon, then he would find a gold mine. The Indians talked freely of it. Do you believe it could be true?"

"If gold is nurtured by the sun," he replied, "as the old alchemists say, then surely the lands around the Equator must be veined with rich seams of it. I sailed to the Orinoco myself, in just such a hope. Let me see."

They bent their heads together over the map, his gray one, and hers, with her hood pushed back to reveal her smooth brown hair. The time slipped by as Ralegh pointed out places to her, and told her more of the mountains and the jewel-bright birds, the crystal-clear waters and endless skies of the Americas. Kate listened to Ralegh's every word, her eyes shining, and for a few moments it was as if she were with her father again.

At last she sighed and said, "I must go. Sebastian will be awake, and missing me. And I have things to get ready." She gazed at him ruefully. "In two days' time I must go to the palace of Whitehall."

"You? To Whitehall? But I thought you hated the court."

"I do. But I've been invited to take part in a masque, led by the Queen. There is to be a rehearsal in the Banqueting Hall the day after tomorrow."

"Does your husband approve?"

She hesitated. "He has reminded me how important it is to stay in favor with those in power."

Ralegh said quietly, "He is right, of course. Have you told him yet that you visit me?"

She met his eyes. "No."

There was silence for a few moments, except for the sounds made by the Tower's workmen rising up through the half-open window, the noise of the armorers and the coin-makers who worked within the grim walls. Ralegh began to fold up the map. "Perhaps you should consider it. But then I am afraid he might forbid your visits. Thank you, my dear, for letting me see this." He held the map out to her, but she said, "Oh, you must keep it! My father once told me that he wanted you to have it. He said that if you were ever given the chance to go on another expedition, you might wish to take it with you. He said that no man stood a better chance than you, of finding gold in the New World. He also said that none deserved it more."

Ralegh smiled and shook his head. "I'm afraid I shall never be free."

"You will," she said fervently, picking up her basket and pulling her hood over her hair once more. "You will be free. You have so many friends who care for you, who fight for justice for you."

"My enemies are more powerful than my friends," he answered quietly. "At least for the moment. But perhaps, for me, gold and freedom, if they come at all, will come hand in hand."

She went still. "What do you mean?"

He went to check that the door was shut. Then he came back to her. "There are so many ways," he said, "of looking for gold. Some search on the banks of the Orinoco; others labor in a dark laboratory, nurturing their secret concoctions over a fire."

"You are talking about alchemy again?"

"Indeed, yes. And I had a good teacher in the art. Dr. John Dee. Last December, just before he died, he was sick, and confined to his house in Mortlake. He was unable to visit me. But Kate, he sent me this letter."

Going over to an oak chest, he unlocked it with an iron key and reached deep down into the piles of folded garments to draw out a piece of paper. "Please," he said to her. "Read it."

"To Auriel." Her voice was low and sweet. *"Can the glories of the past be reborn? Can gold grow from the cold earth? Soon I will write again, with news of such treasure, such golden hopes: the elixir indeed. The Black Bird is hoping that within twelve months he will drink golden wine with you once more..."*

She looked up. "The black bird? I don't understand. And who is Auriel?"

"Auriel was one of Dee's angelic spirits. It was also his secret name for me. I don't understand all of it either, Kate. But much of it is in alchemical language. Dee was trying to tell me, I think, that he believed he had discovered the secret of the Philosopher's Stone. And that he hoped I would soon be free..." He gazed at the letter, touching it as if to coax out some hidden meaning. "He promised to write again. But soon afterwards he died."

"Oh," she whispered, "how cruel. To have your hopes raised with such talk of gold and freedom."

"For a while I was encouraged to hope," he said. "But with the news of Dee's death, I wiped it from my mind. Gold and freedom together—an impossible dream. I am Auriel, yet I shall never be free. Never..."

She clasped her hands together. "You should be free. You must tell the King's councillors again that you are quite innocent of the crimes they charged you with. To accuse you of colluding with Spain! Only a fool could think you, of all people, guilty of such a thing." She spoke passionately, and Ralegh lifted a finger to his lips, to remind her that Governor Waad's spies were never far away.

"I was afraid," he said, "when I got this letter, that it had been tampered with. Afraid, too, that it might even have been a forgery, to tempt me into trouble. So please, Kate, say nothing of it, to anyone."

"Of course. I hope you know that you can trust me to be silent. But what if Dr. Dee *did* write to you again, as he said he would? And what if the second letter never reached you?"

"Of that I am afraid also. That he died, perhaps, before it could be dispatched. And that somebody else—who might or might not understand its meaning—has got it."

She said fiercely, "If only I could *help*."

He took her hand again and pressed it. "You help me, my dear, by visiting me in this bleak place. But now you must leave. I do not want to cause you trouble."

She nodded. "I must go and prepare to be a goddess at court in two days' time."

"You will play the part excellently. I only wish I could see it all. Kate, thank you for coming. Your visits hearten me greatly."

She went out to rejoin her waiting maid. Ralegh limped back to his desk and returned to the writing of his "History of the World." Kate left the grim Tower with Bess, and they were rowed upriver as the gray November clouds chased across the sky. She listened to the lonely crying of the seabirds as they winged their way inland from the salt marshes to the east, and Ralegh's words seemed to echo again and again in her head.

"I am Auriel, yet I shall never be free. Never..."

16.

There is in our chemistry a certain noble substance. In the beginning thereof is wretchedness and vinegar, but in its ending joy with gladness.

Therefore I have supposed that the same will happen to me, namely that I shall suffer great difficulty, grief and weariness at first, but in the end shall come to glimpse pleasanter and easier things.

MICHAEL MAIER (1568–1622)
PHYSICIAN AND ALCHEMIST TO RUDOLPH II

THE NEXT DAY, AT FIRST LIGHT, THE PRINCE'S MEN came for Pelham, as they had promised. It was a clear, bright dawn, with a light fall of snow crisping the ground, and a frost mercifully giving some solidity to the muddy trackway of the Strand as the mounted cavalcade, with Pelham riding the horse they had brought for him, made its jangling way beneath the pennants of Prince Henry to the Palace of St. James.

Pelham was searched at the gates, and his sword was removed. "A formality," they apologized, but he knew it was not, and accepted it.

They rode through the grounds of the palace to find the Prince on horseback, in the tiltyard between the Friary garden and the chapel, practicing at the joust with his friends. Pelham had seen him before, of course, from afar. He recognized instantly the tall, slender figure with the bright tawny hair and regal bearing.

Pelham's escorts dismounted, as did Pelham, and they waited in the low winter sunlight, beside the tiltyard. The young Prince, handing his lance to an attendant, rode toward them on his chestnut mount. "Come close," he said. Pelham approached and bowed, feeling the old shame at his dragging leg. He remained with his head lowered until the Prince, from his saddle, commanded him to stand upright, and said, in his light, even voice, "Master Francis Pelham. I have heard that you are a veteran of the Azores expedition, and that you acquitted yourself with honor against the Spaniards at Fayal. I would like you to tell me about it. Will you follow me?"

Pelham lifted his head higher, perhaps, than he had done for a long time.

The Prince and his entourage made their way to the newly built riding school to the west of the palace yard, with Pelham and his escort following. There the Prince's companions continued to school their mounts in the pale light falling from high windows, while Prince Henry sat at one of the trestle tables set against the wall and ordered Pelham to join him there.

Pelham told him of the voyage to the Azores twelve years ago, when he was only nineteen: how Essex and Ralegh had inspired the whole company with their valor. He hesitated before pronouncing their names, for Essex had died a traitor's death eight years ago, and Ralegh was imprisoned. But Prince Henry raised his hand—which Pelham noted was adorned not with jewels but with the calluses of a swordsman—and said, "Please don't be afraid to mention their names. Essex in his day was one of the Queen's greatest soldiers. And as for Ralegh, I think that none but my father would keep such a bird in a cage."

His lip curled in scorn as he mentioned his father. Pelham was shocked, but hid it. One of the Prince's attendants, the grizzled old soldier Spenser, pressed Pelham next about the attack on Fayal, wanting to know every detail about English and Spanish sailing tactics, the English gunnery, and the Spaniards' responses. A servant brought wine, and as they drank Prince Henry and his men listened closely to Pelham's replies, discussing his answers with passion. He noted how they talked of Spain and her Catholic allies with loathing, but spoke with nothing but admiration of the King of France, and Prince Maurice of Nassau.

Prince Henry talked openly about his longing to sail the seas and do battle himself with the Spaniards. "As you did," he said earnestly to Pelham, and Pelham felt like a nineteen-year-old again, being praised by Ralegh.

Prince Henry's mounted companions had begun an intricate maneuver under the tutelage of the Prince's Master of Stables, a youthful-looking Scotsman called Duncan. For a while the lofty school was filled with the jingle of harness and with the rhythmic beat of hooves. Pelham watched their skill with wonder. Prince Henry, clearly also stirred by the display, had got to his feet, the better to assess them. The slanting rays of winter sunlight glinted on his tawny hair, and his eyes flashed fire as he turned to face his seated entourage and said, "With such companions, what could I not do? I will not marry the Spanish princess, as my father has ordered. I will lead a great army against the Spaniards rather than make peace with them, ever."

Pelham, watching him, thought, If this Prince were King, there would be no limit to what he could achieve...

He felt, just for a moment, as though all the Prince's attendants had turned to look at him, Pelham, gauging his reaction to the Prince's defiant words.

And then, suddenly, Prince Henry picked up the goblet of wine from which he had been drinking and slammed it back down on the table, so hard that the wine flew out in dark droplets across the table. Duncan, hearing it, halted the horses. Henry's attendants rushed to his side as the Prince drew his hand across his forehead and whispered, "I see it again. I see poison, and death..."

"Nay, my lord," said the gruff soldier called Spenser quickly, gripping his shoulder, "there is nothing to fear. We have all drunk the same wine, and we are well; don't you see?"

The Prince's hands covered his face. "It is in my stars, that I will die of poison; of this I am sure..."

They led him away quickly, out through the great doors of the riding school into the cold winter air.

Pelham had risen, as did everyone else, while the Prince was escorted from the hall. The riders dismounted in silence and prepared to lead their horses away. Pelham sat again, unsure of what to do, what was expected of him. Another of the Prince's men came to sit next to him, to whom Pelham had been introduced earlier: John Lovett, Henry's chief clerk: slim, exquisitely dressed, watchful.

"Our Prince," said Lovett to Pelham quietly, "is of a sensitive disposition. His character is without doubt brave, manly, as you have seen—in fact wholly admirable—"

"Oh, yes."

"All of us here are devoted to him."

"Indeed," said Pelham fervently.

Lovett rested his hands on the table. Pelham saw that he wore a single ring, a large ruby set in gold, on the little finger of his right hand. Lovett went on, "Prince Henry has a certain...I dare not call it a weakness, perhaps a vulnerability. He has been brought up to be wary of plots and plotters. In himself he is well able to defend his own cause—he would lead an army into battle, he would fight any number of men single-handed. He is a superb and courageous swordsman and athlete."

Pelham nodded, waiting.

"But what he is very much afraid of," went on Lovett softly, "are those enemies against whom he cannot fight. He is afraid of sorcerers, of poisoners; of those who would use hellish spells to bring down evil on him in the dark. And there is so little we, his friends and advisers, can do to protect him against such fears. I wanted you to know all this."

Pelham said, spreading out his hands, "I am honored beyond measure to have been taken into your confidence. If there is anything, anything at all I can do . . ."

"You have helped us already, by coming here today. Prince Henry is eager to talk with anyone with experience of fighting the Spaniards, at sea or on land. He feels that his father—and, indeed, his country—have dealt harshly with people such as you."

Pelham felt a rush of emotion.

"We are Prince Henry's day-to-day guardians," went on

Lovett. "We look all the time for men we can trust. You are employed as a seeker of recusants, are you not?"

"Yes. Yes . . ."

Lovett leaned closer and said, "Your worth should be recognized more fully. Perhaps you could be of use to the Prince at some time in the future. Would you be prepared to serve him?"

"With all my heart," replied Pelham fervently.

An attendant had opened the big double doors to let out the remaining horses. The cold air swept in. Lovett got to his feet. "I must attend to my duties," he said. "The Prince goes to the court at Whitehall this afternoon."

Pelham, too, rose. "Yes. Of course . . ."

"If you go to the west gate," said Lovett, "you will find your previous escort waiting to take you home. Thank you for coming here today." He smiled. "You will hear from us again."

So PELHAM MADE HIS WAY OUT INTO THE COLD LATE morning. The clouds had gathered, and more snow was beginning to fall; and yet he could see the gardeners still working like wraiths between the bare trees.

He looked up at the leaden sky and breathed in deeply. Kind words from the Prince and his attendants would not pay his debts. But Lovett had, surely, been offering him some sort of work, very soon, at St. James's Palace. His spirits soared.

He walked on through the park to the west gate, where he had to stop for a few moments as several men and a horse-drawn cart laden with sawn-up branches crossed his path. The horse's hooves were slipping on the newly fallen snow. As he waited there a man in a long, pale coat with a wide-brimmed hat pulled low over his face appeared at his side and said, "My men will be out of your way very soon."

Pelham had jumped at the man's voice, which possessed a strange, whistling resonance, as if his vocal cords had been damaged. He said, "Think nothing of it. But I'm surprised your men are still at work, on such a cold and treacherous day."

The man smiled. "My gardeners would work every day,

and every night, too, for Prince Henry. And treacherous? To-day? Oh, no." The grave smile continued to illuminate his face. "The stars, you see, are auspicious for our toil. And the Prince knows it is so." The man was watching the progress of his minions as they collected up more felled timber that lay beside the path. "There is a time, you see, according to the stars and the seasons, for everything."

Pelham listened, though he knew it was time for him to go. He said, his despair returning suddenly as the west gate beck-oned, "Tell me. Are you ever asked to predict the prospects of some voyage to far-off seas? Would you know in advance, from the stars, whether or not a ship would return safely?"

The man regarded him thoughtfully. "I can forecast an aus-picious date for embarkation. Men have consulted me over such matters. But as for long voyages, why, those frail ships are at the mercy of winds, currents, hostile sailors; and there are so many uncertainties."

"Yes," said Pelham. "Of course."

"I think," said the man regretfully, "that if you are thinking of asking for such help, then any advice might already be too late."

He nodded and moved on, after his men. Pelham set off to-ward the gate. A horse and escort were waiting for him, as Lovett had promised. And as he rode on his way homeward, his troubles once more assailed him.

BY NOON THE SNOW HAD STOPPED, BUT THE SKIES were still heavy. Down by Whitehall stairs a private barge, canopied against the elements, banged against the wooden jetty as the rowers banked their oars. A liveried footman jumped out first to secure the rope, and then to lend his hand to a small, middle-aged man in an unornamented doublet and cloak of black, who scrambled with awkwardness and some distaste from the confines of the rocking boat. Two more liv-eried men followed, offering him their arms. He brushed them aside in irritation and set off toward the palace of Whitehall, with his attendants following hurriedly behind.

He was short, of crooked stature, and walked awkwardly,

even in his haste. He was an unprepossessing figure; but nevertheless the crowds thronging the waterside between the palace buildings and the water's edge made way for him like the waves of the sea parting on either side of his path as he pressed on through the well-trodden snow toward a gate where the porters bowed their heads low. He passed the line of guards with their halberds and headed into Whitehall's labyrinth of buildings and courtyards with hardly a glance about him at the magnificence to be seen all around. He was a constant attender here, with no need to stare, as did the visitors who traversed the public way through the palace, or the many Scotsmen who had followed James and his northern lords south, to beg, in the opinion of the scornful English, for undeserved, unearned favors.

Servants deferentially hurried to open doors for him, for he was the chief and most subtle of James's servants, Sir Robert Cecil, Master of the Wards and Lord Treasurer of the Realm, who had learned to overcome the outward defects of his unprepossessing appearance by dominating those around him with his mental powers, which were unsurpassed. He entered the high chamber where others already sat at a table that was covered with documents and ledgers; and he reflected, perhaps, that though the House of Commons liked to think it had some say in the affairs of government on the rare occasions when it met, it was these men who ran the country: Charles Howard, the Lord Admiral; Chief Secretary Scrope; Archbishop Cranborne; and Henry Howard, the Earl of Northampton, distinctive with his hooded eyes and his long gown of black. The Earl of Northampton had been absent from London for a short while. He was, on Cecil's entry, the last to stand, and the first to sit down, almost before Cecil did. Cecil noted that also.

Lately the long-standing rivalry between Cecil and Northampton had found expression in a more tangible form. Their retainers had taken to fighting, in armed bands, out in the city's streets at night. The violence had become something of a court scandal. The other week one of Northampton's men had been badly injured, knifed in a running battle, and the King had summoned both men to express his disapproval. He had told them, in his broad Scots accent, how important it was that they work in harmony.

Later that night one of Cecil's men, the one suspected of stabbing Northampton's man, had been found dead—drowned, it appeared—on the muddy bank of the Thames by Dowgate. The two lords, in the Council chamber, maintained a frosty civility, but no one was fooled.

Now Cecil allowed the silence to reign briefly; then he looked at every man in turn and said, "Nothing must endanger our peaceful relations with Spain. There is talk of war, even now, even though the treaty between Spain and the Dutch has been signed. My lords, there are those who would plunge our country into the catastrophic hostilities which threaten all of Europe now that the Duke of Julich is dead. France talks of a holy war, and presses King James to join a Protestant alliance; but we must remain apart. And before the end of the year, the marriage arrangements between Prince Henry and the Infanta must be finalized."

He looked round again, meeting eyes, reading thoughts. "This is the will of the King," he said.

Then he drew some papers toward him. Clerks and servants were summoned, to write notes, to deliver messages, to pour wine; and the routine business of the Privy Council of England commenced.

17.

───────────⁂───────────

*Gold is of all metals the most precious, and it is the tincture of
redness; because it tingeth and transforms every body. It is calcined and dissolved without profit, and is a medicine rejoicing,
and conserving the body in youth.*

JĀBIR IBN HAYYĀN (C.721 A.D.–C.815)
ALCHEMIST

AT NIGHTFALL IT BEGAN TO SNOW AGAIN, BUT THE
heat was stifling inside the workshop of Master Tobias
Jebb, silversmith, on Ludgate Hill, where it was almost time
to close up the shop.

The two other prentice boys had already been sent off for
their meager supper, but Master Tobias, sweating over his fur-
nace, had told Robin Green, his youngest assistant, that he
must stay behind to hold a beautiful silver drinking vessel for
him while he affixed the handles. Robin's heart sank. There
would be no food left for him. But he braced himself to do the
job aright, waiting while stern Master Tobias prepared the sol-
der; and as he waited he remembered how last night his master, mellowed a little by the spiced wine his wife had prepared
for him, had talked with his learned friends long into the night
about Hermes Trismegistus, and the making of the Philoso-

pher's Stone. Robin had eavesdropped, crouching at the top of the stairs. And as he listened he forgot the cold and his hunger.

He sometimes wondered if Master Tobias had sensed Robin's youthful ardor for learning when he chose him four years ago from the ranks of the orphans at the Foundling Hospital—had seen it, perhaps, in the hungry eyes of the thin-faced twelve-year-old boy who had gazed at him as he and his half-starved fellows were lined up for his inspection. Tobias chose his apprentices from the hospital, Robin had heard tell, because then he had no one to answer to.

Robin had been in the Foundling Hospital from infancy, having no knowledge of his mother. As with his fellow unfortunates, the parish clerks and beadles made him pay out his gratitude in silent suffering. The orphans were fed on messes concocted from the offal that the butchers of Houndsditch could not give away. Those who survived infancy were not left in idleness for long, for sin fills empty minds, or so the clerics said. Robin and his fellow inmates, when big enough, were kept busy at such tasks as breaking coals, and pulling rags to pieces, and they were also given lessons, chiefly in the Bible and the evilness of their ways. Here lay Robin's salvation. For he discovered, early on, that he had a hunger for learning.

He made few friends in the Foundling Hospital, but kept to himself, struggling to read the stern texts that the masters provided, and to make what he could of the bleak world that surrounded him. From the age of ten or so, the other inmates started to be picked out and sent into the world to earn their keep: the stoutest as barge boys or carriers' lads; the smallest as sweeps or linkboys. The prettiest, there were rumors, were taken away quietly to such places as Lord Hunsdon's brothel in Hoxton, no doubt in return for a fat fee paid in secret to the hospital's master.

As for Robin, he was neither pretty nor hefty, and was constantly overlooked by these ungentle masters, until Tobias Jebb the silversmith turned up, looking for an apprentice. And he chose Robin.

At Master Tobias's, Robin was often hungry and cold, frequently beaten, and always overworked. But what he learned, from listening, and from secretly borrowing the silversmith's books to read by candlelight into the early hours, was more valuable, he told himself, than any earthly riches.

Robin dreamed of someday becoming a magus. Of knowing all the secrets for himself. This, he reminded himself, was his time of trial. He read in his master's books about the significance of gold, both real and allegorical; how it represented the highest, purest state of matter, to which in time all elements would naturally be transformed.

He knew that gold was a substance miraculously resistant to tarnish, corrosion, and fire. Surely it was the ultimate expression of beauty and purity on earth; and yet the true aim of alchemy, the magi said, was not the attainment of wealth, but the perfection of the human soul. The transmutation of base metals into gold was but the forerunner of spiritual redemption.

Robin longed to discover the secret of this transmutation. The Philosopher's Stone.

The silversmith's stern words of reprimand dragged him back to the present: the vase was finished now, the handles secured. Tobias had once let Robin try some handlework, and had beaten him afterward, because the boy had set one of the handles crookedly on the little silver trinket vase. After the beating Robin realized that his master had forgotten all about the vase. Normally it would be melted down and used again. But Robin took it—this was one of his few sins—and kept it with his secret things, hidden under his straw mattress in the attic.

Tobias was starting to take off his heavy apron. "When you've cleaned my tools, Robin," he ordered, "you must sweep and scrub the floor. Don't leave it filthy like last time. And I don't want you sloping off till it's done. Do you understand?"

Robin had never sloped off, ever, before completing his tasks punctiliously. He had never left the floor dirty. But he bowed his head in acknowledgment and went to clean all the used implements in the washhouse adjoining the workroom.

And it was there, as he cleaned and polished the molds and soldering irons with water and pumice, that he heard one of Tobias's friends, the elderly Cassius Barnes, who often came to talk to the silversmith of philosophy and other learned matters late into the night, come rushing in with the news that Jacob Underwood the apothecary was dead.

Robin stopped what he was doing and moved closer to the almost-shut door.

"Dead?" repeated Tobias sharply. "How?"

"It was an attempt at robbery, they think," said Cassius Barnes. "And then he was stabbed to death, brutally. They even hacked off a finger, perhaps in an attempt to make him talk. His shop was ransacked, so it's hard to tell what was missing. But apparently he was talking earlier about a recipe for gold, and his friends wonder if it might be this recipe that his murderers were after."

"A recipe for gold?"

"Yes. Encrypted in a letter to someone called Auriel. A customer came to his shop and offered to sell it to him."

"Did you say *Auriel*?" Something in Tobias's voice—a kind of awe—made Robin peer through the crack between the door and the wall. His crusty old master looked transformed. Stunned.

"Yes, indeed," said Cassius. "Though Underwood was laughing about it."

"Then neither this man trying to sell this letter, nor Underwood himself, can have *known*..."

"Exactly." Cassius looked round and lifted an admonishing finger. "Exactly, my friend. Neither of the fools know what you and I have heard. That Dr. Dee himself told close friends on his deathbed that he had found the recipe for gold. And had sent it for safekeeping to someone—not an angel, but a man. A friend whom he called Auriel."

DOWN BY THE RIVER AT DEPTFORD, THE NIGHT HAD brought a cessation of activity amongst the docks and storehouses, except for a single late coal barge unloading its cargo by the light of a lantern. Snow still fell sporadically, to settle on the wharves and on the hulls of the new ships being built, the *Trade's Increase* and the *Peppercorn*, which seemed to bear, in their soaring structures, the promise of fabulous journeys to the East, in search of treasures.

And here were places of incoming treasures, the several well-guarded warehouses belonging to the foremost lords of the realm; amongst them that of the heir to the throne. For this was where Prince Henry's quest for Italian artifacts and precious porcelain and glassware from farther east—Turkey, Arabia, the Orient, even—had its first landing, before being transported onward to St. James's Palace, which Henry saw as the birthplace of a renaissance for England, a storehouse of precious objects from around the world, to enrich his court, and his future reign.

When Prince Henry's father was crowned King of England six years ago, he received, among many other presents, a suit of armor wonderfully adorned with jewels and enamel work from Japan. The King scarcely looked at it. Now it lay forgotten, unwanted, in some storeroom. Prince Henry had resolved then that he would make up, in every way, for the graceless philistinism of his father. The treasures of the whole world would be garnered and cherished by him. Once he became king.

The Prince's warehouse was locked and barred, and in darkness. The night watchman had passed by a quarter of an hour ago, and was due to return in twenty minutes, but he would in fact be longer, for as he passed by the warehouse he had been felled by a blow to the back of the head.

Inside the Prince's warehouse, his two assailants, Ned and Pat, moved quietly, carrying a taper each. Pat, an expert at housebreaking, had managed to force open a small side door, using a crowbar and a picklock; and now the two intruders stepped quickly from one packing case to another. The warehouse was half empty, and every sound echoed. They moved as quietly as they could, talking in low voices only when they had to. They soon learned to recognize the cases containing art treasures; they were carefully roped, often with the straw that protected their fragile contents poking out between the slats.

Ned whispered, "Are you sure about this?"

"Quite sure. Six crates arrived by ship today, for Prince Henry. They were examined and signed for by just one man. The man you mentioned. John Lovett."

They decided to take one side of the hall each. It was Ned who stopped by a group of crates covered loosely in a sheet of canvas. He pulled it aside. There were six of the stout wooden boxes, padlocked shut.

Ned gave a low whistle to Pat, who loped over and tested the weight of the boxes. He got his crowbar and pulled the slats of one crate a little apart, then bent to peer through the opening. "Metal," whispered Pat over his shoulder.

"Open it further."

"People will know..."

"Make it look as though it's been damaged accidentally."

Pat gave a twist to his crowbar, and a plank cracked loudly. They stood very still, but all was silence. Pat pulled the broken plank aside and looked in.

"Guns," he said.

Ned bent and looked also. Wheel-lock pistols, carefully packed in wadding. He turned to Pat. "Six crates of them? Are they all the same, do you think?"

Pat tested each box for weight and nodded. "Could be twenty or thirty pistols in each. And they're new. Foreign, I would guess." He pointed to the little ink stamp on the corner of each crate—a crude drawing of a rainbow. "Every gunmaker has his mark, and that isn't a London one. I heard there have been more consignments like this lately, Ned. Many more."

They left, then, knowing it might not be long before the felled watchman was discovered, and hailed a boat upriver, pretending to have walked from a Greenwich tavern. They laughed and joked as they were ferried back to the city; but all the time Ned was thinking, Guns for Prince Henry? Or for John Lovett?

Sarah Lovett had told him that her husband made a fortune in gold out of imported paintings, which she suspected didn't even exist. The gold, she said, came from the Prince's loyal friends. Was it to pay for those guns? And were the guns for John Lovett? Or for Prince Henry himself? Why import weapons so secretly?

The snow was falling more steadily now, outlining the roofs of the city, softening the harsh bulk of St. Paul's cathedral. They alighted at Paul's Wharf, and Ned paid off the boatman. Pat looked around assessingly, then said to Ned, "I've been offered work at Deptford. I know one of the foremen. The one who told me about the boxes. The pay's not bad, for this time of the year."

Ned, who'd been checking the change in his pocket, turned to him slowly. "What about Rose Alley, and my brother? He misses you, Pat. He was saying only today that he's not seen you there for a while."

"No." The big Irishman's face darkened. "Nor likely to either. That bitch Alice has been telling lies about me again."

Ned's heart sank. His brother needed all the friends he could get. "Are you sure?"

"Completely sure. It's because I turned her down once. She swore to get even. No surer way to make a woman's heart go hard as flint against you."

Ned said quietly, "I'm sorry my brother has not the sense to value you."

"Deptford's not far away. He can always send for me if he needs me. So can you."

Ned nodded. "If you do decide to work at Deptford, will you let me know if there are any more consignments of guns for Prince Henry?"

"Of course."

"And listen for any talk about a man called John Lovett?"

"Is he a thieving government crook?"

Ned laughed. "Yes. Yes, I think he is."

"Then it will be a pleasure." Pat gave him a mocking little salute, and Ned set off back to Rose Alley, where he collected Barnabas from Tew the cook. He went not to his room over the stable but to the bakehouse, where the oven glowed gently, and Underwood's crucible, filled with Matthew's wine and the long-since dissolved pellets of dung, sat warm and winking at him.

He rubbed Barnabas's head and put more coals in the oven. Then he pulled out his Auriel letter and gazed at it.

He didn't know what was going on, but he would have to make up his mind what to tell Northampton, because he was due to meet him tomorrow, at Whitehall. The Earl's patience would be running out. Especially if he knew by now that one of the men he had set to watch Ned had been killed.

A knock on the door broke into the silence. It was too tentative for Pat, or Matthew. Could it be Alice? He frowned.

The knocking started again. He went to unbolt the door and flung it open, to see a scrawny boy who shivered in the snow. It was Robin Green, the silversmith's lad. Mentally he cursed again.

"What the hell are you doing here? How did you know where I lived?"

The lad looked as pale and thin as Ned remembered in his big coat that hung loosely round his scrawny frame. But his eyes were bright with eagerness. "I—I followed you the other day, sir. After the riot."

"Why?"

"I wanted to try and find out more for you, about Auriel."

"Dear God." Ned hauled him inside and closed the door. "I told you to forget about Auriel. If the name means anything—anything at all—it means not gold, not alchemy, but trouble. Do you understand?"

Robin looked crestfallen. "But I had to tell you what I've just found out. What I heard Master Tobias saying..."

"Ah, yes. The esteemed silversmith. Who works his apprentices like slaves, and feeds them less than he would his dog." Ned was tired, and angry at this intrusion when above all he needed to think.

"Please. Listen," begged the boy. "Tobias was telling his friend—who is also interested in alchemy—about a rumor that shortly before his death Dr. Dee had found the secret of gold! And Dee told his friends that he had passed the secret on to someone he called Auriel..."

Ned drew a deep breath. "So he was talking with angels. A pleasant enough illusion on one's deathbed."

"No, no, you don't understand. Everybody knows that the angel Auriel was one of Dee's angelic spirits. But from the way Master Tobias and his friend were talking, they clearly had reason to believe that Auriel was a real person. A friend of Dr. Dee's."

Ned was staring at him. A real person. As he himself had started to suspect. "Did they have any idea who?"

"I don't think they did. But please—may I see your letter again? It might help me to understand!"

Ned, who had hidden the letter under his doublet when he went to open the door, eased it out again. "I've told you," he said warningly as he started to unfold it. "It's all nonsense. It must be."

But Robin wasn't listening. He didn't even take the letter. Instead he was gazing at the crucible in the corner. He went over to it and breathed, "It's working!"

Ned, bewildered, said, "It's just wine and dung. Nothing's happened. There's nothing to see."

"Nothing? This is the beginning of everything. Of creation. The flask, with Sol and Luna inside it: light and shadow, sulfur and quicksilver. Flamel's vessel of the grave... You can see, in there, if you look, the two components, mingling yet separate: masculine and feminine, like smoke wreathing in still air, just as Flamel said."

He took the letter, which a bemused Ned still held, and scanned it quickly. *"In spiritus vini is the base material first engulfed, then nurtured in a sealed vessel on the consecrated athanor...* What next? *Let the earthly part be well calcined...* I think you're supposed to add a condensing chamber, and collect the liquid, like so—you don't mind, do you, if I do it?"

He put the letter down and from under his big coat he pulled out a shabby canvas bag which clanked as he put it on a workbench. Then he emptied it, spreading out the contents. There were glass tubes, condensing dishes, little pottery vessels, and an array of corks and stoppers. "I've just borrowed them," he explained anxiously to Ned, on seeing his expression, "for a few days, from my master. That's all..." As he spoke he was already connecting another glass vessel to Ned's crucible by using the tubes and corks. He stood back in satisfaction. Then he opened the oven door, put in more coals, and started to work the leather bellows.

Ned said, "You'll burn it. It will overheat."

Robin turned back to him. "No. It's all right. We need heat, to separate the mercury from the salt through instruments of fire. It says so in Master Tobias's books. There's one book in particular that he values, *The Journey,* by an old alchemist called Wolfram; I've heard him read it aloud to friends. I wish I could borrow it, but he always locks it away in his safe before I can look at it. I know we have to carry out the process in the consecrated athanor. The athanor that bears the sign that nurtures many pilgrims, it says in your letter. I don't know what that means—the sign of the Cross, perhaps?"

"Scallop shells. The symbol of St. James of Compostella."

"Of course! Anyway, this oven will do as our athanor. And then, you see, the Noble Prince will be laid low."

Ned was gazing at him. "Tell me about the Noble Prince."

Robin's brow furrowed. "I think," he said, "that the Noble Prince is the result of the conjunction of philosopher's mercury and sulfur, in the final stages of the Great Operation. *'A princely being is nurtured from the precious egg of the alchemists.'* That's what Master Tobias said."

"So it is all allegorical nonsense."

"Oh, no," said Robin, distressed. "No, how can you think it?"

Ned narrowed his nostrils at the stink coming from the crucible. A vapor was already rising and condensing, dripping down into the separate vessel Robin had connected up. "What about the lion?" asked Ned, pointing at the little picture inscribed on his letter.

"The Lion," said Robin, "is the guardian of sacred places. He is the most revered of creatures; and yet, in alchemical terms, he must die for the Philosopher's Stone to come to fruition. I learned that also, in a book of Master Tobias's."

There was a sudden stink of charred earth. Thick smoke rose from the crucible. Barnabas whimpered and Ned rushed to open the door to let out the foul stench. "For God's sake. Are you trying to suffocate us all?"

"No. This is right. *Fire will be kindled close to the lair of the Scorpion* . . ."

"What is the Scorpion?"

"The Scorpion, I think, represents this black oil here, at the base of the crucible. Scorpions are supposed to spit out an evil-smelling oil which is the only remedy against their venom."

Robin's face was sooty with smoke, but his eyes glowed with happiness. Reaching for the small quantity of distilled liquid he'd just drawn off, he poured it into the black matter in the crucible. There was a sizzling sound, and again the stink of the burning mixture filled the room. Ned stood by the open door to drag fresh air into his lungs. *The Lion must die*... That phrase rang over and over in his mind. Robin added more of the distilled liquid, then placed the crucible once more on the hot oven and watched with satisfaction as the mixture bubbled, and dried out, and turned once more to cinders. Robin avidly studied the Auriel letter again.

"*Then must the actuated mercury be added*... That's what we must do next."

"I haven't got any actuated mercury."

"I think it means any sort of alcohol. Wine will do. Thanks." He took the leather bottle Ned rather dazedly pointed out, and poured its contents over the burned mess, half-filling the crucible. Robin sealed it up with a cork, glanced once more at the Auriel letter and murmured to himself, "*Then must the actuated mercury be added, in the fashion of navicularius*'—I don't know what that means—'*in judicious incitement to princely war.*' Judicious. I think that means the oven must be kept low," he explained to Ned, "until the next stage, while the elements fight each other in the crucible. One of them has to die for the other to survive."

"Isn't all this supposed to take years?"

Robin shook his head emphatically. "Ficino said that a moment can be like a year, and a lifetime just the blinking of an eye, in the life of an adept. It says so in—"

"In one of Master Tobias's books? You cannot really believe all this."

"But it's true, don't you see? I can make it work! I'll come again tomorrow..."

"Oh, no." Ned had his hands on the boy's shoulders and was propelling him into the street. Out there, as the snow whirled round them both, he said, slowly, clearly, "Don't come back. I'm telling you all this for your own good. I want you to go away and forget everything about Auriel. I wish I'd never gone into that damned apothecary's shop."

Robin let out an exclamation. "I meant to tell you. Master Underwood is dead! He was robbed, and killed. They thought he had gold . . ."

Ned stepped back in shock. Then he said tiredly, running his hand through his hair, "London is a violent place. But we know that already, I think. Now go, and don't tell anyone—do you understand?—anyone about all this."

Robin turned and walked slowly away into the wintry night, his thin shoulders hunched in dejection beneath his outsize coat. The beggars at the corner of the street watched him go, then turned in silence back to their fire.

NED WENT BACK INTO THE BAKEHOUSE AND LOCKED the door. He went to the oven to damp down the coals, wafting away the smoke and the stench with his hands. The crucible, half full of wine and charred dung, barely simmered on the stove. But the bitter odor of the burning residue lingered still.

Tomorrow he had to go and see Northampton. How much should he tell him, about Sarah Lovett's accusations? About the secret crates of foreign pistols, signed for by her husband and stored in Prince Henry's warehouse, so close to Northampton's own, at Deptford?

He would tell him enough to keep himself alive. Especially as, today, an invitation had arrived for him, to St. James's Palace.

And it was signed by John Lovett.

18.

*Say to the court, it glows
And shines like rotten wood*

Sir Walter Ralegh (c.1554–1618)
"The Lie"

T HE MAGICIAN FROM THE ORIENT CLIMBED UP ONTO
the stage of the Banqueting Hall and began to declaim
some of the most execrable verse that Ned Warriner had ever
heard.

It was the final rehearsal for the masque that was to be per-
formed in front of the King during the Christmas festival. But
the harmony to be expected so soon after the feast of Cecilia,
the saint who had drawn the angels down to earth with her
singing, was absent. Above the magician, the heaven that had
been built of silken clouds, gilt stars, and swooping plaster angels was still being adjusted by the carpenters, whose hammering drowned out a good deal of the verse, while the hall
itself was thronged with the usual array of clamoring
courtiers, petitioners, and hangers-on, all of whom continued
whatever business they were about without paying any attention to the preparations on the stage.

Ned Warriner sat cross-legged on the floor of a small ante-room off the main hall, which was being used also by the masque's musicians to tune and store their instruments. To pass the time he tossed dice with three of Northampton's servants, who had been his escort ever since he arrived there. They had made it quite clear that any attempt on his part to reject their company would be resisted.

Some musicians with sackbuts and hautboys were wailing discordantly in the main hall. Northampton was late. Northampton liked toying with people. At least Ned had got this far, safely. He knew that Northampton's men could easily have dispatched him by now, if the Earl had willed it. Ned had gambled that he was still of more use to his old master alive than dead; though every nerve, every sinew of his body was taut as he glanced round toward the open door leading to the Banqueting Hall.

"Don't even think of trying to leave us," said one of Northampton's men. "Not before the game's over. Your throw."

Ned casually tossed a double five and pulled the coins toward him. "I just wondered if Northampton might have found some more exciting entertainment for the day."

"More exciting than you, Warriner?" drawled another. "Hardly. You must have been an unforgettable bedfellow for the old man. Perhaps you'd like to describe to us exactly what you used to do for him——"

Ned leaped to his feet, fists clenched. Northampton's men were on their feet, too, surrounding him.

Ned raised his hands in truce and sat cross-legged again. The game of dice continued.

Out on the stage in the main hall, which Ned could glimpse through the open door, the magician had finished his speech. With a rattling of chains and creaking of ropes, and more muttered cursing from the carpenters, an artificial mountain draped in green silk was towed onto the stage, accompanied by music from some out-of-tune trumpets high up in the gallery. A cluster of cupids climbed out of a Stygian cave at the mountain's base and began to run up and down the stairs hewn into the mountain's side, scattering handfuls of golden dust. Ned thought, looking at the scantily dressed youths, that if they did not tempt Northampton into showing himself, nothing would.

Then, just as he was turning back to the dice game, he saw someone else striding rapidly through the throng in the Banqueting Hall toward this very room. Not Northampton, but Pelham. As Ned slowly got to his feet, his old enemy was standing in the doorway, his face dark with anger, and disbelief.

Ned's captors stood also and ranged themselves behind him.

"Well. Francis Pelham," said Ned. "Still torturing and killing Catholics?"

Pelham said, "I cannot believe, Warriner, I cannot believe that you are here, at liberty."

"Why shouldn't I be?"

"The Catholic prisoner, Ashworth—you helped him escape, two years ago."

Ned said coldly, "Your imagination is running wild, Pelham. Though I'll tell you this: I'm glad to hear of anyone escaping the clutches of fanatics like you."

Pelham breathed, "He was an enemy of the State. A servant of the Pope..." The sudden squeal of trumpets from the gallery drowned out some of his words. "I swear I will have you put in the Tower, Warriner. Where you belong."

Ned said wearily, "For God's sake. I don't know what you're talking about, and neither does anyone else. You are making an almighty fool of yourself, Pelham." He turned back to Northampton's men, but Pelham grabbed his shoulder and swung him round.

"A fool of myself? Let me tell you that I have an appointment with Waad, here, later today, to arrange a warrant for your arrest; but I've a mind to call the guards myself, now, to take you into custody."

Pelham was already looking round agitatedly. Ned was thinking, Damn it, damn it, he's going to get someone to arrest me here and now; they're going to be fighting over the honor of taking me to prison.

And then came reprieve, for as the music of the masque filled the hall anew, Ned realized that Northampton had arrived at last. Resplendent yet sinister in black velvet, adorned with many jewels, the old Earl was standing just outside the entrance to the anteroom, watching Pelham's back.

Pelham, realizing no one was looking at him anymore, turned and saw Northampton there. He bowed tightly and muttered with bitterness, so only Ned could hear, "Ah. *Now* I understand."

And he backed out of the room, still bowing to Northampton; but the last look he cast at Ned was one of hatred.

Northampton gestured to his men to stand farther away, but he beckoned Ned closer. "I set you a task, Warriner. You appear to be procrastinating."

"My lord. The matter is not as straightforward as it seems—"

"It seems straightforward enough to me. Come, Ned. You are a soldier. You have killed men. I thought we understood each other. Trusted each other."

Ned remembered Northampton's heated flesh, his hot, dry lips on his own. He had to fight not to let his revulsion show. He said, "If you wish to describe it in that way." He added, with a slight bow, "My lord."

Northampton went on, "These are dangerous times. Death goes unnoticed. Why, only the other day one of my own men was found washed up on the river shore, with half his face blown away. It seems easy enough, this murder business."

Ned continued to meet his gaze. "Perhaps, my lord. But when the victim is a man of some prominence, murder is a clumsy weapon. Sometimes the truth can be more devastating."

"Truth? All I want is Lovett dead," said Northampton flatly. "Didn't I make that clear? If you still want my protection—and judging by what I heard of Pelham's outburst earlier, you are soon going to be very much in need of it—you had better carry out my orders, and quickly. Otherwise I will be tempted to think you are of no more use to me."

He turned to go. Ned sprang after him. "My lord, did you know that Lovett is importing weapons illegally, in Prince Henry's name?"

Northampton pursed his lips. The shadows from the candles exaggerated all the gaunt planes and hollows of his lined face.

"What weapons? A few swords? A few lances for the Prince's boyish tourneys at St. James's Palace?"

"A little more, my lord. Lovett is arranging for considerable quantities of firearms to be imported—from France, I think—and stored at the Prince's warehouse at Deptford. Close to your own. I have seen just a few of them. They are being signed for by Lovett, as art imports. Something is being planned. And I hope to find out more, very soon. I have been inside St. James's Palace, and there Lovett's wife confided in me. She has promised to let me have more information when I go there again. I have another invitation. In a few days' time."

Northampton had drawn closer. He was gripping Ned by the shoulders. His breath, scented with cinnamon lozenges, was pungent. "Does Cecil know any of this? Did you see any of his spies there?"

"If Cecil has any spies at the palace, they are lying low. I was fortunate, I think, to obtain this information from Lovett's wife."

Northampton stepped back, and his thin lips curled in a malicious gleam. "She took a fancy to you, did she? Well, well. You *are* trying hard. I do hope that this is not a desperate play for time. I will give you a little longer, then, to bring me news of real importance about Lovett and his master the Prince. But if I find out you are lying, Warriner, then I will send in someone else to do what you have failed to do." He swung round impatiently as a clarion call of trumpets in the main hall announced the climax of the masque, then turned back to Ned. "By the way, I can see that Francis Pelham might become rather a thorn in your side. Did you know—because I don't think *he* does—that Pelham's pretty little wife visits the prisoner Ralegh in the Tower? Ralegh—and all his friends— are being watched closely at the moment by Cecil's men. She should take more care."

Ned felt cold. The trumpets made a vicious jangling in his brain. He said, "My lord, Kate Pelham has always been close to Ralegh. He was a friend of her father's."

Northampton raised his eyebrows. "A friend in the Tower is dangerous to anyone. And I doubt that Pelham takes enough interest in her whereabouts. Their marriage cannot be very satisfactory, to either of them. She makes secret visits, and so does he. I heard the other day that he had been seen slipping out of the house of a whore in Candlewick Street.'

Ned stayed very still.

"I found much amusement in this story," went on Northampton, "for, you see, this particular whore, whether he knows it or not, is a Spaniard by birth, and a secret Catholic. Inappropriate, don't you think, for a recusant hunter?"

He looked round, to where his servants waited for him, by the door. "Report back to me, Warriner. About those guns, and Lovett, and the Prince. Otherwise I will take action of my own. Do I make myself clear?"

He left the room, and his servants went ahead, clearing a path for him through the crowds in the Banqueting Hall.

Ned braced himself to leave also. And then he saw Kate.

The twelve goddesses of the masque, draped in gauze and samite, had sung their final song of victory, and now they glided one by one down the wide stairs that led from stage to floor, led by the Queen. Her courtiers gathered round to applaud her. The remaining goddesses dispersed, talking to one another and to their friends in the hall. One of them was Kate Pelham. She was conversing with her neighbor, the lady Arbella Stuart, about some detail of the stitching on her sleeve; he could see her holding out the pale green fabric and pointing to it. Her smooth brown hair was drawn up beneath a gauze headdress adorned with seed pearls; her brow was slightly puckered by a frown, and a soft blush tinged her cheeks.

When he had met her, over three weeks ago, in the garden of her house, she had been simply dressed, with her hair falling loose, like a country girl. Now she was as exquisite as any of the noblewomen who surrounded her.

The musicians were starting to play a coranto, signaling the start of the dancing that always followed a masque. The music master was shouting instructions, telling the Queen's attendants where to stand, how to move. Kate was in their midst. She had not seen him.

• • •

NED, LOOKING ROUND, PICKED UP A LUTE THAT ONE of the musicians had left leaning against a wall. He went to the doorway and played some loud, jarring chords on it.

The coranto had started. Most people ignored him. But Kate had turned, and he knew the moment she saw him, because the color drained from her face, leaving her skin translucent. Her green eyes were dark in the whiteness of her face, just as they had looked on the day he had told her he had to leave England. She'd said simply, "How will I live, without you?"

He played another chord. A challenge. She moved out of the bright circle of dancers toward him.

He played louder, backing into the room, and she followed him in.

"Ned." Her voice throbbed with emotion. With tension. "What are you thinking of? What are you doing here?"

He put down the lute, so hard that all its strings vibrated. He pushed the door shut so they were all alone, and took her hands, to pull her close to him.

"You said you couldn't live without me. But you married Pelham. For God's sake. Francis Pelham."

She looked back at the door, as if to escape him. There were tears in her eyes. She tried to pull away. "Ned, you are hurting me."

He said urgently, because he could see he was about to lose her, "I know you don't want to see me anymore. You've made that quite clear. But I just need to *know*. Why didn't you wait for me? Was it because I'd not got enough money?"

"You know that is not true..."

"Was it because I wasn't good enough for you? Kate Revill, related to the Earl of Shrewsbury, lady-in-waiting to the Queen..." He waved toward the hall, from where the music drifted through the closed door. He said, more quietly, "You used to laugh with me at that kind of empty spectacle. You used to despise it, and say you never, ever wanted to be part of it all. But now you are one of the Queen's ladies, and you tell me *No more poetry...*"

She drew her hands away. "Ned," she said quietly. "Why are you doing this to me?"

He remembered how she came to him that first night in his humble rooms by the Temple, cloaked and hooded, radiant with love. She had wept in his arms afterwards and told him she never wanted to leave him.

"You should have told me," he said. "About the boy."

Her eyes widened. In shock. In fear.

"Kate, Kate," he said. "I know that he is mine."

She drew her hand across her eyes. "This is no good," she whispered. "Ned, I must go."

Head held high, she pulled open the door and went swiftly back toward the dancers in the main hall.

Ned watched her go. Anyone except Pelham . . . But Ned was lying to himself, he knew. Anyone at all would be as bad.

NED WENT HOME TO ROSE ALLEY, WHERE OLD TEW had given Barnabas an enormous shinbone to keep him happy in Ned's absence. Ned took Barnabas and locked himself in the bakehouse, where the fire in the oven was almost out, though the crucible still glowed faintly, with its mixture of horse dung and Matthew's wine vaporizing and condensing and running back down the sides.

He marveled at the fact that it was doing what it was supposed to do—unlike almost everything else in his life—and pushed a few more coals in the oven, to keep himself warm. Barnabas settled himself on the floor with his bone. Ned sat on the stone bench.

So he had managed to extend a little the time of safety Northampton had granted him. But what was the point? Northampton would still want him eliminated when his usefulness was at an end. Kate would still be married to Pelham. The crates of guns with their curious rainbow mark would quietly continue their journey to some unseen destination; an illegal trade in imported arms was nothing new . . .

He stood up suddenly. The rainbow.

"Increase the fire till the glorious rainbow of the East appears, which is the Cauda Pavonis . . ."

It was in his Auriel letter. He reached inside his jerkin for it. But the letter wasn't there.

He got to his feet, searching his pockets and the lining of his doublet.

There was a hammering at his door. And a man's voice. "Ned! Ned!"

Ned went to pull back the bolts. It was Matthew, a fading bruise on his forehead the only sign now of the attack he had suffered.

"What in Christ's name are you doing in there, Ned?" he demanded. "There are some foul smells coming out of the window." He glanced suspiciously at the crucible. "What's that?"

"I'm working on a remedy," said Ned wearily, "for hangovers. It will make my fortune."

Matthew wrinkled his nose. "Fortune my arse. Come and eat with us. Tell us your news. You must be hungry."

"No, I'm not. Really."

"The others are there. Steen wants you to look at some ballads he's written. They need your touch in the closing lines, he says. They're filthy, but they're not nearly as good as yours—" He was trying to peer past Ned at the crucible.

"I'll take a look at them tomorrow."

Matthew nodded and started to go, then turned back suddenly. "Red wigs."

"What?"

"I almost forgot. Davey's blundered again. Turned up with a cartload of red wigs. But red isn't fashionable anymore at court. Any ideas, Ned?"

"I'll think about it," Ned promised.

Once more Matthew was about to go, then suddenly remembered something else. "Davey told me someone was here asking for you earlier. Of course Davey told him that anyone who comes here asking questions without good reason risks getting his throat slit. The stranger said that he was an old friend of yours, but he wouldn't give his name. He said, *'Tell Ned to remember the Street of Gold.'* Then he sloped off."

Ned shook his head in puzzlement. The only Street of Gold he knew was in Prague. Who would have sought him out from there?

The minute Matthew had gone, Ned started hunting again, beneath the stone benches and amongst the scattered ballads he'd scribbled for Matthew. He went up to his room above the stables and searched there, but again, there was no sign, and he was beginning to realize that there wouldn't be; because he'd already guessed what had happened to it. Who had taken it.

19.

As guilefull Goldsmith that by secret skill,
With golden foyle doth finely over spred
Some baser metall, which commend he will
Unto the vulgar for good gold insted,
He much more goodly glosse thereon doth shed,
To hide his falshood, then if it were trew.

EDMUND SPENSER (C.1552–1599)
THE FAERIE QUEENE, BOOK 4, CANTO V V.15

IT WAS THE NEXT DAY, THE FIRST DAY OF DECEMBER,
and because of the extra demand for his wares at this time of
approaching festivities, Master Tobias Jebb had his apprentices working even later than usual at his workshop in
Ludgate.

Robin was hungry and weary. He had been up late the
night before, trying to decipher Ned's Auriel letter by candlelight. He was hoping to get it back to Ned that evening, hoping
Ned would forgive him for borrowing it. Robin had studied
the letter with care and was more than ever convinced that it
was of great value.

But the hours went by with agonizing slowness as Tobias,
who had just completed a set of silver dishes for one of his
rich clients, supervised while Robin and the other apprentice,
Will Frewin, plated them with gold leaf.

They had done it often before; but still the silversmith

watched them with an eagle eye as they soaked linen rags in a solution of chloride of gold and burned the rags to ashes, then rubbed the ashes on the surface of each silver dish until they started to gleam palely with gold.

It was a pretty trick, and legitimate enough, if the honorable silversmith told his customer what he had done. Of course Tobias, being honorable, always did. But when he turned to mix more of the chloride solution, Will Frewin, who had been sly and overfriendly with Robin of late, winked at him and whispered, "We could fool a few people with these gold dishes, eh, Robin? Make our fortune."

Robin, who did not like Frewin, ignored him and continued silently to rub at the silver dish he was holding with the ash-blackened cloth until its surface turned slowly to gold. He was hoping that with Ned's letter he had something better than trickery.

At last the silversmith considered the dishes to be worthy of his rich client, and he locked them into the oak chest that he used to safeguard valuable articles overnight. Frewin was told to go and fetch coals in for Mistress Jebb's oven. Robin was ordered to tidy away and sweep the floor.

And then, Tobias told Robin he was not finished yet; there was no supper for him until he went on an errand to the Wool Wharf, over a mile away, and collected a new planishing hammer that he had ordered from a metalsmith there.

THE COLD DECEMBER NIGHT WAS TAKING HOLD OF the city. Darkness had fallen, relieved only a little by the light of the moon, and a mist was rising dankly from the river. The last of the snow had gone, but the air was still raw. Robin hurried through the city to the Wool Wharf as quickly as he could to collect the little hammer, which he put deep in his inside pocket; then, feeling quite faint with hunger, for he had eaten nothing but a crust of bread and some thin gruel at noon, he set off back, hoping there would be something left of the meager supper Mistress Jebb reluctantly offered her husband's apprentices. He was thinking also of Ned and his letter as he ran; and so it was some time before he realized he had taken a wrong turning.

He did not know where he was. When he saw the dark bulk of the Tower looming ahead, he realized he must have been heading east instead of west. He was further confused by the fact that the dark street ahead of him was blocked by a slow-moving cart being pulled uphill from the river by two great horses. The cart was covered with a tarpaulin, and guarded front and back by six burly, bearded men carrying sticks, who looked around fiercely every step of the way. Robin, guessing they were up to no good, backed into a doorway as they drew near.

Then the cart became stuck as a wheel caught in a rut. The men had to shove hard to free it; the sweat gleamed on their brows, and they swore aloud, though Robin noticed that they were careful not to raise their voices. As they tugged and pushed at the cart, the tarpaulin slid off, and Robin saw the gleam of metal. Of gun barrels—cannon—so close to him that he could see the markings on them.

Someone cursed, and pulled back the tarpaulin hastily to conceal the contents of the cart. At that moment another man came riding up. They clearly knew him, for they turned to him deferentially and began to give a few words of explanation. This horseman was not dressed roughly, like them, but was clad in the sober and well-tailored garments of a gentleman. He dismounted and walked round the cart, assessing the situation. Robin pressed back farther into the doorway. But this man, the sharp-eyed newcomer, saw him.

He came slowly toward Robin. His face was thin and cold. He had pale, gray-blue eyes. He caught Robin by the shoulder. "What are you doing here, boy?"

Robin's teeth were chattering. "Nothing, sir. Please—I'm on an errand for my master—I'll be late . . ."

"Why are you hiding, then?"

"I only thought to get out of the way, sir—"

Robin's well-dressed inquisitor cuffed him lightly with his right hand, and Robin saw a ruby ring on his little finger that glinted like blood. "Didn't anyone tell you it's dangerous to be out on the streets after curfew? Now get out of here quickly, boy. There's nothing for you."

Choking with fear, Robin squeezed past the cart and ran all the way back through the dark streets of the city.

WILL FREWIN HAD BEEN WATCHING ROBIN CLOSELY for the last few days, and as soon as Robin had been sent off on his errand, Will went to rummage through Robin's meager possessions in the tiny attic room next to his own.

Will came from a respectable family. His father was a coal trader, and had paid good money to secure this apprenticeship for Will. Will resented being saddled with the poor workhouse boy Robin, who nevertheless contrived to be Will's superior at every task.

All the while listening out for footsteps on the stairs, Will hunted quickly through the threadbare clothes in Robin's battered oak chest. At the bottom, carefully wrapped in a ragged blanket, he found some glass tubing, and a small pelican—a spouted glass vessel of some value that he recognized as one of Master Tobias's. Will grinned to himself. "Got you," he breathed. After that Will went to investigate Robin's straw mattress. He found nothing underneath it. But as he pushed it back he realized there was a slit in the ticking of the mattress; and when he slid his hand inside, he found a book of Master Tobias's on the alchemist's art. And a folded, crumpled letter.

I NEVER EXPECTED," SAID THE SILVERSMITH HEAVILY, "I never dreamt that I would have my generosity to a workhouse orphan repaid in such a way."

Robin had returned at last from his errand to find Tobias Jebb waiting for him with a constable standing on either side. Robin shrank back in terror.

"Sir," he said, "I did what you asked. I have the planishing hammer here. I'm sorry I took so long . . ."

Tobias pointed, and Robin saw on the table the equipment and the alchemy book he was going to take to Ned. He said desperately, "I was only going to *borrow* them . . ."

The constables moved forward. Master Tobias held up his hand. "One moment." Then he moved closer to the quaking Robin. "I also found something else that I think you have stolen. And I want to know exactly where you got it from."

Robin saw, with utter despair, that his master was holding Ned's Auriel letter. He said, "A friend lent it to me. Please. You must let me return it to him..."

Tobias Jebb smiled grimly. "As I thought. You have stolen this also. Who is this so-called friend whom you robbed?"

"I—I do not remember his name..."

Tobias took Robin by the ear and twisted him round to face him fully. "I wish to know where you got this letter. This letter that bears the lion symbol of John Dee himself, yes, and his motto: *Qui non intelligit aut discat aut taceat.* I think that a spell in prison might change your mind about telling me how you really came into the possession of a letter written by Dr. Dee. I will give you one last chance to tell me from whom you stole this letter."

"I cannot." The pain from his ear was almost unbearable. "I do not know his name—"

"Do you suffer the same loss of memory regarding where he lives?"

"Yes! I mean—I do not know where he lives..."

Tobias thrust him aside so harshly he stumbled to his knees. Then the silversmith called to the constables to take him away on a charge of theft.

As Robin was hauled out of the room, with a constable on either side, he was aware of Will Frewin grinning at him as he watched from the shadows; and of Master Tobias, holding Ned's Auriel letter closer to the candlelight, and scrutinizing it with a kind of ardor burning in his eyes.

SINCE DAWN FRANCIS PELHAM HAD BEEN WORKING assiduously at what he did best: getting answers from those who preferred to stay silent.

His visit to Prince Henry's palace had made him feel that the battle he fought against recusants was a battle worth winning. This morning had come a brief note from one of his many contacts to say that old Lady Montague had just died, and Pelham knew—everyone knew—that she was a shelterer of priests. Her house in Southwark, close by the bridge, was known as "little Rome" to her neighbors, and it was rumored that beyond an intricate network of secret chambers and locked doors she had a tiny chapel with a pulpit, where candles burned day and night to illuminate idolatrous plaster figures. She welcomed the Jesuits, it was said, who came by ship to Gravesend; they were rowed to her house at dead of night, to take rest and refreshment there before riding off to spread their Romish poison throughout the English countryside.

And everyone knew old Lady Montague was protected. She had powerful friends at court, not least of them Queen Anne, who celebrated mass regularly in her own private chapel in Greenwich. As a foreigner, the Queen had to be allowed this perfidy; but that she should be allowed to extend her protection to English subjects was, in Pelham's mind, a bitter wrong.

Now Lady Montague was dead. And Pelham, together with several stout assistants, had the permission of no less a person than Sir William Waad, controller of the State's recusant hunters, to carry out a search of her house.

So at the dead hour before dawn, he battered at the door in the name of the King, cleared the house of its remaining occupants—a housekeeper, a maid, and two manservants, who were glad to leave without being charged—and set his three stout men to roam about the house. It was work they were accustomed to. They prowled from room to room, tapping walls, lighting fires to smoke out any recesses in the great chimneys, looking for holes driven into paneled walls through which water or thin gruel could be fed to a priest by night.

At first they worked quietly, their ears attuned for any noise, any movement that was not the scurrying of rats beneath the floorboards. But they found nothing, and as dawn began to creep over the city, Pelham grew increasingly agitated. He had been so sure he would find something here; something to restore his diminishing fortunes and raise him in the favor of his masters.

Outside, the streets of Bankside were coming to life.

Tradesmen's drays rumbled along the lane, and from the river came the sound of watermen's cries. Pelham ordered his men to put caution aside, because soon Lady Montague's powerful relatives would arrive to take possession of the house, and his chance would have gone. He curtly commanded them to rip sections of paneling from the walls, to drag great beds aside and heave up floorboards. They worked for another hour. As sunlight filtered through the narrow windows to reveal the disarray within, they paused to rest, weary in their labors. Pelham was close to despair.

And then he heard a smothered cough.

Pelham pointed silently to the section of the wall from which he judged the sound to have come. His men set to work with renewed fervor, to tear aside the piece of paneling that had sounded solid to their taps, but was soon revealed to be a cunningly contrived false one. They flung it to the ground and saw a narrow opening, a tunnel only four feet long, between rooms. At the end, where the tunnel widened out just a little, was a priest, hunched and shaking with fear. They were almost smothered by the stink of his body, of his ordure. There was an empty water jug at his side, and a pewter plate stained with dried gravy, perhaps days old.

Pelham's men dragged him out of his hole. He was elderly, and his body was withered and shrunken beneath his loose priest's garb. He fell over as Pelham's men pulled him to his feet and lay there immobile, his knees bent up to his white-bristled chin. It was most likely, thought Pelham, backing away from the stench of him, that he was not capable of standing after his close confinement. Yet he was managing to pray aloud as he lay there, muttering the confiteor and the mea culpa as Pelham's men made a makeshift carrier with two of the poles they'd used for hole-prodding and a knotted linen sheet from one of the beds. Pelham guessed that by the time they had done with him in the Tower he would wish he had died in that hole.

PELHAM'S INSTRUCTIONS WERE THAT IF HE FOUND anything he was to report immediately to Waad, at Whitehall. So, leaving his men to take the prisoner to the Marshalsea prison, he took a boat upriver from London Bridge, mentally rehearsing his report, deducing that the capture of this priest would bring praise, and more solid reward in the way of money. Perhaps, even, the priest would betray others under questioning, thus adding to the benefits for Pelham. He tried to stop his mind racing as the boatman rowed him steadily past Blackfriars and the Temple Gardens to Whitehall Stairs, but he could not help but be hopeful.

Even less could his hope be stilled when he heard, on asking for Governor Waad, that no lesser person than Sir Robert Cecil—the King's Lord Treasurer and Chief Secretary—wished to see him first.

The news of Pelham's success must have traveled fast, even through Whitehall's labyrinthine passages. Was he about to be thanked personally by one of the most powerful men in the kingdom for today's work? It appeared so, for he found himself escorted along candlelit passageways and up sets of stairs to one of the inner sanctums of the palace, the room where the Privy Council met, but where today its chief member, Robert Cecil, sat alone behind the big table.

Pelham bowed low. Servants and clerks hovered at a distance. Through the single window he could see the church spires of the city gleaming in the pale winter sunlight.

Cecil said at last, "Well, now. I hear you are a recusant hunter, Master Pelham."

Some called Cecil the cleverest man in England; he was certainly the richest, for he fared well in his services to the state. Pelham bowed his head again. "My lord, I have the honor to serve Sir William Waad in that capacity."

Cecil's delicate fingers were toying with the quill pen on the table before him. "I have been hearing lately that some of your assistants, Master Pelham, are a little too ardent in the pursuit of recusants."

Pelham was astounded. He said, "My lord, my lord. I did not realize one could be too assiduous in pursuit of one's civic and moral duty."

Cecil thinned his lips. "We are not at war with those of the Catholic faith, Master Pelham. We are not at war with anyone.

His Majesty the King is anxious for peace in his realm. Unless a man refuses to swear the oath of loyalty, then lenience is the order of the day. Do you comprehend me? The unnecessary persecution of Catholics is causing problems with our friends at home and abroad."

Catholics. Friends abroad. *Spaniards*...Pelham drew a deep breath. "My lord, my only desire is to serve the King and his servants. Always."

Cecil had drawn some papers toward him and was leafing through them. He looked up again suddenly. "Sir William Waad tells me that he has no more work for you at present, Master Pelham. He thanks you for your assistance in the past, but regrets he can employ you no more as a recusant hunter. We must adapt to the times we live in. No doubt you will find alternative employment elsewhere, very soon. Good day to you."

That was it. No chance for appeal, for argument. A servant was already holding open the door. Pelham limped out, thinking bitterly, This is because of the Spanish marriage. King James wants Prince Henry to marry the Catholic Infanta, as does Cecil, because the Infanta will bring with her a dowry of Spanish gold...

Somehow, he could not remember how, he made his way out of the warren of courtyards and buildings that made up Whitehall Palace and found himself down by the riverside again. And then, he began to despair. He had no work. And unless he could find some way soon to pay off his mounting debts to the moneylender—unless his ship came in—he was quite ruined.

20.

&

Study me then, you who shall lovers bee
At the next world, that is, at the next Spring:
For I am every dead thing,
In whom love wrought new Alchimie.

JOHN DONNE (1572–1631)
A NOCTURNALL UPON ST LUCIE'S DAY

LATE THAT NIGHT, AS PRESAGED BY THE BLEAK EAST-
erly wind, it started to snow again. Candlelight gleamed
behind the shuttered windows of the big houses at the bottom
of Ludgate, close by the old city wall. Traders were closing up
their stalls for the night. Diligent city wives with their maids
in tow, having scoured the shops for end-of-day bargains,
were starting off home, setting their faces to the bitter wind.
The rich burghers and their ladies were wearing their furs,
while the beggars shivered in rags in doorways.

The great tower of half-derelict St. Paul's, somber
guardian of the city, reared foursquare into the blackness of
the night. Apprentices scurried along Cheapside, finishing the
last of their masters' business. There were no riots today, no
fights with the ubiquitous Scots, no brawls even between the
serving men of the lords of the realm. It was too cold for such

diversions. Today was a day for getting work done and for hurrying home to the fireside, or to the congeniality of the tavern.

Ned Warriner rivaled any of his fellow citizens in purposefulness as he marched up Ludgate Hill with Barnabas at his heels, his feathered hat pulled low, his cloak drawn tight against the east wind that whistled through the lanes of London. He was going to get his Auriel letter back. He slowed down as he drew near to the sign of Master Tobias Jebb, silversmith by appointment to the King. The shutters were not closed yet. Candlelight still shone from within.

An apprentice came hurrying out from round the back of Tobias's shop, carrying a bucketful of coal. Ned placed himself in front of him, startling the lad so he almost dropped the bucket, and said, "Where is the other boy? Robin?"

Frewin shot him a sly look. Then he said, "They've arrested him. He's in the Wood Street Counter."

"On what charge?"

"He's been stealing from Master Tobias. He deserves everything that's coming to him."

With that, the boy hurried on. Ned's first thought was that the odd, learned apprentice would fare badly in the stinking Wood Street prison.

And his second: Where is my letter?

He looked up at the candlelight blazing from Tobias Jebb's establishment. Either Robin had the Auriel letter on him when he was arrested—in which case the authorities would have it by now—or it would be in there, somewhere. He realized the apprentice boy had left the door to the workshop ajar. Ned moved quickly toward it and pressed himself against the wall by the doorway so he could look inside.

A single candle gleamed in a holder on the wall. The place had been tidied for the night, the tools and materials all put away on shelves: the hammers and tongs, the calipers and soldering irons, the pumice and paste used for polishing the finished wares.

Set against the far wall was a tall oak cabinet with a stout lock. Ned guessed this was where valuable silverware would be kept overnight. What else might a prosperous silversmith keep in such a place? Cash? The secrets of his art? A letter purporting to be about gold, from John Dee?

He heard the hurrying footsteps of the apprentice returning. He slid quickly away back into the darkness and went home angrily through the fast-settling snow. Curfew had rung as he was leaving Jebb's shop, and the city's gates were now locked and guarded, so he had to turn north to where the city wall had crumbled into ruins. The snow gave everything a different perspective, and muffled all sounds.

As he drew near to Rose Alley, he saw that the beggars had for once left their fire and were clustered round someone, begging for money. Their rags were like the stark black robes of monks against the whiteness; their faces were gaunt, their hands stretched out clawlike around their prey. "Alms. Give us alms," they chanted hoarsely.

And Ned saw as he got closer that the person they had in their midst was Kate. He strode forward and pushed two of the clamoring beggars aside. The others muttered protests but backed away, hands raised quickly in appeasement as Ned confronted them, one after the other.

Kate was clutching her fur-lined cloak to her chin as if it would offer her some protection, but her hood had fallen down, and her long brown hair, unpinned, had tumbled all around her shoulders. Her green eyes were blazing in defiance, just as they had when she was a child in trouble; but Ned saw that she was trembling.

Ned drew her away from the sullen beggars, who were settling once more round their fire. He said to her, "They would not have harmed you. But others might have done. What are you doing here? You should not come alone to a place like this."

Kate began to shiver violently. "I came to find you."

"To find *me*? I assumed after our meeting at Whitehall yesterday that you never wanted to see me again."

She bowed her head, then lifted it. "I had to see you, about Francis. To beg you, to implore you to leave him alone."

Ned drew his hand across his forehead. "Of course. Francis. Your husband. What am I supposed to have done now?"

She gazed up at him. "He has been dismissed from his job. But I'm forgetting. You will know that already, won't you?"

"If I denied that I was responsible," he said heavily, "I don't suppose you would believe me for one minute. I didn't know he'd been dismissed. I think you credit me with powers I'm nowhere near to possessing."

"I know that you are working again for the Earl of Northampton, who despises recusant seekers and would gladly make mischief for them."

He was silent.

"Please," she went on in a low voice, "I know you hate Francis, I know you hate me for marrying him. But Ned, my little boy is sick. He needs medicines, doctors—"

"Our little boy," he said. "Our child, Kate."

She glanced up at him, wide-eyed again with fear.

"I won't tell your husband," he said tiredly. "What good would it do?"

"None," she whispered, "none at all...Ned, for Sebastian's sake, not for mine, I beg you to stop destroying Francis, who thinks the child is his, and loves him as much as I do. Leave us alone, Ned, and let us try to save something from the sorry mess that you and I have made of our lives. *Please...*"

He was silent still, his eyes never leaving her face. Then he said, *"They flee from me, that sometime did me seek..."*

"Stop it," she said. "Stop it." She looked away into the distance, where the beggars crouched once more, silent, round their fire, and he saw the tears in her eyes.

"Kate," he said, taking her by the arms, "why did you marry him? Why did you marry Francis Pelham, of all people?"

She shook herself free. "You have already decided, I think, that I married him for money. Isn't it enough that without him I would have been disgraced, and our child fatherless? I thought you were never coming back."

"But I told you I would return."

"Someday, yes. But how long was I meant to wait? And now you are working for the Earl of Northampton again. I remember you once swore to me that you would not take another penny from him. Ever."

"Kate, I need his protection, to stay here in London..."

"Then don't stay," she said bitterly. "Go. And leave my husband alone. That is all. That is what I came to say."

They gazed at each other in the dim glow of the light that escaped from the shuttered windows of Matthew's house. The muffled sound of voices and laughter issued from within as the usual carousing got under way.

She drew her cloak tight. Her face was pale with cold. "I must go. My absence will be noted. Will you remember, Ned, what I said?"

"I never forget anything that you say. But you cannot go back on your own. You should never have come here by yourself."

"I cannot use Francis's servants. They spy on me."

"You must let me see you safely home—"

"No!" Then she said, more quietly, "I cannot afford for us to be seen together. I will be all right." But in her glance at the silent beggars he saw the remnants of her fear, and he said, "Wait."

He hurried to the house and hauled out Davey and little Pentinck. He told them to escort Kate home and to guard her well. They were intrigued and willing, especially when they saw how pretty she was.

Ned did not want her to go, not like this. He drew Kate aside and said, "One more thing. I know you don't want advice from me. But you must stop visiting Ralegh."

She lifted her head. She said, "In that I will defy you willingly. Sometimes I think he is the only true friend I have."

Ned cursed himself for his ineptitude. He watched her disappear down the snow-covered street with her escort, and turned with a heavy heart to go into his brother's crowded house, where he drank too much, and sang them songs to make them laugh, though laughter was the last thing on his mind.

AT ST. JAMES'S PALACE, HUMPHREYS AND HIS GARdeners had been busy, in spite of the snow that had fallen. At Humphreys's direction, some of the rows of mulberry saplings, subject to so much care, had been dug from their temporary home, and their tender root-balls wrapped one by one in sacking that was secured round their stems with twine. Four horse-drawn carts had come to the gates to be laden with these twiggy bundles, and Humphreys had supervised Nicholas and his other gardeners closely in this, bidding them handle the young plants with as much care as they would a babe. For these mulberries, raised alongside those already established at St. James's, were going to travel farther afield. To and fro in the fading afternoon light Humphreys had trudged from the snow-covered earth beds to the carts, talking in a low voice all the while, to himself, and his plants, and his men, while the carters, high on their perches, had waited motionless, their breath misting in the cold air.

After a while John Lovett came to watch, and he stamped his booted feet in the cold and looked at his timepiece as Humphreys halted first one then another of his laden gardeners, to straighten a twisted branch or secure a loose piece of sacking; "For otherwise," he explained fretfully to Lovett, "the frost will pierce the roots and kill them; they are too young, too tender for this transportation; they should have been left in their winter beds till spring." But Lovett brushed the air impatiently with his hand, no doubt wishing he could brush Humphreys aside also, and said, "They are needed now. Do you understand? Spring will be too late."

Humphreys replied with asperity, "Very well. Very well. But unless they are going to temperate climes, they will not survive the winter."

"Is that the last of them?" Lovett called out as Nicholas laid another bundle of little trees on a brimming cart. Nicholas nodded, not looking at him. Lovett turned back to Humphreys and answered, "Listen. I know you are anxious. But they will be planted in sheltered sites, as you advised. Even I know that mulberries will not survive in a harsh climate."

Humphreys, still looking unhappy, said nothing but watched as the carters gathered up their horses' reins. Lovett, meanwhile, his impatience lessening now that the business was done, gave the carters their orders and stood back in satisfaction as the laden wagons began to lurch on their way down the snowy track. Humphreys, however, gazed sadly after them, until his trees were out of sight, and Lovett, after telling him he wanted to see him inside as soon as he was finished, turned and hurried back to St. James's Palace.

Humphreys told his gardeners they could go. The light was almost gone, and their work was finished for the day. But Nicholas, who had watched Lovett as he walked swiftly away, looked one last time round the snow-covered garden, reluctant to go back to his lonely room in the palace annex.

Humphreys's gardeners were kind to him, but they left at night, to stay elsewhere. The palace servants, if he tried to join them, laughed at him, mocked him always, pretended to throw themselves about and make choking sounds as he did when his affliction struck him. He did not blame them, for his own father could not bear to acknowledge or even to look at him. He burned with longing to be as they were, to do as they did.

Humphreys had told Nicholas that he could make him better. Humphreys was like a magician; he knew so much, about the plants, and the stars, and the workings of the body and the mind. Nicholas always did his best to do exactly what Humphreys told him. But the waiting was hard.

Nicholas helped Humphreys to tidy away the last of the straw with which they had been protecting the tenderer plants against the cold. But as he hurried to and fro, Humphreys put out his hand to stop him.

"Look," he said. "Have you seen how full the moon is?"

Nicholas looked up and blinked in the moon's brightness. "Will the moon make me better, Master Humphreys?"

Humphreys put down the implements he held. "Now," he said, "I have told you what will make you better, Nicholas, have I not?"

"Yes," replied the boy. "But I did not know that it would take so long."

"Then you must learn more patience. And perseverance."

Nicholas hung his head like a child; a strange sight, for he towered over Humphreys and yet seemed more helpless than an infant as he twisted his great hands together. Such strong hands, young but callused and roughened with the work he did; and yet he touched the plants so carefully, and tended them just as Humphreys instructed.

Humphreys told him it was time for him to go. Then he locked up his tools and left the palace; but instead of going home to his mother, who would chide him for being late, he turned north to Holborn village, and took the way that led between ploughed fields, smelling of frozen earth, to the old church that lay in rural isolation between the villages of Holborn and Clerkenwell: the church of St. Etheldreda's, that had since the time of King Henry VIII provided a haven for the Spanish ambassador and his staff, and a refuge for the many English Catholics who went there in secret to celebrate mass.

He was clearly known there, for a clerk who was a Spaniard invited him in. And when he came out again he was carrying a purseful of gold.

F OUR DAYS LATER, ON THE SEVENTH OF DECEMBER, Francis Pelham was tramping around London, looking for work. It was a week since he had been dismissed. He had expected his name and his reputation for honesty to speak for him; but instead he found doors closing. He had known he was not generally liked; he knew that his puritan ways made less scrupulous people uncomfortable with him. But he had not realized that he was unemployable.

He set off toward the river at Billingsgate, where the winter sun gleamed on the clustered ships, and the air was filled with the shouts of the dockhands unloading Scandinavian timber and bales of dyed wool from Bruges. He walked along the wharf to the office of the Virginia Company.

He had come, he told them, in case there was news of the *Rose* at last. The clerks looked at one another, and he could tell what the news was to be.

The *Rose,* he was told, had been wrecked off the Bahama islands. This report had been confirmed by a ship that came into Deptford just yesterday.

Pelham went dizzily out into the cold winter sun, amidst the noise and bustle of the wharf. He had no hope now of paying off his debts. Unless he sold the house.

Still dazed, he went to visit the scarred woman Martha in Candlewick Street, but even there, he failed in what he set out to do, there in that darkened room where the candles burned with the scent of incense, and her attentions were a scourging to his tormented soul; so he went on to a tavern and did something he had not done for many years. He sought oblivion in drink.

He arrived home at last to find Kate and Sebastian together in the parlor. Kate was telling a story to their son, but she broke off when he came in.

She looked beautiful, with her soft brown hair coiled at the nape of her neck, and her mother's pearls gleaming at her throat. Pelham suddenly remembered how much he had loved her, how much he had wanted her when first they met; he tried to tell her so, but she said quietly, with disgust, "You have been drinking."

Sebastian began to cry. She gathered the child into her arms and left the room in a swirl of silks. Pelham wondered if, as well as the wine on his breath, she had detected the smell of the whore on him.

He slumped in a chair and put his head in his hands, and let despair overwhelm him.

21.

Ralegh doth the time bestride
He sits 'twixt wind and tide

BALLAD, "SIR WALTER RALEGH," 1601 (ANON.)

EACH DAY AT THE TOWER OF LONDON, CROWDS OF people gathered three times to see old Ralegh pace round the high wall. It was a good jest, this, and one that the people of London appreciated, for Governor Waad had built this very wall a year ago to stop the people of London seeing their captive hero; but nothing daunted, Ralegh climbed Waad's new wall and walked round on it every day, at nine and at one and during the last hour of daylight.

And Waad dared to do nothing. Each time he appeared, the people standing along the riverside cheered their old, limping hero, and longed for the days of good Queen Bess. As they left, they secretly cursed those who had put such a valiant man in prison.

On the afternoon of the tenth of December, when the winter light was almost gone, Sir Walter Ralegh, having completed his last circuit in the biting east wind, made his way back down to his room, where he was told that he had a visitor.

Kate Pelham was inside, gazing out through the window with her back to the door. She turned quickly as he entered, and smiled at him.

"I cannot stay long," she said. "But I have brought you some new quill pens, as you asked." She was already searching through the basket she had put down on the window seat. "And here is some raspberry cordial, to ease your sore throat."

He took the items she offered, thanking her and placing them on his desk. Then he put his hand on her shoulder, and felt how she was trembling.

"Something has upset you," he said. "Or someone."

"No. No, it is nothing . . ." But he saw the sparkle of fresh tears in her eyes, though she quickly turned away from him and wiped them away.

"How is your son?"

"He is well." She smiled. "Sebastian is very well, and full of mischief."

Ralegh looked around, and made a decision. "Come with me. Let me show you something that might divert you a little, as it diverts me. An old man's pastime, if you like."

He picked up a lantern to light their way through the afternoon dusk, and took her outside into the walled prison garden. He led her to the little stone hut in the far corner beyond the apple trees, once used for keeping hens. William Waad—making yet another error in his treatment of his most famous prisoner—had once, in a moment of madness, told Ralegh he could use this hut as a garden retreat. Ralegh used it not only for his writing, but for another, more esoteric pursuit.

As Ralegh hung his lantern from a hook in the rafters, Kate saw that there was a stove in one corner which Ralegh had transformed into an alchemist's athanor. On the shelf beside it were arrayed his pots and crucibles and refining dishes. Yet Ralegh's current interest, he told Kate, centered not on making gold, but rather on its analysis. He had a collection of ore samples from the New World, he explained, which sailors and explorers had brought to him over the years, hoping that gold might be found therein. Now he showed her some of the samples he'd been working on, how he analyzed them in this tiny laboratory for traces of gold and other minerals. He was pleased to see that she looked happier, and distracted from her griefs.

"Here," he said, holding out to her a small piece of rock, "is some gold-bearing ore from Guiana. A few days ago, following an old recipe, I took twelve grains of it and heated it in a crucible together with half an ounce of filed lead and a quarter of sandever."

"What happened?"

"I managed to extract from it a whole grain of gold."

He passed the dull rock to her, and she took it in her hands, fascinated. "It's like trying to make gold," she said. "Only more real. How I wish I, too, could go exploring. Could visit the lands where these minerals are found. As you must wish you could go again..." She handed him back the ore, reluctantly.

He took it and said, "There are, you know, other ways of making gold."

Her smooth brow furrowed a little. "Of course. You are thinking of the letter Dr. Dee said he was going to send you: the letter that he promised would contain the secret of gold."

He put his finger to his lips. "These walls have ears. How much time do you have, Kate?"

"I can stay a little longer. My maid will wait for me."

He led her back through the gathering darkness to his room in the Tower, where he closed the door and made her sit down at his desk. She watched him, her eyes wide and troubled.

"Kate," he said, "I have something most important to ask you. Do you remember what I told you? How once my old friend John Dee wrote that as well as sending me the secret of gold, he would also tell me about a plan to set me free?"

"Of course I remember. Did you ever hear any more of it?"

He went to check again that the door was closed, and sat close to her. He replied, in a low voice, "No. But do you remember how in the letter Dee mentioned someone called the Black Bird?"

"Yes. I do." She was listening intently.

"It was the name," he said, "for a good old friend of mine,

a seafarer, a brave comrade. We sailed to Cadiz together. And I have just heard that after a long absence the Black Bird—whose real name is Alvaric Johnson—will be back in London again, before Christmas. If anyone at all knows about the plan mentioned by Dee, Johnson will." He hesitated. "Kate, I should not be asking you this, I know I should not, but..."

"You want me to take a message to him," she said. "Of course I will."

"It is too much to expect..."

"My father would have told me it was my duty," she said simply. "You have been so good to me. How could I not help you?"

"Wait," he said. "Let me write something. It will not take long. I want to tell him that the golden wine is still there for the drinking."

He sat at his desk and wrote a letter, which he sealed and handed to Kate with the instruction that Johnson was known at the chandler's shop at the corner of Bearward Lane, halfway along Petty Wales.

"I will find it. When should I go?"

"I was told that he would be back in London by the twenty-first of December. Wait till then. Remember that you must go by daylight. And take servants with you! The area is unsafe after dark. I really should not ask you—"

"I have already told you I will do it."

"You are your father's daughter." He hugged her briefly and called to the warders to escort her out; and so Kate left the Tower with Ralegh's letter, addressed to the Black Bird, hidden beneath her cloak.

As DARKNESS FELL RALEGH LIT MORE CANDLES AND sat at his desk, to work; but he found himself unable to write. His memories engulfed him, memories, among others, of Alvaric Johnson, the Black Bird, who had, like so many brave English sailors, been forced into unemployment since the ending of the war with Spain. At Cadiz thirteen years ago Johnson had fought joyously at Ralegh's side as the English ships' guns tore into the Spanish galleons in the harbor. The

English soldiers had marched on the terrified town and in the sacking of it had found cask upon cask of a rare Spanish liquor, which the locals called golden wine. Johnson had secured a cask for Ralegh and his men. On board his flagship that night, as the hulls of the enemy galleons still burned, they had drunk to the glory of England, the defeat of the Spaniards, and death to all traitors.

Now Ralegh unfolded his crumpled letter from Dee, received almost a year ago, which he kept always with him.

"To Auriel. Can the glories of the past be reborn? Can gold grow from the cold earth? Soon I will write again, with news of such treasure, such golden hopes: the elixir indeed. The Black Bird is hoping that within twelve months he will drink golden wine with you once more..."

Had Dee written to him again? If so, where was the letter?

He walked restlessly round his room as darkness fell and felt a fresh shaft of anxiety over the letter he had given to Kate. He was putting her in jeopardy by making her his messenger. And yet he had to act. He had to find out what Alvaric Johnson had in mind. For this year—the year in which Dee had told him he would be freed—was almost at an end.

He yearned for liberty. That was why Dee called him his Auriel. The old magus knew that, like an angelic spirit, Ralegh longed to be free, soaring high above the confines of this stone prison.

22.

No wound, which warlike hand of enemy
Inflicts with dint of sword, so sore doth light,
As doth the poysnous sting, which infamy
Infixeth in the name of noble wight.

EDMUND SPENSER (C. 1552–1599)
THE FAERIE QUEENE, BOOK 6: CANTO VI V.1

IT WAS THE TWELFTH OF DECEMBER, AND THE SNOW
had gone, but a vicious wind scattered the dry leaves into
heaps around St. James's Park and whistled against the walls
of the Prince's palace. Inside, Francis Pelham, cold as ice,
waited in the great hall along with other petitioners and
hangers-on, as the brief winter day drew to its close.

Most of the petitioners sat with their heads bowed on the
oak benches ranged against the walls. Not so Pelham. He
walked to and fro, his boots sounding out his distinctive un-
even tread against the stone-flagged floor. Around him the
shadows flickered like living things, for the wind penetrated
the ancient casements, causing the candles to dance uneasily
in their sconces. Two soldiers in Prince Henry's green and silver livery stood at the door that guarded the passage to the
courtyard, with their halberds raised. It struck Pelham that it
could be as difficult to get out as to come in.

He had thought that he had friends here. *We badly need men we can trust,* Lovett had said. But it appeared Pelham had been mistaken in his estimation of their need for him.

"They told me to come here," he said again and again to those who questioned him. "Spenser, and Lovett..."

"For what purpose?"

He hesitated. "I thought they might have work for me. In the service of the Prince."

"Have you got an invitation? A letter?"

"No..."

Then had ensued the long wait in the hall with the other, silently resigned petitioners. He was cold, he was hungry, and above all he wished he had never come.

Someone called his name at last. He was led up some stairs and along a gallery to an empty chamber, where at least there was a fire. He sensed he was closer to the heart of the palace, closer to Prince Henry's presence. As he waited, he thought that he could hear the faint sound of a lute being tuned in an adjoining room, but he did not try to listen further, for he despised music.

He waited alone, warming his hands before the fire. He heard footsteps and turned, hoping to see Spenser, or Lovett, or even the Prince himself; but no, it was Richard Mapperley, the Prince's chaplain, escorted by two clerks.

Mapperley was younger than Pelham, but taller, and thinner, almost sinister in appearance, with his pale waxen complexion, his domed forehead, and dark clerical robes. His tone was cool as he said, "Be so good as to leave your petition for the Prince with me. I will see that he gets it."

Pelham said, "But I have no petition. I came in hope of seeing Prince Henry's chief clerk, or even the Prince himself."

"Do you have a written invitation?"

"Not written, no! But the last time I was here, I was invited to come again..."

Mapperley cut in, "Do you have an appointment?"

"No."

"In that case, I suggest you go home and write stating your business. The Prince and all his chief officers are all far too

busy to see anyone without an appointment. I will get someone to show you out."

"But—"

Mapperley said tersely, "You should be more careful of the
company you keep in the city, Master Pelham." Pelham's head
jerked up. Mapperley went on, slowly and deliberately, "You
were seen coming out of the house of a Catholic whore."

Pelham colored, then paled to whiteness. Another servant
was summoned to show him out, so he found himself retracing
all his halting steps. As he followed his guide into the main
hall, several people engaged in animated conversation were
moving so purposefully across his path that he was forced to
step aside. And he saw someone he knew in their midst, with
his lute slung over his shoulder.

Pelham lurched forward. "*Warriner.* What are you doing
here?"

The group ground to a halt. Gazes, both curious and mocking, turned on him from all around the hall. Ned Warriner
faced him, slowly. He said, "I was invited."

Pelham felt all his frustration, all his disappointment exploding inside him. He knew in that moment who it must have
been who had revealed the tale of the whore to the Prince's
servants. "This man," he expostulated, turning to them all,
"don't you know who he *is*?" He looked around in despair at
the cynical sea of faces that surrounded him. Someone
laughed openly, goading him beyond endurance. "Don't you
know," he pressed on, "who he works for?"

Someone stepped forward and said coldly, "This man is a
former soldier and a musician. He's traveled in Europe. He is
about to play for the Prince." They all started to move on, but
Pelham rushed forward and barred their way, declaring, "He
is a spy! At court everyone knows him, not for his pretty
songs, but because he is Northampton's lackey, Northampton's whore..."

He had their attention at last. Everyone knew that the Earl
of Northampton was no friend of Prince Henry. Pelham went
on desperately, "He'll be here to pass information back to the
Earl. Ask him. Ask him..."

He had not realized his posture was threatening, but it must have been, for two men were holding him back, and in his agitation he started to struggle. Ned had stepped out from the crowd to face him, the skin around his mouth white. Pelham broke free from his captors and made for him; they grappled with each other and were pulled apart, still struggling, Pelham perhaps more fiercely than his old enemy. Held tightly at last by two guards, he spat out, "A soldier? A musician? Warriner, you are a traitor. You should never have been allowed to return from exile."

Ned, too, was captive. "And you, Pelham," he said flatly, "should have been gaoled long ago for the persecution of innocent men. At least you've been stopped from making any more victims suffer."

"*Victims*? Do you mean recusants? It must have been you. You who cost me my job. Damn you..." Pelham lunged again. Breaking free of his captors, he lashed at Ned and caught his face with his fist, breaking the skin on his cheekbone. Ned, who was still held tightly, kicked out, catching Pelham on the leg and toppling him; now Ned was free, too, standing over Pelham with his fists clenched and his blue eyes blazing and the bright blood trickling down his cheek. One of the Prince's guards called out, pointing to the fallen Pelham, "Get that madman out of here."

Pelham was dragged away unceremoniously. Ned shrugged, and straightened his doublet, and held his kerchief to his bleeding cheek. Then it was his turn to face the guards who had gathered around him with their hands on their swords, and blank hostility in their eyes.

THEY LED PELHAM OUT INTO THE GROUNDS, AND told him to leave forthwith. He straightened his clothes and set off toward the gate, burning with mortification.

Because it was almost dark, he did not see Henry's head gardener until he was almost upon him. In spite of the poor light, and the bitter cold, Stephen Humphreys was examining some rows of plants in the lee of a yew hedge. A big, slow youth carrying a spade followed his every move. Humphreys turned to Pelham, his eyes expressionless beneath his protuberant forehead, and he said, "The stars were not auspicious, then. For your ship."

Pelham pulled up. "No. No, they weren't. How did you know?"

"I hear all sorts of things. Next time, you must calculate such ventures with more care." Humphreys lifted a finger. "Everything grows or prospers according to its planetary season, whether you talk of people, or plants, or voyages. It is impossible to fight the influence of the stars. Only think how the marigold opens out in the sun, how a woman's cycle waxes and wanes with the moon, like the tides; there is no gainsaying the power of the heavenly bodies." He looked round the garden, then pointed to the silvery shrub at his feet. "Take this plant, the lavender. Mercury rules it, and so it is potent for diseases of the head and brain. But it is not safe to use it where the body is replete with blood and humors, because of the mercurial spirit with which it is possessed."

He wandered on, up and down the rows of plants, with the tall young simpleton dogging his footsteps. Pelham, realizing the man was no longer aware of him, pulled his collar up against the cold and hurried off, his face set against the biting easterly wind, leaving Humphreys rambling to himself and his minion. He knew he was going home to face the prospect of his ruin. But as he limped toward the gates, he heard his name called, and he turned to see John Lovett, Henry's chief clerk, running toward him, out of breath.

"Master Pelham. Please stop. Please come with me. I am afraid there has been a mistake; I did not know, I was not told that you were here. Will you accept my heartfelt apologies? Will you come back inside with me? We need to talk."

IT WAS NED WARRINER'S TURN TO PACE IN SOLITUDE, for he had been taken, roughly, to a distant chamber of the palace, where he was locked inside. He cleaned his bloodied cheek as best he could with his handkerchief, wincing at the rawness of the cut, and assessed his situation.

He still had his lute, and it was unharmed, thank God. He

struck some plaintive chords, then crossed the room and looked out the window, where dusk was rapidly falling.

He guessed that Pelham's visit to the palace would also have an inauspicious ending, but that was little consolation.

He heard the bolt being drawn back on the outside of the door. In came the grizzled old soldier Spenser, pompous and perspiring in his ancient leather doublet, in which no doubt he would claim to have fought many Spaniards. His equally ancient sword clanked at his side. Ned put down his lute and turned tiredly to face him. Spenser was breathing hard.

"To indulge in a common brawl, here in His Highness's palace—it is unforgivable! Is it true that you are one of Northampton's lackeys?"

"I once worked for the Earl before I traveled abroad."

"And now?"

Ned folded his arms and shrugged. "Now I am trying to earn my living by my music."

"That is not what I asked. Are you still working for Northampton?"

Ned did not reply. Spenser lurched forward, shaking his finger menacingly. "Answer me, damn you. Are you here as his spy, as Francis Pelham declared?"

Ned raised his hands to warn him off. "Do I look like a spy? Have I had a chance to learn any secrets here?"

"Yes," said Spenser shortly, "to your first question, and no to the second, now and forever; you will get no chances to learn secrets here. I told them on your first visit that you were sly and decadent, and that you were not to be trusted. You will leave this place, now. And, by God, you will not come back."

So HERE WAS ANOTHER UNCEREMONIOUS EXIT; FOR, like Pelham before him, Ned Warriner was escorted along the passageway and down the stairs to the nearest doorway, through which he was hustled out into the courtyard. At one point, as he was marched through the almost dark gardens, he saw the odd-looking gardener in the distance, tending his plants with the tall epileptic youth following him, carrying stakes and a spade over his broad shoulders. Then he was hurried on again, toward the palace's boundary wall, and out through the high gate.

Darkness was falling quickly. Ned remembered that tomorrow was St. Lucie's Day: a time to grieve the failing of light and the onset of midwinter. Ned's surly escort marched him some way along the lane, to make sure he had no ideas about returning, then left him and turned back into the palace grounds where the gates crashed shut. Ned stood there, with the emptiness of the countryside enfolding him, and a sporadic wind making the bushes in the hedgerow shiver. A bright moon shone overhead: a hunter's moon.

He had not even seen Sarah Lovett, from whom he had hoped for so much more. And her husband, John Lovett, now knew Ned for what he was: Northampton's spy.

Another failure. Thanks to Pelham.

He set off to walk home across St. James's Fields, in the direction of the cottages and lighted lanes of Charing village; but then he heard footsteps coming up behind him. He turned swiftly, heart beating hard; then someone he didn't recognize sprang out at him and held a knife to his throat, while another man came up also and checked him for weapons. "You will come with us, Ned Warriner," he was told.

It was a night for surprises.

PELHAM FOUND HIMSELF IN AN UPSTAIRS ROOM OF the rambling palace, but this time there were no scowling guards, no interminable waits in freezing cold halls. Instead he was ushered into a richly furnished anteroom by John Lovett himself, and urged to sit before the log fire. A servant hovered to pour him spiced wine.

"I am so sorry," Lovett was saying, taking his own glass of wine and at the same time gesturing to the servant to leave the room. "I am afraid there has been a misunderstanding. The Prince's chaplain is overzealous in his duties. He heard rumors about your meetings with the Catholic woman in Candlewick Street. And I fear he has misinterpreted them."

Pelham said in a low voice, "If you feel I should leave,

sir—that I am not worthy to be here—then I will go instantly."
He started to stand up again, but Lovett put out his hand to
stop him rising.

"Look. It's hardly a hanging matter to visit a whore, even
if she is a Papist. Though I told Mapperley you'd surely gone
to try to convert her."

Pelham sat heavily, folding his hands together. "That is not
true, I'm afraid. I did sin with the woman."

"For God's sake," said Lovett irritably. "I don't care if
you've had carnal relations with the Spanish ambassador and
all his staff at Ely Place; I just said it to shut Mapperley up,
and anyone else who's heard the tale. Now, listen to me. If I
had known that you were coming here, then this—misunderstanding—would never have arisen."

"I should have sent a message first. I just wanted you to
know that I have not forgotten what you said. 'There is always
room,' you told me, 'for people who wish to serve the Prince.'
You said that you needed loyal people."

Lovett leaned forward. "And so we do. But I thought you
were already fully employed."

"No longer." Pelham briefly explained the termination of
his post as a recusant hunter. Now that peace had been made
between Spain and the Netherlands, he explained, Cecil
wished for a further thawing in relations between Spain and
England. Accordingly Cecil had ordered that the questioning
and holding of secret Catholics be moderated.

"Ah, the fool," said Lovett bitterly. "The crookbacked little
fool." He got up and paced the room. "Nothing has changed.
These peace treaties are only pieces of paper. Spain and the
Papacy will always be bitter enemies of England. We should
be striking at their poisonous Catholic hearts; we should have
supported the Protestant Dutch; we should be helping King
Henri of France at Julich, where even now he is drawing up
his armies to oppose the Catholic forces of the Hapsburg Empire." He turned back to Pelham. "I am sorry. Sometimes I
find it hard to stay calm on these matters."

Pelham said earnestly, "Please don't apologize. I understand."

Lovett walked over to the window and glanced out into the

darkness of the courtyard. "I heard that you are in trouble. That you are in debt." He lifted his hand to silence Pelham's stammering reply. "It is nothing to be ashamed of, that you have not been rewarded well enough in your work. I would like to help you." Lovett sat down again. "But just for the moment, I must ask you to be patient. The Prince leaves tomorrow morning for hunting at Royston with his father. He could be there for some days, and I, of course, must be with him. But I will not forget you. As soon as we return here to prepare for the Christmas festival, I will be in touch."

Pelham felt an instant's sickening disappointment. He had begun to hope for something now.

But he voiced appropriate expressions of gratitude, and was shown out, with courtesy, into the gardens again. A servant with a lantern guided him to the main gate. There was no one about except the guards, huddled round their brazier. He pulled his cloak around his shoulders and set off into the night.

Time, now, to deal with Warriner.

23.

Meanwhile she of the Peacocks Flesh did Eate
And Dranke the Greene Lyons Blood with that fine Meate,
Which Mercurie, bearing the Dart of Passion,
Brought in a Golden Cupp of Babilon.

GEORGE RIPLEY (D.C.1490)
"CANTILENA" V.17

SET AMIDST THE CLUSTER OF HOUSES AT CHARING village, close by the place where three centuries ago King Edward I had set up the stone cross to mark the procession of his wife's coffin to Westminster Abbey, there stood an inn called the White Swan, a respectable establishment used by men from the country who had business at Whitehall and needed lodgings for the night. It was to the doorway of this inn, in the darkness, that Ned Warriner was marched.

At least, he thought, they had not brought him here to murder him. That would have been far more easily done in the country lanes they had just left.

"Get up those stairs," the man with the knife said softly in his ear. The knife pricked the back of his neck. Ned raised his hands and climbed, with his escort behind him. At the door of a private chamber, one of the men knocked, then opened the door and pushed him through. Ned stumbled across the threshold. As he pulled himself up he saw in the bright candlelight a maid who was pretending to sew but was watching Ned's unceremonious arrival avidly. Ned heard the door close behind him as his escort disappeared. Then he heard another door to a small inner chamber open on his right, and he turned to see Sarah Lovett standing there.

He drew a deep breath. He said to her, "Why have I been brought here?"

Instead of answering, she told her maid to go. It was then that he smelled the strong wine on her breath; though he had known, from looking at her, and from seeing the decanter and goblets on the oak chest by the window, that she had been drinking. She replied at last, "I heard you would be at the palace today. I asked my men to look out for you. I trust"—she pointed to his cut cheek—"that they were not responsible for your injury."

"Surprisingly, no." He was still angry. "Did you tell them to escort me here at knifepoint?"

"I told them to make sure you got here."

"And so I am here. Why are you here?"

She shrugged, and toyed with the fine pearls at her neck. "Sometimes I like to be private. Sometimes I like to be as far from that hellhole of a palace as possible."

"Does your husband give his permission?"

"Why should he object? I often stay here. It makes it easier to visit my physician, or the seamstress in Cheapside who makes my gowns. It is a tedious journey in bad weather, and the hours of daylight are so short. My husband knows that if darkness has fallen and the palace gates are locked, then I will spend the night here with my servants. He does not complain. In fact he is glad, because then he can take one of the serving girls to his bed. I always know. I can smell the sluts between my sheets the next day."

She laughed and turned to the oak chest, on which sat the decanter of wine. There were two goblets, one half full. She drained that one and refilled them both. She carried one to Ned, and as she gave it to him he saw that her hand was unsteady. He took the glass from her but did not drink.

She touched his lute, which was strapped to his back still.

"How did your music go today, Master Warriner? Did the Prince enjoy it?"

"I didn't play," he said. "I was dismissed."

"Why?"

"The Prince's advisers decided I wasn't trustworthy."

She laughed a bitter laugh. "Not trustworthy? Tell me, out of that circle of hangers-on, of sycophants, of fanatics, which one of them is? They all serve their own interests—that old fool Spenser, who thinks he is still fighting single-handed a whole army of Spaniards; or the unctuous Mapperley, who preaches against sin but cries out in his dreams with secret lust. Or Henry's young friends, Duncan and the other gallants, who are with him only to absorb some of his power, and his money. They would all leave him in the flash of an eye if they thought they could do better for themselves elsewhere. And as for my husband, he's busy lining his own pockets as usual."

Oh, the tricks of fate. It had been a long, circuitous route, tonight, to what he was after.

Ned said slowly, "You told me, when we met before, that your husband has other interests. Besides his work for the Prince."

"Indeed. And I could tell you were intrigued. That is why I summoned you. Well, partly why . . ." She laughed and drank more of her wine; her dark eyes glittered dangerously. "I can see the way you are looking at me," she breathed. "I know you are wondering why I want to tell you such things. But why not? Why should I not tell everyone about my husband?" She pulled up her sleeve. Ned drew in his breath. There were ugly bruises on her wrist and forearm.

"He did that to me. My husband. He calls me a drunken whore. But it's he who has made me so." She pulled her sleeve down again and walked the room distractedly before turning back to him. "Which of them hurt *you*?" She pointed again to the fresh cut on his cheek. "Was it *him*?"

"It was an accident."

She shook her head disbelievingly. "He is stealing," she said. "I told you, didn't I?"

"You told me about the gold he gets. For the paintings that the Prince imports."

She came closer and touched his hand. "I don't think those paintings exist. I think my husband is keeping the gold for himself. I'm telling you these things because I want my husband ruined. Are you surprised that I hate him so?"

"I thought you'd told me." He pointed to her bruises.

"That's not all," she said. She drank again. "I was made to marry him—oh, that's nothing unusual, I know, but he never, ever cared for me. When our only child was born," she went on, "when our son was born seventeen years ago, at first he loved him. But as the child grew out of infancy, and my husband saw how he was afflicted, he turned away from him, and from me. He said the boy was not his."

She was suddenly quite calm. "I hated him for that. Hated him. Because I had been faithful until then, and I loved the boy. I still do . . . I made sure he could stay near me. I see him every day. So does my husband, probably, but he pretends the boy doesn't exist." She turned to pour herself more wine. "Nicholas is seventeen. He is feeble in his mind, but strong enough when he is not laid low by his epilepsy. He works now for the mad gardener Humphreys, who is kind to him, in his way. At least his strength is thus put to some use."

Humphreys's servant. The child of John and Sarah Lovett. Ned said, "I have seen him there."

"I believe you have noticed a lot of things. I think you have your own reasons for gaining access to the palace. But I still trust you, more than I would any of the men who surround the Prince."

"Then tell me about your husband. About the paintings, and the gold."

She pressed her hand to her brow. "He has always been involved in corruption at the royal dockyards. It's all so easy for him; he used to work there, you see, and now has the excuse of supervising the goods imported for Prince Henry. It's easily done; a question of altered paperwork, of bribes offered for silence, a share in the proceeds. Men come to my husband, and when I can, I listen. I overheard some of them the other day. These men were telling him they had moved some goods, as he had ordered. They talked, first, of 'the paintings,' but then—they lowered their voices, but I could still hear—they were talking of armaments. Pistols; powder; cannon. My husband listened and gave them some orders, which I could not hear; but he was angry with them for accosting him at St. James's. He said that they were never, ever, to come to him again without prior instruction; that he would contact them when he was ready."

"Who were they?"

"I don't know. I didn't recognize them. After a while they talked about the two new ships at Deptford that are almost ready to be launched. I know there's to be a grand ceremony, shortly after the Christmas festival. The King will be there, and Prince Henry. So naturally my husband is involved in the arrangements. That will keep him busy, now that the mulberries have gone. It was through the mulberries, of course, that he acquired his gold."

She had paused to reach for more wine. His hand fastened over hers, to stop her drinking. "Explain," he said.

She laughed. She ran her hand up and down his arm. "Wouldn't you like to know, master musician? But how much would you like to know? What can you offer me in return?" She was moving closer to him, lifting her hands to his shoulders.

He tried to hold her away. "Sarah..."

"My husband is getting gold," she said. "It comes to him secretly, by courier, from around the country. In return for those wretched mulberry plants. I've watched that strange, ugly man Humphreys, who is in charge of their growing; I have seen how they are dispatched, at the dead of winter, when no person in their senses would think of such a task."

He said, "Why pay gold for mulberries? Surely, surely no plant is so valuable."

"Perhaps it's not the mulberries they are paying for, but the letters that go with them."

Ned gripped her arm. "What sort of letters?"

"I thought at first they were just instructions. On how to grow the trees, how to nurture silkworms on them—some scheme to make money, of course..."

Her voice trailed away. She wanted more wine. This time Ned let her fill up her goblet, and he took some himself, before asking, "Have you seen any of these letters?"

"No. I looked in my husband's office, but they are sealed, well before dispatch. That's why I started to wonder about them."

"Do you think the Prince himself is in any way involved with this mulberry scheme?"

"He knows about the trees, of course. You realize, don't you, how superstitious he is? They've told him that mulberries, widely planted, will bring him good fortune. But they bring my husband the best fortune of all." She seemed distracted; she toyed with a strand of her hair.

Ned said, "Sarah. Listen to me. I need to see one of those letters. And I need a list of the people they are going to."

She was laughing at him again. "What will you do to reward me? To make it worth my while to get the letter, and the list for you?"

"I thought you wanted your husband exposed for what he was. Isn't that enough?"

"Perhaps. When will you come to see me again?"

"I cannot come to the palace. They would not allow me in."

"Then where can I get in touch with you?"

He thought quickly. "There's a tavern called the Crown, in Shoe Lane. You can leave a message there."

"Very well. The Crown. I shall do it. And you can reward me now. In advance."

He knew there was danger here, in her drunkenness, her scheming; but she was kissing him, and after a few moments she leaned to blow out the candles.

He told himself, as she guided his hand to her breasts, that he would leave, in a few moments; that he would take her to the inner bedchamber and persuade her to rest there, while he went and called for her maid. But she drew him with her, and she leaned back on the richly embroidered counterpane and pulled back her skirt, with a rustling of silk. Her thighs, above the stockings she wore, were smooth and pale. She let them fall apart and placed her hand on her own flesh. The wine was roaring in Ned's head.

"This is the other reason why I summoned you," she said, stroking herself softly. "Come..."

* * *

L ATE THOUGH IT WAS WHEN NED GOT BACK TO ROSE
Alley, Matthew was not there, but his men crowded round
him and pulled him into the house to regale him with the tale
of how a black-clad Puritan man with a limp had come asking
after him earlier, and not as a friend. He had looked, little
Pentinck told Ned eagerly, as if he would like to murder Ned
if he'd found him.

They'd played with the intruder for a while, pretending they
didn't know who he was talking about; then they sent him to
the tumbledown house at the end of the lane where two old
ravaged whores lived, telling him he'd find Ned there, but to
make sure to offer plenty of money first to get in. They had
watched as the man went in with his coins ready, and came
rushing out again shortly afterward, his face incandescent with
rage. They told Ned how he stood for a while in the street, his
fists clenched, as if he would take on Matthew's crew single-
handedly, as well as the whores, and all the beggars round their
fire. Then he turned and went limping off toward Ludgate.

Matthew himself had arrived while they regaled Ned with
this news. Matthew managed a smile as he listened, but his
face was haggard. He collected a dish of stew from the cauldron in the kitchen and sat down to eat.

Ned pulled up a seat next to him. "Matthew, I've been
meaning to speak to you. Business isn't good, is it?"

Matthew's smile collapsed. "Good? It's going from bad to
worse. This morning Steen told me he needs even more
money to keep my patch clear of the damned constables. And
I can't afford it, Ned."

Ned knew that Scrivener Steen paid off the local authorities—the constables, the night watchmen, and the local justices—on a regular basis to keep their noses out of Matthew's
affairs. Now he said sharply, "Are you sure you know which
side Steen is on?" He wouldn't put it past the scoundrelly ex-
lawyer to take money from all sides and pocket it himself.

"Oh, Steen's always taken his own cut. I know that. But so
far he's been loyal enough. This is his home; he doesn't want

to see me ruined. But he says we're up against strong opposition. God help me, but someone's determined to take over my patch, Ned. Most likely that bloodthirsty gang of thieves in Whitefriars."

The ancient liberty of Whitefriars, which adjoined the bank of the Thames to the west of the Fleet, was an old Carmelite monastery which since the Dissolution had come under the jurisdiction of neither Westminster nor the city. Instead it had become the refuge of the most desperate of London's criminals.

"And the worst thing of all," said Matthew heavily, "is that whoever it is knows exactly what my plans are. Anytime I'm about to shift some goods, or I hear of a place ripe for plunder, someone's there before me." He glanced round the room at his band of companions and lowered his voice. "It does bad things to you, Ned, thinking there might be a traitor among your friends. The other night Alice told me she had her doubts about Pat and his Irishmen." He hesitated. "We've not seen them around for a few days."

"I've heard Pat and his friends are working down at the docks. You know he and his men have to take whatever employment they can find around this time of the year. And you know, surely, that Pat would never betray you. Ever."

Matthew scratched his bristled chin and frowned. "I don't know. I went with Davey yesterday to Cheapside with some nice bolts of cloth we'd got hold of down at the wharf. A stallholder who owes me a favor was going to sell them for me. But we were stopped by the constables as we went through Ludgate. We had to make a hell of a run for it, and leave the stuff. Somebody had told them we were coming, there's no doubt. Another month of business like the last one and I'm ruined."

WHEN NED FINALLY GOT TO HIS ROOM OVER THE stables, he stretched himself out on his bed and lay staring into the dark. He slept at last, only to dream of lions and angels, their features hideously distorted, drifting in and out of a thicket of mulberry trees that caught fire. In his dream he was running toward the burning thicket, because he knew, and no one else did, that the Prince was there, and only Ned could save him. But as fast as he ran, he was getting no nearer, until suddenly he found that he was on board a ship, sailing along a great river between burning banks, and in the distance he heard the roar of gunpowder. "It is the Scorpion," someone whispered in his ear, pointing to the black, sinister creature emerging from the flames.

"No," he answered, "no, the Scorpion is the King of Spain, it is in my letter..." He reached into his pocket, but then he remembered he didn't have it anymore, and the flames were stretching closer, across the water.

And then he saw Kate, running to him across the deck of the ship. Her hair was flying loose, as it used to when she was a child. She was carrying a small wheel-lock pistol, a beautiful thing, like the one Northampton's man had carried, with a walnut stock adorned with carved ebony panels. Ned was trying to warn her that she must hide, she must get into safety.

But then he realized she was pointing the pistol at him.

A T AROUND NOON THE NEXT DAY JOHN LOVETT RE-
turned on horseback to St. James's Palace from the city, his boots laden with the grime of the road, his cheeks flushed from the thin east wind. There was not just, though, the smell of the road, of his mount, on his clothes; Spenser, old soldier that he was, could detect the scent of gunpowder and gunmetal clinging to him when he met Lovett at the stables. As if Lovett knew this, he went straight to his rooms to change from his riding clothes. He washed his hands also, then went to find his wife.

She was seated at the spinet in the empty music room. She had been playing in a desultory fashion, but she stopped when he came in and sat very still, without turning. He dragged her up by the wrists. She cried out, because he was hurting her. "Tell me," he said. "Tell me what happened last night, you whore."

She shook her head, and he hit her. He hit her again, but she kept her bitter silence through it all, until he said, "If you don't tell me about it, I will get rid of the young lout you saddled me with and told me was mine. The gardener's boy. I will send him far away."

Her eyes blazed then with hatred, but she whispered, "As I think you already know, I met the man who was here yesterday. The lute player. Warriner."

Lovett said, "And what did you do with him? You whore." He hit her again.

When she'd recovered she gave him a look of utter contempt. "What do you think?"

Lovett twisted her arm. "You are a faithless whore, and loose-tongued, too. Tell me this: Did he ask any questions? About me, or the palace, or the Prince?"

Tears of pain had come to her eyes, but she still stared at him defiantly. "Why should he? He is a musician. Anyway, I kept him too busy for any talk on such tedious matters."

Lovett hissed, "Go to your room, damn you."

He pushed her to the door, then went down the passageway and gave urgent orders to one of the guards. Some moments later Humphreys was escorted in. Lovett shut the door and stood with his back to it, assessing the newcomer. Humphreys looked resigned. Lovett said, "We are forever on the lookout for enemies here. Do you understand me? If anyone comes asking questions about anything at all, even something as trivial as the plants you raise in the garden, you must come to tell me. Have I made myself clear?"

Humphreys said gently, "Trivial? Trivial, you say? I do not understand, my lord. I do not think the young Prince would call my work trivial. Plants are evidence of the health of the ground beneath our feet; they are the fruit of the earth's womb..."

Lovett said, with concealed exasperation, "Yes, yes, we know how important it all is, and this is why we don't want people asking questions, don't want people interfering. Those mulberry saplings, for instance, and their distribution throughout the southern counties—they are part of a vital scheme that could be ruined by interlopers."

"Vital, indeed"—Humphreys nodded earnestly—"for the mulberries bring down life-giving forces from the heavens to protect the young Prince Henry."

"Yes," said Lovett, his patience visibly cracking. "Yes.

You've told us all that. Has anyone been asking about these mulberry trees? About the way in which they are being delivered around the countryside, with the letters of instruction?"

"Letters of instruction? No. It is all a secret. You said it was to be secret."

"Yes. We did. But you must let us know if anything unusual happens, if anyone is asking questions, because they might be the Prince's enemies. Do you understand me?"

"I have told you. The plants carry their own protection. They issue forth good portents, to shield the Prince from all harm . . ."

Lovett raised his clenched fist, put it to his forehead, and sat back heavily in his chair. "God damn you," he said quietly, "if the Spaniards had not tried to strangle you, I think I would have done it myself." He gestured toward the door. "Go. Just go."

Humphreys left, his expression wounded.

And then Lovett, who paid informers not only at the White Swan Inn at Charing, but also at other places throughout the city, began to ask more questions about the traveling musician called Ned Warriner.

THE EXHILARATION PELHAM HAD EXPERIENCED AFter knocking down Ned at St. James had vanished with his fruitless foray to Rose Alley to hunt for his enemy. He was tired of sleepless nights over money troubles, of Kate's silent but constant reproach. His only consolation was his little boy, whom he loved. But at last he had a lifeline thrown to him, for the next morning he was invited to call on Robert Mansell, Treasurer of the Navy, at his office in Deptford; and there he was offered a job as clerk of the shipyard. Someone, said Mansell, speaking to him vaguely from behind the paperwork on his desk, had spoken highly of him.

Pelham felt sure that it must have been Lovett, who he knew once worked in the navy office. He was filled with an immense gratitude that in the stinking pit of corruption that enveloped both city and court, there were people who valued his honesty.

The post did not come with a vast salary, but it was enough to fend off the moneylender, to keep his wife, who hated him, in silk gowns, and to keep his son, whom he loved, happy and well.

24.

*Separate the earth from the fire, and the subtle from the gross,
softly and with great prudence.*

THE EMERALD TABLET (ATTR. HERMES TRISMEGISTUS)

W ELL, NED. COME TO LOOK FOR A SAFE PASSAGE
out of England?"

Ned was at Deptford docks. As the tide raced high and
gulls wheeled overhead, he had walked along the riverside
amidst the coiled ropes and piles of timber until he saw the familiar gaunt, black-haired figure he was seeking. Pat was
heaving barrels of tar from the wharf steps up to a dray
manned by two of his colleagues from Bride's Fields, but he
stopped when he saw Ned and grinned, dusting his big hands
on his canvas breeches.

"A safe passage?" Ned shook his head. "Things aren't quite
that desperate yet. But can you get me one at short notice?"

"Of a certainty. It's a sound enough notion, to plan your
exile while you're still a free man." As he talked he was drawing Ned aside, away from the other laborers. "Listen, Ned.
I've been watching out for the man you mentioned. John

Lovett. The Prince's secretary. He's been down here a few times. But he seems more interested in those two new East Indiamen"—he gestured toward the ships being built, farther down the riverside—"than in any more imports of so-called art for his royal master. As for the Prince's warehouse, security there is tighter than ever since you and I paid our visit. There's a watchman on guard all night now. If any goods similar to those we saw have arrived, then I've not seen them."

Someone was shouting for him; he nodded to Ned and went back to join his comrades as they heaved up more barrels to the waiting dray.

Ned walked on, and watched the men working on the hulls of the almost finished East Indiamen, the *Trade's Increase* and the smaller *Peppercorn*. They worked in haste, making the most of the fine weather, for they were to be launched in the presence of the royal family on the day after Christmas.

And Lovett was interested in the progress of these ships. His wife had already mentioned this to Ned; but no doubt he was involved in the organization of the launch ceremony, in which Prince Henry, who since childhood had always harbored a love of ships and seafaring, would surely play a prominent part.

He went to look more closely at the *Peppercorn,* where carpenters planed the decks, and gangs of laborers prepared the slipway for its launch. He thought of the places this ship would sail to: of the wide seas, and warm spice islands. If he failed in everything, here, then perhaps such a venture would be a suitable exile for him. There were stray dogs roaming the wharves, looking for scraps, chasing gulls. He'd left Barnabas again with old Tew, with whom his dog had established a close and food-fueled friendship. He stood awhile longer in the winter sun, watching the work of the fitters and dockmen.

And then, he saw someone in the distance. A familiar figure, with cropped fair hair and black clothes, walking purposefully along the wharf in spite of the limp that marked his stride. Francis Pelham. Ned moved out of sight quickly, his pulse racing. Then when Pelham had moved on, he approached a nearby yard worker and said, "That man who just went by, in black. Do you know what his business is here?"

The man looked where he was pointing, then said with the scorn of the manual worker for the clerical, "Him? He's just been appointed. Something to do with accounts. Paperwork. Mansell showed him round yesterday."

At first Ned could not believe it: that Pelham had survived his evident disgrace at St. James's, to the extent that he had obtained a job here, at the dockyard, where Sarah Lovett had told Ned that her husband was still involved in corruption. He suddenly wondered: Had Lovett secured Pelham's appointment?

NED HAD PROMISED HIS BROTHER HE WOULD CALL AT the workshop of his printer friend, Summers, in Paternoster Row, to collect some ballads the printer had been preparing. By the time he got there, dusk was gathering.

Summers, stooped from bending over his press, his hands black with ink, went to collect the bundles of printed sheets and handed them over.

"Not bad," he chuckled. "Did you write them? Not bad at all. I especially liked this one—'The Court Shepherdess.'"

"With her mantle tucked up high
She tended all her flock
So buxom and alluringly
She cast aside her smock . . .

"Who's the shepherdess, I wonder? Could be any one of the fine ladies at court. Tell Matthew I'll sell plenty for him. But we could do with something about the plague. It's struck again."

Ned leafed through the top sheets, checking the quality. "I thought it was too cold for the plague."

"There's always the occasional outbreak, even in the dead of winter. It's taken a rich silversmith this time. In Ludgate. You could write a good rhyme about that, couldn't you? Death lying in wait for the unwary . . ."

Ned slammed down his sheets. Some fell to the floor. "What was his name?"

"Jebb. Tobias Jebb. Hey, watch those, the ink might still be wet—"

Ned was heading for the door. "Listen, Summers, do you mind if I collect these later?"

"But Matthew asked for them specially! He said they had to be ready by today—"

Ned had already gone, striding off toward Ludgate through the crowds of early-evening shoppers and tradesmen. He pulled up, panting, outside Tobias Jebb's shop, but no lights shone from within, and he saw what he knew he would see: the dreaded plague cross daubed on the door, the house boarded up with planking, and nails across all the windows.

He gazed at this scene of devastation. A neighbor carrying a lantern called out, "I'd get away from there if I were you. Can't you see the plague has visited?"

Ned turned. "Are they all dead?"

"They will be by now. You know what happens. Once the plague doctor has confirmed the contagion, they're shut in with bread and water for as long as it takes." The neighbor glanced up at the house and crossed himself surreptitiously. "No one's heard anything all day. They'll be along for the bodies tomorrow."

"Who was in there?"

"Master Jebb and his wife. Oh, and one of the prentice boys."

"What was the boy's name?"

"It was young Will Frewin. He was screaming for help after the doctor came and gave his verdict. Then they boarded the house up, and we heard him again. Dreadful, it was. He was trying to tear the planking away with his bare hands. But of course they always make sure there's no escape. The other apprentice is in prison on a charge of stealing, otherwise he'd be dead, too."

"What about Jebb's servants?"

"They didn't live there. They're being confined to their own houses."

As far as Ned knew, no one could inflict the plague on somebody else, unless they were infected themselves. But the letter to Auriel seemed to bring death in its wake. Albertus had died, and Underwood the apothecary. Robin had stolen the letter and was now in prison. But before he was taken away, did Tobias Jebb perhaps get to see it?

The neighbor had gone inside, while Ned stood there. Had Tobias Jebb talked about the Auriel letter? Did he, too, need to be silenced?

He stood there gazing up at the house with its doom-laden cross painted over the door. He walked round the side to investigate the other windows and the door to the workshop. All possible entrances had been sealed up with planks of wood, solidly hammered in place with great iron nails; a thorough job indeed.

Darkness had taken hold of the city. Farther up on Cheapside, the shop owners and stall holders were lighting lamps and candles which brightened the December gloom as the last citizens hurried home. But Jebb's shop was in darkness, and silence. The fear of death could almost be felt. The plague, they said. Was it true? Or was it simply an opportunity to have a house sealed up, and people silenced?

He walked round to the back, looked quickly to see if anyone was watching, and investigated more windows and doors, until at last he found a weakness—a place where the planks had been nailed less tightly over a narrow window, so he was able to get his hands underneath the wood and wrench it away. The sound of the splitting timber seemed enough to wake the dead; but he waited a few moments and still saw no one, heard nothing. Checking the street again for watchers, he prized away the shutter beneath and, getting astride the ledge, carefully eased himself in.

It took him some time to adjust to the blackness. He thought he heard things moving, rustling in the dark: rats, or perhaps just the sounds of old timbers settling into the silence of death.

And then he caught sight, in the shadows, of someone staring at him.

It was a woman, fully clad, sagging on a wooden seat. Her features were pale and waxen. Her teeth were bared in a rictus of a grin. A corpse.

His eyes were growing used to the darkness. He looked all around and saw, slumped across the table, a middle-aged man, clad in the robe of a prosperous tradesman. This must be Master Tobias, the silversmith. His arms were sprawled, his head lolled on its side. His eyes stared, and a trickle of vomit ran from his thin lips.

Ned stepped back, and in the darkness nearly stumbled over the body of the boy. The other apprentice, Frewin. He lay on the floor, with his hands still reaching out toward the door. His fingers were bloody from tearing at the nails and wood that had confined him. His mouth was wide open, as if he were still crying out in terror.

Ned almost expected them to turn their mask-like faces toward him, to reach out for him; he felt they must be able to hear his beating heart, the racing of his pulse. Racing, not because of the corpses—he had been a soldier, he had seen enough of those—but because he could see, anyone could see, they had not died of the plague. Their skin was unmarked by blotches or buboes.

And where Master Tobias's left hand was spread out on the table, in a pool of drying blood, Ned could see that his little finger had been amputated.

Ned started to walk around. Rows of books had been swept from the shelves on one wall and were scattered across the floor. It was possible that one of the victims, in a last struggle for life, had brought them down. But it was possible, too, that someone was searching for something. He went through to the workshop, where he'd looked on his last visit there. Adjusting his eyes to the deeper darkness, he saw that the heavy oak safe had been forced open, and everything in it strewn across the floor: more papers and books, even some silver dishes that must have been put in there overnight for safekeeping. He knelt and started looking through the books and papers, searching amongst Master Tobias's vital recipes, his orders and receipts. There was no sign of his letter.

He pushed the papers aside. Perhaps Robin still had it. Perhaps it had been destroyed.

He looked again at the books that had been pulled from the wooden cabinet, picking them up, one by one, with the stubbornness of desperation, not really knowing what he was looking for, only knowing that there must be something there, some reason for all these deaths.

One book, a worn, vellum-bound volume with a small padlock and leather strap holding it closed, lay a little apart from the others. He held it up in the gloom and read the letters, engraved in gilt on its spine. *"The Journey."*

He remembered Robin saying, "There's one book in particular that he values, *The Journey,* by an old alchemist called Wolfram..."

He forced the lock open. Inside, pressed between the first pages, were two folded sheets of paper.

His Auriel letter. He put it swiftly inside his jerkin. Was this what the killers had been looking for?

Getting to his feet, he turned and took one last look at the slumped bodies, at the silent workshop, at the scattered books and papers. The fetid smell of death filled the air. He climbed quickly out of the narrow window by which he'd entered, closed the shutter, and pushed the planks back into place.

He stood there in the street, breathing hard to draw the fresh night air into his lungs. And then, close by, he heard a muffled sob. He pressed himself back into the darkness, thinking of the boy with bloodied hands who was weeping as he died. Then he heard the sound again; and he saw, hiding in the shadows, a small, hunched figure, shaking with grief. It was Robin Green, Master Jebb's apprentice.

Ned pulled him out and raised him to his feet. He could only just recognize him, because his face was a ghastly mask, with raw stumps where his ears should have been. They had been sliced off, as the law ordained for thieves. The wounds had been roughly cauterized, but the flesh was still raw, and oozing foul matter.

The boy was whimpering with pain and fear. Ned, still holding him, said, "What are you doing here? You will die, out in this cold, with those wounds untended."

"I was going to come to you," Robin sobbed. "In Rose Alley. But first I had to try to find the letter. I was only going to keep it for one night, but Master Tobias took it from me, and now he's dead."

"I've got the letter, Robin. I'll explain later. When you and I are well away from here. All right?"

Ned put his hand through the lad's arm to speed him out of that desolate place. They went to the wall by Amen Corner and scrambled through the ruins; then hurried on, past the bonfire with its beggars, into Rose Alley, where Robin had come only a short while ago to tell him with such ardor that his Auriel letter must indeed have been written by Dr. Dee. They turned the corner past Matthew's house, where Ned noted with surprise that the door had been left wide open; they went on, down toward the stables, only by now Ned was running, and Robin was panting after him, because Ned could see the smoke, and smell the stink of burning timber and straw. And as he ran, he could see it, the stable building, with its upper story, where Ned's room was, an inferno crowned by flames that leaped into the black winter sky.

Matthew and his friends, Davey and Pentinck and Black Petrie's coalmen, and even plump old Luke, were running to and fro with leather buckets filled from the street pump which Tew was working like one demented. But the fire had taken a fierce hold, and there was nothing they could do, except throw their water at the lower story, and beat at the flames, and try to stop it all spreading to the timber buildings nearby.

And instruments of fire will be kindled...

Ned ran up to Tew. "Where is Barnabas?" He had to shout it again because the old cook was half deaf; at last Tew shouted back that he was in Ned's room, above the stable; he had put him there earlier, he said, while he went out for food; and Ned was running toward the outer staircase, which still stood, except for at the top, where the flames were starting to devour the timber steps and the handrail. He charged up the first few steps, already coughing at the smoke and the heat, when Matthew thundered up behind him and grabbed his arm.

"You can't go up there, lad! Are you mad?"

For answer Ned shook himself free and staggered on up, but the flames were rushing down to meet him. With a great cracking sound, the side of the building began to collapse. The staircase rail broke free under Ned's hand; the steps gave way, and Ned fell, arms flailing, into the debris.

Burning to ashes, he thought as the heat engulfed him.

25.

The thumb, in chiromancy, we give Venus:
The forefinger to Jove; the midst to Saturn;
The ring to Sol; the least to Mercury.

BEN JONSON (1572–1637)
THE ALCHEMIST, ACT I, SCENE 3

NED OPENED HIS EYES SLOWLY. HE WAS LYING IN bed in the attic of Matthew's house. A fire had been lit in the grate, but it was still cold. Rain beat against a tiny window let into the slanting roof above him, through which gray daylight filtered.

He turned his head and saw Matthew, sitting on a stool close to his bed. Next to his brother was Robin, his thin face desperately pale against the scarred red stumps of his ears. Both of them were watching him anxiously. He realized that his hands, resting on the grimy blanket that covered him, were bandaged. They hurt, badly. He must have been clinging to the burning wreckage of the staircase as he fell. Pushing back the blanket, noting that he was clad in loose breeches and a linen shirt—his brother's, he guessed—he tried to get himself up by swinging his legs out of the bed; but as he put his right foot to the ground, a sharp pain shot up his calf, making him fall back. He saw then that his foot was bandaged, like his hands.

"Stay still, lad," advised Matthew.

Ned shut his eyes. "I don't think I'm capable of doing anything else. How long have I been here?"

"Only a night and a day."

"A night and a *day*?"

"Well, most of the day. It's almost three in the afternoon. The fire was last night. We all thought you were done for—there was a piece of burning timber fell across your foot, trapping you. But Robin here ran into the wreckage you'd landed in and pulled you out. Those boots of yours saved you from worse damage, but your right foot's badly bruised. Dr. Luke came straightaway, to put dressings on your burns. He made you swallow a sleeping draught, 'cause you were shouting like a lunatic about fire and ashes."

"What happened to Barnabas?" said Ned. He sat up again abruptly.

Matthew pulled at his bushy black beard and frowned. "Dead," he said apologetically. "I'm sorry, Ned. It was the dog barking that first told us of the fire. We did our best to save the place and get him out; you saw how we were running with bucket after bucket from the pump, but it was too late."

Ned bowed his head.

"Old Tew only put him in there for a little while," explained Matthew, "because he had to go to the Shambles for meat for our supper, and he knew the butchers there wouldn't let a great dog like him anywhere near. So he found the spare key and locked him up in your room. He was a good dog," went on Matthew. He blew his nose.

Ned looked up at him suddenly. "Do you have any idea who did it?"

Matthew hesitated. "It could have been an accident. A spark from a lantern, or something."

Ned gazed at him steadily. "I left nothing alight. Who did it?"

Matthew looked uncomfortable. "There were a couple of strangers round Rose Alley late yesterday afternoon, asking Petrie and one or two others about you, where you lived.

Petrie told them to clear off, but apparently they came across Pentinck, and you know what he's like. Before any of us could stop him he told them you had the room above the stable. He meant no harm." He frowned. "Though we've given him dire warnings since. Anyway, they must have come back later. When it was dark. Perhaps they were sent by that fellow who was here looking for you the other night."

Ned clenched his bandaged hands, then stopped, because they hurt. That had been his first, instant reaction. That it was Pelham, after revenge. But now, he wasn't so sure.

"Yes," he said. "That will be it. Did Luke say how long it will be before I can walk again?"

"He said you must rest your injured foot, you mustn't walk on it, but he doesn't think there's anything broken. A week or so, he said, and it'll be as good as new. Your hands will take a little longer. You can stay here for as long as you want, of course. It was Davey's room, but he's moved next door with Luke. And I've already told your friend he can share with Pentinck." He gestured to Robin. "He saved you."

Matthew stood up then, and patted Robin on the shoulder, saying he had business to see to, but he'd be back again shortly, and he'd have food sent up. As soon as he'd gone, and the door was shut behind him, Robin leaned forward, his hands clasped tightly before him. He whispered, "I've got your letter safe, Ned. I took it from your pocket when you were hurt."

Ned pulled himself up against his pillow. "You've not told anyone here about it, have you?"

"Of course not!" Robin started to rub at one of his scarred ear stumps, then winced.

"Has Luke seen to your ears?" asked Ned more gently.

"Yes. He's given me a salve for them. He says they'll be all right. Ned, I'm so sorry I took your letter the other day. I only borrowed it to try to help you. I was going to bring it back to you straightaway."

"But then Tobias Jebb got hold of it."

"Yes. But he's dead now, and you've got the letter back!" Robin was desperately anxious for Ned to forgive him. "Have you thought," he went on, drawing closer, "that everything that's happened—Master Tobias's death, the fire—could be because of your letter?"

Ned said, "Your master died of the plague. The fire was an accident."

Robin was shaking his head. "Perhaps. But people will stop at nothing to get the secret of gold. The house of the magus Agrippa was burned to the ground when the rumor spread that he'd found it; people killed one another, after he died, to get hold of his writings, though they never found his secrets. Ned, have you looked after your crucible?"

"If the bakehouse is still standing, it's there. But Robin, it's just a stinking mess, of wine and charred dung. The oven probably went out long ago."

"Just let me check it for you," pleaded Robin. "It will do no harm."

Ned raised his hand in a weary gesture of resignation. "Very well. Matthew will have a key. You said you'd got my letter. Let me have it."

Robin nodded and reached inside his jerkin to pull out the folded sheets of paper. As he did so, something came out with them and fell to the floor: a little silver vase, scarcely two inches high, with crooked handles set on either side. Robin snatched it up and was guiltily pushing it back in his pocket when Ned said, "What's that?"

"It's nothing," Robin said quickly. "I made it months ago. Master Tobias was teaching Will and me how to fix on handles, but mine were crooked, and so he beat me." He blushed. "I was meant to put it back in to be remelted, but I didn't, and then it was too late. Master Tobias would have accused me of stealing it, you see. So I kept it. It's my talisman."

He put it away and handed Ned the Auriel letter. While Robin rubbed, scowling, at his cheeks, in an effort to alleviate the pain of his ear stumps, Ned unfolded it and glanced over the all-too-familiar words.

He felt sure now that people were dying because of this letter. Tobias Jebb's ransacked house had told him that. And the murderers were being protected. But why? And on whose orders?

The boy was watching him eagerly, his eyes pain-bright.

"I've been trying to remember," he said, "exactly what Master Tobias said when he took it from me. He was sure, you know, that your letter was written by Dr. Dee. Just as I told you. He said the lion symbol was Dee's. Just there—do you see it?" He leaned across to point it out. "And the Latin—"

Ned said, *"Qui non intelligit aut discat aut taceat."*

"Yes. Again, Master Tobias said that was John Dee's motto. 'He who does not understand should learn or be silent.' I saw my master's hands shaking with excitement as he read that."

"Did anyone else apart from you hear him saying all this?"

"The constables were close by." Robin's voice faltered a little. "And Will Frewin. He was the apprentice, who spied on me..."

The one who lay dead, thought Ned. Who had been screaming to get out.

"But none of them," went on Robin, "would have *under-stood...*"

Ned held the letter higher to catch the sparse daylight. If only he himself understood the contents of the letter a little more. "Robin," he said, "I know I asked you before. But what else could the word 'Scorpion' mean, in alchemy?"

Robin's face brightened. "I know that the Scorpion is used by some of the old alchemists as a symbol for the process of separation. The signs of the zodiac can be used, you see, to indicate the various stages of transformation. And the Scorpion, meaning separation, comes after Libra, which means sublimation."

Ned nodded, as if he understood, but really he understood nothing. He ran his finger farther down the spidery writing. "What about this, then? *'When the emblem of Morus is strewn throughout the land, then is the time for the rebirth...'* Have you any idea what *morus* means?"

Robin frowned. "I've not come across it in any of my master's books. But I do know that *morus* is the Latin word for the mulberry tree."

Ned said, *"No.* It cannot be..."

Robin looked at him, amazed at his vehemence. "But it is. I'm sure of it."

Ned said urgently, "Do you happen to know, did your learned Master Tobias ever mention to anyone that there was an alchemical significance in the language of ships, or dockyards?"

"Ships?" Robin shook his head in puzzlement. "No. Why should ships and dockyards have anything to do with alchemy?"

"No reason. No reason at all."

But Lovett had been involved with the mulberries. He'd been paid gold for them. And Lovett's wife had said, *"The launch ceremony will keep him busy, now that the mulberries have gone..."*

"Robin. I want you to find out everything you can for me, about the meaning of this letter. I want you to give me every possible alchemical interpretation of every single word. Can you do it?"

Robin's face fell. "I'm not sure I can, without the help of Master Tobias's books."

"I've got some books. And there are the ones you borrowed, to show to me."

"They'll have been destroyed, in the fire."

"No they won't. They were in the bakehouse. They'll still be there. Will you go and get them, and bring them here? I need your help."

Robin got up. "I can see if the crucible is still all right."

"You can do what you like with the crucible. But don't be long. And remember not to say a word about all this to anyone—my brother and all his crooked friends included."

Robin nodded and hurried to the door, his eyes shining with eagerness.

NED LAY BACK WEARILY AGAINST HIS PILLOWS. Barnabas was dead. He had a useless leg and burned hands. And someone was trying to kill everyone who came into contact with this letter. He held it up to the fast-fading light. *"When the emblem of Morus is strewn throughout the land, then is the time for the rebirth..."*

Mulberries. He thought of smooth-tongued Lovett, who, according to his wife, was shadily transmuting mulberries into gold.

Was it possible that Lovett's involvement in the corruption at the dockyard—and perhaps, even, his signing for those guns paid for with the mulberry gold—was also concealed in the Auriel letter? But why? And why would John Dee be writing about it? How had he *known*?

He remembered suddenly that Pelham had just started work at the Deptford dockyard. He put the letter down. His head throbbed; he thought he could still smell the burning timbers that had engulfed him. He missed Barnabas.

Later Luke, still relatively sober, came to examine his injuries, and to recommend the use of tobacco as a remedy. "Inhalation of the smoke soothes the brain," he explained, "and reduces the phlegmatic humors throughout the body." He had lit his own pipe, and raised it encouragingly as he spoke. "You may try mine if you wish. The savages of Peru share pipes nightly, after eating. They believe that drinking the smoke brings visions of paradise, and at the same time prolongs an active life."

Ned coughed and waved his arms about to dispel the fumes. "Perhaps some other time. Luke, will the boy be all right? Are his scars healing properly?"

The plump old doctor frowned. "It's a truly barbaric punishment, isn't it? What did he do? Steal a few coins from his master, who from the looks of the lad kept him half starved anyway?"

"Something like that."

"He'll be all right. The stumps look ugly, but the cauterization is usually pretty effective. They'll heal if he keeps them clean. And he needs to be kept busy. That's the solution."

He was looking at the door, clearly anxious to get to the tavern, but Ned pulled himself up on the bed and said, "Luke. One more thing. Do you know of any reason—medical, superstitious, anything at all—for the removal of a dead man's finger? Especially the little finger?"

Luke frowned. "I'm not sure. Of course, the touch of a hanged man is reckoned by some to be a cure-all for many illnesses. You'll have seen how sick people cluster round a dead man's body when he's cut down from the scaffold. But the little finger? I don't know of any medical significance to it.

Though I know as a matter of interest that astrologers believe the little finger is ruled by Mercury."

Mercury. Prince Henry's ruling planet, according to Humphreys, and the planet under which the mulberry tree thrived. A while ago he would have dismissed it as superstitious nonsense.

"Is each finger ruled by a different planet, then?"

"Indeed, yes. According to tradition, the thumb belongs to Venus, the forefinger to Jove, the middle one to Saturn, and the ring finger to the Sun. If you believe in such things, which many do."

"So I'm beginning to realize." Ned shut his eyes briefly.

Luke said, "You are tired. I'll leave you to rest."

"Luke. If you can find out any reason for the removal of the little finger, some sort of ritual, or magic—anything at all— will you let me know?"

"Of course."

As SOON AS LUKE HAD GONE, NED EASED HIMSELF onto his good leg and tried to walk around, but the pain from his bruised right foot was excruciating. He went quickly back to his bed when he heard someone coming up the stairs. It was Alice, in a flowery, low-cut gown which clung to her full bosom. She carried a bowl of soup, which she put on the table next to his bed. Then she sat down beside him.

"Where is Matthew?" he asked pointedly, thinking of Pat, and how Alice had blackened his name with his brother.

She shrugged and handed him the soup. "Drinking himself silly, as usual at this time of night," she said. "Ned, someone wanted you hurt. Badly."

The strong perfume she wore all but stifled him. As bad as the fumes from Luke's tobacco. He put the soup bowl back on the table. "It was an accident," he said. "Barnabas should never have been left locked in up there with a lighted candle. He must have knocked it over."

"I don't think so." She was gazing at him steadily. "I think, Ned, that you've been asking for trouble, by getting mixed up with the wrong people."

"One doesn't come to Rose Alley for pious company."

Her heavy-lidded eyes flashed with anger. "That's not what I meant, and you know it. There's that Kate Pelham, for one. She'll bring bad luck to you, Ned."

Ned said wearily, "Alice, it is none of your business. And Kate Pelham wants nothing to do with me."

"Doesn't she?" She leaned forward so her plump shoulders and breasts were almost touching him. "She came here to speak to you that time. She lowered herself to visit Rose Alley. And the people who are tailing her will no doubt have found out where you live, too."

"What do you mean, the people who are tailing her?"

She shrugged again. "I don't know who they are. Her husband's spies? Government men? I saw her the other day. She'd been to visit someone, a friend, I suppose, in Blackfriars. She was walking home across the Fleet Bridge with her maidservant. And she was being followed by two men. Whenever she stopped, they stopped, too. Once she turned round to say something to her maid, and I saw the two men hide in an alley until she moved on again. She's in trouble, Ned. And she'll lead them to you, here."

He wondered, with a kind of bleak anger, if they were Northampton's men. "She'll lead them nowhere," he said. "She doesn't want anything to do with me. She thinks my lifestyle is—unsavory."

Alice reached to touch his cheek. He turned his face away and asked her to go; he said he was tired.

Her eyes flashed with disappointment as she drew away from him. She said, "It's because I'm not a fine lady, isn't it?"

"Alice," he said, "Alice, I'm Matthew's brother."

"Your brother," she said with contempt, "is a fool."

He said quietly, "I don't happen to think so. And I think he deserves some loyalty."

"Ned." She knelt swiftly at his side. "See here. This is no place for you or me. I've got a little money put by. I could arrange for us to go away together, far away. Just tell me when you've had enough of all this bloody misery—"

He said, angry, "If I've given you any encouragement to think I might say yes, then I apologize."

She had gone pale. "It's an offer you'd do well to accept, Ned."

"Are you threatening me?"

She stood up, silent, rebellious. He went on, in a low voice, "What happened between us was a mistake, Alice. I do not want it to happen again. I don't like the way you treat my brother and his friends. How can I make things plainer?"

A man's voice roared cheerfully from the bottom of the stairs. It was Matthew, calling for Alice. "Damn you," she said in a low voice. She left, in a swirl of skirts and perfume, her face tight with anger. Ned lay back in utter exhaustion and remembered what Northampton had told him about Kate becoming too friendly with the prisoner Ralegh.

Was that why she was being followed? Who by?

When Alice's footsteps had died away, he tried once more, desperately, to pull himself to his feet, to walk again, but he could not; his injured foot would not bear his weight. He fell back onto the bed and gazed through the little window into the darkness. Overhead the moon went sailing through the clouds, mocking him.

He wanted to play his lute, but of course he couldn't.

He wished Barnabas were there.

L ATE THOUGH IT WAS, A PEDDLER WAS TRAVELING A southern upland road on foot with his packhorse. He followed an ancient track, worn deep by countless feet, and lined with oaks whose branches shone with crystals of frost. Owls hooted from distant thickets, floating like moths above the branches. Mysterious creatures scuttled in dead bracken that had been turned to silver. The peddler's horse carried woven willow panniers laden with saplings: mulberry saplings, whose roots were bound with sacking to protect them against the cold night air.

At the inns where he ate and rested, people asked him about his saplings, and when he explained that they were for the nurturing of silkworms, some tried to buy them from him. "Can I make silk, too, peddler? Is it really so easy? Do I just have to plant a tree?"

"No," said the peddler, "it is not easy."

"Why not?"

So he would explain to them. "You need earth of the right temperament, properly enriched, and bathed in the sun's rays at the appropriate time of day. And the trees must be planted with Mercury at retrograde, so the planet's powerful beams nourish the soil."

And so on, until his listeners, bored, laughed at him for a fool and turned away. But the peddler just continued on his journey, smiling, with his trusty horse and his willow panniers gradually emptying; he tramped on by night and by day, because he had a list, engraved on his mind, of some twenty or more people who would not laugh at him, but who would be expecting these saplings. And a letter.

When the emblem of Morus is strewn throughout the land, then is the time for the rebirth...

He had been told to tell them that more detailed instructions would shortly follow. They were to make themselves ready.

He had been told by those who gave him his orders that if he was interrogated by hostile men, then he was to kill himself rather than answer their questions. He was warned that he would be tortured, if captured; was advised that his captors would not allow him to remain silent; and was it not better to die a swift, clean death than to face certain agony, after which he would anyway surely die?

So he kept within his doublet a little phial of mercury poison. Death would be quick and painless, they assured him. And the mercury: how fitting, he thought, for it was that very planet that ruled the fragile, silk-bestowing mulberry tree.

He had been told to say, if asked for his name, that he was known simply as the Crow.

AS DAWN ROSE COLDLY THE NEXT MORNING OVER ST. James's Palace, Stephen Humphreys, in the Friary Garden, was watching more piles of raked-up leaves smoldering in the morning mist. His gardeners moved about him, wraith-like, silent, absorbed in their work, even when a messenger came to tell Humphreys about another fire: a burning building this time, wherein lodged a lute player who was reputed to dabble in alchemy.

Humphreys shook his head, frowning. "Men who investigate the secrets of fire and gold," he said, "should protect themselves accordingly. What was his name?"

The man told him.

"And where did you say he lived?"

"In the midst of a den of thieves close to the Fleet, called Rose Alley."

Humphreys nodded and paid the messenger, who departed. But then someone else came to seek Humphreys's attention, the young Nicholas Lovett, who hurried toward him from the house, his demeanor and clumsy carriage denoting his agitation.

"Master Humphreys, I was late because I was talking to my mother—"

Humphreys put out his hand in a gesture intended to calm him. "There's no need to apologize. I understand. Is your mother well?"

"Well enough. She asked me about the mulberry trees. The ones I dug up for you, Master Humphreys. She wants to know where they are going."

Humphreys put his head on one side. "Now, Nicholas," he said, "I wonder why she is interested in mulberries?"

Nicholas frowned. Then his big, simple face brightened. "She said a friend wanted to know! But she told me it was to be a secret—"

"You know you can trust me," Humphreys reassured him. "I will find out for you, very soon, where the mulberry plants are going. We want your mother to be happy. But you must tell me, Nicholas, what else she asks you. Then we can truly help your mother. Will you promise? It will be our secret."

"Yes," said the youth. "Oh, yes."

Humphreys showed him how to lay the paving stones for the herb garden, and left him working there, absorbed. He knew that Sarah Lovett had been punished by her husband for bedding the lute player, who had twice visited the palace. He guessed that the lute player had been punished also. By fire.

But did Lovett know that his wife was interested in the mulberries? Who had put her up to asking such questions?

There had been too much talk lately. About mulberries, and gold. It brought ill luck. Only the other night a learned silversmith who talked about a letter that too many people wanted had died. All his household had died, too, except for one apprentice boy, who had sought refuge, Humphreys had learned, in the very place where he was least likely to be safe.

He went back to his task of pruning an espaliered apple tree that grew against the south-facing wall. As he cut back the limbs that grew awry, and tied other, softer stems into place, he began to sing to himself, in his strange, whistling voice,

> *"The dragon devours himself,*
> *And the black raven is dead;*
> *Metal yet liquid,*
> *Matter yet spirit,*
> *Cold yet engulfed in flames..."*

It was the song Ned Warriner had sung, on his first visit to Prince Henry's palace.

DOWN BY THE RIVER AT DEPTFORD, WHERE THE smells of tar and varnish filled the air, the new ships for the East India Company, the *Trade's Increase* and the *Peppercorn*, were nearing completion. The last timbers were being hammered into place on their decks, the last of the caulking applied. Master Phineas Pett, shipbuilder to the King, was walking up and down the dockside in the blustery west wind, watching the joiners and carpenters who swarmed like ants over the ships he had designed. He assessed the final stages with proprietorial pride.

Francis Pelham was there as well, in a lesser role. This was his fourth day there. His chief duty, he had learned, was to keep the records of the incoming and outgoing supplies there at the King's dockyard; and accordingly, in his office, he had laid out in meticulous order the heavy registers, the delivery notes, and the many receipts to be signed and recorded and filed. As he went about his work he still limped, but his step was lighter.

At dawn that morning, before reaching his new place of work, he had called at Lombard Street to arrange a new contract for the payment of his debts to the moneylender there. He had told Kate that she was not to worry about the cost of the payments to the physician who attended Sebastian.

He had been honored, when he first made himself known at the dockyard three days ago, to be shown his office and introduced to his tasks by Sir Robert Mansell himself. From the start Pelham had been eager to learn as much as he could about his new job, but Mansell seemed unconcerned with details.

"Just sign for the supplies that come through," Mansell said somewhat abstractedly, showing Pelham the consignment sheet for some timber being unloaded from a moored Swedish cog. "Then copy the details into the registers and pass them on to the clerks for payment."

Pelham had frowned a little. "But I must check that everything is in order, surely? That the goods have actually been delivered; that they are correct in every specification?"

Mansell gave him a sideways glance and rubbed his nose. "You can rest assured, Master Pelham," he said, "that everything will be correct. Your part in these matters is a mere formality."

Pelham bowed his head. They had walked out along the wharf, where Mansell showed him the remaining offices and gave him the keys he would need. Pelham, with the salt wind in his face, and the shouts of the Deptford shipbuilders echoing around him, had felt as close that day as he had done for many a long year to the half-forgotten dreams of his youth.

They had paused for a while by the smaller ship, the *Peppercorn,* which stood high on its building blocks above the slipway. There they discussed beam and depth ratios, and the relative virtues of Scandinavian pine and British oak. It was then that Pelham decided it would be worthwhile to investigate the prices of timber being brought into the port, for many foreign ships—notably the Baltic cogs—were built largely of pine, less than half the price of oak. He had spent the morning of his fourth day there making detailed notes of prices, and talking to the chief carpenters, after which he went to inspect the latest delivery docket on his desk, which he had noted was for barrels of gunpowder. "Just sign them," Mansell had said airily. But anyone could have told him that Francis Pelham took a pride in doing everything properly. Anyone could have told him that once Pelham had been entrusted with a job, he would not be prepared to compromise that trust. So he took the docket and walked on down the wharf to the warehouse where the gunpowder was stored prior to being sent on to its destination.

He asked a young clerk, the only member of staff present, to show him the barrels of gunpowder indicated on his docket. The clerk was offhand with him, almost surly. He pointed to a section of the storeroom and said, "They should be somewhere over there."

"Where are your records?" asked Pelham. The clerk opened a register for him, then said he had other matters to attend to and quickly walked off.

Pelham inspected the register, which indeed matched his docket. Then he went to find the barrels, stamped with a delivery number, and counted again and again. At least a quarter of them were missing.

He hunted around for the young clerk, who was nowhere to be seen. He asked two other clerks he found in another part of the store about the barrels, but they told him it was none of their business. He went to look for Mansell, but was told that he had gone up to the city to dine with Sir Thomas Smith of the East India Company. No one knew when, or if, he would be back that day.

Pelham went back to his desk. He began to make his own lists, and limped around the dockyard asking questions. Although even his zeal was momentarily curtailed when he went to introduce himself to the Clerk of the Ordnance, and met with the clerk's response. "Pelham. Pelham...I know that name. Your wife is a good friend of Sir Walter Ralegh, isn't she?"

Pelham frowned. "She knew him a long time ago," he said. "When she was only a child. Her father was acquainted with

Sir Walter before his imprisonment. But my wife is not his friend."

"I see," said the man hastily. "I misunderstood . . ."

"You did," replied Pelham curtly, and went on his way.

Asking questions.

26.

~❧~

Sondry vessels maad of erthe and glas,
Our urinals and our descensories,
Violes, crosslets and sublymatories,
Cucurbites and alembikes eek...

GEOFFREY CHAUCER (C.1342–1400)
CANONES YEOMANS TALE

WHENEVER HE WAS LEFT ALONE, NED TRAMPED around the confined space of his attic room, forcing himself hour by hour to increase the weight he was putting on his injured foot. He wasn't alone often, because Matthew's friends were attentive, taking it in turns to carry up Ned's food, along with the news of the town. Davey arrived one day with an unexpected present, a clutch of broadsheets bearing salacious pictures of ladies of the town to amuse him. Later Matthew brought a more practical gift—some secondhand leather boots. Stolen, Ned assumed.

Robin was a constant visitor. He had a pallet in Pentinck's room, and Matthew had found the boy a black leather cap with ear flaps, a little like those worn by the sergeants at the Tower, which covered the healing stumps of his ears, and protected them from the vicious December cold that had closed in on the city.

While Ned ate his meals up in the attic room, Robin would sit at his side and report to him concerning the bakehouse and the crucible, which he went to tend at least three or four times a day. He talked of baths and distillations and cohobations, which Ned listened to with painful concentration, asking him to repeat certain phrases while he checked them with his letter. Robin told Ned eagerly that the third operation, the Digestion, was now complete. He had taken alchemical water, he said, and added it to the recalcined earth, which once more had to undergo the painstaking process of condensation and putrefaction until the Crow was attained; at which point Ned raised his hand in protest and said, "Stop. You're ahead of me. What is alchemical water?"

"Dew," explained Robin patiently. "I've been collecting it by laying clean cloths on bushes at night, in an old garden down by the Fleet, and squeezing them out the next morning."

"And the Crow? How do crows fit into all this?"

"It's the next stage," Robin told him. "Master Agrippa wrote that *'the blackness of the Crow demonstrates the perfect putrefaction of the seed.'* I think, I hope, that the crucible is almost ready for the putrefaction. May I see your letter again, to check if I've missed anything?"

Ned gave it to him. "I know I keep asking this. But have you discovered anything yet in that letter about dockyards? Any symbol, or archaic alchemical word?"

Robin glanced up from the letter. "There's nothing I can see. But look. Here's the bit about the Crow. *'Now, from the putrefaction of the dead carcass of hope, a fruitful Crow will be generated, base at first, but which little by little stretching out his wings will begin to fly with his precious seeds, aided by Attramentum.'* The Crow, being black, is the alchemical term for the Nigredo, the dark stage of melancholy and death which all the alchemists agree is essential for creation to take place. Isn't it wonderful?"

"What is *attramentum*?"

"It's the alchemist's name for black ink."

"Black ink..." Ned put his hand to his head. "Why don't they use ordinary words?"

• • •

D R. LUKE CAME UP AT REGULAR INTERVALS, ALWAYS out of breath from the stairs, to change Ned's dressings and apply more salves, a process that took variable amounts of time, according to how inebriated he was. Ned's hands were healing quickly.

Matthew came up often, sometimes after his late-night drinking bouts, to encourage Ned's return to good health volubly, and to tell him the latest gossip of the streets, in an endeavor to rekindle his brother's ballad-writing career. Ned listened, and held up his bandaged hands, and said that as soon as he was better, he would compose a whole bookful of ballads.

"Something jolly to sell on the streets," Matthew suggested. "Songs they can sing in the taverns over Christmastide."

Ned tried to ask him how business was, and if he was keeping his enemies at bay. But Matthew always said business couldn't be better and changed the subject.

Alice came only rarely, clearly harboring a grudge over his rejection of her attentions. She occasionally brought him his food, which she slammed down on the table by his bed. She said accusingly once as she was going, "That prentice lad of yours. He spends a lot of time in the old bakehouse. Did you give him the key? He seems secretive whenever anyone asks him about his visits there."

Ned said, "He's embarrassed by his appearance. His ears. Perhaps he'd rather be shut away on his own than in company."

She put her head on one side, disbelievingly, and left.

By the time there was just over a week to go till Christmas, Ned was at last able to put his weight on his foot, and Luke removed the bandages from his hands. Ned waited till the usual carousings began below, as Matthew's cronies, the spoils of their day assessed and locked up, began their celebrations. Though in spite of Matthew's assurances to the contrary, business, from what Ned could find out, had continued to deteriorate.

Ned listened for a while to the merriment, then pulled on his coat and hat, eased on the secondhand boots his brother had given him, and set off quietly down the back stairs.

Time was fast running out, especially if Northampton had learned by now that his spy had been unceremoniously kicked out of St. James's Palace. Ned needed to see Sarah Lovett, who had promised to find out more about the mulberry letters. He needed to see Kate, to convince her that her friendship with Ralegh was bringing her into danger. And he wanted to find out if Pat had learned anything else about Lovett's secret activities at the dockyard.

But first of all he intended to find out why Tobias Jebb had died.

A T THE REQUEST OF THE PRIVY COUNCIL, THE ROYAL College of Physicians had, five years ago, drawn up a list of actions to be taken by the local authorities in the event of an outbreak of the plague. Any new cases of the disease were to be reported within each parish by the locally appointed searchers and watchers, whose job it was also to see that the quarantines were not broken. A grim job indeed when it involved locking in the living with the dying.

Part of the parish searcher's job was to ensure that each reported plague victim had not, in fact, died of old age or murder. This information had then to be passed on to the Clerk of the Parish, who kept the records. Ned Warriner knew this; and so, that night, through the wind and the rain that set the street signs swinging and blew out the householders' lanterns until the blackness was almost all-enveloping, he went asking questions. Finally he walked to Gudrun Lane off West Cheap, limping like Pelham because of his injured foot; and there he knocked at the door of the house belonging to the Clerk of the Parish.

He missed Barnabas loping at his heels. He turned round, almost expecting to see him there, delayed by a rat hole, perhaps, or some interesting item of food; but of course the street was empty. He knocked again. A sudden squall of rain stung his face as he waited.

At last a manservant half-opened the door and looked at Ned with suspicion. Ned said, "My name is Warriner. Tell your master I'm here. I think he will see me."

The manservant closed the door, and for a few moments Ned's confidence seemed misplaced. Then the door was opened once more, this time by the Clerk of the Parish, Thomas Crabtree.

He looked irritated, and nervous. "Well, Warriner? What do you want?"

"I want you to check your registers," said Ned, "for the details of the death of the silversmith Tobias Jebb. Of the plague."

Crabtree had in the past been one of Northampton's paid informers. Ned knew it was a fact he was anxious to keep secret. He blustered, "I cannot. I have company. Perhaps if you come again in the morning—"

Ned said quietly, "Now. Unless you want the parish to know you used to take money from Northampton."

With the utmost reluctance Crabtree beckoned Ned into the hallway and went off, his face dark with annoyance. He came back some moments later carrying a heavy register, which he put on the table and started to look through. He looked up at Ned, his expression a mixture of anger and triumph. "What was his name? Jebb? There's nothing written here."

"But he died of the plague. He and his wife. It was only a few days ago. The house was sealed up and marked."

"I told you. His name is not here."

"I've just visited the searcher who had the house boarded up. He said you gave orders for the burial."

Crabtree colored. "There must have been an error, then, in the paperwork. I didn't realize there had been a plague case."

"Even though you arranged for the bodies to be taken to the plague pit by St. Bartholomew's Hospital? At night?"

"Damn you, *I can't remember* . . ."

Ned turned on his heel and walked away into the darkness. He was sure now that the murder of Tobias Jebb and his wife had been orchestrated by someone in a position of power: someone with the ability to subvert all the officials of the parish.

• • •

THE NEXT DAY, AT NOON, NED WAS AN ANONYMOUS part of the bustle outside the premises of a fashionable seamstress in Cordwainer Street, where horses, shoppers, and hurrying grooms jostled for space in the busy lane. Freshly shaven, clad in a loose cloak and a wide-brimmed hat, Ned called at the side door of the seamstress's large house and was ushered past the ground-floor rooms, full of cutters, assistant seamstresses, and rolls of cambric and satin, to a back stairway, where he was led up to a private room on the first floor.

Sarah Lovett let Ned in, then locked the door. "You got my message, then. I remembered what you said, about reaching you at the Crown." She wore a simple gown of dark blue silk trimmed with cream lace. Her dark hair was bound up in a half-net; its color was still lustrous, but he could see streaks of gray.

She sat on one of the chairs before the fire and beckoned to him to sit facing her. "My husband found out. About our last meeting." Ned sprang to his feet, but she beckoned to him to sit again. "Oh, it's all right—he just thinks that you are one of my many lovers. Ned, I've more news for you, and this was the only place I could think of where we wouldn't be spied on. Men aren't allowed in here, except by invitation. I've sent the groom away for an hour—he's one of my husband's informers, of course. We have perhaps twenty minutes, while my new gown is measured and cut."

"You said you had news for me."

"Indeed. Oh, indeed." She reached into the pocket of her gown and held out a sheet of paper to him—but almost immediately she pulled it back again. "Your hands," she said. "What has happened to your hands?"

She had noticed the shiny red scarring. "It's nothing," he said.

"But you won't be able to play your lute."

"Not for a while. Some would say it's no great loss."

"I would disagree." She smiled ruefully. "Still, it's nothing, indeed, to what my husband would do to you if he knew you were here, with me." She coughed, covering her mouth with a lace-edged handkerchief. He thought that she looked pale and tired. "Here you are." She held out the paper again. "These are the names of the people to whom the mulberries are being delivered. They are sending my husband gold in return."

Ned scanned the list quickly. From his time at court, he recognized a few as the names of country gentlemen, the kind who came to London when Parliament was summoned, though those occasions were rare these days. But there was nothing linking these names, as far as he knew. Nothing to arouse particular suspicion. "Did you get a copy of the letter that was sent with the saplings?"

"Yes," she said. "But I don't understand a word." She held out another piece of paper. He took it and read, *"When the emblem of Morus is strewn throughout the land, then is the time for the rebirth."*

It was what he almost expected to find, yet reading the exact phrase that was in his Auriel letter still stunned him. It was a moment before he could speak.

She was watching him carefully. "Well? Do you understand it?"

He looked up at last. "I wish I did. Have all the mulberry plants been dispatched?"

"I think so. And I've seen the gold coming in, as payment."

"Do you think the Prince knows anything about it?"

"Yes," she said. "That's one of the things I wanted to tell you. Henry must know about the gold. It's locked up by my husband in the Prince's treasury. And the Prince himself signs for it, each time it comes in. So much money, for half-dead plants, sent out in the middle of winter . . ."

Ned said carefully, "Do you think that's all this is? Something done for profit?"

"Why, yes. What else?" She laughed bitterly. "Money is all my husband cares about. And presumably the Prince is pleased enough with the filling of his coffers."

"I wonder how the gardener, Humphreys, feels about the money that's being made through his skills."

She gave a little shiver. "Who knows? He is a strange, strange man. I think he is making his own efforts to find out where those trees are going. I saw him looking once at the records of dispatch, which my husband had left out when he was suddenly called away. He pretended he was searching for my husband, but he made no further efforts to find him, and just hurried off." She shivered again. "Something about him makes me uneasy, though I know I should be grateful to Humphreys. He keeps my son occupied. He makes him feel useful. He's told him he will get better. Poor Nicholas. I hope Stephen Humphreys has not raised my son's hopes that his father will learn to love him."

A sudden shaft of winter sunlight fell on her face, on the outline of her breasts beneath her gown. She looked older by daylight, tired and sad though still beautiful. He felt pity for her; though clearly she felt none for herself.

He said, "Do you think your husband is still involved in corruption at the dockyards?"

"Of course he is. You might as well call it stealing. I told you I'd heard some of the messengers who come to him, with their news about shipbuilding materials that disappear into thin air. Supplies that never quite match the tally sheets. 'Wastage,' they call it. And I found out something else for you. You asked me to see if I could learn anything about someone called Francis Pelham. Well, I've discovered that my husband was responsible for his appointment recently at the Deptford shipyard. I found letters he wrote, recommending Pelham to Mansell."

Ned's heart was beating faster. "You must be careful. If your husband found you going through his papers, if he knew you were telling me these things..."

"I'm hoping," she said softly, drawing nearer, "that you're duly grateful for the risks I'm taking."

"Of course I am. You know I am."

"How grateful?" She was drawing closer to him. Her mood of bitterness had changed; she was smiling, amused. "As grateful as you were last time we were here?"

"Sarah," he said warningly, "you have already told me your husband knows of our last meeting. If he were to guess that you are seeing me again, what would he do?"

"Nothing," she said, "that he hasn't done already. It's like a game between us. To think that I used to dream, before I was married, of love and children..." She laughed again, mocking herself. "Ah, Ned. You should have children, you know. There must be someone that you love, somewhere."

"Once, perhaps," he said. "But it was a long time ago. A mistake."

"You must be all of twenty-five, twenty-six—and you think yourself so learned in love. I'm thirty-four, and my husband has been beating me throughout our marriage. How is that for being old?"

"There must be someone you can go to. Your family, your friends; someone who will help you."

"What's the point? He'd find me. Besides, I told you. I manage to contrive my own kind of amusement. My compensations, if you like..." She lifted his hands and looked again at the burn scars on them. "Your poor hands. I would have tended them for you."

"Sarah, I must go." He withdrew his hands from her grasp and reached behind her for the door, but she barred his way.

"Come to see me at St. James's Palace," she said. "I will find out more for you. If you promise to ruin my husband."

He shook his head. "How can I get inside the palace? Even if I hadn't already been kicked out for being Northampton's spy, it's far too dangerous for you."

She thought quickly. "Come on Christmas Eve. There will be lots of visitors there—actors, and musicians, and mummers. It's the one night of the year when the Prince permits a little festivity, God help us. If you carry your lute, and come in some disguise, you should get in easily amongst all the others."

"I will do my best." He turned to leave again, but she went quickly over to the window and looked out. "You cannot go down there yet. Duncan, the Prince's Master of Horse, is out there, waiting for his wife. She had a fitting at the same time as me. She might be a while yet."

Ned swore softly. Duncan would recognize him. "There must be a back way," he said, "in a place like this."

"Not from this part of the house. There is only one way out. Past Duncan and his men."

Ned moved back into the room, away from her. "You should have told me this."

She shrugged, a little smile on her face.

"I cannot stay here," he said flatly. "I have things to do. I'll have to take a chance on Duncan and the others recognizing me."

She stood in front of the door. "If you try to get past me, I shall scream. I shall call Duncan up and tell him that you assaulted me."

His pity for her evaporated. She was pulling away her headdress, so that her hair fell down, and she began to unbutton the bodice of her dress. Ned said, his face still set, "If you force me, you might not enjoy this."

"Oh, I will," she said softly, moving toward him.

27.

The head of the Crowe that token call wee,
And some men call it the Crowes bill;
Some call it the ashes of the Hermes tree,
And thus they name it after their will.

GEORGE RIPLEY (D.C. 1490)
"BOOK OF THE TWELVE GATES"

BY THE TIME NED LEFT THE HOUSE OF THE SEAM-
stress, there was no sign of Duncan or his attendants. He
wondered if Duncan had really been there, or if Sarah Lovett
had been lying. He stepped out into the rain and wind and
breathed deeply.

Putrefaction, mortification. Blackness indeed.

He could still smell the perfume of Sarah Lovett in his nostrils; could hear the rustle of silk in his ears as she moved beneath him. As he had warned her, he had been angry and had
hurt her in taking her; but she made no protest. If anything she
encouraged him. He had wondered if this was how the beatings had started, with her husband.

Yet the things she'd told him. The Prince. *The time for the
rebirth*...

He heard the din from Matthew's house before he got
there. In spite of the rain, his brother was holding a party

that was spilling out onto the street. Some whores from the Crown had been invited, and they'd brought friends, so the shrill chatter of the women competed with the sounds of clashing tankards, and of furniture falling over, because Tew and Davey were fighting over some insult Davey had hurled at Tew's culinary efforts, and the cook had for once heard.

If Matthew was facing ruin, he and his companions were making the best of it.

Ned pushed into the melee, asking for Luke, because he had more questions for the doctor.

"He's out on the town," Davey called. "Went off hours ago with some friends. He could be at the Three Grapes, or the Black Bull. Are you joining us?"

"Perhaps later."

Ned went out again, wondering which tavern to try first; whether it was worth trying any, if Luke had been drinking for hours. Then he saw Robin, running toward him from the bakehouse. The boy's thin face was alight with excitement.

"Ned," Robin said. "You must come and look. It's the crucible."

Ned, weary, said, "Is it really necessary? Right at this moment?"

"Yes," said Robin. His voice betrayed his eagerness. "Please. Now."

So Ned followed Robin down the lane to the bakehouse, where Robin unlocked the door and went straight to the oven. The glow of the coals lit up the boy's eager face as he crouched over his crucible, so that he looked every inch the magician's imp with his soot-stained face, his huge dark eyes, and the healing stumps where his ears used to be. The satanic stink of sulfurous chemicals filled the air.

Robin turned to Ned, breathless with excitement. "Yesterday the mixture was in danger of drying out, so I remembered what your letter said. I've been making notes from it, every time you showed it to me. So I knew to add some actuated mercury." He held out a flask.

"Actuated mercury? I don't even know what it is. Or how to get it."

"I knew!" Robin was hopping up and down. "I got it from Dr. Luke. See?"

He uncorked the phial and held it out. Ned sniffed and backed away quickly. "That's piss."

"That's right! But not just anyone's—it had to belong to someone born under the sign of Aries."

"Of course."

"I knew Dr. Luke would have some," went on Robin, undeterred by Ned's expression. "He examines it, to detect people's illnesses."

"Whose is it?" asked Ned suspiciously.

"I don't know." Robin shrugged. "But as long as his patient's birth sign was Aries, it doesn't matter! I added it, and warmed the crucible again, and then I began to work on the perfect putrefaction of the seed, like in your letter—Dr. Dee's letter!" He closed his eyes and quoted, *"Next cast the native birds of righteousness into a prison with the alien beast—cinis et lixivium..."*

Ned drew his letter out and gazed first at it, then at Robin. "You know it all by heart."

"Oh, yes. Well, almost every word. *Cinis et lixivium*—that's ashes and liquor. And then I added antimony..."

Ned was still poring over his letter. "Yes, I see it. *Scrupulous antimony*. What's that?"

"I wasn't sure, but I know that *scrupulus* means a quarter ounce, so that's the quantity I added. Of antimony, which I got from an apothecary. And look!"

He left Ned holding his letter and picked up the crucible. Its base was filled with a black, tar-like substance. "You have," Robin announced reverently, "attained the Crow."

Ned thrust one hand through his hair. "Right. And what precisely do I do with it?"

"You start work on the next stage, which is to attain the Cauda Pavonis. The Peacock's Tail. Let me just see the letter again..."

Ned handed it to him. Robin ran his finger down it eagerly. *"A fruitful crow will be generated,"* he read aloud, *"base at first, but which little by little stretching out his wings will begin to fly with his precious seeds..."*

Robin looked up from the letter. "We'll need more glass tubing. And a bath, to keep the crucible warm in. And more coals, for the athanor. I might have to ask Dr. Luke for some more actuated mercury."

Ned had taken the letter back from him. "There's a bit more here about your actuated mercury. 'Actuated mercury must be added in the fashion of *navicularius*.' What does *navicularius* mean in alchemy?"

Robin hung his head. "I don't exactly know. But it seems to have worked anyway."

"I know that *navicularius* is Latin for shipmaster. Robin, I've asked you this before. But do ships, or dockyards, have anything at all to do with alchemy?"

"Not as far as I know," said Robin, frowning. "I don't know anything about ships. I've only been down to the wharves once. And then I was nearly killed."

Ned drew a deep breath and leaned back, watching him. "For a mere prentice lad, you've led an eventful life. What happened?"

"It was when I had to go on an errand for Master Tobias. I saw something I shouldn't have done, down by Billingsgate. I'd got lost, but afterwards I realized where I was, because I recognized the church of All Hallows. There was a horse wagon coming up from the river, in a hurry, but the men with it had to stop the horses because the cover was slipping off the wagon. And I saw the muzzles of cannon poking out, gleaming new. It was late in the evening, and the horses' hooves were muffled. They were stealing them from the dockyard, I'm quite sure."

Ned had gone still. "Did they see you?"

"Yes. They covered the cannon up quickly and dragged me out from where I was hiding. I thought they would kill me. One of them questioned me. He seemed to be in charge. The others were rough men, but he was different. He spoke, not like a thief but like a gentleman. He wore a ruby ring on the little finger of his right hand. The ruby reminded me of blood. He told me to go."

A ruby ring, like the one worn by John Lovett. *Navicularius*—the shipmaster. Stolen ammunition. Not pistols this time, but cannon . . .

Ned said to Robin, "Go back to Matthew's. Join the party. You've had enough of all this for one night."

"But—"

"Go."

When he'd gone, Ned locked the door, then turned and gazed at the crucible. Its contents glowed blackly, like oil. A shaft of moonlight from the window suddenly fell on it, and he thought, just for a moment, that he saw colors, deep at its heart.

He looked at his letter again.

"Increase the fire till the glorious rainbow of the East appears, which is the Cauda Pavonis..."

He went impulsively to the oven and put in more coals. Then he sat on the stone bench nearest to the crucible and gazed into it once more, watching the shifting, glutinous blackness in the moonlight. No colors there. But he thought, for a moment, that he saw the face of old Albertus gazing back at him; then realized it was his own reflection.

He pulled himself away and blew out the candles. He started to call Barnabas's name, and pulled himself up, remembering.

He felt he was sinking deeper into blackness with every step.

Nigredo.

AFTER LEAVING NED, ROBIN OBEDIENTLY SCURRIED back along Rose Alley to the back stairs of Matthew's noisy house, where he started to climb to the small room he shared with Pentinck, on the floor below Ned's. It was dark there. He wished he'd thought to bring a candle, and he jumped when a woman came out of a doorway and exclaimed, "Jesus, Robin. You gave me a shock. Where are you hurrying off to?"

It was Alice. Robin ground to a halt and backed up against the wall, his heart thudding. "To my room," he stammered.

He thought that Alice was beautiful. Dangerous, but beautiful. He knew that she was Matthew's mistress. He'd heard whispered talk among the others—when they were quite sure Matthew couldn't hear—about the other men she'd been friendly with from time to time. About the things she did with them. Alice, with her beautiful golden hair, and her ripe breasts, which he could see rising and falling. And her full lips, which she was moistening with her tongue...

"So early? I thought you'd be enjoying yourself at the party. Don't you like company?"

"Yes. Yes!" he stammered. "But I have things to do." From down below came the roar of Matthew's friends, the soaring of busy fiddles, and Matthew's bellowing laugh.

Her hand fastened round his wrist. "Nothing so important that you can't come and talk to me first," she said. "I'm lonely, Robin. Where's Ned?"

He looked around desperately. "He's busy somewhere."

"I thought he might be. No doubt he's still in that bake-house where the two of you spend so much time. And I'm longing to hear about it all. But I won't keep you long." She drew one finger gently along his soot-stained cheekbone. "Unless you want me to."

THERE WAS, TO THE NORTH OF THE WOOL WHARF AND the west of the Tower, a low tavern known as the Galleon, which was frequented by mariners temporarily ashore, and in particular favored by privateers; men who in the days of Elizabeth had sailed forth against Spain to rob her ships of gold. Now England was at peace with Spain, but many of her mariners were not.

No Elizabethan sea captain was as well set up as the pirate Easton, with his eleven ships, or Captain Bard with his twenty-two, all fully armed and crewed, and ready to run to the safe harbors of Bantry Bay if the forces of law and order should be after them; a circumstance unlikely indeed, because those who should have upheld maritime law turned a blind eye to the activities of the privateers, in return for a fat slice of their profits.

This quarter to the north of the Wool Wharf was the London lair of the pirates. This was where covered carts came up laden from the river at midnight, and woe betide anyone who interfered, or tried to spy on them—as Robin Green, who had escaped lightly because of his youth and obvious ignorance, knew to his cost. For the carts that came up here brought goods that were not for the eyes of the customs men, but were to be stowed in deep cellars, and behind locked doors; they were sometimes goods stolen from the Spanish, but more often from others nearer home.

Tonight in the Galleon, surrounded by his cronies, was an old sailor just returned to London, who had been known, in his younger days before age turned his jet-black hair and beard a faded gray, as the Black Bird. His real name was Alvaric Johnson, and he often told the story of how he drank the famous golden wine, the finest liquor in Spain, with Ralegh after the taking of Cadiz. He was more than bitter against those who had locked old Ralegh away. He continued the fight against Spain in his own way, as a privateer.

Tonight, knowing in advance of his return, a man of some influence had sought him out. Johnson was used to that; he was familiar with money changing hands; with figures in authority coming to him by night, to benefit in secret from his ships' acquisitions. And Johnson had met this particular man before. He was well dressed, with a fine green velvet doublet showing beneath his plain cloak, and he spoke in a soft, well-educated voice. He was here to ascertain if Johnson could provide him with what he needed, and had evidently decided that he could.

"There is a cellar," this man told Johnson, "in an empty house at Crab Lane, near to the Tower. It has been made freshly secure. My men will show it to you, and give you the keys. Will you be able to convey the goods in question there on the night before the Christmas feast?"

Johnson knew that the goods in question were armaments, intended for the naval dockyard. There was bribery and corruption everywhere; that was not his problem.

The man was waiting for Johnson's reply. Johnson kept him waiting for a few moments, then said, "It can be done. Just as my men have done everything else you've asked. As long as you're sure there won't be any trouble. I'm too damned old for hanging."

"Everything," said the man quietly, "has been arranged."

They all drank to one another's health with more wine which the cloaked man paid for; until the candles burned low. And then the man went out alone, into the bone-biting cold, and Johnson saw that he was smiling.

NED HAD TRACKED DOWN LUKE IN THE BLACK BULL, a low inn at the corner of Faitour Lane. He was pitifully drunk. Of his companions there was no sign.

Ned hauled him outside into the night. Luke was promptly sick, retching into the gutter. Ned took him to the pump in the nearby stable yard and pushed his head under it while he worked the handle and the icy water came gushing out. Then he walked him to and fro, to and fro, until the old doctor was able to talk sense again.

"Must—be—ill," Luke was muttering as the water dripped down his wispy white locks. "My head . . ."

"Too much bad ale. And worse friends," Ned replied curtly.

He took him back to the Crown, sat him before the roaring fire, and ordered some food for him. When Luke had eaten a little of the bread and cheese, Ned leaned toward him and said, "Luke. If you wanted to kill someone without leaving a trace, what would you use?"

Luke frowned and rubbed his forehead. "Without leaving a trace? It would have to be poison, of course. Slow poison. Arsenic is the best. Not too much; a full dose would cause convulsions, discoloration of the face, be too obvious. Far cleverer to use small doses regularly, over several months. No one would ever know."

Ned said decisively, "That wouldn't do. I was thinking of something that was immediate but unidentifiable. What if, say, instead of swallowing something, you were forced to breathe in some kind of poison? Could that be fatal?"

"Well, now." Luke scratched his head again, his rheumy blue eyes abstracted. He gazed longingly at Ned's ale; Ned ordered him a mug of the Crown's weakest brew, warmed and spiced. Luke drank deeply, then leaned back, closing his eyes.

"Poison," Ned reminded him. "Luke, this is really important."

Luke nodded. "Let me see. Lead fumes can kill. But that can take months. The most toxic vapor of all comes from the roasting of sulfide ores. If a man were forced to breathe in the fumes, why, then, his lungs would collapse, and his heart would stop. Almost immediately. No one can survive the inhalation of pure mercury."

"I thought you said sulfide ores."

"I did. If heated, you see, the ores give off mercury vapor."

Mercury. Prince Henry's ruling planet. The planet that ruled the little finger, and the mulberry tree...

"And it wouldn't leave any trace?"

"None that was visible, no." Luke was perspiring visibly. Ned pushed the loaf of bread toward him. "Eat some of this and you'll feel better. And have a little more ale; at least it's a decent brew, won't poison you like the stuff you were downing at that last place. Just one more question, Luke, and then I'll let you go home to your bed. You didn't happen to find out any further medical reason, did you, for people to have their fingers amputated, either before or after death?"

Luke grimaced as he chewed on the dry bread. "Fingers? No. I remember you asking me. Little fingers...Unless it had something to do with some strange ritual. Some talisman, perhaps. Though after you last asked me, I remember thinking how it reminded me of a little trick the Spaniards used to get up to with their prisoners. Didn't you hear talk of it when you fought in the Low Countries? They used to saw off their prisoners' fingers one at a time, to make them talk. I saw a few men out there with the telltale stumps. They were the lucky ones who survived."

"You served out there for a while, didn't you?"

"Yes. I was a doctor with the English forces for a couple of years, before the old Queen died. Then I came home again. I'd seen enough. The Spaniards were brutes. If the finger trick didn't work—and you'd be surprised how much agony the amputating of one finger can put a man through—they used to half-strangle their prisoners to get what they wanted out of them. Those who survived bore the scars for life."

"What sort of scars?"

"What you'd expect from a rope. A raised, ugly weal—red

at first, fading to white with time, but it never goes." Luke reached for more ale, but Ned put his hand over his to stop him.

"In a moment. Listen. You didn't, did you, come across someone on the English side called Stephen Humphreys? He was tortured in that very way by the Spaniards."

Luke pondered a little, shook his head. "Humphreys? No. I don't remember the name. But I was only there till 1602, and the war went on till 1604, when King James made his peace with the damned Spaniards and abandoned our Dutch allies to their fate. If you really want to track down the doings of your Humphreys, I know of some old soldiers who once served there. They are regulars at the tavern at the end of Old Dean's Lane: the Cock. Do you know it?"

"No," said Ned, "but I'll find it. I'll take you back home now, Luke. You'll feel better for a good night's sleep."

Luke got stiffly to his feet. "So would you, from the looks of you," he answered.

28.

Full many great calamities and rare
This feeble brest endured hath, but none
Equall to this.

EDMUND SPENSER (C.1552–1599)
THE FAERIE QUEENE, BOOK 4: CANTO 7, V.14

THE NEXT MORNING KATE PELHAM STOOD IN HER
garden, where a breeze from the river rustled amongst the
winter-bare plants: the empty husks of poppy and columbine,
the withered leaves of gilliflowers and cranesbill. She thought
of Ralegh, tramping round his Tower prison, dreaming of far-
off seas, far-off places. She pulled out from her pocket the
sealed letter with which Ralegh had entrusted her, and turned
it in her hands.

"I want to tell him that the golden wine is still there for the
drinking," Ralegh had told her.

It was eight o'clock. Ralegh had said that she was to deliver the letter to the chandler's shop at the corner of Bearward Lane today. Four days before Christmas.

Sebastian was in the care of his nurse. Pelham was preparing to go to his new place of work; he would be leaving soon.

She went to the servants' room to find her maid, and told her that shortly they would be going to the city, by boat.

"To the Tower again, mistress?"

"Almost as far, Bess. To the Wool Wharf."

Then she went to her room to put on her cloak and pattens, to protect her shoes against the mud; and it was there that her husband found her. His face was pale with anger.

She said, "I thought you had gone."

"Is this what you do, the minute I depart? You go out and leave your son alone?"

"I left him with his nurse," she said.

"I have just been to his room. He is ill. He can scarcely breathe. How can you leave him?"

She ran to her son and found him struggling for breath. Pelham had already sent for the doctor, who came and said there was little he could do, for one so young; he recommended camphor, but the stronger medicines, he said, were not suitable for a child not yet two years old. They would have to wait for the attack to pass. He would return later. Sebastian tried to inhale a camphor vapor, which his nurse prepared at the doctor's instruction, but Sebastian was upset and frightened, which made his breathing worse, and he was crying for his mother. Kate held him close, as white-faced as Pelham had been, silently accepting her husband's final rebukes as he left at last for work.

Sebastian's crying lessened as she cradled him. His breathing began to ease. Ralegh's letter lay heavy in her pocket.

She stayed with her son and waited for the doctor's return. Sometimes Sebastian slept; sometimes he awoke and cried fitfully. The hours passed. By the time the doctor arrived in the late afternoon, Sebastian's breathing had eased, but the skies were darkening, and the servants were lighting the candles.

Leaving Sebastian's nurse in charge, she called Bess and told the housekeeper, Pelham's spy, that she needed to collect some medicine for Sebastian. Then, as night closed in, she and her maid took a boat downriver to the Wool Wharf. As they alighted, Kate pulled her cloak round herself instinctively.

Ralegh had warned her that this neighborhood came alive

after dark. Men were gathering on lamplit corners, watching to see what was happening, exchanging news. The taverns were beginning to fill up.

The area, being so near to the river and the docks, had a maritime air. Many of the men wore bright if ragged clothes, and jewels or gold hoops in their ears. She was aware of attracting attention in her well-made garments. She felt vulnerable, even with Bess close at her side.

She was almost at the place where Ralegh had told her that the chandler's shop should be, halfway along Petty Wales. The stalls and shops down this street were still busy, especially those of the food vendors; they would normally be open for trade late into the evening; but as she walked onward, she saw to her dismay that the chandler's shop was already shuttered and dark.

She turned to tell Bess they must hurry back to the wharf. They would have to come again tomorrow. But just then a man stepped out of the shadows of a side alley, and then another man also, barring her way. She guessed at first they were out to rob her, and yet they were soberly dressed, and spoke well, not like the other men who were around this place.

The first one folded his arms, and said, "This is a mighty strange place, mistress, for a lady like you."

"I had some business here," she answered defiantly. "At the chandler's shop."

"Well, well. Out shopping, are we? No manservant with you. And a maid who's just vanished into the shadows. An unusual outing, wouldn't you say, for a lady of your quality?"

The men were moving in on her. The street seemed to have emptied.

The second man said, "Master Cobb the chandler is known to be friendly with pirates, and, often enough, is up to no good. What was your real reason for visiting him?"

She held her head up high. "As I said. It was a matter of business. My father was a seafarer. He had some sextants and charts that I was thinking of selling. I thought Master Cobb might be able to dispose of them for me—"

"We think," said the first man softly, "that you are lying.

We think that you have a letter for Master Cobb. You had better come with us, Mistress Kate Pelham."

THE COCK TAVERN, AT THE CORNER OF OLD DEAN'S Lane and the Shambles, was a place unused to strangers, and Ned, on his arrival there, was watched with hostility at first by the tavern's regulars. But as he reached for his ale someone noticed the fresh scarring on his hands, and a few more questions led to the other drinkers discovering that he had been a mercenary in the Low Countries for two years. By the time he'd finished two pints of the Cock's powerful brew, they had accepted him as one of themselves. As Luke had informed him last night, this was a gathering place for old soldiers, and some of the men were survivors of the Ostend siege.

Ned knew that it had taken Spinola three years to reduce the great coastal stronghold of Ostend to rubble before the Dutch and their English allies were finally defeated by the peace treaty.

"I heard," Ned said, "that some of the English soldiers were captured and tortured by the Spaniards as they attempted to get help for the town. In the last months of the war."

"That's right," said one man. "They'd gone out at night, for food and supplies. The townsfolk were starving. The supply ships hadn't been able to get through for weeks. I saw those brave soldiers set off under cover of darkness. But they never came back. The damned Spaniards surrounded them and took them into their camp. There they were tortured, half-strangled, and burned at the stake. And all the while our King and his councillors here in London, fat and comfortable in their palaces, were making peace with the King of Spain. They died, those soldiers. All of them."

Someone else started talking about the warfare round Sluys. Ned summoned more ale and realized he was being watched by a crippled old soldier at a nearby table, who was beckoning him over. The man's breath was foul with tobacco smoke as he drew Ned close and whispered, "It's not true.

What he said, about Ostend. Not everyone on that rescue mission died. One of them who escaped was the man who bloody well betrayed us all."

"Betrayed you all?" Ned turned to him slowly. "How do you know? Were you there with them?"

"Yes. I went out on that sortie. The traitor was an Englishman. And he'd slipped word to the Spaniards in advance that we were going to leave Ostend that night to try to get help from Prince Maurice at Sluys. This Englishman, damn him, must have been a secret Catholic; probably in the pay of Spain all the time . . ." He spat into the rushes that were strewn across the floor.

"If he was working for the Spaniards," said Ned, "why did they torture him?"

"They had to make it look good, didn't they, Spinola's men? And I think that in their own way they despised the bastard, for betraying his comrades. So he was half-garotted, like the rest of us, while the Spaniards questioned us about Dutch plans and supplies." He reached for his beaker of ale, which Ned had had refilled for him. "Halfway through the questioning, this traitor, who was senseless by then, was taken outside. Our Spanish guards told us he'd betrayed us. Said he was an agent of theirs. They laughed at us for being stupid enough to include him in our plans. They said he was dead—they didn't like traitors either, they said—but I know he was alive, damn him. I know he survived it all, because I met him again."

Ned was breathing hard. "Where?"

"It was some months later, after the peace, at Sluys. I was waiting for a ship back to England. It was dirty weather, no ships could get into harbor. But I saw him there, I recognized him, with the scar livid around his neck. And he saw me. God damn him, we knew each other well enough. He vanished into the crowd as soon as our eyes met, and it was like two cursed souls meeting in hell."

Ned said quietly, "Did you know this man's name?"

"The Spaniards," said the old man with contempt, "called him Stefano."

Ned was silent a moment. Then he said, "There were

supposed to be no survivors. You have not told me how you escaped."

The old soldier looked round quickly. "Don't let the others know. I'm only telling you all this because I think you're after Stefano. I slew a fellow soldier to get away. A young Dutchman. After the first day of torture, they chained us in pairs for the night. I had a knife still hidden in my clothes. I killed the young lad I was chained to, and severed his hand." He looked at Ned challengingly, as if daring him to express surprise and horror.

Ned said, "I was a soldier once. I know what war is like."

The man nodded, assessing him. "So I got away," he said. "The guards didn't expect anyone even to try to escape. The rest of them were burned alive. At least I spared the young Dutchman that." He suddenly gripped Ned's arm. "Is he still alive, that Stefano? Because if he is, find him for me and I'll kill him myself."

Ned bought the man more ale, and left the tavern soon afterwards. The night had turned cold and frosty. He stood a moment, gazing up at the stars.

Could Stefano be Stephen Humphreys? And was he still working for Spain?

THE NEXT MORNING, IN THE OPEN DOORWAY OF A tall house in Woodruff Lane stood a French merchant by the name of Bertholt Hugrance, who imported fine silk cloth from the continent. A well-dressed, handsome man of middle age, he was bidding farewell to a group of friends as one by one they turned and walked quickly up the street, past the derelict house of the Friars of the Cross. As the last one departed Master Hugrance was about to close his door with relief against the chilly air, when someone came forward from the street and said, "Master Hugrance. May I speak with you?"

Hugrance turned, and a shadow crossed his face, though his voice was calm. "Ned Warriner. It's been a long time. Should I be afraid to see you here?"

"I am not working as a spy for anyone. I would guess you have been celebrating mass privately in there, with your friends, one of whom was no doubt a clandestine priest, but that is not why I have come."

Master Hugrance gazed at him a moment longer, then opened the door and led him into a small parlor. "There were rumors, Ned. When you left the country two years ago, people said that you knew more than a little about old Evan Ashworth's escape from his guards on his way to the Tower." Hugrance closed the parlor door and looked at him. "I hear Ashworth escaped to the continent, and is still playing his lute splendidly at the mansion of a wealthy banker in Turin. You were good to him, always. And to me. You warned me on at least two occasions when Francis Pelham was about to descend on my home."

"I used to warn all the Catholics I knew when Pelham was about to descend on them. It's a habit that's hard to break."

"You're not here for that reason now?"

"No. Oh, no. I'm here this time to ask you a favor." Ned sat down in the chair his host indicated, and took the proffered glass of sweet marsala wine. "Master Hugrance, I need to know more about a man called Stephen Humphreys, who works as a gardener at St. James's Palace. I need to know if he has Catholic sympathies."

Master Hugrance frowned. "Are you asking me to betray a fellow Catholic?"

"This man, if what I've heard is true, betrayed many English soldiers and led them to a cruel death by torture at the siege of Ostend. I think you would find such an act hard to condone in any man, whatever his religion. Will you help me? As I've helped you in the past?"

"On one condition," said Master Hugrance, a little wearily. "If you should find out that there's more to this than meets the eye, more than you are telling me—and that any inquiries of mine are liable to get me incriminated—will you give me due warning, so that I can escape to France?"

Ned stood up. "If that's the case, then I'll be coming with you," he said.

He went outside and stood on Woodruff Lane, in the cold,

clear air. And then he saw a familiar tall, dark-haired figure loping toward him.

"Pat," he said. "Any news? Matthew misses you."

"And I miss him," said the big Irishman. "But not the whore who shares his bed. Ned, there's something you ought to know."

Ned tensed. "News from the dockyard?"

Pat shook his head. "No. Not guns. Not ships. Something else. I heard it on the streets this morning. Francis Pelham's wife has been arrested and taken to the Wood Street Counter."

Ned put his hand to his forehead. He said, slowly, "I wish you could have brought me better news. With what is she charged?"

"There are no charges yet. But they say she was going to visit a chandler called Cobb, down by the Wool Wharf. To be sure, everyone knows Cobb's got his fingers deep in the business of stolen goods from the shipyards. The word is that she had something to deliver to him, a message, but she wouldn't say who had given it to her. So they took her in for questioning."

Just for a moment Ned felt such blinding rage that he could scarcely think. Kate, being used as a messenger. For whom? Had Pelham got her involved in this?

He looked round, and wondered how long it would take him to get to Wood Street.

Pat said, "It's no good going there this minute, Ned. She is being questioned by the magistrates' men. It could take hours, they say."

Ned breathed, "Very well. Then there are other places I must visit."

29.

What freezings have I felt, what dark days seen!
What old December's bareness everywhere!

WILLIAM SHAKESPEARE (1564–1616)
SONNET 97

FRANCIS PELHAM WAS PACING THE COURTYARD OF
the Tower of London, where the low winter sun crept over
the battlements, and the ravens wheeled croaking overhead.
He walked like one of the King's caged lions in the dungeon
below, because his wife had been disgraced on account of her
visits to this place. Her visits to see the traitor Ralegh.

They had come last night to tell him, and this morning he
was preparing himself to visit her, in prison. To cross the grim
portals of the Counter in Wood Street, to pass by the turnkeys
and gaolers who knew him so well. First, though, he had business here.

He turned as he heard his name called. It was Sir Walter
Ralegh, coming haltingly toward him, leaning on his stick.
Pelham would still have recognized him as the brave sea cap-
tain who had been one of the commanders of the Azores ex-

pedition twelve years ago, but life had dealt harshly with both of them.

Ralegh drew near. "Pelham," he said. "They told me you were here. I must explain, about your wife—"

Pelham braced his shoulders. "Sir Walter," he cut in. "I must tell you that on my marriage to Katherine Revill I forbade any further contact between herself and you. Yet I find that she has disobeyed me, and with such consequences . . ." He rubbed his clenched fist to his temple. "Sir, you must tell them that her visits to you were made in all innocence, in her ignorance, even; you will, I am sure, wish to see that she is freed immediately. You are not entirely without friends of influence—"

"Stop," Ralegh was saying. "Stop, Pelham. Aren't you aware that they have arrested her because of the letter?"

Pelham stepped back. "What letter?"

Ralegh made a despairing gesture. "I was foolish. I asked her to deliver a message to an old friend. She was intercepted with it. And they will be questioning her, just as they have questioned me. They are always trying to link me to plots . . ."

Pelham was incredulous. "A plot? You say there is a plot, and my wife is involved?"

"If there is one," said Ralegh heavily, "it is not of my making, and your wife knows nothing of it. Nothing at all. But she was carrying my letter."

Pelham was already turning and striding off, calling to the guard to let him out. He was thinking, Damn her, damn her, she will quite ruin me; isn't it enough that her father's enterprise has already almost done so?

He felt like disowning her, as he'd known upright men to disown their wives after learning they were secret Catholics, secret priest-lovers.

HE HAD BEEN TOLD THAT AT THE WOOD STREET Counter they were holding Kate in the upper rooms known as the Master's Side, a place Pelham knew well, for it was there where Catholics were detained for questioning, if they were wealthy enough to avoid the horrors of the grim cells below. The shame of his wife being there all but over-whelmed him. There would be questions to answer, papers to sign, money to be paid to the magistrates, if her release was imminent.

But first he went from the Tower to his office at the Dept-ford dockyard, to check on the paperwork that awaited him, and to tell his colleagues that he would be absent for an hour or two longer. He guessed that the other clerks would be glad to see him gone, for his questions and his dogged searches through the records for the missing stores had endeared him to no one. Though if they thought he would not do his duty, then they did not know Francis Pelham.

So he called in at the dockyard office, where candles burned against the midwinter gloom. Outside, it was starting to rain. He told the junior clerks that he would be back shortly, and also told them which registers he would require for inves-tigation on his return. They greeted this news with barely con-cealed surliness, but he repeated his instructions and made them acknowledge them, to make sure they had no excuses for failing to comply. Then he went out to the wharf, where carts rumbled by laden with timbers and canvas sheeting; where sailors shouted and gulls cried high over the choppy waters of the Thames. The rain was coming down heavily now, so he fastened his cloak and pulled down his hat, and was turning his thoughts with the utmost grimness to the Wood Street Counter, and his wife there, when he saw Ned Warriner com-ing toward him.

Pelham wanted to lash out at him. But Warriner, whose face was pale and unshaven, and who looked as if he had not slept for days, came toward him with his hands raised in ap-peasement and said, as the rain lashed down, "Pelham. I have come about your wife. You must help her. You must get her out of that place."

Pelham's bitter laughter filled the air. "Oh, this is rich. You. You traitor, Northampton's spy—you come to tell me that my wife's arrest is *my fault*? I am on my way to the prison now. I will do for her what I can, though I am not sure what. Get out of my way."

But Ned, still pale, wiped the rain from his face with the

back of his hand and stood his ground. "You know what you can do. You must tell the authorities that your wife has been an unwitting accomplice, in the corruption that surrounds this place. You must explain her innocence, inform them how she has been used..."

Pelham stared at him. "Listen to me, Warriner. Your ignorance—your *arrogance*—astounds me as much as ever. You clearly have no idea that my wife has been arrested because she's been carrying secret letters for that traitor in the Tower."

"She's been carrying letters for *Ralegh*?"

"That's right. You should make sure of your facts, Warriner."

Ned said quickly, "She probably did it in all innocence. As an act of friendship. She has a great regard for Ralegh—he was her father's friend."

Pelham was gazing at him stonily. "Do you mind telling me what business this is of yours?"

"She was my companion once. In childhood. My father was once her father's friend. I cannot believe she is guilty of any wrongdoing."

"Your father," said Pelham, "was a crook who killed himself out of shame at what he had become. As for my wife's wrongdoing, she has persistently lied to me about her visits to Ralegh, which I expressly forbade on our marriage. Why should she not have deceived me in other ways?"

"Just tell me one thing. Are you going to help her?"

"Why? When she has brought me nothing but disgrace and trouble?"

Ned said quietly, "If you will not help her, then I will."

He turned and walked off into the pouring rain, leaving Pelham standing, staring after him.

Childhood companions?

IT WAS DARK BY THE TIME PELHAM, DRENCHED FROM the rain, finally reached the prison in Wood Street. Kate was in a private room with a fire and candles, but the walls were bare stone, and a chill draught seeped through the high window.

She was seated, but stood up when she heard him come in,

and faced him in silence. He began to question her about the letter Ralegh had given her. At first she tried to say that she had written the letter herself, and it was not from Ralegh at all. But Pelham replied that Ralegh himself had told him that he had given it to her. She said nothing more after that, not even when Pelham rebuked her bitterly for visiting Ralegh against his express command. "At such a time," he said. "For all this to happen at such a time. This was my chance to prove myself, and now I will be a laughingstock. My wife, consorting with a convicted traitor..."

When he had finished, she replied in a low voice, "Ralegh was a good friend to my father. It was my duty to visit him."

"Your duty, madam," he said, "is to me. And you would have done better to remember it."

They argued; he hit her. She almost fell, and sat in the chair again with her back to him, holding her cheek. In the distance they heard a prisoner's cry of distress, echoing through the vaulted stone passageways; then there was silence. He stood there, breathing hard. He said, "Has Warriner been here yet?"

She turned to him quickly then, and he saw that her eyes were wide with apprehension. "No," she said. "Why should he visit me?"

"That is my question precisely. What is Warriner to you?"

She shook her head and said nothing.

"What is Warriner to you?" he repeated. "Is he your lover? Answer me."

She met his gaze staunchly. "I have hardly spoken with him since he returned from the war."

"Did you know he was Northampton's spy? Did you know he was Northampton's *lover*?"

"I think there are few of us who have no secrets to hide, from our youth."

"I mean *now*," he said, banging his clenched fist into his palm. "Since his return, he has become the old man's whore again; didn't you realize the whole court knew it, and laughed about it?"

He saw the color drain so rapidly from her face that he thought she might faint. But she stood up and said, "Leave me. If you have any decency left in you at all, just leave me."

He turned and left the room.

He signed papers to acknowledge responsibility for her. He paid money for her accommodation and her food, there in the Master's Side, and said that he would send her maid to stay with her, for as long as her imprisonment lasted. Kate would be there, he understood, for at least another night. Tomorrow she would be brought before the magistrates again, and a decision would be made as to whether or not charges would be laid.

Pelham could not bring himself to ask what the charges would be.

He went home through the dark wet night to arrange for Kate's maid Bess to go to her mistress with clothes and other necessities. He hugged Sebastian, who wanted to know when his mother was coming home. He helped his little son to set up his toy soldiers around his bed. "Can I be a soldier soon?" Sebastian asked.

"You will," Pelham assured him, holding him tight, "someday be as good a soldier as the greatest of the King's knights."

Then Pelham was called down to the hallway, because he had a visitor, Duprais the moneylender. Pelham was surprised, and displeased, that the man should pay this intrusive visit to his home; but Duprais raised his hand to stay his protests, and told him he had come to say that sadly a large sum of money was now overdue. Pelham took Duprais to his study and locked the door. "Please explain," Pelham said. And Duprais told him that he must foreclose unless two hundred pounds was received in the next three days.

"Three days? But we agreed. I told you that I have a new post at the dockyard, with regular pay; we decided that I would pay off this debt, stage by stage."

"Did we? I thought, sir, that the debt was overdue already."

Pelham said, "But I have no money."

"Three days," said Duprais softly. "It is a business necessity, I fear."

SINCE THE THIRTEENTH CENTURY THE TOWER OF London had contained a menagerie for the amusement of the monarch and his friends. King James was particularly fascinated by the lions, whose quarters were situated just west of the middle tower. They had a yard paved with Purbeck stone, and they were let out of their dens, to exercise in this yard, through wooden doors which could be raised by their keepers with ropes and pulleys.

In the summer of that year, the lioness had whelped, and the progress of her cubs had been a source of fascination for the King. He was there tonight, the evening of the twenty-third December, with his retinue of noblemen and courtiers; discussing with William Waad, the lieutenant of the Tower, the welfare of these young lions during the cold weather.

The Earl of Northampton was in the King's party, watching, with the others, as the lioness groomed the young ones, while the male lion prowled restlessly, turning his amber eyes on the onlookers. The smell of the animals' pelts, damp from the rain, and of their ordure, was overpowering; Northampton, dressed in a fur-lined overgown of black bombazine against the cold and the rain, held a scented pomander to his nose, and turned with relief to follow the King as he eventually announced his departure for the state barge that waited by the Tower steps to take him and his entourage back to Whitehall.

Servants held torches high, to light their way, but Northampton did not see the figure that came out of the darkness, until he was almost at his side.

"My lord..."

An insistent, a familiar voice. Northampton turned, frowning. "Warriner. I have been waiting to hear from you."

Warriner looked tired and ragged. Out of place. Northampton gestured to him to step back, into the shadow of the Tower wall, and joined him there. "Well? The last I heard, you'd been kicked out of St. James's Palace. You don't appear to be having much success, Warriner."

"My lord, I'm still getting vital information, from Lovett's wife. There are things going on, involving Lovett and his partners. I'm meeting Sarah Lovett tomorrow night."

Northampton's eyes narrowed. "Perhaps you ought to know that, for Lovett's wife, time is running out." He saw the tension round Warriner's jaw.

"What do you mean?"

"She is dying. Didn't you know? She is mortally ill."

The cough. The pallor, thought Ned.

"Oh, she puts on a good appearance," went on Northampton, "on the days when she is in remission. No one would guess. But her doctors have told her she has not long to live. So her usefulness is limited. As, perhaps, is yours."

"My lord, I think you will find it worth the wait. You see, I think I'm uncovering a scheme that involves the Prince himself."

A gleam of interest. Then, "Letting your imagination carry you away again, Warriner?"

"I think not, my lord. I just have two requests."

"And they are?"

"Firstly, a little more time. And secondly, your help for Kate Pelham. She has been arrested."

"Pelham's wife? Why should I help her?"

"I think she has been used, my lord. As an innocent messenger, by the plotters. If I'm to make progress, I need her to be free—"

Northampton gazed at him a moment. "For you also, I think time is running out," he said softly.

Then he turned, with a swirl of his rich cloak, and swept back into the circle of torchlight that illuminated the King and his attendants as they descended to the royal barge.

30.

———————————— ✦

The alchemist should be discreet and silent, revealing to no one the result of his operations.

ALBERTUS MAGNUS (C.1193–1280)
LIBELLUS DE ALCHIMIA

EARLIER THAT SAME EVENING, MATTHEW WARRINER had been having problems with Alice. "Do you know," he said, as he lay back on his bed and watched Alice brushing her hair, "do you know, for a while I even thought you were after bedding my little brother."

Alice turned slowly. She was naked, and still warm from Matthew's bed. Her breasts were full and rosy in the half-light. "Him?" she said. "He's losing his wits."

"Alice, Alice, what makes you say that?"

"He thinks he can make gold."

"Gold?" Matthew was more interested in how Alice's dark nipples were stiffening now in the cold. "Come here," he said, but she shook her head and continued brushing her long fair curls. He got up, aroused again, and pulled her back to the bed.

"Yes, gold," she said. "Let go of me, Matt Warriner. What

did you think Ned was doing in that bakehouse that he keeps locked up so well?"

Matthew, caressing her breasts, said, "He's trying to discover a remedy for hangovers. He told me so. Come here—"

"Are you stupid?" she asked scornfully, pulling herself up on one elbow and gazing down at him. "Yes. Of course you are. He was lying to you. Your brother is trying to make gold. Like the alchemists."

"You mean the Philosopher's Stone," corrected Matthew. "Alchemists try and make the Philosopher's Stone, which will turn everything into gold. How do you know what Ned's up to?"

"His little helper Robin told me all about it. See here."

She pushed him away and scrambled off the bed again. Matthew fell back with an oath, while Alice rummaged in the pocket of her gown, which lay in a heap on the floor. She turned and waved some sheets of paper at Matthew. "Look. Robin's got it all written down, how to make gold, or the Philosopher's Stone, or whatever, and I've been copying it. I'm about halfway through. I know where there's another key to the bakehouse, so I go in there when no one's around. He might have the recipe for gold, Matthew! Why don't you see whether it's true or not, whether some fool will pay good money for it? For God's sake, do you always want to live in a filthy place like Rose Alley?" She waved her hand around to indicate the cobwebs, the dirt, the peeling plaster.

"Yes," he said. But he heaved himself off the bed and lunged toward the papers she held. She lifted them high above her head.

"What are they worth to you?" she demanded.

"A pretty necklace. A new gown, perhaps."

"Come on. More than that, you old skinflint. At the very least you could make a ballad sheet of it and sell it all round London for a fortune. *Two* new gowns, Matt."

He threw himself back on the bed. "I've not got any money. Tell me when Ned and his young friend have made lots of gold. Then I might be interested. Come here."

She was getting impatient. "Jesus, Matt, if you're not interested, there are others who will be. All right, it's nonsense, but it will fool a few people. It's something to do with someone called Auriel. Listen to me. If you won't try to make money, then I will, damn you for being coarse and stupid!"

He dragged her lazily back to bed and began to fondle her again. "Stupid, maybe. Coarse, yes." He bent and reached between her legs. "But don't you like it? How coarse would you like me to be?"

She shoved him away and began to pull on her clothes, struggling with the buttons.

"I'll show you," she muttered. "Damn you, I'll show you."

The door slammed after her. Matthew Warriner cursed, loudly and colorfully.

IT WAS LATER THAT NIGHT, WHEN HE WAS IN HIS CUPS, that Matthew thought again of what Alice had said. He'd gone to the Star tavern in Fetter Lane, and someone there was laughing at him because he'd been trying to sell the landlord a cartload of sea coal that was little more than dust. Earlier he'd argued with Davey about buying up the coal because Davey had told him from the start it was worthless. Matthew was secretly willing to admit he'd been wrong, but even so he didn't like being laughed at. And he was having to face up to the fact that he was just about ruined. He'd got fed up of bribing the local constables, and finding they did nothing to protect his trade. Rivals were moving in on his patch; if his men tried to steal, someone was there before them; if they tried to sell pilfered goods, they were offered such meager money that it was hardly worth their while to transport the stuff.

Someone was behind all this.

Because he was desperate, he'd been thinking a little more about what Alice had said. About his brother, and the secret of gold. In fact he'd tried to find Ned, to ask him about it, but Ned was out, and Matthew's interest had grown as the night wore on. Usually he laughed at people who boasted of making gold, but his brother was no fool, and Matthew already knew he was up to something odd in that bakehouse.

"You'll never make your fortune unless you learn to gull

your customers with a little more skill," pointed out a jeering stranger in the Star, who'd heard of Matthew's failed efforts to sell the coal.

Matthew was angry, and more than a little drunk. "Soon," he said, meeing the stranger's gaze belligerently, "soon, I'll be more than rich. Someone I know—someone I know very well—has got the secret of making gold."

His tormentor grinned. "Has he, now? He must be remarkably clever."

"He is! He's going to make his fortune. He's got the secret in a letter!"

"Oh, yes?" the stranger mocked. "Who's the letter to? Mephistopheles?"

"No," objected Matthew, "no, it's to—to—somebody's name, an odd name, ending in 'l' . . ." He scratched his head. "Damn it to hell, I can't remember." Everyone around him was laughing. But later, someone else he didn't know came up to him and drew him to one side.

"I hear you're selling a cartload of sea coal," he said. "I'll have it. And what was that about the letter?"

"It was a letter to Auriel!" said Matthew at last, with triumph. "Yes, that's it. To Auriel!"

The stranger kindly told him he was surely mad, or drunk, but a good fellow despite that for all his delusions. They struck a deal for the coal, and then the man offered to buy Matthew more ale at a better tavern than this, where the women could be had for free; and so Matthew, still smarting after Alice's rebuff, went with his new friend to some drinking den he didn't know. There were no free women in sight yet— the stranger said they'd be arriving later—but there were some mummers. Matthew always liked mummers, especially at this time of year, just before Christmas. He laughed as the jester pranced around the tavern with his bells, telling bawdy jokes and singing, while the knight and the Turk bowed and made speeches and waved their wooden swords, until at last the big Turk pretended to die, lying on his back and waving his legs in the air. Everyone applauded. Matthew's new friend tossed them some money, and Matthew, who thought the jester's songs almost as good as those of his friend Irish Pat, whom he sorely missed, laughed and clapped with the rest of them, and forgot all about his brother, and Auriel.

AFTER A WHILE MATTHEW TOLD HIS NEW COMPAN-
ion he must set off home. At least he'd be able to tell Davey he'd sold the damned coal. But as he trudged away from the lights of Fetter Lane in the rain, he heard footsteps coming up rapidly behind him.

He cursed himself for having ventured out this far, without a few of his companions at his side. And he'd had too much ale for much speed. He tried to increase his pace, but the footsteps quickened also.

He turned suddenly to confront his pursuer, but with a bellow of rage he realized that others were coming up from all around. Someone grabbed his arms, and he felt the point of a knife at the back of his neck.

He saw that the men were in strange costumes, and wore masks. The mummers had followed him. Was this a joke? The jester, whose eyes glittered behind his fool's mask, stood in front of him and said, "You were talking, Master Warriner, about the secret of gold, and a spirit called Auriel."

The big Turk who'd died and kicked his legs in the air stood at a distance, resting the point of his sword on the ground. Matthew was sweating despite the cold and rain. "What if I was? It's rubbish, all that stuff about making gold. Everyone knows that."

"But someone you know clearly believes he possesses the secret." It was St. George who spoke this time. His helmet gleamed in the rain. "And you said earlier, in the tavern, that he had a letter containing the recipe. You said it was addressed to Auriel."

The man who bought the coal must have talked.

"Perhaps I said so. Perhaps I was lying."

"It's not the sort of thing someone would make up. Who is your friend with the letter?"

"I told you. It was lies, all lies—let me go, damn you—"

He tried to run, but they had him still by his arms, and the man with the knife held its point at his throat. Their foolish costumes and grinning masks frightened him more than anything he'd ever seen.

"Let me go," he blustered, "damn you to hell, or I'll call the Watch—"

They laughed. "Call away," they said. "Call away."

A T AROUND THE SAME TIME, ROBIN GREEN, APPRENtice magus, was scurrying back to the bakehouse through the pouring rain from the direction of Fleet Street, where he'd been to an apothecary's to buy a new warming bath for his precious crucible. He was daring to hope that after subjecting the contents to putrefaction and condensation over and over again, as the liquid returned to the body, the Crow would become the Peacock; and *Cauda Pavonis* would be his, the last stage before the attainment of Silver Luna, the White Stone.

His step quickened as he turned up Shoe Lane. His big frieze coat flapped round his skinny shanks as he ran, and his leather cap with ear flaps streamed with rain. When he reached Rose Alley, and saw the candlelight seeping out of the bakehouse window, he thought joyfully, It's Ned. He's come to look at the crucible at last. How pleased he will be that it's going so well.

The door was unlocked. He pushed it open and saw not Ned but Alice, bending over the sheet of notes he had left on the workbench; the notes he had made from Ned's precious Auriel letter, which Ned had told him, over and over, never to let anyone see.

She turned to him slowly and smiled at him. His heart beat fast. He was remembering what had happened the last time she smiled at him like that.

"Alice. How did you get in?" he blurted out at last, still clutching his parcels to his chest.

She swung a key from her finger. "There's a spare key, my love. In Matthew's house. Don't look so worried. Didn't you enjoy yourself the other night?"

Robin was stricken. "I didn't mean to—we shouldn't have . . . Does Matthew know?"

She touched his cheek with her finger. "Matthew," she

said, "has cleared off without telling anyone where. I think he's got another woman. You wouldn't find yourself another woman, Robin, would you? I was sorry when you didn't come back to me, like I asked you to. I was disappointed."

Robin stammered, "Please. You shouldn't be here. This is private—"

"Your efforts to make gold, you mean?" She took his parcels from him and carefully put them down. "It's interesting, Robin. Really interesting. I think you are so clever."

She sat back on the bench and began to open her bodice, looking up at him slyly as she did so. As he watched her full breasts tumble out, with their dark crests already tightening, he caught his breath, and the blood surged to his face.

"You must go," he whispered.

But she beckoned him closer and whispered to him to caress her body with his mouth. He found himself unable to disobey; found the heat suffusing him as she reached out to touch him. To stroke him, through his clothes. "Now, Robin," she whispered, "you have been a bad boy. You have neglected me. Let us have no more excuses..."

She began to unbutton his breeches and fondle him there; and so Robin was lost again, in Alice's arms. And some time later he was left alone, flushed and exhausted as she quietly stole out. He pulled himself to his feet, and in a kind of atonement went to prepare the crucible for sublimation in its new bath.

But as he worked, his hands were trembling, because after all he had just attained a sublimation of his own, and he was bitterly ashamed.

WHY, ALICE. THIS IS A SURPRISE."
    Aiken Summers, Matthew's printer friend, was sitting at the table in his workroom in Paternoster Row, surrounded by heaps of printed ballads and fly sheets. His hands and bristled jaw were, as ever, smudged with ink. When Alice came in alone, her cloak dark from the rain, his expression was speculative, and lecherous.

He put down the sheet he was examining and came toward

her. "May I take your cloak? Can I offer you some refreshment?" He looked suddenly at the door. "Isn't Matthew with you?"

"No." She pushed back her wet hood but kept on her cloak, because she didn't intend staying for long. "He'll have drunk himself senseless somewhere. He'll be back soon with an aching head or the clap."

"Pity." Aiken put his head on one side. "He'd promised me some more material."

"Well, I might have something for you, Aiken. How do you fancy printing something about the secret of making gold?"

"Alice, dear Alice, it's been done before." He sighed. "Too many times, believe me."

"This one's good," insisted Alice. She tossed back her loose hair, scattering raindrops. "There are lots of interesting bits. Stuff about the stars, and angels. Interested?"

"I might be," he said, wary. "I'd have to see it all first."

"Oh, no. I know you, Master Summers. You'd copy it and print it anyway, and pay me nothing."

"I can't pay anything without seeing it," he repeated.

"Listen, then," she said impatiently. "I'll give you an idea of how it goes." She pulled a crumpled sheet of notes out of her pocket. *"To Auriel, I will give the gift of gold . . .* And then there's bits about earth and fire, and sulfur—all that sort of thing. People will love it. Now, how much will you offer me?"

He scratched his chin, adding more ink to the smudges already there. "Offer you? My dear Alice, it sounds absolute nonsense," he said.

Alice started stuffing her papers back into the pocket of her skirt. "Then I'll find someone else to give me gold for it. You see if I don't."

T HAT EVENING THERE WAS A BRAWL IN THE SHADOW of St. Paul's Cathedral. It had started in an alehouse in Paternoster Row, with an imagined insult, followed by a challenge. Both combatants were quickly joined by their colleagues, gathering out of the neighboring taverns and brothels like the warriors sown from dragon's teeth who confronted

Jason and his Argonauts, and within a quarter of an hour two bands of armed, trained men were fighting with deadly intent beneath the cathedral's eaves as the rain sluiced down, their swords swinging, their boots slipping in the mud.

The night watchmen kept well away, for they knew this was not a battle of the criminal fraternities, but stemmed from the traditional warfare between men of two rival factions, those who served my Lord Cecil, and those of Northampton. The personal exchanges between the two great men in the Council Chamber became, more often than not, translated later into bloodshed on the streets of London; and anyone with any sense stayed well out of the way.

One of Northampton's men was carried away, bleeding badly from a sword thrust to the chest. His colleagues, with a roar, mounted a fresh attack on their enemies. Daggers had been drawn, as well as swords. Where men fell in the mud of the cathedral yard they thrust upward, hacking and slashing, until they could stagger to their feet again. The long blades clashed together, gleaming wetly in the heavy rain, and the sound of oaths and jarring metal echoed round the cold gray walls of the derelict building. Another man fell, screaming as the tendons of his forearm were sliced through. But still the battle went on.

And then someone rode up on horseback and commanded them to halt.

The newcomer's air of authority was such that they all reluctantly obeyed. He was a courtier: a servant of the Privy Council. There had been orders, this man told them curtly, from their masters. There was to be a truce forthwith. A situation had arisen which was too serious for the great men of the city to waste their resources and their servants in this fashion. All true servants of the Crown were to unite in these dangerous times against the hidden traitors in their midst.

A plot. The whispered murmur rippled through the exhausted combatants. *A Spanish plot . . .*

There had been rumors for a while now that Cecil's men were looking for a cryptic letter that betrayed, some said, a Jesuit conspiracy, backed by the Spaniards. Others, more cynical, said, No, Cecil's men were hunting for a recipe for gold.

As if the little hunchback Cecil did not make enough gold already, out of taxes and enclosures, and grants from the King for his great palace at Hatfield.

There were restless murmurs to this effect from Northampton's men. But the courtier who had halted their warfare put up his hand again and announced that the Earl of Northampton, who recognized the imminent danger to the state, wanted his men to know that he had resolved to join forces with Cecil in maintaining the security of the realm. Everyone was to be on their guard for treachery. It was crucial that the plotters were discovered by the twenty-sixth of December—the day of the ship launch. In three days' time.

Did Cecil want them alive? someone called out.

Preferably, but dead would suffice.

31.

If, as in water stir'd more circles bee
Produc'd by one, love such additions take,
Those like so many spheares, but one heaven make,
For, they are all concentrique unto thee.

JOHN DONNE (1572–1631)
"LOVE'S GROWTH"

IT WAS LATE BY THE TIME NED REACHED THE WOOD Street Counter. He went up to the barred window through which the nighttime guardian of the gaol peered, and when the turnkey asked for his name, he kept his face in the shadows and thrust money at him instead. He was taken to the Master's Side, to an upstairs chamber furnished only with a bed and chair, where Kate sat, her dark head bowed over some crumpled embroidery at which she doggedly stabbed. She did not look up when the door opened, but her maid, who was laying wood on the fire, rose when Ned came in, looked at her mistress, and left the room. The turnkey left also, locking the door behind him.

Ned said, "Kate." She was still plying her needle, almost ferociously. He thought at first that she had not heard him come in.

But then she lifted her head. Her soft brown hair hung in

disarray past her shoulders. Her gown was of pale gray silk, with no adornment except a narrow lace collar. His breath caught in his throat, because she was so beautiful. Slowly she stood up, and all her sewing slipped in an untidy heap to the floor. Her gaze, as her clear eyes met his, was expressionless.

"Kate," he said quietly, "you hate embroidery."

"I asked them," she said, "what I was supposed to do in this place. They told me to pray, or study, or sew. The latter seemed to me to be marginally less a waste of time than everything else." She gazed up at him, and he saw the fresh bruising on her cheek. "I do not know why you have come."

He wanted to kill the person who had bruised her face.

"What else could I do? We were once friends," he said.

"Yes. Once."

Her coldness smote him. "I would have come earlier," he said, "but I have been trying to find out why they've put you in here. You are suspected of plotting with Ralegh, but I know that cannot be so, I know he is simply a very good friend of yours. Please tell me everything that has happened. I might be able to help you."

"You might be able to help me? You, or your master Northampton?"

He said quietly, "Is that why you cannot bear the sight of me?"

She sat down again and picked up her embroidery. Then she raised her eyes to his. "I heard you shared his bed again. Is he paying you well?"

"Northampton knows nothing at all of this." He looked round quickly, grabbed a stool, and dragged it close. "Listen. I learned that you were carrying a letter for Ralegh, and that the letter imperils you. Kate, Kate, you are too close to dangerous things."

She trembled, just a little. "I thought," she said, "that it was just a letter to an old friend."

"You didn't," he replied. "You must have known there was much more to it than that. What have you told the magistrates?"

"At first I told them it was I who wrote it. But that was a mistake, because Ralegh had already confessed to Cecil's men that he gave it to me. I think he was trying to help me."

"What happened to the letter?"

"Is all this going straight to Northampton?"

Ned caught his breath. "No. I don't talk to him. I just sleep with him. Share his whores. If that's what you choose to believe. What happened to the letter?" When she remained silent he said, "Oh, Kate. Who else do you think is going to help you?"

"What a sad plight I am in," she said softly.

"Think of your son. *Our* son."

For the first time, she looked anguished. "Do you think that there is ever a moment when I don't think of him?" He waited, and she went on at last, "Well. The letter. As I suspected it to be dangerous, I gave it to my maid Bess to look after, when we set out on our errand. I told her that if I was apprehended—which I was—she was to hurry away and destroy it. She tried to do so, but she was caught with it. So Governor Waad will have read it by now, and Cecil, and all of poor Ralegh's enemies..."

"Do you know what was in it?"

She drew a deep breath. "Yes. You are right. It is dangerous. There is a plot to free Ralegh."

"Tell me," he said. "Quickly. The gaoler might come back anytime." He glanced at the door.

"It is all," she said, "in a way, about secret letters. Sir Walter told me that John Dee wrote to him at the end of last year, promising that he would send him the secret of gold, and also telling him that there were plans to set him free."

"John Dee wrote to Ralegh? About gold, and some escape plan? Are you quite sure?"

"Absolutely. Wasn't I always good at remembering things?"

"Yes," he said quietly. "Tell me what you can remember about this first letter."

"He showed it to me," said Kate. "I can remember most of it. *'Can the glories of the past be reborn? Can gold grow from the cold earth? Soon I will write again, with news of such treasure, such golden hopes; the elixir indeed...'* It was addressed to Auriel."

Ned let out a low exclamation. "Auriel?"

"Yes. Dĭdn't I explain? 'Auriel' was Dee's secret name for Ralegh. They wrote to each other in some sort of code, always. They both knew there were spies everywhere."

Ned had got to his feet. He pressed his palm to his forehead. "Auriel is Ralegh. Oh, dear God, I should have known. If only I'd known . . ."

Kate was watching him. She said quietly, "I've been foolish, haven't I, Ned? I suppose this means I am in danger, too."

"I'll help you," he said, turning to her. "I will protect you. Because now, at least, I'm beginning to understand what it all means. But I should have guessed. It's some sort of plot, Kate. Not only to free Ralegh, but to set up an insurrection that will perhaps unseat the King."

She stood up also. "Like the Powder Treason?" She was very pale.

"Like the Powder Treason. Only instead of gunpowder, they talk of mulberries, lions, and noble princes. And stealing from the dockyards." She looked at him sharply. He pressed on, "Tell me again what you can remember of that first letter from Dee to Ralegh. *Can the glories of the past . . .*"

She recited it for him once more, frowning in concentration. "Apparently Dee promised to write to Ralegh again. But the letter never came. And then, of course, Dee died. Ralegh was afraid, because by then he'd heard rumors that the first letter had been intercepted and copied by Governor Waad's men before it was allowed to reach him—in which case the contents would have gone straight to Cecil. And if that second letter was ever sent, Cecil would be watching for it. Ralegh was worried that if it revealed a plan to free him, then his enemies might use it to press for his execution."

Ned put his hands on her shoulders. "Kate, Cecil never got that second letter."

"How can you be sure? Did Northampton tell you?"

Ned shook his head. "No. I know, because I've got it."

She sat down again. "Oh, Ned. Are you sure?"

He pulled the Auriel letter out of his jerkin. He sat next to her and showed her the two crumpled pages, and explained in a low voice what he understood of it, so far. He read out to her the parts he did not understand, about doleful *planities,* and *attramentum,* and *Mercator.*

She gazed at it, absorbing it silently.

"I think," he went on, "that the Lion must represent the King. The Noble Prince must be Henry. The Scorpion, surely, is Spain—it was Walsingham's code word for the Spaniards, Cecil's also. Auriel, I know now, is Ralegh—he is set to rise, in other words, to be freed again. But 'Mercator'—it means 'merchant,' of course, in Latin, and there is a mapmaker of that name, but I cannot find out anywhere what it signifies in this context. *Behold, Mercator grows to full size with great fanfares and explosions...*"

"Ned," she said, "how did you get hold of this letter?"

She listened as he outlined the story of how he won it, in the dice game at the Three Tuns. So long ago, it seemed now. He told her, too, how he suspected that people who had talked of it were being killed.

She pressed her hand to her temple in a gesture of anxiety he remembered so well from her childhood, but her beautiful voice was quite steady. "Yes, well," she said. "People would be desperate to get it, wouldn't they? Both Cecil's men and the plotters."

He nodded. "I need to know more about the letter Ralegh asked you to deliver. Who was it to?"

"It was addressed to someone called the Black Bird, an old sailor friend of Ralegh's. His real name is Alvaric Johnson; Ralegh told me he still sails the Irish seas from time to time as a privateer, and his London base is in Bearward Lane."

"What did the letter to Johnson say?"

"I did not see it. It was sealed. But he told me that he wanted to tell Johnson—the Black Bird—that the golden wine is still there for the drinking."

"So Ralegh," said Ned slowly, "must have guessed that his friend Johnson would be involved in a plot to rescue him from the Tower. And he was asking if Johnson had his instructions yet. Ralegh must have known that all this was dangerous. He had no right to ask you to deliver this letter."

Kate shook her head. "Ralegh has been so good to me,

Ned. If I had followed his instructions, and gone by daylight, I would have been safe. But I was late, and there were men there, officials of some sort, who questioned me, and seemed to know what I was doing there—" She broke off and gazed at Ned, realization dawning. "They did know, didn't they? They knew I would be coming. And what I would be carrying."

He remembered what Alice had told him about the men tailing Kate. No doubt they had been watching her for some time.

Ned said, "You were probably overheard, in the Tower. There are spyholes and listening grilles everywhere. As well as intercepting his letters, they will watch Ralegh and his visitors constantly. The public still revere him. As a potential figurehead for any revolt, he must be just about the most dangerous man in the kingdom as far as King James and Cecil are concerned."

"Apart from Prince Henry," she said.

He looked at her quickly. "Yes. Apart from the Prince."

"Poor Sir Walter." She pressed her hands together and bowed her head, in a gesture of concentration that he remembered well. "If it is a plot, then I am in trouble, aren't I?"

"No," he said. "No! You are just Ralegh's innocent friend. He asked you to deliver a letter to an old comrade, that's all. You needn't be afraid. You'll soon be free."

She pushed her hair back from her forehead and said, "How do you know? When you tell Northampton all this, tonight, will he offer to protect me? As a favor to you?"

She walked across to the fire and turned her back on him, her arms folded tightly.

"Kate," he said. "I am not proud of my association with Northampton. But he is a powerful man. I needed his protection, if I was to come back safely to England."

She still would not meet his eyes. "Why bother to return? After so long?"

"Because I heard you had a son."

She had tears in her eyes now. "You left, Ned, so suddenly. And then I heard nothing, nothing at all from you."

"I heard you had married Pelham," he said.

"I had no *choice*."

"Just as perhaps I had no choice other than to work for Northampton again. And it's not what you think, Kate. Those days are long since over. They were over when I first met you. All I wanted was to take you and Sebastian far away, from Pelham, from Northampton..."

"You should not have run such a risk. You are in such danger here."

"I can cope with that," he replied bitterly. "Better than I coped with hearing the news that you'd married Pelham."

She spread her hands out in a gesture of impotence, of despair. "When my father died, I was alone, and without help. Francis came often to visit me. He had always considered himself a friend of my father's. He offered to help me with my father's affairs. At first I refused him. I told him not to call. But when you left me, I was weak, and afraid. I did not think you would ever come back."

"And you must have discovered by then that you were pregnant. Kate, you should have told me. I would have returned."

"To face prison, possibly death? Of course you couldn't return. But I was alone, Ned, with a child on the way; and Pelham offered my only hope of protection. I used him. I am not proud of it, but I used him."

He pulled her to him. He touched the bruise on her cheek and said, "I will kill them for this, for putting you in here."

She tried to smile, but was trembling in his embrace. "Oh, Ned, Ned, you don't change, do you? You'll only get yourself exiled again. Or killed."

"I don't care," he said. "Who hurt you? One of the turnkeys? Or the magistrates' men?"

She whispered, "It was Francis."

"I will have to kill him," he said.

"He was agitated; he was anxious about everything he has to do, in his new job."

"Is that an *excuse*?"

She shook her head. He drew her into his arms and cradled her to him, kissing her forehead. He said, "I love you. I've always loved you. Never anyone else."

He could hear the warder knocking at the door. His grip tightened. "When you're free," he whispered, "as soon as this is over, then we'll go away together, overseas, somewhere safe. You and me and Sebastian."

She smiled, and wiped her eyes with her handkerchief.

He left her with an answering smile, but as the warder led him down the grim corridors, and the door closed on her imprisonment, his heart was heavy.

He knew now that the well-worn letter he had inside his doublet was the one that Dee had written to Ralegh—Auriel—to tell him about some dangerous plot to free him, and presumably, to unseat the King in a widespread uprising. Before the end of the year.

Today was the twenty-third of December. And Kate was unwittingly implicated in something that threatened to be every bit as deadly as the Gunpowder Plot four years ago. As was he.

32.

When he (the alchemist) expects the reward of his labors, births of gold, youth and immortality, after all his time and expense, at length old, ragged, rich only in misery, and so miserable that he will sell his soul for three farthings, he falls upon ill courses.

HENRY CORNELIUS AGRIPPA (1486–1535)
THE VANITY OF SCIENCES AND ARTS

I WAS THERE," CONFIDED THE OLD MARINER, DRAWING closer to Ned and pulling the clay pipe out from between his tobacco-stained teeth. "I was there, on Ralegh's ship."

After leaving the prison Ned had walked quickly down Candlewick Street to the Wool Wharf, where sailors gathered in the various taverns. He'd asked if anyone remembered the sea battle of Cadiz, thirteen years ago, and found this aging sailor, noted for his reminiscences.

He told Ned how Ralegh and Essex and their men had burned the Spanish ships at anchor in the great port. "All their great galleons," he said, his weathered face alight. "It was as if the sea was on fire. The Spaniards were destroyed. Essex's soldiers marched on Cadiz and looted it. Johnson's men brought sackloads of booty back to our ship."

"Was that Alvaric Johnson?"

"The same. Ralegh called him his trustiest comrade. They

brought gifts from the sacked town specially for Ralegh, because all the men loved him. Gold and jewels, food and liquor... That night we feasted, and drank the famous golden wine of Cadiz."

"So there was really golden wine?"

"Oh, yes," said the old mariner, smacking his lips at the memory. "There were barrels full of the stuff, brought from the governor's palace. It was the sweetest liquor you ever did taste."

Ned drank more ale with them and heard more reminiscences, then went on his way homeward as the night clouds gathered and the rain fell once more.

"The golden wine is still there for the drinking..."

What was being planned? What had Dee heard, that he was trying to let Ralegh know in his letters?

Stolen arms and gunpowder. Pelham and the docks. The ship launch on the twenty-sixth, in three days' time.

A bunch of drunken apprentices were making their way home along Old Fish Street. He stepped to one side and wondered again about Robin's story of the cartload of cannon, directed by Lovett, being surreptitiously transported up from the river in the direction of the Tower. Close to Alvaric Johnson's lair in Bearward Lane.

He knew of someone else who lived in the shadow of the Tower, in Crab Lane: the deputy Spanish ambassador Fabrio, who had taken on much of the responsibility for his master's work now that old Ambassador Zuniga, in frail health and fearful of the plague, had retired far from the city to the country village of Highgate. *The Scorpion will be blown from his lair. Auriel shall rise again...*

He imagined trying to explain what he had learned, what he suspected, to Northampton. *"I have not killed Lovett yet because I have a letter to someone called Auriel. It looks like a letter about alchemy, but I think it's a plot to kill the King. I think that Lovett is involved; but perhaps he is the least, the very least part of it. Perhaps he is merely obeying orders..."*

From Prince Henry?

Tomorrow night, Christmas Eve, he was due to meet Sarah Lovett at St. James's Palace. Tomorrow night seemed a long, long time away.

He drew his hand across his face to wipe the rain away, and wondered if there was anyone he could trust.

HE HAD JUST CROSSED THE FLEET BRIDGE WHEN HE became certain that he was being followed. Clumsily, by an amateur. He walked on a little, then swiftly sidestepped into a doorway and pressed himself back into the darkness. As the footsteps came closer, splashing through the mud and rain, he moved out and pushed his pursuer up against the wall, holding his knife against his neck.

The man whimpered with fear. He was of middle age, and thin, so thin, clad in an old purple doublet and a ragged and rain-soaked cloak. His hair, a faded gingery red, hung in lank streaks below his hat.

"Don't kill me!" he whimpered. His breath reeked of alcohol. "Master Ned, don't you remember me? We used to go drinking together, in Prague; I'd heard you were back in London, so I've been looking for you, everywhere."

"Lazarus," breathed Ned. He put away his knife and shook his head in resignation. "Lazarus, the Scotsman from Prague. I cannot think, in God's name, why you should be searching for me. Where are you hiding out? Why did you come back?"

"I was homesick," said the Scot, scratching his nose.

"So the streets of Prague proved too hot for you, did they? I remember your trick with the pewter bowl coated with a smear of candle wax."

"Ah, yes!" breathed Lazarus. "The *transmutation*." He grinned toothily. "It always worked, that one."

"You old rogue," said Ned. "Worked? You mean you hid a few gold filings beneath a coating of wax, then you'd heat the bowl, mutter some gibberish, and show people the gold sparkling in the melted grease. Gold you'd conjured out of thin air, you said. Then you sold people some sham recipe, and another cheap pewter bowl, and disappeared. You're still using the same tricks, I take it? As well as the false name?"

"The name Lazarus has served me well enough for the last

twenty years! I told you—I had to call myself something learned, something ancient, or no one would believe in me."

"And they do now, do they? What happened to you in Prague? Did you have to run?"

"I missed London," said Lazarus plaintively. "So I thought I'd come back to pursue my studies."

"Your various frauds, you mean?"

"No, Master Ned! I'm almost there, I tell you; I'm on the very brink of making the Philosopher's Stone! But I need someone to subsidize me; a gent with a fair tongue, and a bit of money, to help me set up as necessary."

"Lazarus," said Ned, "to be associated with me is the last thing you want, believe me. I have no money. And if you thought I was in trouble in Prague, it's nothing compared to the trouble I'm in now."

"I'll help you, then! I'm living in Whitefriars—I've got some good friends there."

Ned frowned. The vicious criminals who made Whitefriars—also known as Alsatia—a no-man's-territory for everyone else were the gang that Matthew suspected of moving in and wrecking his business.

"Good friends? I'm surprised you're still alive, if you've taken to living in that hellhole. Anyway, I thought they hated the Scots."

"I've told them I'm half-Polish. *Kocham Londyn*—I love London! And the Duke himself protects me."

"Last time I heard, the leader of the Alsatian rabble was a toothless old dame who went round putting curses on everyone."

Lazarus shook his head. "That was years ago. They got rid of her. They've elected a new leader now, a new Duke of Alsatia; he's a superstitious old fool who believes I bring him luck. And he employs me to work on the secret of making gold."

"I've had my fill of gold," breathed Ned. "And tricksters. Understand?"

Lazarus glanced at him slyly. "I have my uses. Is your brother Matthew Warriner?"

"Yes," said Ned, instantly wary. "I share his house. What of him?"

"I'd get out of his house, if I were you. And warn him. The Duke's after his patch, wants to expand his business."

Ned swore softly. "I knew it. My brother and his men will fight back."

"It's too late. The Alsatian gang have got all the information they need to finish your brother off."

"What information? And who did they get it from?"

Lazarus glanced nervously at the expression on his face. "Someone who knows your brother—"

"*Who*, damn you?" He clutched the Scotsman by the shoulders.

"I can't remember the name! But I do know it was a woman."

"A *woman*?"

"Yes. I've seen her with the Duke. She's young. Bonny, with long yellow hair."

Alice. Ned stepped back, drawing his hand across his forehead. Alice was the traitor. He had to get back, to warn Matthew.

Lazarus whined, "I'm doing you a favor, Ned, telling you all this!"

"Then I'll do you a favor, damn you. I'll offer you some free advice. If I were you I'd clear off abroad again. They tend not to like fraudulent Scotsmen in London."

"They will when I've made my gold!" called out Lazarus. Ned was already striding off down the street. "They will, Master Ned!"

Without turning, Ned raised his hand in an elementary gesture of dismissal. *"Qui non intelligit aut discat aut taceat,"* he called out. "Either learn some sense or shut up." He went on his way toward Rose Alley, leaving the Scotsman far behind. Lazarus gazed sorrowfully after him, and then he clutched his head suddenly, exclaiming,

"Qui non intelligit... But that's what Dr. Dee used to say. I know it. I used to visit Dr. Dee at his house in Mortlake, long ago. Master Ned! Master Ned! Wait for me. What do you know of Dr. Dee?"

But Ned was out of sight, thinking about betrayal.

Alice.

W E'D QUARRELED WITH MATTHEW," EXPLAINED Davey anxiously to Ned. "Over a cartload of sea coal he bought. We told him it was rubbish."

"Rubbish," echoed little Pentinck sorrowfully.

Ned had got back to Rose Alley to find that his brother was missing, and nobody could find him.

Davey went on, "He said he'd sell it by himself. We haven't seen him since."

Alice was missing, too. Perhaps it was as well for her. Ned went out with the others to search for Matthew, scouring the streets, and the banks of the Fleet also, because someone had thought they'd heard shouting from there earlier that night. They found nothing.

Ned told himself that his brother's disappearance could not have anything to do with the Auriel letter, because Matthew didn't know anything about it. Did he?

Y OU TOLD US YOU HAD SOMETHING SPECIAL, ALICE. But this is rubbish. You've lied to us. And we don't like liars."

Alice had arranged to meet some of the Whitefriars gang—the Duke of Alsatia's men—in a tavern off Cheapside. The same place where she had been meeting them regularly, and taking money from them in return for betraying Matthew's plans.

But now Matthew's business was ruined. And they were threatening to tell him about her treachery, unless she could offer them something else.

So she'd shown them what she'd copied so far, of Ned's letter about gold; but they'd flung it aside as worthless.

There were three of them, the Duke's henchmen. At first they'd been friendly enough, chatting with her, pouring her wine. But now their expressions were ugly. She said angrily, "I've never lied to you! Never! I've helped you destroy Matt

Warriner. I've helped you move in on his territory until he has nothing left. This is the last thing I shall do for you. If you don't want this letter, someone else will!"

She wished she hadn't had the wine. She was tired, and felt ill. "I'm going out for some air," she said.

She got outside just in time to be sick, all over the muddied paving stones around the entrance. She was almost certain, now, that she was pregnant. She leaned back against the wall, weak and dizzy. And then someone else was there, guiding her away from the doorway. She bent to vomit again, and as soon as she'd finished the stranger offered her a clean linen kerchief to wipe her face, and his arm to lean on. Another of the Duke's men? If so she didn't recognize him. And for the moment she was past caring. He led her away from the inn until they were in a quiet alleyway. After checking to see they weren't being followed, he said to her, "You choose dangerous company."

He was a strange-looking, ugly man, with colorless hair, and pale blue eyes that gazed at her from beneath a protruding forehead. His voice was hoarse, as if he had been ill and speaking strained him. She pushed him away, said curtly, "Nothing I can't handle, mister. I'll be on my way."

But he blocked her path. "I'm afraid you are too valuable," he said, "for me to let you go, so soon."

"Don't be stupid. Let me past."

But the ugly man did not move, and something in his look made her shiver. "Who the hell are you?" she demanded. "Are you one of the Whitefriars men?"

"Oh, no. I want to be your friend. And I see riches in store for you, Alice," he went on steadily. "Great riches. You have some power, some secret knowledge within your heart . . ."

She laughed again, but uneasily this time. "Jesus. You're talking madness." Her head was spinning.

"I can help you. We can help each other."

She got away from him just in time to be sick once more. He held her in the darkness as she retched into the gutter. Then he led her to the pump down the street so she could bathe her face and rinse her mouth.

She was weak by now, almost too weak to stand, so he took her to a lodging house just down the road, better than most, to a room with clean linen on the bed and fresh rushes on the floor. He ordered her a posset with white bread, to help her get over the nausea. He locked the door to their room, and he told her, in his strange voice, that she knew quite well how she could repay him.

While he talked, he was taking his coat off. Now that he was in his shirt and breeches, she could see that he was younger than she'd first thought, younger and stronger. She gasped aloud when she saw the terrible scar round his neck and cried out that he must be a hanged man, surely; some sort of ghost, come to haunt her. But he smiled and said, No, it was the Spaniards, and could she not imagine his suffering?—and by now he was sitting on the bed beside her, and undressing her, and touching her.

He worked with a skill that she found startling in one of so strange an appearance. He hurt her, at times, but before she could protest the pain would be taken over by a fresh kind of pleasure, and when she had gasped aloud, over and over, and it was finished, she curled over into the pillows, feeling sick again, and ashamed. But this man was not ready to rest, for he tugged at her shoulder and said, "Now tell me. Tell me about the letter to Auriel, Alice. You were trying to sell it earlier."

She saw that he had her papers in his hand. The notes she'd made from what Robin had written, about the gold. He must have found them amongst her clothes. She jerked into alertness again, cursing herself. "It's nothing," she said. "It's nonsense." She tried to get up. But he pulled her back to face him, roughly this time. She tried to push him away, but he gripped her wrists, and his pale eyes hardened.

"I did not ask you," he said, "for your opinion; which is, in fact, as worthless and as stupid as I would expect from someone like you. I asked you to tell me about this letter you have copied. The letter you told Summers about, and were trying to sell at the inn. I want to know where you saw the original. Who has got it now."

And so, as he hurt her more, she told him everything she

knew, which was not, in truth, a great deal, but she suffered enough for trying to withhold any part of it. She told him about Ned and Robin, and the notes they scribbled, the books they studied as they worked in the old bakehouse in Rose Alley.

"Ned the lute player," he said.

She nodded. She told him how they were trying to make gold, which as everyone knew was a charlatan's trick. It was all trickery. But the man appeared satisfied enough with what she could remember to tell him.

It was when the questioning came to an end that she grew really frightened, for she realized, then, that he would have no more use for her.

"Matt," she whispered, "oh, Matt..."

IT WAS LATER THAT SAME NIGHT, BY THE RIVER AT Deptford. The tide flowed in at full spate past the docks where the new East Indiamen, *Trade's Increase* and *Peppercorn,* stood in readiness, their wooden hulls laid bare to the December night.

All was silent, except for the steady tread of the watchman on the path, and the slapping of the tide against the wharves. But in the offices, a candle flickered as it was borne from room to room. Francis Pelham was searching for some documents that he knew were missing, for despite everything, he had not forgotten his duty. He had been going through the files now for over two hours, and he was not finding what he wanted.

He was looking for proof that his new job, in which he'd started so eagerly only five days ago, had not failed him, as everything else in his life seemed to have done. He wanted to be reassured that the vital records which he'd marked for Mansell's attention, because of the many errors that lay within, were still in the place where surely he had locked them. And yet, though he looked again and again, they were not there.

He could think of nowhere else to search. At last he locked

up and went outside, and told the watchman he was leaving. He was aware as he walked away of the watchman gazing after him with suspicion, and dislike.

Pelham set off toward the city, tramping along the wharves, where heaps of tarry ropes lay coiled, and rats scuttled. He passed a coal boat that was being unladen, its lamps swinging as black-faced laborers hauled coal sacks off on pulleys, their endeavors somehow unearthly in this dead hour after midnight. He walked on, his head down, as they swung the sacks along rhythmically to one another, chanting their old song:

"Five more to go, ho,
Bring the coal in..."

And then he felt a hand on his shoulder, and he spun round, reaching for his sword. He found himself looking into the face of a big coalman clad in a coat of rough canvas, whose eyes glittered in his black-streaked face. The coalman said to him, "Why do men dream of gold, when they can have silver?"

Pelham stared at him. "What do you mean? What are you talking about?"

"You are trying too hard, Master Pelham. Stop looking for trouble, and you will find that your problems will vanish like—why, like the dawn mist on the river, when the sun comes up."

"Four more to go, ho..."

The coalman grinned and put his hands on his hips. Pelham gasped, and cried hoarsely, "Who are you? Who sent you?"

"You ask too many questions, Master Pelham. Remember it. Too many questions."

And then the man had gone, or rather, he was no longer identifiable, for he had melted back amongst the other men. There were at least a dozen of them, black of face and hand, all clad in loose canvas coats, swinging the sacks of coal one by one to the dockside.

> *"Three more to go, ho,*
> *Bring the coal in..."*

Pelham, stunned, stumbled on into the night.

ANOTHER MEETING, THIS TIME IN A PRIVATE ROOM OF Whitehall, and this time not by chance.

Cecil and Northampton sat facing each other at a long, polished table that gleamed in the light from the gold-plated candelabra. A fire of cherry wood burned in the grate. A decanter of wine and two glasses were set between them, but neither man drank. Their servants waited outside.

"There is a man," Northampton was saying as he fingered his glass with his jeweled hand, "whom I think you might find it profitable to question. His name is Warriner."

"Ned Warriner? Wasn't he a servant of yours?"

There was just enough deliberate hesitation before the word "servant" to make Northampton flush with anger. But he smiled, and answered, "Indeed. Until he made too much trouble for himself. He wisely chose to travel abroad. But now he is back. He has been visiting Mistress Kate Pelham, Ralegh's close friend. He has been asking too many questions. But I think he might be useful. For a while."

Cecil nodded. "How best to find him?"

"Set Kate Pelham free. He will be quickly on her trail. Watch him for a while. And then—he is expecting to meet me again. The time and the place are not decided yet."

"Is he expendable?"

Northampton smiled a little, showing his teeth. "Once we have found out what he is up to—yes, he is. Infinitely so, my lord. Infinitely so."

33.

Whatever seeds each man cultivates will grow to maturity and bear in him their own fruit. So does the magus wed earth to heaven: that is, he weds lower things to the endowments and powers of higher things.

PICO DELLA MIRANDOLA (1463–1494)
"ORATION ON THE DIGNITY OF MAN"

IT WAS THE NEXT MORNING, THE DAY BEFORE CHRIST-
mas, and there was still no sign of Matthew. Ned had left Davey and the others searching as far afield as Holborn, and promised to join them later. By nine o'clock he himself was sitting in the parlor of the silk merchant Hugrance's house in Woodruff Lane. Overnight the wind had turned colder; snow had fallen just before dawn, and now shafts of wintry sunlight pierced the diamond-paned windows to illuminate oak-paneled walls and carved furniture scented with beeswax. A fire crackled in the grate. Outside the bells of St. Olave's by the Tower pealed the hour, and a coalman could be heard shouting his wares as his cart rumbled along in the direction of the Tower, its wheels muffled by the snow.

"It's true," Hugrance was saying as he paced up and down his parlor, "it's true, you see. I have checked up on the man you mentioned, Stephen Humphreys, and I have found out two things. Firstly, he has, as you suspected, more than once visited the church of St. Etheldreda, which houses the Spanish embassy."

"The ambassador doesn't live there though, does he?"

"No. The ambassador is in poor health. He lives in seclusion, waiting for his replacement to arrive. His deputy, Fabrio, lives in Crab Lane near the Tower, from where he conducts most of the embassy's business. But some of the embassy clerks are still based at St. Etheldreda's. And everyone knows that secret English Catholics are made welcome there, for mass."

Ned's heart was beating fast. "So Humphreys goes there. You mentioned two things. The second?"

"Secondly . . ." Hugrance was frowning and shaking his head. "He writes to Robert Cecil. About plants."

Ned let out his breath. "Humphreys is a gardener of high reputation. Perhaps even higher than I thought. He traveled Europe studying botany, when his soldiering was over. I know that he worked in the Earl of Shrewsbury's gardens, before he was appointed by Prince Henry—"

"And Cecil, of course," interposed Hugrance, "is spending some of his vast fortune on his new garden at Hatfield. Most likely he is consulting this man Humphreys. Perhaps he's even trying to entice him away from the Prince's service."

"But why should Humphreys be visiting the Spanish Embassy?"

"Perhaps, quite simply, he is a secret Catholic. Many are."

Ned nodded and stood up. "Thank you. I am most grateful."

Bertholt Hugrance pressed him to spiced wine, and a late breakfast, if he wished to share his modest table. But Ned shook his head and went out into the street, where the sunshine and the snow had transformed the city into a place of wonders. He stood there in the sharply delineated shadow of the derelict House of the Friars of the Cross, just inside the old London wall, wondering.

He was almost sure now that Stephen Humphreys was Stefano, the traitor who had secretly aided the Spanish in their capture of Ostend. But surely Cecil, with his far-reaching network of spies, would not have anything to do with a man who was suspected of betraying English soldiers to the Spaniards? With a man who, moreover, secretly visited the Spanish Embassy?

Every time Ned felt he was on the verge of understanding something, the picture shifted again: like a trick of mirrors and shadows he had once seen in a tent at a traveling fair. But perhaps John Dee had understood. John Dee had tried to warn his old friend Ralegh that within twelve months he would be freed by secret friends, at the same time, perhaps, as some attack on Spain: a blow comparable to that inflicted thirteen years ago by Ralegh and his comrades on Cadiz.

A blow against the Spaniards that might rock the peace efforts of the Privy Council, and might undermine the rule of the King himself, who so desperately sought the Spanish treaty, and the Spanish marriage, for his son, and who wished above all to remain apart from the growing Cleves-Julich crisis in Europe. What was being planned? And how did John Dee come to learn about it all in the last months of his life, in such detail that he could write to the prisoner Ralegh and offer him hope of imminent freedom?

Ned was due to meet Sarah Lovett that night at St. James's, in the guise of a traveling musician, unrecognizable, he hoped, amongst the mummers and songsters who would be there on the eve of Christmas in this rare celebration that the Prince allowed as a concession to the needs of the servants. But first he had to see Kate. He had to know if anything was being done to help her. He set off through the streets, where the winter sun shone on children playing in the fresh fallen snow, and hot chestnut sellers called out their wares, and the citizens of London hurried to make the last of their purchases before the festival. The men were carrying boughs of greenery, or hauling Yule logs or children on sledges. The city wives with their red-cheeked servants bore baskets of festive fare, their breath steaming in the cold air.

The Wood Street prison loomed dark and forbidding over the narrow lane, where dogs rooted in the snow, digging out scraps. Ned went up to the turnkey's grille and got his coins ready to buy his way in to the Master's Side where Kate was kept. At first he was told curtly that she was not allowed visitors, but he put down more coins and was shown at last to the vaulted inner hall from where a passageway led down to the notorious Hole. The Hole was a vast underground dungeon in which the poorest prisoners were pushed together without privacy, in the noisome dark. Ned knew of men who had died there. If the prison fever did not get them, then the cold, or the state of starvation in which many of them lived, did.

"She is not in there, is she?" he asked, catching the guard by the arm. "Damn you, surely she's not been put down there..."

The guard shrugged. "She's been moved from her room in the Master's Side. We're trying to find where she's been sent. You'll have to wait."

Ned walked to and fro to keep himself warm. He thought he could hear the moans of the sick. The smell of damp air and unwashed bodies permeated the cold stone. One hour, two hours went by. He asked again and again where Kate was, when he would be allowed to see her, only to be told, "We're making inquiries."

At last he saw a guard coming, who told him she had been taken before the magistrates again, at Newgate, to answer more questions.

He said, "You could have told me this earlier. I have been waiting over two hours."

The man shrugged. "You didn't have to wait. Nobody promised you anything."

Resisting the impulse to hit him, Ned went out to the entrance of the prison. He stopped abruptly when he saw three sergeants there talking to the turnkey, and backed away; out of sight, but not out of earshot.

"We're here to ask about one of your prisoners, Mistress Pelham," a sergeant was saying.

"Not another one after her!" The turnkey made a gesture of exasperation.

Another of the sergeants stepped forward. "Why? Has someone else been asking about her?"

"Oh, yes. Some fellow who's been waiting for hours to see her. Was here last night as well. And he's not her husband, I can tell you that."

"Where is he now?"

The turnkey looked around. "He was here, just a moment ago."

But Ned had heard enough. A group of guards had arrived just then, escorting a new, vociferous prisoner who was struggling; he slipped round the noisy group and was soon walking quickly away from the prison, turning off down the snow-filled side alleys that led to West Cheap, mingling with the crowds who clustered in that broad thoroughfare. He stopped at last, breathing hard.

Were they after him? Was this Pelham's doing?

Hitching his cloak around his shoulders, almost welcoming the bitterly cold air after the stench of the prison, Ned walked slowly but carefully for a while, checking at every turning to see if he was being followed. Of the sergeants there was no sign.

At Newgate, where that day's cases were being heard by the justices, he could find no sign of Kate. He paid out more money; the clerk checked his registers and said, yes, she had been up before the bench yesterday, but her name was not down for a hearing today. He was tired, and growing impatient with Ned's questions. Today there were many more cases than usual to be heard, because tomorrow, Christmas Day, was a holiday.

Ned ate at an alehouse nearby, and by the time he left through the city's gates the short winter's day was coming to an end. He walked westward, past Holborn village and Barnard's Inn, along the snowy wooded lanes that led into the country. As the orange sun dropped like a ball of fire beyond the distant horizon, he came at last to the Prince's palace, where the bare elms and yews were laden with snow, and frosted roofs gleamed against a pewter sky. He could hear the music, before he reached the high gate, and the sounds of people laughing; rare indeed for this somber place. He pulled his feathered hat low and, holding out his lute by way of passport, told the Prince's guards he was a musician, at which they let him through. They pointed him in the direction of the inner courtyard, where pitch torches blazed from their iron brackets around the walls, and the colorful costumes of a group of mummers glittered in garish hues against the snow. Servants and courtiers stood around, warmly dressed against the cold, rubbing their hands by open braziers as they laughed at the mummers' antics and drank spiced wine. He could not see Humphreys. Nor was there any sign of Prince Henry and his chief advisers. After a brief courtesy visit they would, Ned guessed, have probably retreated to the sanctity of the chapel. The atmosphere was the lighter for their absence; and Ned felt a little safer, though he still kept to the shadows.

He hoped that Sarah Lovett would be watching for him from some upstairs window. He hoped that Northampton had been lying, when he said she was desperately ill. As he waited for her he watched the mummers, who were presenting the play of St. George and the dragon with much exaggeration of the bloodier scenes. A jester pranced round the audience, bells jingling, his cap held out for money as he made his irreverent quips. Then Ned noticed Humphreys's helper, Nicholas Lovett. The youth had been absorbed in watching the play, but now some men—palace servants, Ned guessed, released from their duties for the evening—had moved in to persecute the lad, waving torches before his eyes, snapping their fingers at him. One of the torches was swung dangerously close to Ned's face. Ned grabbed the wrist of the man who held it and said, "For God's sake. Leave him alone."

They swore at him and brandished their torches in front of Nicholas once more. Ned snatched a torch and doused it in a water butt. "Leave him." He held the hissing stave in his hand like a club.

They hesitated, but the distraction of a fresh barrel of ale being broached nearby helped them decide Ned wasn't worth the trouble. They went off, jeering at him over their shoulders. The boy stammered his thanks, and Ned nodded curtly.

"I should be with them," said Nicholas, pointing to the mummers. "With them. Then no one would have troubled me. No one understands, you see. Nobody cares that my mother has been taken away."

He gazed at Ned with wide, distressed eyes. Ned put his hand on his shoulder. "What did you say, Nicholas?"

"My mother has been taken away," repeated the boy. "She was sick. And they would not let me see her before she went."

"Where have they taken her?"

"I don't know. They said she would not be coming back. I wanted to tell her that I was sorry, for the things they made me do . . ." Nicholas stumbled away, leaving Ned standing there in the darkness.

Just then one of the doors that led off the courtyard was flung open, and a man came striding out, with several guards in his wake. It was John Lovett, and he was making straight for Ned.

"Stop him," he was calling out. "Stop that man."

Ned was already running, making for the pool of blackness that lay beyond the stable block.

Lovett's men were catching up with him as he dived out of sight. He guessed it was only a matter of moments before they caught him. Lovett would have told everyone he was Northampton's spy. But then, looking back from his hiding place, he saw that some of the guards had confronted Nicholas Lovett and were questioning him, angrily gesticulating. Perhaps they'd seen him talking to Ned? He saw Nicholas raise a finger to point, and heard him say, in a voice that was surprisingly clear, "He went that way. Toward the chapel." He pointed in the opposite direction to where Ned crouched.

They hesitated fractionally, then spun round and headed away again.

Ned uttered a brief prayer of gratitude to Nicholas, who, whether knowing it or not, had saved him. He plunged into the labyrinth of the garden that Humphreys had not yet tamed, twisting between the snow-laden shrubs and winter beds. He found a wet path where the snow had not settled, to disguise his trail like a fox running before the hounds; then he came to the wall, where he heaved himself over with the last of his strength, and fell into the drifted snow on the other side. He lay there winded. Sarah Lovett, his one ally, gone. Sick, as Northampton had told him. Nicholas had said she would not be coming back.

And of Humphreys, there had been no sign.

• • •

HE LAY LOW IN THE WOODS FOR A LITTLE WHILE, IN case of pursuit, but there was nothing but silence out here. He started to limp homeward to Rose Alley beneath the full moon. His way was through the fields and silent woods that lay between the palace and the city. He thought he could hear dogs barking in the distance, and he imagined once that he caught sight of Barnabas's luminous eyes watching him from the shadows amongst the snow-laden trees. But it was a fox, who stopped and gazed at him with amber eyes as he went by.

He trudged on into Shoe Lane where the houses began, and the taverns with their lights, though he kept to the darkness wherever he could. He heard the crackling of frost, and the occasional sliding of snow from roofs. He reached Rose Alley at last, now transformed into a place of beauty, which of all things it was not. The moon shone down. Robin's *Silver Luna*.

He called first at Matthew's house, hoping against hope that his brother would have returned, but there was no one except old Tew, stirring some witches' brew of rank-smelling stew. He leaned toward Ned.

"They're all out," Tew said. "All of them. Still looking for your brother."

"Is Alice back yet?" shouted Ned.

"Is Alice what?"

"I said, is Alice back yet?"

"Alice is out, too. D'you want some food?" Tew pointed to the cauldron.

"Perhaps in a while."

He wandered out again, aimlessly. The house was unnaturally quiet without the presence of his brother and his friends. He saw a gleam of light from the bakehouse window and tried the door. It was unlocked. Robin, who had been bending over the oven, turned with a look on his face that was half guilt, half fear—who was he expecting? wondered Ned—but when he saw it was Ned, his eyes lit up with pleasure, and he said, "Ned, Ned, you must see this. It's happening."

Ned stepped inside and closed the door. "What, exactly?"

Robin moved back and pointed to the crucible.

And Ned, weary as he was, caught his breath and widened his eyes, and drew closer; for within the glass vessel, which he himself had filled so long ago, it seemed now, with dung and sour wine, a garden was growing. Colors bloomed rainbow-bright in the vapor that emanated from the gently bubbling liquid; iridescent, like sunlight on oiled water. He sat on the bench close by and watched in silence, while Robin sat next to him and gazed, too, resting his chin in his hands.

At last Robin said quietly, *"When the putrefaction of our seed has been thus completed, the fire may be increased till glorious colors appear, which the sons of the hermetic art have called Cauda Pavonis, or the Peacock's Tail. These colors come and go, as heat is tenderly administered; until all is of a beautiful green..."*

Ned said, "That's not in my letter. Is it?"

"No. Trithemius wrote it," explained Robin. His thin face was still alight with wonder. He was watching the crucible as if he was afraid it might suddenly disappear. "Master Tobias possessed some of his writings, and I learned them by heart because they were so beautiful."

"Robin, it's not real. It's just trickery."

Robin didn't reply. Instead he stood up to put a few more coals carefully in the oven; then he turned to Ned. "Next we must work toward Silver Luna. Let me see your letter." Ned pulled it out and handed it to him silently. Robin read aloud, *"Increase the fire till the glorious rainbow of the East appears... Behold, Mercator grows to full size with great fanfares and explosions. Accordingly you must heat and ripen the princely white tincture..."*

Ned knew that it was all an illusion. But just for a few moments, it was easier to let the archaic language and the beauty of what was happening in the crucible fill his mind.

The colors still leaped and sparkled around the old cob-webbed walls of the bakehouse, turning it briefly into a fairy-tale cave, a place of magic, of unearthly powers.

He said, "I thought these matters took years. Lifetimes,

even. I thought you had to repeat the same process over and over again."

"Trithemius said, *In the hands of an adept, as much can be achieved in a minute as in a century.* I am no adept. But Dr. Dee was. And he has written it all down here." He touched Ned's letter with reverence. "There are only two more stages to attain: the White Stone—that is Silver Luna—and the Red. The Philosopher's Stone. I must stay here with the crucible. I cannot let anything go wrong at this stage."

Ned got up. The colors in the glass vessel were fading, but the boy's face was still rapt. Ned would never convince him this was not real. "Robin," he said, "remember, now more than ever, it's absolutely vital that no one knows about the letter except you and me."

Was it the light from the crucible reddening the air, or was Robin blushing? "Of course," the boy replied.

Ned went back to Matthew's house, where his brother's companions had returned in low spirits and were gathered round the table eating Tew's fare in silence. Ned pulled up a chair and joined them. "Any news?"

They told him they were going to look again for Matthew later; but Dr. Luke drew Ned aside and told him quietly that someone had been there searching not for Matthew, but for him. For Ned.

Ned stopped eating. Lovett's man? Or Northampton's?

"He told me you were to meet him by Paul's Wharf," continued Luke. "At ten. But finish your food first. You look as though you need it."

"Did he give his name?"

"No, but he said you would know him. He was well dressed, in some nobleman's livery, and spoke with a stammer. He said to tell you that he wants to help you."

Ned pushed his plate aside.

"Your meal—"

"I'll eat it later," Ned said.

As he set off again into the night, he wondered whose side Simon Thurstan was on. He did not expect it to be his.

He suddenly remembered that tomorrow was Christmas Day.

• • •

AFTER THE SNOW, THE RIVERSIDE WAS SILENT, THE
warehouses deserted. At Paul's Wharf, where the moored
wherries of the traders and watermen were bobbing as the tide
ebbed, Ned stood in the doorway of a boarded-up warehouse
and waited, and watched. It was nearly ten o'clock. A chill
mist rose, filling his lungs with icy air and making strange
phantom shapes amongst the high buildings that edged the
river. At first he thought it was his imagination similarly playing tricks, but then he heard it more clearly—the splashing of
oars on the water.

A boat was coming downriver. The waterman appeared,
standing at the prow like Charon. With a single oar he guided
his vessel up to the steps. A tall, cloaked figure scrambled out
awkwardly, handed over some coins, and sent the boat on its
way, back into the darkness.

Ned stepped forward. Ever ungainly, Simon stumbled as
he climbed the rest of the stairs and muttered a curse; then he
saw Ned and raised his hand in greeting. "Ned. It's g-good to
see you." His scarred face was blue with cold. He clasped
Ned's hands in his own, which were clad in good leather
gloves, lined with fur. "Northampton told me to make c-
contact with you. He says that Kate is safe. And he is going to
help you both leave the country. As soon as possible."

Ned absorbed this. Then he said, "What if I don't want to
leave?"

Simon frowned. "But surely this is everything you asked
for! The chance to leave the country, with K-Kate . . ."

"Doesn't he want to see me first? Doesn't he want to know
what I've discovered for him?"

"About the corruption that you suspected?"

Ned said, "It's worse than corruption, Simon."

Simon looked anxiously around the mist-shrouded
wharves. "Ned, I think he knows everything already. He said
to tell you not to worry. He's arranged a passage for you, from
Gravesend, with Kate—"

In the darkness Ned thought he heard footsteps; they were
muffled by the snow, but swift. "What's going on, Simon?"

"Oh, Ned," responded Simon softly. "You always were too stubborn for your own good."

Ned thought that he saw shadows moving, between the warehouses. Simon saw them too; he lifted his hand. Ned realized it was a signal, and that the shadows he'd seen between the old warehouses were closing in on him.

He whirled round. Below him, where the gray river lapped against the wharf, he saw the lines of moored boats. He sprang down, landing in one with a crash that almost winded him, and sent the little boat rocking violently. He went half-leaping, half-crawling along from one boat to the next. He could hear Simon's men shouting, running, cursing, holding up lanterns to try to follow his progress from above, but soon they had lost him in the darkness. He doubled back, jumping from boat to boat; then he found a ladder. He scrambled up it, the rungs tearing at his hands. Crouching low, he went running into a tiny alley that led between the warehouses. One of Simon's men saw him from afar and raised a shout, but Ned swerved into the open doorway of a deserted tenement and waited while his pursuers went pounding by.

Ned came slowly out of his hiding place. He saw Simon pacing the wharf, pounding one fur-clad fist into the other in anger as he scoured the darkness for the sight of his men bringing in his prisoner. He was all alone.

Ned was on Simon in an instant, dragging him back into the shadows, twisting his arm up behind his back while his other arm was around his neck.

"Now, tell me, Simon. Tell me why Northampton sent you here, with this false offer of a safe passage abroad with Kate. What does he really want me for?"

Simon was choking. "I cannot speak, I cannot breathe, damn you . . ."

Ned whirled him round, pushed him back against the wall, and pressed a knife to his throat. "Is this better?"

Simon swallowed, his face gray. He said, "Northampton wants to question you. About a plot at the docks, and Prince Henry. For God's sake be careful with that thing . . ."

The knife had nicked his skin. Bright blood gleamed.

"You're safe as long as you keep talking, Simon. Didn't

they ever tell you that? Where were you and your men ordered to take me?"

"To-to the Tower—"

"The Tower. And the rack, no doubt. I would have been quite an important prisoner, wouldn't I, Simon? But Northampton has not got the power, surely, to put unconvicted prisoners in the Tower for questioning?"

"No. B-but Cecil does—"

"Ah. We are getting somewhere now, I believe. So Cecil wants me also?"

Simon was silent.

"Cecil and Northampton, the old enemies, have combined forces," breathed Ned. "So, Simon, things are getting serious."

He still had the knife point at Simon's throat. Simon was watching him with wide, frightened eyes. "Let me go, Ned, and I'll help you," he pleaded. "I'll g-get you out of the country. I swear it. And the woman. Kate. This isn't your quarrel, yours or mine. Take the knife away, let me breathe, and we'll talk properly . . ."

Ned released his grip just a tiny fraction. Simon pushed him away and shouted out to his men, but broke off on a note of surprise as Ned lunged toward him with his knife hilt gripped in both hands and drove the deadly blade as hard as he could into Simon's chest.

Simon's eyes, as they met his, were filled with amazement, then horror. He reached with fumbling fingers for the hilt, but Ned put one hand hard against Simon's chest and with the other heaved the blade out. Blood spurted. Simon, his face turning gray, started to sink to his knees.

Ned wiped his blade swiftly on Simon's cloak, then seized him by the shoulders, dragged him to the wharfside, and rolled him over the edge. There was a heavy splash. A moored boat bobbed in the waves. And Ned was running through the streets, though he knew he would not be safe anywhere now. Northampton and Cecil . . .

And they knew about Kate. She was in danger also.

He set off, running, for his brother's house; but he knew, as he turned the corner into Rose Alley and skidded to a halt, that he should have seen this, should have seen this coming.

• • •

THE STREET AT THE END OF SHOE LANE WAS DE-
serted. even at this late hour there should have been
drinkers clustered round the tavern door, and whores watching
from their window.

But the tavern door was firmly closed, and the whores'
window shuttered up. Even the beggars' brazier was abandoned. Ned walked on carefully, keeping to the shadows in the
ominous silence. And then he saw the bakehouse.

Solid stone though it was, it was wrecked. Its door and
window were smashed in, its roof ruined, its walls blackened
with fire. And Matthew's house, that comfortable fortress of
lawlessness, was surrounded by constables of the parish, who
were also swarming in and out through the torn-off door.

Of Matthew's gang, there was no sign. Black Petrie's
warehouse was silent.

Ned pressed himself back into the darkness, his heart thudding. Did Simon know this was going to happen? Was this
part of a concerted attempt by Cecil and his allies, who now
included Northampton, to get Ned and his letter, and destroy
any possible refuge for him?

He saw someone running toward him: a familiar figure
wearing a leather cap with earflaps and a coat that was too big
for him. Robin.

"Ned. Ned. Is it really you?" Robin's face was streaked
with tears.

Ned pulled him quickly into cover. "Tell me what's happened."

"Matthew is dead," sobbed Robin. "They've found his
body. Then the constables came. I went to hide, but I heard the
shouting as they broke in. The constables were asking everyone, the beggars, Black Petrie's men, anyone they could get
hold of, about the bakehouse, and Alice . . ."

"Alice?"

Robin's face was a picture of misery. He was cradling a
wrapped bundle to his chest. "They said that Alice is dead,
too. They said she'd been trying to sell the secret of gold."

Ned breathed, "How did Alice have the secret to sell on?"

Robin could hardly speak. "It's all my fault. I talked to her. I'm sorry, Ned. She read my notes, from your letter—"

Ned ran his hand through his hair. "*Why?* Why did you let her see them, damn you?"

"She invited me to her room. And then . . ." Robin broke off and hung his head.

"*Then?*"

Robin's silence spoke for him. Ned said, bitterly, "Was she worth it? No, don't bother to answer. Did Davey and the others manage to get away in time?"

"Yes. The warning was raised as soon as the sergeants appeared at the other end of Shoe Lane. They ran."

"As we must. If we're to stand any chance at all." He looked up and down the street, pressing Robin back into the darkness as a fresh gang of constables went hurrying by.

Robin whispered, "I still have the crucible, Ned. I have it, here." He patted the bundle inside his jerkin. "If I keep it warm, it might survive for a little while longer."

Ned said grimly, "I think you and I will be lucky to survive for a little while longer. Come *on.*"

"Where are we going?"

"To Bride's Fields, and the squatters' camp. Where I might still have some friends. For God's sake, run."

34.

For they to whom I used to applie
The faithfull service of my learned skill...
They all corrupted through the rust of time.

EDMUND SPENSER (C.1552–1599)
"THE TEARES OF THE MUSES"

FRANCIS PELHAM HAD SPENT THE DAY BEFORE Christmas in a state of gathering agitation. At his desk at the Deptford docks that morning, he sat down to a pile of papers to which more were brought every quarter hour by the clerks and provisions officers. They were eager to get home to their fires, for this room was bitterly cold, in spite of the tiled stove that burned in the corner. But even in their haste to get through the day's business they noticed with surprise that today, instead of putting these papers aside for a later, closer scrutiny, Pelham read them cursorily, then signed them and passed them on.

Stop looking for trouble...

This morning, he asked no questions. How could he? His wife was in gaol, under suspicion of collaborating with the traitor Ralegh. His debtors were threatening to foreclose. Without his job, he was lost.

He signed everything without demur; he asked no more questions about the documents he'd put carefully aside, yesterday, because of the many errors that lay within, but which had since gone missing. He said nothing, but he despised himself for his silence.

When Mansell, Treasurer to the Navy, came in, the clerks jumped to attention. Pelham got up, too. And Mansell started to make his way over to his desk.

"Pelham," said the treasurer, "I heard you were looking for me yesterday. They said you wanted to see me about something."

Pelham forced himself to meet his eye. He wondered if Mansell knew yet, about Kate. "It was a trivial matter, sir." His Protestant conscience grieved him almost more than he could bear. "And it is dealt with now."

"Good." Mansell wandered round Pelham's desk, fingering a file here, a register there. He was richly dressed and groomed; his hands were soft and plump. "So you're settling well into your new work?"

"I hope so, sir."

"I'm sure you are." Mansell was holding a quill pen up to the light and squinting at it. He turned and put it down again, smiling at Pelham. "There's some extra work coming in shortly. I feel you might be just the man to deal with it."

Pelham was silent a moment, waiting, cold.

"It concerns the launching of the two East India ships," went on Mansell, "the day after tomorrow. The King and all the royal family will be here to watch. So we've been asked to help with some extra security—to arrange for a platform to be built overlooking the place where the King will stand, so that His Highness's guards can watch him all the time." He cleared his throat fussily. "You'll have to commandeer some of the dockyard carpenters and make sure that they have access to whatever they need. Do you mind dealing with it, Pelham?"

"Not at all," said Pelham with some relief, "not at all. I will do it to the very best of my ability, sir."

"I'm sure you will," said Mansell. "It's a matter of administration only, but important nonetheless. I'll make sure the chief carpenter reports to you shortly with the plans."

Pelham worked on doggedly for the rest of the day. Later he saw the chief carpenter about the platform for the King's soldiers, and the carpenter also explained to him that the platform had to be strong enough to bear seven ceremonial cannon, to be fired at the moment of the launch. Pelham gave him the necessary authority for the equipment required, and for commandeering the extra workmen, and the carpenter said he and his men would commence work straightaway. There wasn't much daylight left, but the construction could be easily completed on the morning of the ship launch.

Pelham worked at his desk a little longer. By then it was five, long since dark, and people were starting to leave. He himself finished work soon afterwards, and went on his way through the city.

He went to Lombard Street, where Duprais the moneylender lived, to plead for more time. Duprais came to the door to meet him, holding out his hand. "Master Pelham. Well, well, what a pleasure to see you. I am so glad, you know, so glad that you have managed to sort out all your, shall we say, little troubles so successfully."

"Troubles?"

"Your debts, sir, your debts. All paid. So glad."

"Yes," said Pelham dazedly. "Of course. I just thought I would come to you to check if there was anything else to be settled—any paperwork, any bills to be signed . . ."

"No, oh no. Your colleague dealt with all necessary matters this very day."

"My *colleague*?"

"Yes. So obliging. Everything has been paid off. Everything."

"Did my colleague give you his name?"

"Aha." Duprais touched the side of his nose. "You are testing me now, aren't you, Master Pelham? He said not a word more than necessary. He said you had told him that discretion was essential. Isn't that right?"

AFTER THAT PELHAM STUMBLED OUT AND WENT slowly home. The house was silent. He guessed that the nurse would have taken Sebastian up to his room, to prepare him for bed.

He had told Sebastian and all the servants that Kate had been obliged to visit some relatives, to take them her Christmas greetings; but he guessed it would not be long before they heard the truth.

He did some work in his study, checking through his bills in a daze, still scarcely able to comprehend that the loan which had burdened him for so long was totally repaid. He locked his papers away. Then he began to look for the plan the chief carpenter at Deptford had given him that afternoon, the plan of the platform which was being constructed for the King's soldiers and cannon on the day of the launch.

He could not find it. He hunted again, amongst the papers that lay on his desk. He realized that he must have left it in his office at Deptford.

Then he heard someone in the passageway outside. Thinking it to be his housekeeper, he went outside; but he saw Kate, still in her cloak, her cheeks glowing from the cold.

"What are you doing here?" he breathed.

She said quietly, "All the charges against me have been dismissed. I thought you knew. I thought you had paid the money."

"Money?"

"I have been bound over not to offend again. In other words, the charges have been found to be groundless. Wasn't it you who paid the forty pounds to the magistrates to have me released?"

"No," he said, "no..."

But who had paid that money? Ned Warriner? He ground one hand into the palm of his other. "Forty pounds. I will investigate. I do not like to be beholden to anyone." He drew himself up. "Madam, I do not find my own charges against you to be groundless. From now on, you will not leave your chamber without my permission."

She looked paler than ever, except for the faded bruise on her cheek. "I trust you will allow me access to my son. If not, I would be better off in the prison I have just left."

"Enough!" he said. He'd stepped toward her again with his

hand raised, as he had in the prison. He saw her flinch, then brace herself proudly in the candlelight. "Enough," he said again, but more quietly; "you may have the freedom of this house, but you will not leave it until I tell you so. Later we will talk, you and I."

She turned to go upstairs. He went into his study again and shut the door, and rested his head in his hands, in despair.

N ED HAD SUSPECTED FOR SOME TIME THAT HE AND Robin were being followed. Robin was limping, exhausted; but Rose Alley was well behind them, and they had almost reached the thickets of hawthorn and rowanberry that surrounded their destination—the vagrant camp of Bride's Fields.

But as they passed the last of the few lonely cottages where the tannery workers lived, Ned thought again that he could hear hurrying footsteps in pursuit; though when he stopped to look back he saw nothing but a lame beggar crouched in a doorway, while somewhere over by the Fleet a drunkard was singing to an invisible moon.

The mist came up in ever thicker swathes from the river, muffling all sounds. Then he heard more footsteps, close by this time, and a low voice. A dog barked, but was quickly stifled.

It was the silence that fell afterwards that was most ominous. Ned hauled Robin behind a ruined wall and pulled him down to crouch in the half-melted snow. He saw men coming down the empty lane. Men with dogs. Even the drunkard had stopped singing.

Constables? No. They wore ragged, colorful clothes and moth-eaten fur-lined cloaks. Their faces were marked by debauchery. They had three dogs straining on long leashes: long-snouted brutes whose ribs showed through their coats.

He pressed Robin farther back into the shadows.

Robin was looking at his crucible. He tugged at Ned's sleeve. "Ned, Ned! It's gone cold!"

Ned whispered, "You can heat it again. Be quiet."

"But you don't understand. If it goes cold, then it's dead . . ."

One of the men out on the lane looked round sharply. A dog whined, straining at its leash. They had been heard.

The dogs found them moments later. Robin was quickly seized. Ned tried to fight the gang of men, but there were too many of them. Their hands were roped together, and they were hauled southward past the silent taverns and houses of Fleet Street where, if anyone saw them, they took good care not to be seen themselves. Past St. Bride's Church, to where a high stone wall, lichened with age, loomed up from the mist.

He'd already guessed where they were being taken, and by whom.

They had come to the old Carmelite monastery of White-friars, mockingly known as Alsatia. It was the most lawless territory in all of London. And Alice had betrayed Matthew's gang to its leader.

Robin and Ned were pushed toward a big, iron-studded gate set in the wall of the former monastery. One of their escorts thumped his fist on it and called out a password. There was a creaking of bolts, and the gate was flung open. Ned and Robin were bundled through, past three guards who wore ragged military uniforms and carried pistols. One of them thrust a lantern close to their faces and turned to their captors. "Who the devil have you brought in this time?"

Ned started to speak. Someone hit him, hard. He could hear Robin's muffled sobbing behind him; he turned and saw that the boy looked white with fear. Even though his hands were roped he had kept his crucible safe; Ned could just see it, an ill-defined bundle tucked inside his belted doublet. Ned faced his captors once more and called out, "Many citizens of London seek refuge here, in the ancient liberty of White-friars. I want to know why I am being brought here with violence."

Someone laughed and tried to push him on. "Would you have come then if we'd *asked* you? Asked you politely?"

They all laughed this time. But the man with the lantern took his clay pipe from his mouth and said, "Hold on, comrades. We should hear him. As he says, we have a fine tradition."

Ned said, "Thank you. You have brought me here by force. I do not know why. Firstly, I want you to untie these ropes. And secondly, I want a meeting with your Duke."

They laughed again and hauled them through the big old wooden gate. "You'll see the Duke all right. And soon enough. Now move, damn your insolence."

He heard the gate being locked and triple-bolted behind them.

They were pushed along between the ruined buildings of Whitefriars. A small town had been built there out of stone and timber pilfered from the deserted monastery: a melee of ramshackle hovels and lean-to shacks, built alongside the twisting, muddy lanes. There were more substantial buildings, too, crammed together: inns, and cookshops, and the homes of Alsatia's wealthier citizens. Low taverns spilled out light, and the sounds of bawdy songs and muffled laughter came from within. Late though it was, some ragged children stood around the door of one alehouse, their faces gaunt with cold and hunger as they watched the prisoners stumbling by.

At last the little convoy came to the end of a dark lane, where Robin and Ned were hustled through a door and down some stone steps that led to a basement room. One of their captors hung his lantern on a rusty hook, and Ned saw that water ran down the walls—this room was probably below the level of the nearby river, he guessed—and rats scuttled off into the darkness. A crudely made wooden table and stool were the only furnishings.

Someone had pushed Robin down the last of the steps. He stumbled and fell heavily on the stone floor. Ned breathed, "Leave him, damn you. Can't you find someone your size to push around?"

They turned on him as one, their teeth bared. With his hands still bound, there was little he could do. By the time they'd finished with him, Ned, too, was on the floor, his mouth bleeding, his ribs aching from where they had kicked him, until someone at last suggested, with regret, that perhaps they ought to leave him alone because the Duke wanted to see him, preferably alive. And then suddenly there was a commotion, and someone else was running down the stairs into the cellar, pushing their guards aside. "Ned!" the newcomer cried out joyfully. "Ned! They told me you were here!"

It was Lazarus. He had the grace to stand back, abashed, when he saw the state Ned was in. Robin cowered in a corner. Ned slowly stood up. He tasted the blood trickling from his mouth.

"I didn't have much choice in the matter," he said.

Lazarus turned and started to say something, forcefully, to the Duke's men. Ned saw that Robin was crying. He went over to him.

"It's all right," he said. "It's me they want, not you."

"You don't understand!" Robin was gazing sorrowfully at his sealed crucible, which was lying on the floor, unbroken but cold. "It's dead," he whispered. "Oh, Ned. It's dead."

Lazarus was still haranguing the Duke's servants, who clearly knew the Scotsman well enough to listen to him. They untied their captives' ropes and drew back, muttering, as Lazarus clapped his hand on Ned's shoulder. "Don't you worry, now," he said, his enthusiasm a little muted. "There's clearly been a misunderstanding."

"I'm relieved to hear it."

Lazarus hissed some more invective at the Duke's men. "Get going. *Idz sobie*!" One by one they left, the last one muttering sullenly. Lazarus turned back to Ned and rubbed his hands together. "A bit of the Polish," he said. "I mix it in from time to time—it's a devilish tongue, the Polish, you'll remember it, Ned—and that keeps them from remembering I'm half Scots. They don't like the Scots."

"So they're easily tricked, then?"

"They're as stupid as the lowland cattle reivers, my lad, and you can't say more than that." Lazarus was adjusting the lantern hanging from the wall, a satisfied grin on his face. "I'll make sure the Duke soon has you set up more comfortably, don't fret. You and your young friend."

Robin looked up, his eyes wide with fear. "The Duke?"

"The Duke of Alsatia. He rules this place, and he's a good friend of mine, as those ruffians well know." Lazarus waved toward the door cheerily. "I'll be off and tell him you need better quarters, though at this hour he might be senseless with ale, so it could be a while before you hear any more. But I'll see that you come to no harm from these fools. Their leader wants you treated as a very special guest."

"Then he has a strange way of going about it. Lazarus, do something for me, will you? Presumably you can get in and out of this place whenever you like?"

"As easily as the Duke himself!" Lazarus boasted.

"Then find out for me if there's any news about a woman called Kate Pelham, who is in custody at the Wood Street Counter."

"Kate Pelham," repeated Lazarus. "I will!"

He banged on the door, which was opened by Ned's tormentors. Lazarus admonished them, "You leave him be. You hear me?" and then they all left. Ned heard someone bolting the door from the outside.

He began to feel the sickening ache of his bruised ribs. Dimly in the distance he could hear the church bells of London ringing. It was midnight, and Christmas Day. Robin was curled up on the floor exhausted, with the crucible resting in the crook of his arm.

IN THE SHADOW OF THE TOWER, IN BEARWARD LANE, there was another kind of disturbance as midnight struck. At either end of the lane bonfires had been piled up and set alight at the moment the bells of All Hallows began to peal; some thought it was a forerunner of the Christmas Day celebrations, but others, who asked about it from a safe distance, were told that it was a riot against the justices, who had tried to inspect a house in Bearward Lane on account of the rumors of stolen goods hidden there.

The justices had clearly been thwarted. There was no sign of the forces of law and order. The house which belonged to the old pirate Alvaric Johnson was on this street; and as the fires burned at either end, barred hatches to the cellar of his home were being unlocked and raised. Boxes were being heaved up with ropes and pulleys, and laid out, with care: not pirates' treasure, though it was rumored to be here in plenty in the street's deep undervaults, but ships' cannon, and powder, and ammunition; all acquired through a process of stealthy theft week by week and month by month, from the dockyard at Deptford. They were goods which the conscientious Francis Pelham would have recognized only too well, in writing, at least, because they should have been secure in the warehouses of the East India Company.

Instead they were here, in boxes, being loaded onto waiting carts and covered with canvas under the supervision of a man whom even Alvaric Johnson listened to: a tall man with a soft but cultured voice, dressed in a black cape edged with velvet, as if he were in mourning. John Lovett, whose wife, they said, had recently died.

From nearby Crab Lane, where the deputy to the Spanish ambassador, Lucilio Fabrio, lived, the glow of the bonfires could be seen from the upstairs windows. The smell of charred wood and smoke filled the air, mingling with the sullen river mist.

The deputy ambassador Fabrio always shuttered his lower windows and bolted his door at night. The disorder outside reminded him unpleasantly of the anniversary of the Powder Treason a few weeks ago, when guards from the Tower had to be summoned to protect his household against the lawless rioters who threatened it. So from behind his shutters he did not see the men who later lurked around his house and the empty dwelling beside it, assessing their proximity to one another, and talking in low voices.

He did not see how, in the chill darkness some hours before dawn, boxes covered with canvas were brought to this empty house, handled with the utmost care, and taken inside there by men who remained with those boxes, on guard.

He did not see how, at the end of the same dead hour, horse-drawn carts took the ships' cannon, stolen from Deptford, away from Bearward Lane to all the guardian places of the old city: to Aldgate and Bishopsgate, to the postern by the Tower, to Cripplegate and Ludgate: all the ancient bastions of London. There they were unloaded, and concealed.

But they were not expected to be hidden for long.

• • •

A T ST. JAMES'S PALACE, LATE THOUGH IT WAS, THE lamps were still lit, not in seasonal revelry, for the musicians and mummers had gone long ago, but in a mood more akin to a vigil.

Prince Henry, youthful, ardent, was striding to and fro in a ground-floor room, where the shutters had been flung open, so that the bright candles cast a golden glow over some snow-encrusted bushes in the courtyard outside. These bushes were festooned with berries on which the light from within glinted as though on jewels. The Prince had complained of the heat, even though the fire had been allowed to die down. His cheeks were pale and his eyes burned as if with a fever.

"I will not marry the Spanish princess," he was saying. "I will not."

That morning his father the King had told him that the negotiations for the marriage contract were to be set in hand as soon as the twelve days of Christmas were over. Later a missive had come from Cecil, gently reinforcing the wisdom of such an alliance.

Now Henry stopped his pacing and turned to those who accompanied him: Spenser, Duncan, his Master of Horses, and Mapperley. Of his chief servants, only Lovett was not there. "I will not do it!" he repeated.

His advisers clustered in a deferential circle to reassure him. "No," they said, "of course you will not. And soon you will be able to enforce your will on all of them."

He looked at them. "You are right. Soon."

He walked over to the far wall, where a map of Europe had been mounted. "The Catholic Hapsburg forces are gathering," he said, pointing; "but the King of France is massing his troops to defend the Protestant kingdoms against the evils of Papistry. I will be there at his side when the fighting begins, at the head of an English army; and in the meantime our ships will rid the seas of the Spaniards. The stars shine down favorably, I know . . . Is it all arranged?"

"Yes," they said. "Sire, it is late; you are tired. You will need all your strength in the days ahead."

The Prince gazed a moment longer at the map. Then he allowed them to summon his servants, who led him away to his private quarters.

MAPPERLEY LEFT FOR MIDNIGHT PRAYERS IN THE chapel. Duncan left also, to go to his bed. But Spenser continued to pace the room with his gray head bowed in thought. Through the open windows he heard the chapel bell ringing, and in the distance all the bells of London pealed out for Christmas Day. In the courtyard outside a sudden breeze shook the snow-covered bushes so they sparkled in the light cast from the palace windows. Then he stopped his pacing, and his hand flew to his sword, as he heard doors opening and closing in the distance. There were footsteps outside. John Lovett came in and closed the door.

He looked as if he had ridden hard. His clothes smelled of his horse's sweat, and of bonfires. He took off his hat and his black cloak and sat in a chair, drawing his hand across his brow.

Spenser said, "Well?"

"Everything is in place. Everything is ready."

"And no one suspects anything?"

"Johnson has the local justices suitably bribed."

"You are sure? It takes only one person, one person . . ."

"I'm quite sure." Lovett laughed curtly. "How would anyone know? How, by all the saints, would anyone even guess? The privateers will be seeing to everything that is necessary at the house in Crab Street on the day after Christmas. Stirrings at the Scorpion's lair indeed . . ."

"Indeed. Do Johnson and his men know anything else?"

Lovett shook his head. "We decided to keep them in ignorance. Just in case."

They exchanged a look of silent understanding. Then Lovett poured wine for them both, and they changed the subject, starting to discuss the domestic arrangements that had been made at St. James's Palace for the Christmas celebration: the services to be held in the chapel, Prince Henry's attendance later at the court of his father the King, and the tournament to be held the day after, at Whitehall.

Suddenly Lovett went to the unshuttered windows which opened out into the garden and he saw, just a few yards from the house, the gardener Humphreys with a spouted pail of water. He beckoned to Spenser, who looked out also. Spenser, with an exclamation, flung open the nearby door that led outside and strode up to Humphreys.

"What in the name of God are you doing here at this hour? Were you eavesdropping? I tell you, I'll have you dismissed from here, whether the Prince permits it or not."

Lovett was behind him. Humphreys put down his pail and dusted himself down. His pale eyes were mild, almost wounded.

"I was watering the quince trees," he said.

"Watering? Quince trees? For pity's sake, it's one in the morning on Christmas Day. It's the middle of winter, with snow on the ground. Are you completely mad?"

"I have to nourish them with water that has been bathed in the rays of Jupiter," explained Humphreys gently. He pointed up to the bright silver star high in the east of the night sky. "This water is from the lake. It holds the planet's rays, you see, but only for twelve hours, so it must be imparted immediately to the quince trees, at the hour when Jupiter reaches its zenith, or all benefit is gone."

Spenser had his fist raised, as if he would hit him. Lovett held him back.

"I am doing it for Prince Henry," Humphreys went on. "The fruit of the quince tree, properly nourished, is a powerful antidote to poison of all kinds. And quinces that have been grafted under a full moon and nourished with water blessed by Jupiter at midwinter are especially potent."

"Bah!" Spenser strode back into the house in disgust. Lovett followed him, and once inside he bolted and barred every shutter and door.

But Stephen Humphreys carried on calmly, with a beneficent smile on his face as he watered, and the scar on his neck was quite livid in the moonshine.

35.

*Poor themselves, the alchemists promise riches which are not
forthcoming; wise also in their open conceit, they fall into the
ditch which they themselves have digged.*

POPE JOHN XXII
EDICT CONDEMNING ALCHEMY (1317)

DEEP IN THE HEART OF ALSATIA'S WINDING LANES
was a tavern, built in ramshackle fashion using the stones
from the old Carmelite chapter house. Over its door, a crudely
painted sign creaked in the night breeze from the river, and a
lantern illuminated the lettering to proclaim that this was the
Jerusalem Inn. Inside, the drinking had been going on all
night, and in the midst of an atmosphere thick with tobacco
smoke sat the Duke of Alsatia and all his Council. It was four
o'clock, on the morning of Christmas Day.

The Duke was a robber who murdered those who thwarted
him. His Council consisted of bankrupts, gamblers, and more
murderers; of crooked lawyers, a couple of unfrocked priests,
and some old soldiers from the Low Countries, who found
plenteous opportunities here either to fight the forces of law
and order—forces which tried only rarely to intrude on this
self-contained liberty—or to fight one another, a prospect

which looked imminent now, as they swigged their pint pots of Rhenish, and squabbled over dice and cards. Whores in gaudy rags sat watching in the shadows, or went outside from time to time with one or another of the men.

This was the company that turned to face Ned Warriner, who was brought battered, beaten, and weary into the Jerusalem Inn with Robin cowering at his heels. The Duke and his dissipated band made Matthew's assorted friends look like children at play. Lazarus stood amongst them, behind the seated Duke. He gave Ned a wink, but to Ned his smile seemed to waver.

"Master Ned Warriner," announced one of the Duke's guards. Someone pushed Ned forward. "Brought here to the ancient liberty of Whitefriars on your orders. Your grace."

Ned stiffened. They'd said this before, that he'd been brought here for a purpose. Why? Because of the grudge the Duke bore against Matthew? If so, he was in for a rough time.

His escort kicked him. "Lower your head, damn you!"

Ned bowed his head to the Duke, a man perhaps more vicious-looking than the rest of them in that candlelit circle, with his scarred, fleshy face, and his burly body encased in some soldierly garb dating from the age of Elizabeth.

The Duke glared at him through drink-bleared eyes. "Kneel," he said. "On the floor. The lad as well."

Ned got down on his knees. Robin, behind him, followed suit. Ned said, "My lord, I understood that this place was known as the Liberty of Whitefriars. A place of freedom."

"And so it is. Except for Papists and damned Scots."

Ned saw how Lazarus grinned again, but also pulled his hat a little lower over his face.

"I am neither," replied Ned, "nor is my companion. If you will not set us free, then at least tell me why we were brought here."

The Duke scowled and leaned forward. "You're Matthew Warriner's brother, aren't you? He swindled me, did Warriner. Two years ago. Out of ten angels."

Ten angels. Oh, Matthew, thought Ned, you were careless there: to make an enemy of this man, for so paltry a sum. Ned tried to speak again. One of the Duke's henchmen kicked him in the ribs and he doubled up, winded.

"But that," the Duke went on slowly, "is not why you are here." He pushed aside his pot of ale and leaned his elbows on the table, heedless of the spilled wine there, and the scattered tobacco ash. "What we want is gold."

Ned was still struggling to heave air into his lungs. He said, "I have no gold."

The Duke scratched his chin. "That is not," he said, "what I have been led to believe." He turned to someone in the shadows behind him. He said to this indistinct figure, "Remind us all, friend. What you told us. About Matthew Warriner's brother."

The man who came forward was thin and clean-shaven, dressed in black, almost like a cleric. He gazed at Ned, and his face twisted in that familiar, sneering smile.

Scrivener Steen. His brother's former ally. Here, in Alsatia.

Steen turned back to the Duke, to all of them.

"This man was once a spy at court, Northampton's whore," he said in his smooth voice. "And he has something that should belong to better men than he. Something that should belong to our valiant leader." He paused and looked round at them all. "He has the secret of making gold."

Ned got to his feet angrily. "You forgot to tell the Duke you're a born liar, Steen. If I really had the secret of gold, would I have been living in the kind of places I've lived in, dressed like this? I possess no such secret. No one does."

The low murmurs of disappointment around the room started to swell into a growl of anger. The Duke turned to Steen, his expression ugly. "You told me that this man was an alchemist."

Steen said quickly, "He's also a devious trickster. He knows a lot more than he's saying, your grace. You remember the woman Alice, who was passing information to you about Warriner's gang? She told me this man was on the brink of a great discovery. She said he had almost discovered the secret of the Philosopher's Stone, in his laboratory in Rose Alley."

Ned was still breathing hard. So it was true, what Robin

had said. Alice had been betraying his brother. Alice also knew about Ned's crucible, in the bakehouse in Rose Alley— thanks to Robin, who was standing behind him, shoulders hunched, white-faced with dejection.

And it appeared that Steen, like a rat leaving a sinking ship, had also gone over to the Alsatian gang. Between them they had destroyed Matthew. Now it was Ned's turn.

"If the prisoner's no use to us, then give him to the justices!" someone roared.

"No, knife him," called another. "And throw him in the river."

"Throw him *out,* throw him *out* . . ." They banged rhythmically with their pint pots.

Lazarus stood up and screeched amongst the din, "Listen to him! Listen to him, damn you. If you will but give him a chance, he'll tell you how he has the secret of gold—"

"I deny it," said Ned coldly. "No one can make it, least of all me."

The Duke's tiny eyes narrowed still further in the fleshy folds of his face. Lazarus was dancing in agitation at Ned's side.

"Shut up," the Scotsman hissed. "You know more than you're saying. Don't you?" Then, in the face of Ned's continuing silence, he swore at him and swung round to face the company. At the same time he was reaching into the pocket of his faded purple breeches and bringing out a small copper dish. Ned groaned inwardly.

"Your grace. Master Ned Warriner gave me this, for safekeeping. It is a dish that will produce gold whenever you wish; and yet it is merely a sample of what he can achieve! He would have more to show you, whole bricks of gold, but his laboratory in Rose Alley, and his sacred athanor, were destroyed by the King's men. And yet he still has the secret, deep in his heart . . ."

Ned grabbed his arm. "What in hell's name do you think you're doing?"

Lazarus turned on him and whispered out of the corner of his mouth, "Silence, my lad, or you're dead meat."

He stepped forward, holding out the little dish to the Duke

and his companions as if it were made of gold itself. It was, to all appearances, quite empty. But Ned could see inside it the thin coating of wax.

"Now see, lords and ladies," Lazarus was intoning, "see this little dish, prepared by Master Ned Warriner in his alchemist's laboratory! It begs to be heated, to be given the gift of warmth, as a mother bird nurtures her nestlings."

"Lies," said Ned tiredly. "All lies."

"Here is the *Rubedo*," went on Lazarus, "here is the perfect putrefaction of our seed." He was holding the bowl over a lamp with one hand and circling the fingers of the other over it in a dramatic gesture. "Thus the secret of gold is released; thus the egg is hatched; the transformation is complete!"

He held the bowl reverently before the Duke and his men. In the bottom were some glittering particles. "Gold," he announced. "And more can be made, so much more, if our alchemist Master Ned Warriner is given the freedom of the liberty of Alsatia, and is allowed to work here, for your grace!"

The Duke peered greedily at the golden flecks that shone so tantalizingly in the depths of the bowl. "Is it true?" he growled. He looked at Lazarus, then at Ned. "Is it really true?"

Scrivener Steen was watching and listening, his calculating eyes darting from one to the other. Ned stepped forward to speak. But Lazarus elbowed him out of the way.

"Your grace, my friend here is overmodest," explained Lazarus. "But yes, he does indeed have the secret of the Philosopher's Stone! Just give him a few days, and he will provide you with limitless gold—all yours, your grace!"

The Duke's face was flushed with avarice. Slowly he handed back the bowl to Lazarus and scrutinized Ned, hard. Then he turned back to his Council. "Very well. I hereby propose that we give Ned Warriner a few days, as Master Lazarus requests, to show us the secret of alchemy. Are we all agreed?"

"Aye," they called out. "Aye!" They banged their tankards on the table.

Ned looked icily at Lazarus, then back at the Duke. "And if I don't succeed in making gold for you?"

"Then you will die." The Duke smiled slowly. "But you will make gold. And then you will become a freeman of Alsatia, swearing opposition to sign and seal, writ and warrant, sergeant and tipstaff and bailie—"

"And death to Scotsmen and aliens!" shouted one of his companions.

"Death to the little hunchback Cecil!"

"And that old bugger the Earl of Northampton!"

"Likewise the Pope. Damn them all to perdition!"

They all raised their tankards and drank deeply. The Duke said suddenly, "Throw Warriner back in his cell. He's not a freeman of Alsatia yet."

Two of the Duke's guards grabbed Ned roughly by his arms and started to drag him away. The Duke suddenly noticed Robin again.

"Who's that young lad with you?"

"He knows nothing about gold. He just happens to be traveling with me. Let him go."

The Duke had risen, burly, massive-shouldered in his old soldier's garb. With a rolling gait, he came over and gripped Robin's thin face in one hand.

"What happened to your ears, lad? Hey?"

Robin stammered, "My lord, they were cut off. I was found guilty of theft—"

The Duke turned his face roughly this way and that, scowling at his stumps. Then suddenly, he started to laugh. "You're one of us. Damn me, one of us! A crop-eared convict, at— how old? Fifteen? Sixteen? Set him free," he roared to his guards, "find him some food, and a bed, for the rest of the night, and a whore; he can join us at the Christmas feasting tonight!"

Robin gazed in desperation at Ned, looking, if anything, even paler than before. "Go with them," Ned mouthed quietly. "And get away from here as soon as you can. Go to Pat, at Bride's Fields..."

And then Ned was dragged away, with the Duke's last words ringing in his ears.

"You've got seven days to make gold, my friend. If you don't, you're dead."

• • •

NED WOKE THREE HOURS LATER TO THE SOUND OF the door opening, letting in shafts of watery sunlight from the steep staircase beyond. He struggled to get up from the straw mattress that lay in the corner of his cell.

It was Lazarus. He came in carrying a plate of bread and cheese, a jug of wine, and a big, heavy sack over his shoulder. "That boy of yours," he announced. "Looks like he's slipped out of Alsatia in the night. The Duke won't be pleased. He doesn't like it when people turn down his hospitality."

He started to light a fire in the grate in the corner of the room. Ned took a piece of the bread and bit into it, hungrily. Clever Robin. He was going to Bride's Fields, to find Pat. Pat would help him to get out of here.

He looked around, mocking himself. All the constables and sheriffs of the city couldn't get him out of Alsatia. It would take an army.

The bread was stale; he swallowed some wine to wash it down. "If this is the Duke's hospitality, I shouldn't think many are clamoring for it. Were you mad, backing up that crooked lawyer, telling him I could make gold?"

"Mad? At least I'm keeping you alive. I've got plenty more tricks to keep the Duke happy for a day or two—gold coins hidden in clay, silver coated in gold leaf . . . Look, I've brought you some things to get you started." He opened up his bundle, revealing a glass crucible and a warming dish, and several flasks of unidentifiable substances.

Ned gave an exclamation of impatience and started pacing his cell. "I don't believe this."

But Lazarus pressed on, setting a metal grid across the coal fire. He looked back at Ned slyly. "I found out more about your Kate Pelham, by the way."

Ned stopped his pacing. "Well?"

"She's free. They let her out of the Wood Street Counter yesterday. Someone came to pay for her release."

Ned gripped his shoulders. "Who? Why?"

Lazarus tried to pull himself away. "That's all I heard. I thought I'd done well enough."

"Are there any charges still?"

"No charges." He smoothed down his loose robe, wounded. "Now, let's get down to business, shall we? I've got the fire going. And here's a crucible. I need to start it all with the prime material..."

"Wine and dung," said Ned wearily. "I cannot believe that I have to see all this again." He went to gaze out through the grating.

"Here it is!" Lazarus was delving in his sack, pulling out a small canvas bag. "Prime material. Ask me anything you want, about Ficino, Agrippa, Trithemius, even John Dee himself—I'm your man! I met him once, you know."

Ned turned round. "You met John Dee?"

"Oh, yes." Lazarus was vigorously mixing some dark pellets, of dried dung presumably, in the wine from Ned's jug which he'd poured into the crucible. "I went to see him at his house in Mortlake. Just before he died. I had to wait awhile, because he was drawing up a horoscope for someone important—a fine lady from Prince Henry's court. A lady who was partial to wine. And she was bitter—so bitter—against her husband—I heard them talking afterwards. I think she'd gone to ask Dr. Dee for a curse against him."

"What was her name?"

Lazarus frowned. "Lovett. That was it. Mistress Sarah Lovett."

"Oh," said Ned, pressing his hand to his forehead, "keep your wisdom of ancients! This is how John Dee knew, this is how he learned of it all. Sarah Lovett! If only I'd known..." He paced up and down in his agitation.

Lazarus looked up at him warily from poking the coals, and there was pity in his glance as well. "Now, calm yourself, Master Ned. We'll soon make something of this, never fear. We can do it together. Make the red stone."

"I know nothing about it. I cannot make the Philosopher's Stone for the Duke."

Lazarus put his head on one side. "How can you say that?" he inquired quizzically. "When you have the recipe of Dr. Dee himself?"

"How did you know about the letter?"

"I started to wonder when you quoted Dee's motto at me. *Qui non intelligit* . . . Scrivener Steen told me the rest."

And Alice would have told Steen.

"Give it to me," wheedled Lazarus. "If only to keep the Duke happy for a while. Otherwise—his patience is as short, you know, as his temper."

Ned hesitated. Then he pulled out the two tattered sheets of the Auriel letter and gave it to him.

Lazarus gazed at it and sighed with rapture. "*To Auriel, I will give the gift of gold.* The recipe of Dr. Dee himself . . ."

"How long will the Duke give us? When will he realize that it's not going to work?"

"But it *will* work!"

"I said, *How long?*"

"Ah, we can always trick the Duke somehow, you and I. Now, let me see. *In spiritus vini is the base material first engulfed, then nurtured in a sealed vessel on the consecrated athanor, bearing the sign that also nurtures many pilgrims* . . . Sign that nurtures pilgrims? What's that?"

"The scallop shell," said Ned. "The sign of the shrine of St. James in Compostella."

"Of course! I'll find some scallop shells and make our fire a shrine, a consecrated athanor. Now, what's next? *Let the earthly part be well calcined* . . ."

Ned left Lazarus muttering over the Auriel letter. He went to sit at the table, and rested his head in his hands.

Kate was free. But for how long?

Lazarus turned. "*Native birds of righteousness*—what does that mean?"

"It was Robin who was the expert, not me."

"You mean that earless boy of yours knew about it all? Damn, damn: if only I'd known. I'll find him and ask him . . ."

Ned was on his feet instantly. This search for gold was cursed. Everyone wanted it, and it destroyed them. "Don't you dare go near the boy. I warn you, if anything happens to him I'll tell the Duke you're really a Scots fraud, and not half Polish at all. Do you understand?"

Lazarus worked a little more on the crucible in offended silence, until it had reached the odiferous stage which Ned remembered so well.

Then there were thudding footsteps on the stairs outside, and the Duke's guards came in and barked at Lazarus to get out. They stood round Ned and said, "The Duke is not pleased about your young lad spurning his hospitality. And neither are we. Where's he gone?"

"How should I know?"

Someone hit him. Ned hit back. Three of them held him as he struggled, and they taunted him for being Northampton's whore, and by the light of the glowing crucible, they punched him to the floor.

They did things to him that made him long to be far away, or dead, or both.

He tried to remember the names of Dee's seven angels, to take his mind from what was happening. He said them under his breath: Sabathiel, Madimiel, Semeliel; but that did not help either.

And then he realized that Scrivener Steen had come in and was watching silently, his eyes alight with sordid pleasure; and the crucible Lazarus had set up warmed over the fire, issuing forth a sulfurous vapor arising from doleful *planities,* by the names of the seven angels. At last they left him, and kicked him, bruised and shaking, into the corner.

The putrefaction of the dead carcass of hope.

He lay sprawled on the stone floor, wishing he were dead.

36.

The morrow next, so soone as dawning houre
Discovered had the light to living eye,
She forth yssew'd out of her loathed bowre,
With full intent t'avenge that villany.

EDMUND SPENSER (C.1552–1599)
THE FAERIE QUEENE, BOOK 5 CANTO VI, V.35

IN THE NIGHT KATE WAS WOKEN BY SEBASTIAN COUGHing in his sleep. She went to soothe him, and when he was quiet she spent the rest of the night on the truckle bed in his room. She did not sleep again. The silence of the big house, after the noises of the prison, seemed oppressive.

Dawn came, and she pushed back the curtains to see the sun shining on the frozen snow outside. Christmas Day was always a day of quietness and sobriety in Pelham's household: church in the morning and evening, and prayers with the servants before the midday meal was served.

By the time Kate came down to breakfast with Sebastian, she realized her husband had already left the house. She assumed he had gone early to church. She saw that Sebastian was happy with his nurse, then in her husband's absence attended to the matters of the household, for she had learned that routine and work were the best salve for a time of trou-

bles. She asked the steward to bring her all last month's unpaid bills, chiefly for food and coals, and details of the doctor's charges for attending to Sebastian; but he replied, in
some puzzlement at her ignorance, "They have been paid already, madam."

She sat back and looked at him. "Paid? All of them?"

"Why, yes. While you were away visiting your relatives."

"Paid by my husband?"

"Indeed. We went through them yesterday. There are no
arrears."

She put her fingers to her brow, then took them away and
shook her head. "Of course. How stupid of me. He did tell me."

"Yes, madam." The steward bowed and turned to leave.

"Wait. The doctor's bills. Did he pay all of the doctor's
bills?"

"Yes, madam. I saw him do it myself."

She nodded and let him go.

The doctor's bills, amassed over the past year, had been for
over fifty pounds. Only a week ago Pelham had warned her
that his new employment did not pay enough to reduce all his
debts and enable them to live as they were accustomed; not in
a year, not in two years.

The bruise on her cheek throbbed, where Pelham had hit
her in the prison. She put her hand to it quickly.

She thought of Ned, and the things he had told her.

She went to her husband's office, where she had found him
working the night before. She unlocked the door, and then the
drawer to his desk. Pelham did not know she had the keys. He
forgot that the house and all its furniture had been hers before
her marriage.

She looked in the drawer and saw a group of bills docketed
together, all of them marked as paid, with yesterday's date.
She saw a letter of debt to Duprais the moneylender, and she
unfolded it. It was an accounting of the money her husband
had borrowed, which she knew had accumulated interest
steeply over the last two years. She saw it was also signed and
sealed as paid.

Sometime very recently—while she was in the Wood

Street prison, it seemed—her husband had come into a large sum of money. Why? What had he done to earn it?

She unfolded another packet of papers from her husband's desk and read them swiftly, her ears attuned to the sound of her husband's return. She realized that the papers related to the launching tomorrow afternoon of the two new East India-men at Deptford docks. Her husband was, it appeared, to play some part in the associated ceremony.

Pelham had here the full details of the ship launch. She read about the royal guards, the trumpeters' fanfare planned as the King and his family arrived at the ceremony, and the seven cannon that were to be fired to signal the moment of launch-ing. And all the time she was reading it, she was hearing Ned's voice as he read to her from his letter to Auriel; the letter he feared was the lost letter Ralegh expected from his friend John Dee, imparting, in the guise of a recipe for gold, the news of a plot to set the old mariner free, and perhaps topple the King himself from his throne. Before the end of the year.

"Behold, Mercator grows to full size with great fanfares and explosions.... At the spectacle of Silva Luna, raised to bestow libation, the Noble Prince will be elevated, and the Lion shall fall...."

Auriel was Ralegh. She'd been able to tell Ned that. But *Mercator? Silver Luna?*

"Mercator," she was saying to herself, "Mercator." Ned had not been able to decipher the significance of it. He knew, and she knew, that "Mercator" in Latin meant a merchant; but now she was thinking of something else.

Merchant. Trader. Trade, growing to full size. Increasing. She put the papers down sharply on the table.

Trade's Increase...

Her hands were unsteady as she looked back over Pel-ham's papers. She read again the orders he had there, con-cerning the clerks, the trumpeters, the cannonfire that was to signal the launch. *"With great fanfares and explosions..."*

She slammed the papers down, almost knocking them to the floor. This was what Ned was looking for. It was all going to happen at the ship launch tomorrow, and Pelham was involved: Pelham, who had recently been paid a large sum of money which he had kept secret from her, even though it was enough to pay off all his debts, and more.

Her hands had been trembling, but they were quite steady now. She locked the papers away and left the room.

She had to find Ned. She had to tell him all this. But first she had to ensure that Sebastian was safely away from here.

IN COLEMAN STREET, WHICH RAN FROM ST. MARGARET'S Church in Lothbury northward to the city wall at Moorgate, was the mansion of Gilbert, Earl of Shrewsbury, set amidst well-tended lawns and orchards. By dawn the sea coal smoke was rising from the house's lofty chimneys in its multitude of gabled roofs, for this was Christmas Day, and the Earl's servants had been up early to see to the fires, and to air extra chambers for the visitors the Earl was expecting on this day of festivities. They had been informed by the Earl's wife, the Lady Mary, that two unexpected guests had already arrived, relatives of the Earl: they were a young woman and her child, a tiny boy not yet two years old who had, they were told, been ill.

And that morning the Earl had another visitor, a strange and ill-visaged man with a broad-brimmed hat and a pale, loose coat, whom they thought from his speech and manner was mad; but he was not mad, the steward informed them sternly; rather he was a most wise man, well traveled on the continent and learned in the lore of plants and astrology, which often made men seem half-mazed even if they were not so. He had worked for Shrewsbury some time ago, with four of his gardeners, and because it was Christmas Day, he had not come this time to work, but to bid the Earl and all his household seasonal greetings. Afterwards he asked if he could survey the garden, in which he had done so much work; and as the servants watched from the windows of the big house, they saw him wander round the flagged paths, where the morning sun had already melted the snow and glistened on the espaliered pear trees he himself had planted.

The servants saw that this strange man had brought with

him a big, strapping boy of sixteen or seventeen who followed his master everywhere. But he was not as well as he seemed, this boy, for while out in the garden he fell into a fit. They saw him tumbling and thrashing as the epileptic beggars did on London's streets, foaming at the mouth, and they marveled at it. Some kinder souls went out to offer help, and when his seizure was over they carried him in to the servants' hall, and laid him to rest before the fire.

And then Lord Gilbert's guests, his relatives, came to the morning room; a pleasanter task for the servants to tend to them, for the young woman was quiet but courteous, and all the staff, even the stern steward, were enchanted by her little boy, with his black curling hair and rosy cheeks. After eating with good appetite he went out, well wrapped up, into the garden with one of the footmen to play at soldiers marching, while his mother supervised the preparation of some herbal tisane for him in the kitchen. The little boy told everyone he wanted to be a soldier. Even the strange gardener stopped to pat his head and ask his name.

Kate, watching from the window, saw the gardener's face as he straightened up after bending to talk to her son. She felt a sudden unease clutch at her heart, because she felt she had seen him before, though she could not be sure where. She frowned, and shook her head, troubled by some unrecovered memory.

She went outside, to call Sebastian in. The gardener turned his head to smile at her, and she made an effort to smile back. She was being unfair, she knew; but then she saw the scar round his neck and she thought again, I should know him . . .

As a housemaid washed Sebastian's hands, Lord Gilbert came to stand at Kate's side. He said, "That man was a soldier once. He fought bravely in the Netherlands."

"Is that how he came by the terrible scar?"

"Yes. The Spaniards tortured him during the siege of Ostend. His ordeal put an end to his soldiering. Now he is a gardener. He has worked for many great men. At one time Cecil and I vied for his services. You must come here in spring, and you will see our garden at its best. You may visit, my dear Kate, anytime you like."

Kate had been moved by the warm greeting given to her by Shrewsbury and his wife.

"You sent us an invitation, Uncle," she had explained, "as you do year after year; I do hope that we are still welcome, even though we have not seen each other for so long."

"Always welcome," Shrewsbury had said effusively, "always."

Clearly entranced by the little boy, he took Kate and Sebastian to his study, where he showed Sebastian his collection of old daggers and swords encrusted with jewels: all mementos of his illustrious ancestors. Sebastian pointed to them with glee, and chattered to the Lady Mary, about the pretty colors of the precious stones, and of how he wanted a sword himself, like his father's. Lady Mary found some toy weapons for him that had belonged to her children, and Shrewsbury, glancing at his wife with the little boy, said to Kate, "You should leave him for the day with us. More people will be arriving soon; more children. Give the boy a proper Christmas. Better for him than spending the festival at prayer. Stay here yourself. Mary would be delighted."

Kate knew that Shrewsbury and his wife, who had Catholic sympathies, detested her husband and his Puritan lifestyle. "You are very kind," she said. "Uncle, may I leave Sebastian here, just for a little while? There are things I must do. My husband is so busy, with the ship launch planned for tomorrow."

"Leave him by all means. Do what you have to do. Then come back. Join us for as long as you wish."

"I am most grateful." She went to hug Sebastian, and to tell him to be good while she was away. He hugged her back, then was quickly distracted by the toy cannon Lady Mary had found for him.

Kate wrapped herself in her cloak and left the house. Her mind was already racing ahead. She must find Ned. Would he be at Rose Alley? She fervently hoped so. If not, then someone there would know where he was.

She didn't see the gardener until he was almost in front of her. The tall youth, pale from his sickness, hovered at his side. She nodded and would have pressed on, but the gardener stood in her way. He said, "I am surprised that you leave your child unattended."

She was annoyed by this stranger's interference. She said, "Unattended? He is quite safe with my lord Shrewsbury. And I will not be gone for long."

"Safety," he said, almost to himself, "is always a paramount preoccupation for all of us. Your husband is occupied at present with the safety of the King, is he not?"

She stared at him. "He is involved with the ship launch tomorrow, if that's what you mean. Excuse me. I must be on my way."

"The ship launch. Of course. He will be ensuring that there are no stirrings at the Scorpion's Lair. A busy time indeed for all the King's true servants."

He turned to go, with his boy trailing behind him. Kate gazed after him. The Scorpion's Lair? He was surely mad; though she had heard how sometimes these gardeners rambled of stars, of the occult.

Then she remembered where she had seen him before. He had been talking to the guards on the day she was set free from the Wood Street prison. Was it a coincidence?

It must be. She hurried on, to find Ned, to tell him of her fears about the ship launch.

PELHAM HAD NOT BEEN TO CHURCH, AND WAS NOW at Deptford. His duties did indeed press on him, as Kate had told Shrewsbury. Taking one of the few boats to ply the river that day, he had come to collect the plan he had mistakenly left at his office yesterday.

Because it was Christmas Day, the wharves were deserted. He stood out in the open, alone. A light breeze from the river tugged at his cloak as he gazed at the two nearly completed ships. The *Trade's Increase*, in her dry dock, was almost ready. Her deck was coated with snow like sparkling frost.

The *Peppercorn* would be launched from a slipway. The small ship had wedges inserted beneath the hull, preparatory to the removal of her keel blocks. He had seen the men there yesterday, working on either side of the ship, using long ramming poles. Others had been swarming up and down the slip, applying melted tallow to the ramp to ease the ship's passage down to the river.

The bunting already adorning the main mast of the *Peppercorn* shivered in the breeze. A little farther along the wharf was the viewing area where the King and his entourage would gather. Behind it was the almost completed platform, whose hasty construction Pelham had been asked to assist with, from where the King's guard would keep watch on their monarch, and the cannon would be fired to signal the launch.

He walked on to his office in the winter sunshine to collect the plans for the platform. He reached for his key to unlock the door, then stopped.

The door was already ajar. He felt surprise, then anger. The night watchman should have secured it. He went inside and closed the door. It was dark in there and, with the stove gone out, bitterly cold. He lit the candles at his desk, sat down, and started to search amongst his papers.

And then he realized that someone was already there, standing in the shadows, watching him. He let out an exclamation of surprise. It was John Lovett.

He got to his feet quickly. Confused, he said, "Forgive my surprise. I did not think anyone else would be here today."

Lovett stepped forward into the circle of candlelight. He was all in black. "I have just been to church," he explained, "and I have come to check some details of the launch tomorrow."

"I think everything is in order," said Pelham, still startled.

Lovett nodded. "I have the official program, of course, from Sir Thomas Smith of the East India Company. But now I would like to hear your plans, Master Pelham."

He smiled. But Lovett looked and sounded somehow different. His eyes, which before had been so genial, seemed now hooded in the dim candlelight. The knowledge of the anonymous payments Pelham had accepted in exchange for stopping his investigations into the thefts sprang up within him like an ugly worm, but Lovett did not know about them, he could not know...

So Pelham explained to Lovett about the arrangements as he so far knew them; about the careful timing, and the platform that was being swiftly built, under his own supervision, for the King's bodyguard.

Lovett broke in. "How conscientious you are. And your arrival here saves me the trouble of calling on you later, with more instructions. You've been told, haven't you, to ensure that the staging has supports for the seven guns also?"

"Ceremonial guns, yes."

"Indeed. And on the morning of the ship launch, you will personally ensure that a group of armed men, who will come to you for their authority, are given access to the ammunition stores at the rear of the wharf—to which you have the key—as well as access to this gun platform. You will recognize them by the green and silver ribbons they wear, tucked into their breastplates."

Pelham was confused. "I did not know of this. I must check all this with the King's aide."

"That is not necessary," said Lovett softly. "And you will say nothing about them to anyone else. Especially not to any of the King's men."

And it was then, as the candles burned down, and the shadows shifted, and the noise of the Christmas bells from the city seemed to encroach on all his senses like a roaring wave, that Pelham began to feel a growing sense of fear.

"I knew nothing about this—"

"I am giving you your orders now, Master Pelham. And if you have any inclination to question them, you can recall, perhaps, the papers you have recently signed, knowing them to be incorrect, in this very office; the registers you have falsified; the fat fees that have been used, without any protest, as I recall, from you, to pay off your debts. Remember all that, and do as I say."

Pelham's hands were shaking. "I was wrong to do what I did. But this new matter—this affects the security of the King."

"Of course," Lovett went on smoothly. "Always our prime concern. Just as your prime concern is the safety of your little boy. I have given you your orders. You will give the men I have spoken of access to everything they ask for, and say nothing. To anyone."

He left. Pelham sat down, trembling.

He remembered Ned Warriner, whom he hated, warning him that Lovett was involved in corruption at the dockyard. Corruption? Was that all?

What was going to happen at the launch? And was he somehow implicated, he who counted himself the King's most loyal, most upright subject?

He stayed with his head in his hands for a while longer. Then he pulled himself together and went to take a boat up-river as far as London Bridge. The high tide would not permit him to travel any farther. He scrambled out awkwardly, as the wind caught at his cloak and his lame leg ached in the icy wind. And then he stopped, because there was someone he knew there, sitting on an upturned crate, throwing pebbles into the water. It was Humphreys, with his wide-brimmed hat pulled low to shade his eyes against the sunlight dancing off the waves.

Humphreys turned to him and smiled that strange smile. His collar was turned down, displaying to the full the terrible scar inflicted by the Spaniards in the Netherlands. For a minute it seemed to Pelham that Humphreys was sitting there waiting for him. His heart thudded.

"I was looking for someone," Humphreys said to him gently. "But I was too late. The bird has flown; perhaps in pursuit of other prey." The gardener stood up and brushed down the skirts of his coat. "And next I must go to study the vines in a rich man's glasshouse. The vines do not thrive. There is nothing I, nor any human, can do. I told them, I gave warning at the time of their planting last spring, that the stars were not propitious." He turned his head, looking away eastward to the distant masts of the great seafaring vessels. Then he gazed back at Pelham. "Your ship. Has it come home?"

"No," said Pelham. "It is lost for good."

"Ah," said the gardener regretfully. "I am sorry. But the stars have to be favorable, for such a venture to succeed; and the launching of a ship, of any new ship, is a time of great danger."

He got up and turned to go, his shoulders unnaturally bent

for a man of no great age. Pelham called out suddenly, "Stop. What do you mean?"

"Perhaps I mean," Humphreys said, "that I, too, have made mistakes. Now I am going to do what I can to remedy them."

Pelham saw him beckon to a hulk of a lad who loitered nearby, gazing at the ships. The youth came quickly toward him, a look of simple eagerness on his face. Humphreys said to Pelham, "Look to your son," and the two of them set off: the strange, bent gardener, and his young acolyte who towered over him.

Pelham stood there, in confusion. Then he continued his journey home, where he found that his wife was no longer in the house, or Sebastian. She had taken him, the servants said, to her relative, the Earl of Shrewsbury, to celebrate Christmas Day.

Pelham forced a smile. "Of course. She told me. I had forgotten."

But he decided at that moment that Kate was no longer his wife. And his own life was, quite possibly, no longer worth living.

KATE WAS HURRYING ON FOOT THROUGH THE COLD streets of the city and northward up Shoe Lane. The shops and tradesmen's yards were shuttered up, and the snow-covered streets were empty except for people returning from church, or making visits to neighbors, wrapped up well against the cold weather.

She turned up Rose Alley where the beggars gathered round the fire. Last time she was here they had surrounded her, clamoring for alms, but now they stayed where they were, looking up at her in silence. Christmas Day was like any other day for them.

She gazed down the street to the house of Matthew Warriner, and saw that Matthew's house was wrecked, with the shutters hanging loose, and the doors, where they were not scorched by fire, smashed and pulled from their hinges.

She stood, unable to think, to breathe. Then she heard a

man's voice say quietly behind her, "'Tis no use looking for folk in that house, ma'am. No one lives there now, as you see."

She turned and looked into the face of a big, hook-nosed man with dark hair and beard. "I'm Ned's friend, Patrick," he said.

He spoke in a soft Irish voice, and she noticed that he was carrying a lute. Ned's lute. She said, "What has happened to them all?"

"They came in the middle of the night, ma'am."

"Who do you mean? Who did?"

"Enemies. They set fire to the house. Matthew is dead, Alice is dead, God forgive her sins against poor Matthew. They died because they knew too much about the secret of gold. It is indeed a terrible thing, this greed with which so many are infected."

Kate's heart was hammering so loud she thought it would burst. The secret of gold. Dee's letter to Auriel. Dry-throated, she whispered, "And Ned? What has happened to Ned? Please, you must tell me. I must speak to him."

"He is alive. But he is a prisoner of some ruffians in Alsatia."

She let out a low cry.

"He will be safe for a while," Pat went on, "because they want him to make gold. Robin told me so." He indicated a young, thin boy, with an anxious face made grotesque by the scarred red stumps he had for ears, who was gazing at her from Pat's side.

"The hunger for gold," Pat continued, "is why all this happened. The deaths. The burning. A bad business, ma'am." He gestured round the ravaged buildings. "But Ned's lute, at least, was safe. I am keeping it, for when he is free."

Some other men had come silently out of the ruins to join him. Kate recognized ginger-haired Davey as one of the men who had made her welcome on her first visit here; but now he stood looking subdued, holding his hat between his big hands, while little Pentinck hovered at his shoulder. There were other men: gypsies, she guessed, and some laborers whose clothes and skin were ingrained with coal dust. And there was the anxious, kindly-faced old man whom they called Dr. Luke.

"Patrick," she said, "I have to find Ned. How do I get into Whitefriars?"

"You cannot, by yourself. But if you do as we say, we will bring him to you. Soon."

She felt a tiny glimmer of hope, but she did not allow it to last too long.

37.

Thy freedom's complete, as a blade of the huff,
To be cheated and cheat, to be cuff'd and to cuff;
To stride, swear and swagger, to drink till you stagger,
To stare and to stab, and to brandish your dagger
In the cause of your drab.

OATH TO BE REPEATED BY NEW FREEMEN OF ALSATIA

THAT NIGHT NED FORCED HIMSELF TO WALK TO AND fro in his cell, while outside the snow lay white in the early-evening darkness, and the inhabitants of the liberty of Alsatia celebrated Christmas with noisy festivities tempered now and then by drunken exhaustion. As far as he could hear, their celebrations had gone on all day, and looked to be going on all night. Lazarus had told him he would smuggle in a roasted capon or two tonight, when the main feasting began. Ned almost pitied Lazarus's abject attempts to encourage him. He must have seen, must have known how Ned had been treated.

Now Lazarus was bent over the fire in the corner, clutching at the notes he had copied from Ned's Auriel letter and cackling away to himself as he added a drop of this, a pinch of that to his crucible.

"I saw them do this in Prague," he said, putting more coals

on the fire. "Do you remember, Ned? I watched them, in their little houses in the shadow of the castle. Distilling, again and again . . . And so they attained the White Stone, in the Street of Gold, the most beautiful of sights that I've seen in many a long year, until I saw this letter you've got, this letter of Dr. Dee's." He pointed to the letter, which Ned had left on the table.

The noise from some drunken revelers singing outside almost drowned out Lazarus's mutterings. Ned wondered how Robin had fared. Thank God he was out of all this.

There was a crash as the Scots alchemist dropped a brass container he was holding and quickly picked it up again. Ned said, "What in Christ's name are you doing?"

Lazarus glanced sideways at Ned and said, "I spoke to your young boy, Robin, this afternoon."

"You spoke to *Robin*?"

Lazarus nodded. "He's out at Bride's Fields, with the gypsies."

"If anyone saw you—if you endangered him in any way . . ."

"It's all right," said Lazarus, hastily backing away. "I wasn't followed, I swear! I was just checking that he got there safely. And we had a little chat. He's got his own crucible started again, and he advised me to add *flores*. Like the other ingredients in your letter."

"The letter," said Ned, pacing his room, "is not about making gold, Lazarus. I've told Robin again and again . . ."

"That's where you're wrong, my lad. And the boy's the one to unravel all its secrets, believe me! I thought *flores* meant something to do with flowers, but he said no, it was oxide of lead. So I've added some lead filings. See?" He pointed to the crucible. "Your Robin thought his crucible was dead, because it had been cold for so long. But it wasn't. There was just a glimmer of life left in it. He showed it to me. That young apprentice knows what he's doing." He grinned slyly. "And so do I, thanks to your letter from Dr. Dee."

Ned pulled a stool out from beneath the table and sat down to face Lazarus. "You won't give up, will you? If you really believe all this, then tell me: Why is it all so obscure?" He pointed to the letter with his finger. "Why did Dee use words like 'albedo' and 'nurtured'? Did he want his secret to be safe forever?"

Lazarus screwed up his eyes, thinking. "He perhaps wanted his secret to be secure from prying mischief-makers. But it's not as obscure as you think. Anyone who knows anything at all of the Great Art understands that *albedo* means 'the purifying,' which follows the stage of *nigredo,* the symbol of blackness and melancholy. And as for *nurtured,* why, the Stone has a seed, from which it is grown in a sealed vessel. But, mark you, the nurturer has to be one who is an adept in the art, and has come to it by a long and painful process."

"But what does it all *mean*?"

Lazarus touched his temple knowingly. "There are no simple answers, laddie. That's what it means."

Ned suppressed an exclamation of impatience and got up again to gaze through his grating, his only view of the outside world, where fires burned in the street and revelers drifted by. He had failed. His letter, whatever it meant, was worthless to him. He wondered if the guards would come to his cell again tonight.

Lazarus was holding the crucible up to the candlelight with gloating eyes. "Patience, patience. Didn't I say I'd soon have you as rich as your wildest dreams? Look, look how Silver Luna winks at us from the crucible; she's in there, hiding, and soon we'll have the princely white tincture..."

Ned, turning, said caustically, "Didn't you tell Prince Sigismund of Poland you could make silver? And when you failed, he had you thrown into prison."

"It was his fault! He wanted silver coins, merely; the man was never interested in the true secret of the Philosopher's Stone."

Ned laughed. "Your recipe was a vile mixture of arsenic and urine, as I remember."

Lazarus scowled. "Aye. He poured it over me. The ingratitude of the man—"

He broke off as there was a rattling at the door and the bolts were drawn back. Ned turned as it opened and saw the Duke's men. Lazarus stood up hurriedly, attempting to hide his crucible with his voluminous cloak.

A man swaggered toward Ned and said, "You're honored, Master Warriner. The Duke wants you to join in the celebrations."

"What if I have no wish to join them?"

They looked at one another and shrugged. Then two of them stepped forward to hold Ned's arms, and the man who had spoken hit him hard, twice, across the face. Ned, as he reeled, could see Lazarus wincing.

They dragged Ned outside into the lamplit street. It had begun to snow again. Ned told one of the men to take his hand off him; the blows that fell were harder this time.

Out in the street, the cold air whipped into his bruised face. He was dizzy from captivity, and from his injuries. He realized they were escorting him along the street to where the Duke and his companions sat in some state at several great trestle tables, set out in a courtyard lit by hanging lanterns and warmed by blazing fires in iron braziers. Logs of ash sent showers of sparks up into the sky. A pig was roasting on a spit, filling the air with a scent that made Ned reel with its cloying richness. A barrel of wine sat beside the Duke's table, from which tankards were regularly refilled. Torches of pitch-dipped pine flared along the half-ruined street, casting a reddish light on depraved and drunken faces. It was, thought Ned tiredly, like a scene from hell.

His escort pushed him toward the Duke. Ned stumbled to his knees.

"Well, it's my alchemist," roared the Duke as Ned picked himself up. "How goes it with the gold?"

Ned said, "These matters take time, my lord."

"Time?" The Duke scowled. His face was flushed and broken-veined in the leaping firelight. "I don't want excuses, Warriner, damn your eyes! You have that mad fellow to help you, don't you? The Pole?"

He called to a young whore, who was getting wine for one of his henchmen. Then he turned to Ned and patted the seat beside him. "Come. Sit at my side. Take the girl on your knee—yes, that's it—and a pot of wine. And sing me that song that used to go round about Northampton. The one about all his pretty boys dancing naked around his bed. Sing it."

It was an old song. Ned just about remembered it, and he certainly had an appreciative audience. Afterward they pressed food and more wine on him. It was so long since he'd eaten proper food that its richness made him nauseous. At one point Scrivener Steen came past. Ned said, "I knew all lawyers would rot in hell, and here you are."

"Careful," said Steen in his silken voice, his teeth bared in an unpleasant smile.

The whore nestling next to Ned fondled him between his thighs. He found the stale odor of her almost more than he could bear. He drank some of the ale they pushed before him, and they pressed him to sing again, as the torches crackled, and the savory juices from the pig dripped into the flames, and starving dogs snarled and fought over scraps in the shadows. He sang a song in French that sounded lighthearted but was really a virulent curse on drunken Londoners. He hoped no one understood French. Ruined buildings surrounded him in the strange, flickering light, and ruined faces, too, ravaged by drink, and debauchery, and some half-eaten by the pox; he'd thought the places he'd seen in his exile abroad had been bad enough, but this was worse.

The Duke turned and fixed his small, vicious eyes on him. "You have stopped singing, my friend. I do not recall giving you permission to stop."

The Duke's guards were watching. Waiting. Ned sang again.

More meat was being carved in great hunks and carried to each table on wooden platters. Ned was allowed some respite from his singing while the Duke and his companions tore at their meat with fingers and teeth and some fiddlers played. He saw Lazarus dancing with an elderly whore, kicking out his skinny legs and arms in time to the music, his long red hair flying. So much for the crucible.

Then more musicians arrived at the end of the street, escorted by the Duke's men. The Duke regarded them with satisfaction.

"Egyptians," he shouted across to Ned. "We always invite them to Alsatia on Christmas night. They bring luck for the New Year."

Amongst the new arrivals were fiddlers and tambour players in colorful costumes. The Duke ordered them to begin
their music, and they did so. There were dancers also: dark-
eyed girls who whirled and sang in foreign tongues to the wild
music. Some of the Duke's men got up to dance, stamping
their feet in a clumsy attempt to keep up with the fierce
rhythms, grasping after the girls. Then the dancing stopped
for a while, and three of the gypsies played an alien tune
which spoke of far-off, lonely places. Ned, forgotten for the
moment by the Duke and his men, got up to lean against a
wall by himself in the darkness and gazed at the lead fiddler.
And the fiddle player, who had stopped playing now, came
over to him. He had black hair and beard, and a big hooked
nose, and he put his hand on Ned's shoulder and said quietly,
"Christmas greetings to you, Ned."

"Pat," said Ned. "A pity you're so late. You've missed my
singing."

"Then thank God, indeed, for that. Robin told me you were
here." He looked around. "Watch, and wait."

"You'll have to be quick. The Duke promised he'd ask me
to sing again soon."

Pat made a little flourishing bow, with his fiddle dangling
from his hand. "Quick is the word," he said.

The musicians struck up again, and the gypsy girls danced
once more with their tambours and streaming ribbons. It was
close on midnight when one of the girls came to drag Ned into
the dance also, laughing at him, her white teeth flashing. But
within moments she was guiding him into a dark alleyway,
where there were no burning torches. She was not smiling
now. She said, in a low, urgent voice, "Here. Get into these."

She pushed a bundle of gypsy clothing at him: a brightly
colored waistcoat, a red scarf to tie around his waist, and a
wide-brimmed felt hat adorned with ribbons. Then Pat was
there, too, handing him a pennywhistle, the instrument Pat
had once taught him to play; and Ned was led into the midst of
the gypsy troupe, where he joined in with the music until Irish
Pat raised his hand and said to the Duke, who sat in a drunken
stupor with one arm round a girl and his other hand round a
tankard of ale, "Your grace, it is midnight. We must leave."

The Duke roused himself and banged the table. "No, no. Damn you. It's Christmas. The music must go on all night!"

An old Romany man stepped forward. His face was lined with age, and secret knowledge. He said, "It brings ill luck, your grace, to keep the gypsy folk against their will, after midnight."

The Duke waved his hand. "Oh, to hell with you, then, I'm tired of your banshee wailing anyway. Bring my own musicians back!"

And so the great gate to the Duke's liberty of Alsatia was unlocked, and the gypsy troupe thronged through into the Temple Gardens, tambours and whistles still playing, with Ned in their midst.

They fell silent once outside the walls and walked northward past the dark houses and taverns of Fleet Street, through the countryside that lay west of Shoe Lane, to the camp near the old lazar house known as Bride's Fields. The woodlands sparkled with snow, and the hawthorn hedges glistened under the full moon. Later one of the men sang a low song in some foreign language as he tramped.

The derelict land hereabouts had once belonged to St. Bride's Church. Its reputation as the former site of a leper refuge meant that people avoided it, except for those who had nowhere else to go: the peddlers and the tinkers, strolling players and swagmen, and the Egyptians.

Fires glimmered between the derelict buildings. It was Robin who came running out first, to meet the gypsy troupe. He said to Ned, with gladness, "I told Pat where you were. I told him! And I've got your lute safe."

He led Ned to an old byre where dry straw covered the floor and the stars shone through broken rafters overhead. A brazier burned in one corner. Ned's lute was leaning against the wall. Ned picked it up and plucked each string gently. But Robin was still waiting, bursting with impatience. "This is where I sleep," said Robin. "But there's something else. Look."

Ned put his lute down, with care. He knew what he was going to see.

"It's still working," Robin told Ned proudly as he pointed

at the crucible on the brazier, filled with some dark, oily substance. "It wasn't dead after all. That friend of yours, Lazarus, he helped me—"

Then someone else was there, coming up quietly behind him.

Kate.

Ned said, "Later, Robin."

Kate stood with her arms folded tightly, her hair uncovered. Her eyes were dark with emotion, with fear, even; he went up to her and took her in his arms, and he could feel her trembling. "Oh, Kate. What are you doing here? What about Pelham? And Sebastian?"

"Sebastian is safe with my uncle Shrewsbury in Coleman Street," she said. "Pat told me you'd be here."

Robin had slipped quietly outside. Ned drew her close. Her lips were cold from the snow, but he warmed them. At last he drew away. "All the more reason for you not to have come."

"You always told me that I looked for trouble. Even when we were small." She gazed up at him, and the snowflakes whirled about them. "Oh, Ned—" She pointed at the fresh bruises on his face. "Ned. What have they done to you?"

"I was being stubborn."

She gazed at him a moment, then she took his hand and led him across to one of the thatched shelters that stood a little distance from the fires. "They told me we would be safe here for the night," she said.

For a while they sat in the open doorway, watching as the gypsies gathered, to eat, and to make their music.

Ned said, "What about Pelham? Does he think you are at Shrewsbury's house?"

"Yes. And it's because of him that I had to come and see you. Ned, he's involved in the corruption at the dockyard. I know because I found some of his papers, and he's been paid money, so much money. And, Ned, I think I know now what your letter means. Something is going to happen at the launch of the two East India ships at Deptford tomorrow afternoon. Your *Mercator* must refer to the *Trade's Increase*."

"*Mercator*," said Ned slowly. "Merchant—trader . . ."

"Yes!" Kate took his hands. "I think the plotters you told

me about are going to mount some sort of insurrection during the launch ceremony, and at the same time attack the Spaniards somewhere—at their embassy, perhaps?—and set Ralegh free. Ned, it's all going to happen, so soon..."

He gazed into her passionate face. The night breeze lifted the loose tendrils of hair around her neck and shoulders.

"We must get away from all this," he said. "You, and me, and Sebastian."

She nodded and touched his stubbled cheek. "I thought," she said, "just for a moment, that you might say it was your duty to stop all this single-handedly."

"I'm no hero. And I'd be dead just as soon as they realized how much I knew."

The gypsy fiddlers were playing more softly now. The fires across the heath still burned between the lean-to shelters the squatters had made.

"I'll go anywhere with you." She smiled. "We will be travelers. Like the gypsies."

He kissed her hand. He took her inside and began to ease aside her robe, which was soaked with melted snow. "Tomorrow, at dawn, we'll collect Sebastian," he said. "And then we'll find a ship to take us far, far away." He kissed her bare shoulders. "But you are so cold. You must get warm again. Kate, I have loved you always."

Someone had already lit a fire in the hearth, and now Ned piled on more coals, so the flames leaped and cast grotesque shadows around the walls. He came back to Kate and knelt beside her to chafe her cold hands. She was trembling as he lowered her gown from her shoulders and bent to kiss her small breasts, where the nipples were tight and dark.

"Ned," she said, running her hands through his hair, pressing him to her, "Ned..."

"Hush."

They moved into each other's arms on the straw mattress beneath the broken rafters, and as the light of the moon trickled through the window they talked of the places Ned had visited, and would take her to: of the great cities of Europe, and the rivers, and the sea to the south, where the winters were warm, and vines and orange trees clung to the hillside slopes.

They talked of how Sebastian would grow well and strong in the sun, and how they would have more children, many of them, and Ned would teach them to play the lute, and Kate would teach them to sing; and then they stopped talking, except for when Kate saw the bruises on Ned's body, and then she cried, but he kissed her tears away.

Ned awoke two hours before dawn. He dressed and went outside, leaving Kate asleep. The moonlight gleamed on the snow; and as he stood there, and saw Pat and Davey coming up to him, he knew that even here safety was an illusion.

"The boy," said Pat.

"Robin?"

"Yes. I'm afraid he is dead."

Ned felt the cold anger growing as they told him that in the middle of the night Robin had gone out northward through the fields that led to Holborn, with the Scotsman Lazarus.

"With *Lazarus*?"

"Yes. He came here at midnight to find the boy."

"But why did they leave the camp? Why did you let the boy leave the camp?"

Pat put his hand on his shoulder. "Softly, now, Ned. Lazarus and Robin took care to avoid our watchers. But they were, I think, being watched all the way by someone else. Apparently they'd gone to look for mulberry bark by the light of the moon. Some magical nonsense, the Scotsman told us, that had to be done by night."

The emblem of Morus. Oh, thought Ned with bitterness, how his letter was tainted with blood. "So Lazarus is still alive, damn him?"

"Yes. He is in there." He indicated Robin's byre, where a lantern glowed from within.

Ned strode to it and flung open the door and saw Lazarus bent over Robin's brazier and crucible. Lazarus glanced round nervously. "Why, Master Ned—"

Ned pulled him up by his shoulders so his feet left the ground. He could smell the wine on the Scotsman's breath.

"You bastard," said Ned. "You took Robin out in the middle of the night, and now you are drunk, and he is dead."

Lazarus squirmed in his grip. "We had to go out, to look

for mulberry trees! It was in your letter. The emblem of *morus*... Robin said morus meant mulberries, mulberry bark he reckoned, and he'd spotted some earlier, on the heath. Your poor laddie Robin insisted. He guessed the big Irishman wouldn't let us out if we asked, so we just went."

Ned let go of him. Lazarus stumbled and fell to his knees.

"Who was it?" said Ned. "Who took him?"

Lazarus cowered. "It was some of the Duke's men—"

"Which ones?"

"Three or four big brutes, his guards. And that fellow you know was there. Scrivener Steen. He pointed out the boy to them. He said, as he took him, 'Warriner must learn that the Duke does not like his prisoners escaping.'"

"They let *you* go." Ned drew dangerously close again.

"I got away. I ran. But the poor laddie, Robin; they got him first..."

"And they knew where to find him. Damn you, Lazarus, they probably followed you here. How did he die?"

Lazarus hesitated. "I don't think you want to know the details. But after they'd finished with him, they cut his throat. I was hiding, in the bushes, I saw it all; I prayed to God to have pity on the poor lad."

Ned put his hand across his eyes briefly.

Lazarus struggled to his feet and pressed his hands together in entreaty. "I shouldn't have agreed to go out with him, I know. But he insisted, Ned. And we found what we needed, the mulberry bark for the crucible!" He pointed to the glass flask that was set on its stand over the glowing fire. "See, the crucible has reached Silver Luna! Now there is only one more stage before we have the Philosopher's Stone."

Ned pulled the Scotsman up by the shoulders again. Lazarus quaked. Ned said, "Shall I tell you what to do next with your crucible?"

Relief glowed in the red-haired Scotsman's face as he sensed in this a possible reprieve. "Yes, yes! Soon we shall all be rich, Ned, so rich..."

"Take your concoction in there, your silver luna, whatever it is—is it hot?"

"Oh, yes! The mother bird is keeping her nestlings warm."

"Take the flask, the hotter the better, and swallow all the foulness that's in it. I hope, you miserable Scottish Pole, that someday you die in agony and alone, as did Robin."

Lazarus fell back, trembling.

Ned went out. He slammed the door after him. He should have killed him. But enough people had already died.

N ED WOKE KATE WHILE IT WAS STILL DARK. "YOU must go back to Shrewsbury's house, to collect Sebastian," he said. "I will be very near, with Pat and his men. Then the three of us will leave London. Pat will have a boat ready to take us to Gravesend. We will take a ship for France."

He handed her a mug of warm ale, which she sipped gratefully before pulling on her gown and her cloak. Then they went outside together. Dawn was just a lightening, a slight lifting of the blackness in the east. The bonfires of last night were smoldering embers now. She shivered.

"I forgot to tell you, Ned. There was a strange visitor at my uncle Shrewsbury's house, a gardener, with a scar round his neck. Didn't you once mention such a man at Prince Henry's?"

He went very still. "Tell me about him."

She was afraid, then, when she saw the look in his eyes. But she told him how she'd asked Shrewsbury about him; and that Shrewsbury had told her how brave Humphreys had been at Ostend, in withstanding Spanish torture.

"But Ostend *fell*," said Ned. "Many men died cruelly. And I think it was Stephen Humphreys who betrayed them."

She listened intently. "All I know is what Shrewsbury told me. And now he is a gardener, with a high reputation; he has done work for Cecil, at Hatfield."

"As a *gardener*?"

"So I assumed . . ." She was holding her cloak tightly together with her hands, frightened by the look on his face. "But, Ned, there's something else. I only remembered afterwards. I saw this man Humphreys at the Wood Street Counter, when I was held prisoner there. And I was afraid of him. I thought he was watching me."

Ned was holding her by the shoulders, almost hurting her. Humphreys. Was he really working for Cecil? Or was he working for the Spaniards, who gave him gold secretly by night?

And what was he doing at Shrewsbury's house? Was he watching Kate and Sebastian? Who for?

"Did you speak with him?"

"Very briefly. Though his conversation was so odd. He said something about stirrings at the Scorpion's lair. I didn't understand. He seemed half-crazed."

"I've changed my mind," said Ned abruptly. "You must stay here. I am going to get our son."

"No." She was white-faced. "I must come with you!"

"You must not leave this camp. Do you understand?"

"Sebastian—I want to make sure Sebastian is safe."

"He will be. I promise. But I will be better doing this by myself. Stay here. Whatever you do, stay here."

HE SET OFF TOWARD THE CITY WHILE IT WAS STILL dark. The words of his Auriel letter ran ominously through his mind.

"Instruments of fire will be kindled close to the lair of the Scorpion."

He should have realized. He should have guessed, long ago. How much did Stephen Humphreys know?

38.

————————❧————————

*And betimes these gentle knights held many a tournament, and
jousted in jolly fashion, and then returned they to the court to
sing the Christmas carols.*

SIR GAWAIN AND THE GREEN KNIGHT (ANON. FOURTEENTH
CENTURY)

AFTER A SLEEPLESS NIGHT, PELHAM WENT EARLY TO
the dockyard. The wind had changed. The air was milder,
and the snow was melting quickly.

Today was St. Stephen's Day, the day the ships were to be
launched. The final caulking was being applied to the *Trade's
Increase* in her dry dock, while at the slipway for the *Peppercorn,* more melted tallow was being applied to the ways, and
under the ship's keel the tumbler shores were being set up
which would fall away as the vessel was launched.

The section of the riverside along which the King and his
party would walk was being roped off and swept clear of debris. The staging for the King's soldiers, overlooking the
wharf, was almost completed, and had been built strong
enough to hold seven cannon. Pelham walked slowly over to
it, feeling his injured leg dragging. The chief carpenter had

come to him earlier, as Lovett had said he would, to ask for men and supplies. Pelham had silently signed the papers.

He walked away, and went back to his office. He sat down and looked through the papers awaiting him on his desk; and then he put them aside again, in the utmost agitation.

He stood up suddenly. Lovett had hinted at some threat to his child: but Sebastian was safe at Shrewsbury's mansion. Pelham had to report what he suspected—that Lovett was planning some treachery that day.

As he paced his office, someone asked him if he was ill. He was about to deny it, but then he replied that yes, perhaps he was, perhaps he felt some slight perturbation of spirits that presaged a fever coming on. He announced that he would take an hour or so away from the office, to see to some business in town, and then he would return refreshed. As he took his coat and hat and made for the door he saw the other clerks whispering and glancing at him with hostility.

IN AN ATTEMPT TO EMULATE THE TRADITIONS OF HIS English predecessors, King James had arranged a great Christmas tourney at Whitehall Palace.

By ten o'clock, the tiltyard, which ran from the Holbein Gate in the north as far as the riverside entrance, was crowded already with spectators. Tiers of wooden benches had been assembled around three sides of the yard, and at each corner flags and pennants fluttered in the westerly breeze. On the fourth side was the stand where the King himself sat in state beneath a gilded canopy. The Queen was beside him, as were the Princess Elizabeth, and the younger prince, Charles, a sickly child who had been slow to learn to walk. In attendance also was the King's favorite, Robert Carr, resplendent in his silks and lace. The King turned to Carr often to talk, resting his hand on his thigh. He scarcely glanced down at the arena, where the tilters—the Duke of Lennox, the Earl of Pembroke, Sir Thomas Somerset, and Sir Richard Preston—were waiting, on horseback, for the competition to begin.

Francis Pelham, only recently arrived, had pushed his way through the crowded public thoroughfare to the north-facing stand, where he stood close to the entrance through which the competitors were arriving. He watched and waited, taut with anxiety.

Prince Henry came riding into the arena, with all his entourage. He dismounted and knelt, as did his followers, to receive the blessing of his chaplain; then he was in the saddle again, and taking up his lance: a glorious figure in green and silver, his horse likewise adorned. As a fanfare of trumpets sounded and drums rolled, the Prince charged the length of the tiltyard, and his opponent Pembroke did likewise, from the opposite direction. The crowd roared; the dust rose from beneath the pounding hooves of the two galloping horses. As lances clashed, Henry stayed firm, but the Earl of Pembroke went crashing to the ground. Great cheers arose from all around. At both ends, the ranks of armed guards and trained crossbowmen raised their weapons in salute to the young Prince.

"Miles a Deo!" They chanted aloud Henry's chosen knightly title. *"Miles a Deo.* Soldier of God..."

Pelham saw Spenser standing behind the ranks of archers. The old soldier's eyes narrowed in appraisal as the Prince prepared for his second sally. Pelham left his place in the crowded gallery and forced his way through despite the voluble protests of those he disturbed. The Prince had ridden back down to the far end of the tiltyard in preparation for the second charge by the time Pelham reached Spenser. "My lord. A word with you, if you please."

Spenser, turning, looked startled as recognition dawned. "Pelham. What is it?"

"My lord, what I have to say concerns the safety of the Prince and his father. It is vital that we speak in private."

Spenser looked around, then he said, "One minute only. Come with me."

The whole arena was cheering as the Prince thundered to victory over Sir Thomas Somerset, breaking his lance and forcing his surrender. Spenser marched swiftly to the alley alongside the stables, with Pelham limping after him. When they were alone Spenser turned. "Well? Explain yourself."

Pelham was dismayed by the old soldier's antagonism. In

spite of the cool breeze, he found himself perspiring. But he drew a deep breath and was about to speak, when he realized that Spenser was no longer looking at him, but was looking past Pelham's shoulder with eagerness, almost relief. Pelham turned and saw Lovett was there. Lovett glanced at Pelham, then said sharply, "Any problems here?"

Spenser said, "None whatsoever." On seeing the look that passed between Lovett and Spenser, Pelham thought that he had never perhaps felt such despair.

Spenser faced him squarely. "You are a loyal man, Pelham," he said. "Oh, there are people who play the traitor in this land: I talk of the crooked band of self-serving advisers and craven councillors who surround our King. There are highly paid cowards who would urge him to abandon our brave Protestant allies abroad and conspire with the Papist scorpion Spain. But you, I think, are with us."

"He is with us," said Lovett sleekly. His hand tightened on Pelham's arm. "And like us, his loyalty to our Prince, above all others, is unshakable. Isn't that so?"

The crowd roared as the tourney reached its climax. Pelham felt unsteady. He whispered, *"Yes."*

"And your reason for coming here?"

"There was a minor problem," he stammered, "with a shipment of goods, for the Prince. But it can be settled later."

Lovett said, "Good. How is your little son this fine morning, Master Pelham?"

"He is well, thank you, sir, very well."

"Then let us trust he remains so. The winter is such a treacherous time for infants, is it not? Even for those with powerful relatives."

The crowd's roar came again from the tiltyard; Lovett turned to look, then gazed again at Pelham. "Go back to Deptford," he said, "and get on with your work."

Thus Pelham was dismissed, like the minion he was. As the fanfares sounded to herald the next round of tourneying, Pelham stumbled away, back through the yards and buildings of the palace toward the river.

If Spenser also was involved in this treachery, who else

was? Did Lovett know that Sebastian was at Shrewsbury's house?

What was being planned?

The answer to the last of his questions came as he reached the riverside. For there, he heard the news, being exchanged with such excitement, such embellishing with lurid detail. "The Spaniards were torn to pieces—the deputy ambassador quite unrecognizable—blood and bodies scattered between the Tower and the river . . ."

He heard that at nine that morning, an explosion had ripped apart the house of Señor Fabrio, the deputy Spanish ambassador, in Crab Lane.

SHORTLY AFTER DAWN THAT MORNING, NED WARriner had at last reached Petty Wales, and the winding streets that lay between the Tower and the Thames. The bulk of the Tower of London rose threateningly above him. He imagined Ralegh, in his prison room there. Longing for freedom.

Early tradesmen were on the streets, but otherwise all was quiet. This part of the city was occupied by merchants and their families, and by officials who worked at the Tower's Mint and Ordnance, and by the deputy—at present acting—ambassador for Spain, in nearby Crab Lane. Fabrio.

He shook his head, absorbing the humdrum routine of this peaceful part of the city. He told himself he was suffering from a fevered imagination. Or perhaps from the beatings he'd received in Alsatia.

And then, as he approached Crab Lane, he saw something that made his heart race. He could see Fabrio's house from here, well shuttered and still in darkness: no sign yet of activity. But at the adjoining house, he saw the door open. Two men came out, looked quickly up and down the street, then left. Furtively, almost.

Ned drew a little closer, still pressing close to the adjacent buildings for cover; and then he saw someone else, coming down the street, with four men in attendance—a man in a pale, loose coat that he knew well: Stephen Humphreys.

Had he come here for more gold, from Spain?

But Ned saw him go, not to Fabrio's house but to the adjacent building; saw him knock at the door, then turn to his men, saying something, shrugging his shoulders.

And then there was a blinding flash, a great roaring sound; and timbers, tiles, walls, and windows were hurled outward and upward into the still morning air; then another explosion, and another: and before Ned's eyes the houses in Crab Lane disintegrated in a storm of wreckage and dust. He crouched low, his arms over his face, to protect himself. The stench of powder, of destruction, reminded him of war, and for a moment he thought he was back in the Netherlands, remembering the roar of the cannon, and how men had died, screaming, in the battle lines next to him.

No one could have survived. Neither the occupants of the houses, nor those who had been in the street outside.

The debris was raining down now; the sky was dark with the smoke and filth. Farther down the street, householders had come running, to gaze with horror at the wreckage, at the exposed timbers and ruined walls of the houses that were no more; at the half-buried bodies.

Somewhere a woman started screaming, and would not stop.

It had started. What else was going to happen at the ship launch today?

And then he thought, *Sebastian*.

IT WAS A QUIET, SUNNY MORNING IN PROSPEROUS Coleman Street. Some children played with a brightly colored ball. A milkmaid, singing, drove her cow down the broad, tree-lined lane.

But Ned, standing at the tradesman's entrance to the Earl of Shrewsbury's big house, felt as if the darkness were gathering all around. He said to the man who had opened the door to him, "He must still be here. I have authority from his mother, to take him to her." He handed the man some coins.

The manservant frowned. "I thought he'd gone. Wait a moment. I'll check." He came back quickly. "Yes. The little boy has been taken to see the ships that are to be launched this afternoon."

"Taken by whom?"

"By his mother's servants, of course. She sent them to escort him, an hour or so ago."

Was this Pelham's doing? Had Pelham sent for the little boy? No: surely Pelham would have announced himself. And he would not have used Kate's name.

He wondered how he would tell Kate that her son had gone.

The main gates to Shrewsbury's mansion were being hauled open. From the stables at the side of the house came men in the Earl's livery, leading horses out, already saddled and bridled.

Ned said to the servant, "I must speak with the Earl. About the little boy."

"You'll be lucky. He's just been summoned to a meeting of the Privy Council, at Whitehall. A rider came, just before you did. Haven't you heard about the explosion? The house of the deputy Spanish ambassador has been blown up. The King will be desperate to placate the Spaniards."

"I'd heard. Do they know yet who did it?"

"Some privateers have already been arrested. Apparently they'd been stockpiling gunpowder in the empty house next to the deputy ambassador's home for days." He shook his head, frowning. "The Spaniards won't be pleased that their deputy and his whole household have been murdered. It will be a busy time for Lord Cecil and all his messengers, trying to placate them."

He waited for a while, perhaps hoping for more coins; but when none were forthcoming he started to close the gate.

Ned stood there a moment, with his hand over his eyes, as if the sunlight dazzled him.

It had started. And Sebastian was a pawn in the endgame; for the plotters had him.

39.

Therefore keep close of thy tongue and of thy hand
From the officers and governors of the land;
And from other men that they of thy craft nothing know
For in witness thereof they will thee hang and draw.

ELIZABETHAN BALLAD (ANON.)

SOME PAIN IS BEARABLE, AND SOME IS NOT; THUS were discovering the pirates captured within an hour of the explosion and held in the grim stone cellars below the Marshalsea prison. They had been told that soon they would face a short and swift hearing at St. Margaret's Hall in Southwark. The outcome was foreordained. They were told to expect execution by hanging at Deptford at noon that same day, just before the ship launch. Their speedy deaths, before even the dust and rubble had settled in the street of the deputy ambassador's house, would be an appeasement to Spain: news of the executions would be sent forthwith to Madrid, accompanied by the most profound apologies of King James, together with promises of compensation.

There were not many to witness what was happening in the grim depths of the Marshalsea prison that morning. But those present were important enough, chiefly Waad, the lieutenant of the Tower, and other less well-known servants of the Crown, who gathered round as three of the pirates suspected of being ringleaders were separated from their fellows and subjected to His Majesty's justice in the form of a method borrowed from the mighty Spanish Inquisition; for in his younger days Waad had traveled widely, and had seen the refined skill of the Inquisitors in the Spanish Netherlands as they sought out heretics. He had noted the most effective of punishments against men of natural fortitude and stubbornness.

Alvaric Johnson, Ralegh's gallant Black Bird of Cadiz, was hanging in manacles, alongside two of his companions. The three of them had withstood their torment better than the old draper Godwin Phillips had, seven weeks ago. They were not young, but they were used to bearing pain with courage. They were naked, except for their ragged breeches; their sinewed flesh was checkered with old scars and gashes.

Waad was asking them about Ralegh, and the ship launch, and what either had to do with the blowing up of deputy ambassador Fabrio's lodging; but in reply Alvaric Johnson, their spokesman, growled out, "We know nothing. We were told only about the gunpowder. We were told to steal it from the docks, and to hide it in the empty house in Crab Lane."

"Until today. The morning of St. Stephen's Day. When you were told to light the fuses and run. And then what?"

Johnson was silent.

Waad said, "More was to happen at the ship launch. What?"

"I don't know what you're talking about."

"What part was Ralegh to play?"

"Very little, I guess," said the old privateer grimly, "seeing as he is locked in the Bloody Tower, and likely to remain so, God damn those who were responsible for his captivity, bastard traitors all of them."

Johnson knew he was going to die. There was a certain luxury in saying what he thought.

Waad stepped closer. "Sir Walter Ralegh wrote a letter to you, Johnson."

"I know of no letter!"

"No. It was intercepted by loyal men before it reached you. But I will tell you what it said. *'To the Black Bird. The golden wine, I have heard, is still there for the drinking.'* What do you think this letter might mean, Johnson?"

If Johnson had not been suspended by his wrists, he would have shrugged. Instead he laughed.

"You are desperate indeed," he said, "and stupid, to query a man's drinking habits and think you are uncovering a plot. Golden wine? What if I told you it stood for piss? I would piss on you all if I could—what if I told you it meant that?"

His hanging colleagues grinned.

Waad ordered the gaolers to add weights to the shackles on Johnson's feet, so the pirate grimaced in fresh agony as the sinews of his arms were stretched to their extremity. Waad then gave a signal to the two guards who stood on each side of the privateer, and together they put their hands to Johnson's hips and jerked sharply at his suspended body.

Johnson's screaming was thin and pitiful as his shoulders were dislocated. The sweat poured down his face. The gaolers moved to pull at Johnson's body again. One of the other pirates called, "Stop. There is something else. There were cannon, stolen from the shipyard at the same time as the gunpowder."

"Where are they now?"

"They were taken yesterday to various secret places round the city. We know nothing else. Dear God. We would tell you if we did."

Johnson's screams had become agonized gasps. One of Waad's men turned and spoke to him quietly. "I think they mean it, sir. Those in charge would tell them as little as possible of the actual plot, in case they were captured. As they have been."

Waad nodded. "Very well. That will be all. We want them alive for their hanging later."

They were cut down, and Johnson, keening softly in his suffering, was left to lie on the floor. They were all locked in there, in the dark, to await the end which they perhaps wished was upon them already.

• • •

FROM LONDON SECRET MESSENGERS RODE OUT IN various directions with news of the destruction of the house in Crab Lane. Their horses were as ready as they were, for this message had been long awaited; and they rode to the same men who had received the mulberry trees from the roving peddler.

Since the peddler had made his rounds, old weapons had been pulled out of their hiding places; muskets had been oiled and swords sharpened. There had been private summonings of the long-lapsed county militias, who made quiet preparations in quiet places. *The native birds of righteousness.*

A secret army of English Protestant men was preparing to march on London, where the concealed cannon, and many more armed men, were waiting.

They intended to see the Noble Prince elevated, and the Lion fall.

THE CHIEF AND MOST CLEVER OF THE SERVANTS OF King James, Sir Robert Cecil, all too conscious that he did not know as much as he should, was angry with his servants, who had been searching the city for the Auriel letter and had failed. Worse than failure, on occasion those they questioned had had to be silenced.

There was one unlikely man on whom Cecil's last hopes rested. His name was Stephen Humphreys. A minor and damaged spy, he had only yesterday sent a message to Cecil to say that he was close to discovering who had the Auriel letter, and would shortly report with the information; but he gave no names, no places. And as Cecil waited for confirmation that this most unpromising of his spies had actually achieved two major coups, firstly by capturing the owner of the Auriel letter, and secondly by uncovering the detailed plans of the state's enemies; as Cecil waited, feverishly pacing the rooms of his great mansion in the Strand, news came of the catastrophic explosion, in which Stephen Humphreys had been blown to pieces; the deputy Spanish ambassador also.

Cecil was well aware that this was probably only the beginning. The pirates' confessions were sent to him by William Waad; they revealed nothing he did not know. He called to his servants and began to prepare himself for the hangings of the pirates, and the ceremony of the ship launch. But first he had a visit to make.

RALEGH HAD HEARD THE NEARBY EXPLOSION. FOR A moment, as he smelled the stench of powder, and heard the shouts of alarm, the pounding feet of troops racing to the armory for weapons, his spirits surged in wild, unreasoned hope. *"News of such treasure, such golden hopes..."*

But his spirits sank as low as they had ever been when there was a knock at his door and he was told he had a distinguished visitor: the sly hunchback Robert Cecil, whom Ralegh had once believed to be his friend. Their young sons used to play together. But now Ralegh knew that Cecil was his silken-voiced enemy who six years ago had placed suspicions of Ralegh's treachery in the newly crowned King James's heart and caused him to be sentenced to a living death in his cold stone prison.

It was plain to Cecil, on entering the old mariner's prison room in the Tower, that Ralegh was as surprised by the explosion in Crab Lane as anyone; surprised and shocked, too, when Cecil curtly explained Johnson's involvement, and his imminent execution for treason. Ralegh paced his room and declaimed with passion that it was traitors within who drove true and loyal men to such acts of desperation.

But Ralegh did not expand on his theme when invited to do so by a calmly lethal Cecil.

Soon it became clear to Ralegh that Cecil knew all about the first letter sent to him by John Dee. Cecil knew also about the letter Ralegh had tried to send to Johnson using Kate Pelham as his messenger. But Cecil learned no more, for as he suspected, Ralegh had never received the second, the crucial letter that Dee wrote to him, giving final details of the plan to set him free.

Afterwards Cecil told his chief men that they must concentrate all their resources on the ship launch that afternoon; for he had grave fears that the crowds, and the ceremony, could be used to disguise further treachery.

"My lord," said one of his men. "Should you not advise the King to stay away?"

Cecil looked at him sharply. "How would I explain it to him? He would have London turned upside down for traitors. He would order the Star Chamber to summarily execute every minor suspect in the land. His panic would know no bounds. No. We shall not trouble His Majesty the King with our suspicions."

Another asked him if he could question the Prince's men. Or even the Prince.

"No," Cecil replied, "because I might be wrong."

And because someday the Prince would be King of England.

WHEN HE GOT BACK TO HIS HOUSE IN THE STRAND, just before noon, Francis Pelham saw some of Sebastian's wooden soldiers lying by the fireplace in the parlor. He was surprised by how shaken he was to see them. He thought, He will miss his playthings, at Shrewsbury's house.

He prepared himself next to go to Deptford, to attend the launch ceremony; he dressed carefully, in freshly brushed black clothes; and he listened to his steward, who gave him further details of the great explosion that had destroyed the lodgings of the Spanish ambassador's deputy in Crab Lane. It had been the work of privateers, he'd heard, who had been captured, and had confessed to blowing up the Spaniards. The pirates were to be hanged today, so that Spain could be informed of the instant retribution imposed on them.

And Pelham thought, It is over. A single gesture of defiance, a warning to Spain . . . It is over. He began to feel something like hope.

At Deptford the sun was shining on the throng of master shipbuilders and their hands, all working on the two East Indiamen: polishing brass, making final adjustments to the mainmast. At the slipway down which the *Peppercorn* was to be launched, the hardened tallow on the ramps was being coated with a soap of lye and ash to ease the ship's passage. Pelham arrived soon after midday in time to see sweating laborers with poles starting to knock out the keel blocks one by one from beneath the ship's great hull, guided by an overseer with a timepiece. Each blow brought her nearer to the crucial point of launching. Soon the vessel would be ready, with the help of block and tackle, to slide down the ways, with the tumbler blocks falling away around her.

Everywhere, Pelham could see the officials and guards of the East India Company in their blue and gold livery. Everywhere he heard talk of the destruction of the house of the Spanish ambassador's deputy, and of the capture and imminent execution of the pirates who had committed the crime.

He walked on to the place where Lovett's carpenters were setting up the new gun platform, which would dominate both the quayside and the area where the King and his entourage would be. The chief carpenter came up to him and asked him for the keys to the storehouses. The work was almost finished, he told Pelham, but they needed a few more lengths of timber for reinforcements.

Pelham, finding the man's tone peremptory for an underling, said curtly, "I will unlock the door to the storehouse myself."

"I need your keys," the man said, more stubbornly this time. "I'll let you have them when I've finished with them. Sir."

Pelham's anger rose. Then he heard a familiar voice behind him say, "Do as he asks, Master Pelham."

Pelham whirled round and found himself face-to-face with John Lovett.

"Do as he says," repeated Lovett more quietly.

Pelham gave the chief carpenter his keys. The carpenter nodded to Lovett and went on his way. Lovett said, after checking there was no one within earshot, "I hope you are ready to play your part, Pelham. You know, don't you, that seven cannon are to be hoisted onto this platform? To signal the moment of the launch?"

"Yes. Of course."

Lovett drew closer. "At some point, the gunners might require access to the powder stores. You will help them in any way you can. Do you understand? And if it seems to you that those cannon are being prepared for something more than a mere signal, then you will say nothing. Nothing at all."

Pelham looked round wildly. Did Lovett mean the guns would be loaded? If so, they would fire directly into the King's troops.

He said, shaking his head, "I do not understand. I am not sure I can be a part of this."

"You have no choice. You see, we have your little son. Breathe a word of this, Pelham, and we will force you to watch the infant die, slowly. If you still refuse to help us, then we will find someone else who will know what to do."

He looked round. And Pelham saw the faces, in the crowd, watching and ready. Watching *him.* Lovett went on, "The choice is yours." Lovett turned and left.

Pelham, looking round wildly, saw that soldiers were being lined up all along the wharf. A troop of guards came up to him; their captain saluted and said, "Master Pelham? We need your signature, if you please, sir, for access to the powder store." He showed him a warrant. It already bore Lovett's signature. Pelham took the warrant and signed it also.

SEVEN MILES AWAY, IN FRONT OF THE PALACE OF Whitehall, Prince Henry stood amidst a panoply of pennants and banners, with ranks of soldiers on either side. The sun glinted on their swords and armor.

He stood bright-eyed and eager as his courtiers made the final adjustments to his costume, which was a suit of rich emerald silk lined and slashed with pale green satin and adorned with bunches of silver ribbons. His cloak fell back from his shoulders to reveal a jeweled sword at his waist.

A flotilla of barges adorned with silver and green flags lay moored alongside the river stairs, waiting to transport the Prince and his military escort to Deptford. Many thought, though they did not dare to say it, that Prince Henry looked more like a monarch than his father.

The Prince stepped forward, ready to take his place in the

leading barge. His entourage followed: his chaplain Mapperley, his Chief of Horse Duncan, his bodyguard, and his pages,
all of them dressed in his livery of silver and green, with silver
plumes in their hats. The smallest of them, Sebastian Pelham,
not yet two years old, was riding on the shoulders of a stout
man-at-arms, for he was to be a soldier for the day.

40.

"Some few of them suffered."

ROBERT CECIL'S COMMENT ON THE EXECUTION OF SIX
HUNDRED REBELS AT TYBURN IN 1570, AFTER THE UPRISING
OF THE NORTHERN EARLS

THERE HAD BEEN SEVERAL INSTANCES OF MASS EXE-
cutions of pirate bands that year, for the truce in the summer between Spain and the Netherlands had reduced the
freedom of the pirates in the Narrow Seas and had driven
them instead to Irish waters, where the squadrons of pirate
leaders such as Bishop and Easton caused such mayhem in
their assaults on lawful shipping that even the sluggish and
heavily bribed English admirals had to act, by hauling in a
number of minor privateers from their bases of Baltimore and
Crookhaven.

These privateers were usually put on trial and executed en
masse, at Wapping or Deptford, aptly in sight of the great
river and its ships.

And so the hangings of Johnson and his fellows, as a prel-
ude to the launch, were no novelty to the London crowds. The
gallows had been built in haste, close to the timber yard at the

far end of the Deptford wharf, and by noon that day the pirates stood in chains there, all except for Alvaric Johnson, hero of Cadiz, who had been crippled by his questioners, and so lay on the ground tied to a hurdle.

They were due to die with the incoming tide, and the lessening expanse of mudflats at the river's edge, where seabirds clustered and rose wheeling to the skies, must have told them that the time was near. The scaffold was surrounded by soldiers. Three chaplains stood praying with the condemned men, but their solemn words went unheeded as the pirates gazed seaward, with the salt wind in their faces.

The crowds gathered, to watch the men die.

NED WARRINER, MINGLING WITH THE CROWD AT ITS thickest, could see the gallows. Alvaric Johnson was supported now by two soldiers. His face was gray with pain, his limbs oddly twisted. Ned had seen this kind of mutilation before. He wondered what Johnson had told his torturers in his agony. What, indeed, he knew to tell them. Johnson would not taste the golden wine with Ralegh again.

The first of the pirates was being dragged to the scaffold. His arms were tied, but he was struggling, which pleased the crowd; those closest to the scene were cheering him on, and roaring obscenities. Two soldiers tried to hold the condemned man still while the executioner put the noose round his neck, but his efforts to escape made the noose too tight, with the result that as he swung into oblivion, instead of his neck breaking he began to strangle.

Ned turned his back on the man's slow agony and began to push his way along the wharf. He had seen death often, but he preferred the battlefield to the sordid spectacle of a public hanging. He knew from experience that there was always violence flaring round execution scenes; people were often robbed, or stabbed, or both, while whores plied their trade in public. The forces of law and order were focused on the gallows. Everywhere else, in the periphery, people took their chances amongst the unruly mob.

He passed the *Trade's Increase,* waiting in her dry dock

for the tide to rise to the crucial height; and then he reached the *Peppercorn*'s exposed hull. Laborers still worked there, adjusting the bilge blocks, securing the tackle, building up the shoring that would be necessary to keep the vessel stable as she slid down the slipway and her stern lifted with the huge impact of reaching the water. He looked round and saw that the dignitaries were beginning to arrive with their entourages: the Earl of Suffolk, the Lord Admiral Sir Charles Howard, Phineas Pett, and Sir Thomas Smith, governor of the East India Company, who would host the banquet for the King afterwards. The wharf was lined with the King's soldiers and with men of the East India Company, in their blue and gold livery. The state barges of the King and the Prince, accompanied by their ceremonial guard, were expected within the half hour.

On a table covered with rich blue velvet stood a great silver cup, from which the Prince would drink wine as each ship was launched.

At the spectacle of Silver Luna, raised to bestow libation, the Noble Prince will be elevated, and the Lion shall fall...

The tide was rising fast. Musicians with sackbuts and viols were seated by the stairway, tuning their instruments in readiness for the royal family's arrival. On a newly built platform overlooking the landing place were seven gleaming cannon, surrounded by soldiers who were already priming them in preparation for the gunfire that would announce the double launch. Ned recognized them as twelve-pounder culverins. He thought, Why are guns of such a size needed, when no ammunition is to be fired?

He pulled up suddenly. A cold suspicion was starting to form in his mind.

Behind him the roar of the crowd swelled. The second pirate had joined his companion on the scaffold. He was more fortunate: the fall broke his neck. The first one was still writhing in agony as he slowly choked to death. It would soon be time for Alvaric Johnson to die. Half-crippled, blindfolded, the old mariner who had once been Ralegh's friend was already being carried up to the scaffold to have the noose placed around his neck.

Down by the crowded wharf Ned could hear drums rolling. The King's barge, blue-canopied and gilded, was approaching, its banks of oars dipping in and out of the water. Trumpeters clarioned a welcome. Along the quayside marched a large troop of men wearing the green tabards that were the livery of Prince Henry over their breastplates, while silver plumes waved in their glittering helmets.

Ned thought, Surely a ceremonial escort does not consist of perhaps a hundred men, as the Prince's did. He pushed closer. He saw that Henry's soldiers were heavily armed, with short swords in their belts and sheathed pistols.

And they were led by Edward Spenser.

The crowd jeered as the first pirate's sufferings ended at last. His eyes rolled up and his tongue, discolored and swollen, protruded from his mouth. As he was cut down, some of the onlookers scrambled to touch his still-warm body, for the touch of a hanged man's hand was a well-known cure for scrofula, wasting sickness, epilepsy . . .

Epilepsy? Ned knew that something crucial was there, in that connection, but he had no time for that now. He pushed on through the crowd so he had a clearer view of the gun platform, and of the twelve-pounder culverins: guns capable of firing a massively destructive round of shot. The wind was increasing in strength, and the water was growing rough. Very soon, Ned guessed, before the tide was too high, the *Trade's Increase* would have to be set afloat from her dry dock. Then it would be the *Peppercorn*'s turn.

He looked back along the wharf again. Two more pirates danced at the end of their ropes. The crowd was getting its money's worth. And time was running out.

He felt a hand on his shoulder, and heard a soft Irish voice in his ear. "Here we all are, Master Ned. Just as you said."

It was Pat. And he was not alone. Swiftly Ned assessed his forces. There were five of them that he knew: Pat, Davey, little Pentinck, Black Petrie, and old Tew; but there were more men besides, perhaps a dozen of them, all dressed in the canvas shirts and ragged breeches of dockworkers. He did not ask where they had found the clothes.

Even Dr. Luke was there, hovering anxiously in the background looking hot, and troubled, and sober; and Ned was aware, too, of a number of dark gypsy faces around them in the crowd, watching, waiting.

He let out a deep breath and gazed at them all. "Do any of you know anything about cannon, and gunpowder?"

Davey stepped forward and pointed to little Pentinck. "He does," he said. "He used to be a gunner on a privateer."

Ned turned swiftly to Pentinck. "Do you see those cannon? What would you do if you didn't want them to fire? And if you didn't want anyone to notice what you'd done?"

Pentinck's wizened monkey face was taut with concentration. "Charcoal's the answer," he said at last.

"Charcoal?"

"Yes. Add lots of charcoal to the mixture. There's charcoal in the gunpowder anyway. Looks just like the saltpeter in it at first glance. No one will ever know the difference. Except that it won't fire."

"Then that," said Ned, "is what we must do."

Pat was frowning. "How do we get access to the powder stores? And to the cannon? There's not much time."

"I know that," said Ned. "I know. Wait there." He started off toward the warehouses, and then he heard someone, running, behind him, and an arm was round his neck, half-choking him, until he feigned submission, then whipped round, flinging the man to the ground. It was Pelham.

Pelham struggled to pull himself up; he breathed, "Get away from here, damn you, Warriner, haven't you done enough harm?"

Ned hauled him to his feet, gripped him by the shoulders. "There's going to be treachery today. We must stop it. You have to help me."

Pelham, his face gray, said, "I can do nothing. They have Sebastian."

He pointed to Prince Henry's retinue. Amongst his men Ned saw a dozen little pageboys dressed like men-at-arms in miniature green tabards, with tiny swords at their sides and silver plumes in their helmets. Close by was a child too small to walk with the others, so one of the soldiers had let him ride on his shoulders.

So he could be seen.

"Do you think," said Ned quietly, "that I don't care about Kate's son? Listen, Pelham. I think all our lives are pretty well ruined, yours and mine; but let us for God's sake save what we can from all this. I believe we can save the child. Listen. Those cannon are the key to it all. The plotters plan for them to be loaded, to be aimed into the King's men. We must stop them."

Pelham was looking at the new ships swarming with workmen; at the wharves packed with spectators; at the King and his party congregating in their viewing compound. At the seven guns, manned by Prince Henry's men, and aimed at the King's troops.

"You are mad," Pelham said.

"Perhaps," agreed Ned quietly. "But no more so than our enemies. You realize, don't you, that the cannon will only be the start? I think there are many more conspirators, all around the city, around the country, who have been waiting for this day, this signal. They know it because of the mulberries."

"Mulberries." Pelham's voice was bitter with scorn. "Now I know you have lost your wits."

"Perhaps. But we have to do something, or Sebastian and many more will die. Pelham, they'll have the gunpowder and shot set aside, for those cannon. Do you know where it's kept? And do you have access?"

Pelham still looked gray and broken. "Yes. But—"

"Listen to me. You must go with these men of mine to those stores. You have the authority. You will make sure those guns do not do what they are supposed to do—but no one must realize anything is different. Do you understand?"

Pelham looked round almost wildly, as if for escape. Ned said, "This is the boy's only chance. Believe me."

Pelham swallowed and nodded. Pat and the others were waiting close by. Ned beckoned them close and explained. Pelham set off, with Pat and Pentinck and two of Pat's helpers, toward the stores. Ned went over to Dr. Luke, who hovered close by, and pointed out the Prince's retinue, and the small figure in its midst.

"I want you to go over there, Luke. Get as close to that little boy as you can. The one on the soldier's shoulders. Then you must watch, for the moment those gunners prepare for firing..."

Ned continued to outline his instructions, breaking off now and then to watch tensely as Pat's men approached the store-house. He was waiting for someone to stop them, but no one did, for they had Pelham with them. And besides, the attention of the crowds, and all the soldiers, was, for the moment, on the sufferings of the last dying pirate.

Prince Henry stood at the front of his men like a king in waiting; while in the ranks of his pages a small boy perched high on a soldier's shoulders wept for his mother.

CLOSE TO THE DRY DOCK, THE CROWD SURGED REST-lessly, and cries of protest arose. Because the execution of the pirates had taken so long, the tide had come in too far to permit the launch of the *Trade's Increase* without damage to the hull. The onlookers groaned in disappointment, though this was not a rare occurrence at a dry-dock launch, where the timing was always crucial.

But at the *Peppercorn,* high above her slipway, the last of the bilge and keel blocks had been removed, and the overseer signaled to the master shipbuilder that all was ready. The ship-builder nodded and watched, carefully calculating the point at which the final tumbler shores could be removed. Then the straining ropes would be severed with axes, and pulleys would be used to start the ship on her slow descent to the water. If nothing happened to delay it. Ned, who had seen slipway launches before, guessed there was about a quarter of an hour to go before the crucial moment. Prince Henry's soldiers stood in ranks, formidable in their green and silver livery, with Spenser at their head. Ned remembered grimly the weapons his men carried.

He looked toward the gun platform, wondering if Pelham and Pat had gained access to the crucial powder stores; but his view was blocked as a horse-drawn cart went by, laden with the bodies of the dead pirates. The soldiers had to clear a way for it through the crowd, who were pointing and jeering at the sprawled corpses. Ned saw that someone was trying to push through to get to the moving cart, a large, stumbling figure: Nicholas Lovett, moving with a fierce concentration on his round, simple face. The guards were shoving him aside, along with the rest of the curious crowd, but Nicholas was persistent. He was trying to reach the tail of the cart, where the arm of a dead pirate dangled. One guard struck him with the butt end of his pike, knocking him to the ground. Undaunted, Nicholas pulled himself up and tried again to reach the limp bodies.

Ned was right behind him. He caught at him by his sleeve and swung him round to face him.

"Nicholas. The guards will not let you through. You'll get hurt."

Nicholas's eyes widened as he recognized Ned. "But I must touch one of them," he said. "I want to be well."

Ned realized the youth was thinking of the old superstition that the touch of a dead man would cure epilepsy. Ned shook his head. "It's not true, Nicholas. Do you hear me? It's nonsense."

He'd managed to pull the lad to one side as the cart rumbled on and the crowd followed in its wake along the wharf's edge.

"It *is* true," said Nicholas. "Master Humphreys told me. That was why he used to take me out with him to get the fingers."

Ned had stopped breathing. "Fingers?"

"Yes. We went out at night with the other gardeners. Sometimes we were in strange clothes. Mummers' clothes. I was frightened at first but Master Humphreys told me it was all right."

"You were a mummer?"

"Sometimes, yes. There was a soldier, and a fool, and a man, a doctor, who was supposed to make people better." He shivered. "I was dressed up, too, as a Turkish knight. People used to laugh at us all, and they gave us money. But sometimes, it was different. Sometimes the others frightened people, and hurt them. And I had to hurt them, too, but only when they were dead! I had to cut their little fingers off."

Behind them there was a great creaking of chains and ropes as the *Peppercorn* was prepared for release from her restraints.

"It was you," breathed Ned. "You. All the time . . ."

"Only because I was told to! Master Humphreys said it would make me well. He said the cut-off finger of a murdered man is a better cure than anything, because after the murder all of the power of Mercury is concentrated in that one little piece of the body."

Nicholas Lovett. The innocent instrument of Stephen Humphreys. Who had sent the mummers after the men who talked of Auriel.

"Don't tell anyone else," Ned said. "Not ever."

"That's what Master Humphreys said. Do you know where he is? I've been looking for him," said Nicholas, looking around. "But I can't find him anywhere."

"Oh, Nicholas. He's dead, too. Didn't you know?"

Nicholas stared at him with shock in his simple face. "No," he said. "No, you're lying." He turned and ran away into the crowd, who were gathering now round the *Peppercorn,* which would soon begin her grating slide down the narrow ramp toward the churning gray water of the river.

On the gun platform, the artillerymen were preparing to load the seven cannon. Had Pat and his men succeeded in what they were trying to do? There were shouted orders nearby; a small troop of the Prince's soldiers climbed up to surround the guns, and to present arms to the King. Ned guessed they were there to prevent anyone seeing that the cannon were also being loaded with shot. He looked quickly to where Prince Henry stood with his entourage. He tried, but failed, to see one small boy. Of Pat and his men, and of Pelham, there was no sign. Had he failed, yet again?

The soldiers retreated. It was time. He saw the gunners lighting the long cords soaked in saltpeter and holding them to the cannon. Silence fell around the platform. Moments went by. He knew that once ignited, the explosive force of a correct mixture of saltpeter, charcoal, and sulfur within the cannon muzzles would be ferocious. But there was nothing. He pushed closer; saw the gunners' faces; saw their dawning incredulity. The seven great cannon were silent. The gunners spoke hurriedly to one another, their expressions conveying dismay, shock. Someone came with another taper, and they watched and waited in growing anger as this catastrophe unfolded. For one gun not to fire was a mishap. For all seven to fail was a disaster. They would have to be unloaded and charged up again, and that would mean revealing that they were loaded with shot.

Ned felt a hand on his shoulder. Pat said quietly to Ned, "You were right. Those cannon were loaded. But we mixed in the extra charcoal. They'll just think it was the river damp that got to the powder. Someone's head will roll for not storing it properly."

Ned could sense a growing consternation amongst the soldiers and officials who knew what had been supposed to happen; an ominous rumbling, like a distant thunderstorm gathering. The tension around the *Peppercorn,* amongst all the men responsible for her launching, was palpable. Ned said to Pat, urgently, "That was only a part of it. You must take your men and look for Luke. I have sent the doctor to bring the little boy out from the Prince's escort. Kate's son is in terrible danger."

"How will we get him away, in God's name? The boy is a hostage. They will be watching him like hawks."

"I told Luke to go to the Prince's men at the moment the guns failed to fire, and to tell them that the household the boy comes from has just been stricken by the plague. That he must be kept away from the Prince at all costs."

"So they'll want Luke and the boy a million miles away."

"I hope so," said Ned. "I hope so. It will at least give them a chance—" He was already fighting his way toward Prince Henry's men, knowing that Pat and the others would be following close behind.

Then as he pushed through the hundreds of spectators who thronged the riverside, still hoping to see the *Peppercorn* afloat, he saw a line of men, heavily armed, in the blue and gold livery of the East India Company.

They had gathered out of nowhere, it seemed. But clearly they had their orders. Ned saw how with immaculate and purposeful discipline they drew themselves up round the Prince's small army—Spenser's men—until they had surrounded them. The Prince was on the ceremonial dais, talking to his father. If he noticed the swift maneuvering below, he pretended not to.

But he could not ignore Cecil: little Cecil, dressed in black, who came hurrying up the steps to the royal pair and said in his clear ringing voice to the Prince and the King, "Your Royal Highnesses, you are surrounded by treachery! You must leave at once; please permit yourselves to be escorted from here to safety!"

King James grew red, and blustered in his fright and anxiety. Prince Henry was pale and silent. Ned knew the young heir was watching all his hopes evaporate into nothing. The Prince would realize, now, that Cecil and his men had been there watching and waiting. Cecil must have surmised, when the cannon failed to fire, that the guns would have signaled the moment of action. He would know soon enough, when his own men took possession of the guns, that they were loaded, and were meant to fire on the King's men.

Ned heard Spenser shouting to his men. The old soldier was trying to rally his surrounded troops, urging them to defiance. But his soldiers realized, perhaps, as Spenser refused to, that the game was up. A few of them reached for their swords, but within moments Spenser himself was surrounded and was being swiftly marched away. By Cecil's men. And then Ned saw the blue-coated ranks of the East India Company's men drawing out pistols and moving in to disarm all Spenser's followers, making them throw their weapons all in a heap. It was all done so quickly, so cleverly, that many of the crowds still watching the *Peppercorn* poised above her slipway, and hissing their disappointment at the failure of the second launch, would not even have noticed.

And then Ned heard a quiet voice behind him. A voice that froze his blood.

"We can make this easy, Warriner, or difficult. Sadly your friend the doctor is dead. We do not want anyone else to die, you and I. Do we?"

Ned spun round. It was Lovett. He was dressed in the livery of the Prince. His thin, cold face was quite calm, but there was a sheen of sweat on his forehead, and his eyes flickered restlessly down to the child at his side.

For he held Sebastian tightly, his hand digging into the tiny boy's shoulder. Sebastian was pressing his fist to his mouth and was trembling, clearly on the verge of tears.

Ned said, "Let the boy go. Then we'll talk."

Sebastian broke into a sob. "Hush. Hush," said Lovett soothingly, bending over him. But he still gripped the child tightly. He looked up at Ned again. "He can go as soon as you and I have made a deal, Warriner."

Ned said, "With *you*?"

Lovett pursed his lips and frowned. "I don't think you realize," he said, "just how many people there are who would like to kill you. You know too much."

"Let the child go."

"Hear me out first. You and I have so much in common, Warriner. We would work well together. You were responsible for the cannon that did not fire, weren't you? So our plans were wrecked, and Cecil's men were able to move in. And still our foolish, cowardly King suspects absolutely nothing. It is all over. And damn you to hell for it."

Sebastian tried to take a few shaky steps away from his captor, but Lovett intensified his grip on the little boy, and Sebastian began to cry. Ned thought he glimpsed Pat, somewhere in the crowds who were drifting along the quayside behind Lovett's back. But then he was gone. A false hope. He repeated, "Set the child free. Take me instead."

"Warriner, I want you as an ally, not a hostage. You are on our side. Don't you realize that Cecil is in the pay of Spain? He wants peace at any price—even, some would say, at the cost of treachery. After all, he gets gold from Spain."

"Are you claiming Cecil is in the pay of the Spaniards?"

"He always has been. Ever since he decided he wanted the war with our Dutch allies to end."

Hugrance had told Ned about Humphreys, visiting the Spanish Embassy at St. Etheldreda's and coming away with gold. For *Cecil*. And the betrayal at Ostend—Humphreys also, working for Cecil...Ned said heavily, "I had not realized anyone could sink so low and live with himself."

"Ah," rejoined Lovett bitterly, "but Cecil would say that he was acting in England's very best interests. Cecil says that peace is all-important. But we both know there is too high a price to be paid. You and I should not have been on opposing sides. *But there is still time.*"

"No. It is over. And even if your men here had succeeded, how would you have got the rest of the country to support you?"

Lovett looked at him angrily, and with spirit; he said, "My God, Warriner, we already have half the country on our side. People hate the Scottish King and his extravagant court and his self-serving, corrupt councillors. They hate the friendship with Spain, and the prospect of the Spanish marriage for Prince Henry. Didn't you hear how the crowds gathered in Cheapside this morning to cheer the destruction of the deputy ambassador's house? There are countless Protestants within an hour's distance of London who are ready to ride in with their troops and support our cause. So many men have been waiting a long time for this."

Ned said, "For the last time, set the child free. Then I might talk."

"Only if you agree to a deal."

Sebastian was becoming hysterical. Lovett swung him up, fiercely, into his arms, looked around; whether for help, or escape, Ned was never sure, because just then someone else was there, forcing his way through the crowds toward them.

It was Pelham. He charged into Lovett and pulled Sebastian from him, setting him on the ground and shouting at the bewildered little boy to flee. Then Pat and Davey and Pentinck were there, too, and in all the confusion, Pentinck heaved Sebastian up and darted with him into the safety of the crowd; while Pelham flung himself on Lovett and was struggling with him face-to-face. But Lovett got one hand free to draw his pistol from his belt. He fired at point-blank range, and Pelham fell, with blood pouring from a chest wound. Pat and Davey seized Lovett, too late. Ned crouched over Pelham, who was writhing in agony, clutching his bloodstained fingers to his chest. He was choking on his own blood. Ned said, "You've saved your son. Do you hear me, Pelham? You've saved your son's life."

Pelham coughed more blood and fell back, his eyes closed. Ned looked up at the captive Lovett, his anger blazing. In the distance he saw Cecil's soldiers hurrying toward them, their pistols raised.

"We should have been on the same side," Lovett called out to Ned, struggling to free himself from his captors' grip. "The same side, Warriner..."

"Stand back," shouted Ned to Pat and Davey as Cecil's men drew closer, because he could see them taking aim at Lovett with their wheel-lock pistols. "Stand away from him!"

They let Lovett go free, and instantly he threw himself on Ned, slashing at him with a knife he'd drawn from his belt. Ned gripped Lovett's arm to try to disarm him.

"You should have stayed abroad," gasped Lovett, "you should have stuck to your boys and your lecherous old men. At least they paid you well."

He got his hand free and struck again with his knife, catching Ned across the temple. Ned brought his arm up to knock aside Lovett's wrist; but then he heard the crack of gunfire, and Lovett's body jerked upward, and fell back.

Ned sprang away, feeling the blood trickle down his face from the knife cut. He was under no illusion that Cecil's men would not be after him next. He dived to the ground for cover behind a pile of coiled rope, but already they were moving in on him, taking fresh aim.

The crowds had fallen back, shocked by the sound of gunfire, by the sight of blood. Ned saw Davey and Pat hovering uncertainly at a distance, but he called to them, "Get away. Save yourselves. Save the child—"

There was a sudden crash of breaking glass, then a crackle and a blaze of blinding light like the fireworks on the coronation day of James I, but so near, Ned could smell the sulfur. Smoke billowed around, blinding him, choking him.

Dimly he saw Cecil's men, blinded also, reeling back with their hands covering their eyes. Through a gap in the smoke he saw mad Lazarus pulling another large glass phial out from under his cloak and throwing it at them with a howl of glee. It crashed against the wall behind them and there was another outburst of light, like a fountain of fire. As it dimmed, and the noise subsided, Ned was aware of a new, very different sound: the sound of female voices chattering and laughing.

He turned round and saw the Lady Arbella and some of her court friends, attended by servants and pageboys, promenading in all their peacock finery along the wharf toward him, exclaiming with delight at the sight of the ships and the soldiers. There were so many of them that for a while the riverside was filled with the color and vividness of their clothes and sparkling jewels; and as the sulfurous smoke cleared, the soldiers and the commoners alike fell back to gape at them.

"Fireworks," exclaimed the Lady Arbella Stuart, the plain spinster who had once been the focus herself of secretive and foiled plots to place her on the throne. She pointed with delight to the curling fingers of smoke still rising from Lazarus's incendiary display. "How I love fireworks! And all these fine soldiers; I never guessed there would be so many here today. I am so glad that we were in time for the excitement. What does it matter that neither of the ships have been launched?"

Ned felt someone touching his shoulder. He spun round and saw Kate. She paled at the sight of the blood on his hands and face, but her voice was steady as she said, "You have a few moments to get away before Arbella and her friends move on. Pat and his men have Sebastian safe. Please hurry."

Ned pointed to Arbella and her noisy companions in disbelief. "But what is she doing here?"

"I told her there would be fireworks," she said. "Of a sort. And I asked Lazarus to provide them. Now come. Everything is done."

41.

Now cease, my lute. This is the last
Labour that thou and I shall waste,
And ended is that we begun.
Now is this song both sung and past.
My lute, be still, for I have done.

SIR THOMAS WYATT (C.1503–1542)
"MY LUTE, AWAKE"

YOU MUST GET OUT OF HERE," SAID PAT. "OUT OF the country. You know too much. Jesus, man, if they find you they'll string you up from the topmast of the *Peppercorn* the instant they succeed in getting her launched. To be sure, it would be even better entertainment for everyone than watching those poor pirates dance."

In the combination of confusion caused by the fireworks and Arbella, Pat and his men had hurried Ned away from the shipyard and along the river's edge to an empty fisherman's cottage that lay a quarter of a mile away hidden behind a willow thicket on the marshy ground by Deptford Creek. They would be safe there, said Pat in his grave voice, for just a little while. He ordered his men to watch for pursuers from all sides, while indoors tallow candles were lit. The place smelled of the old nets that lay in heaps against one wall. Kate was in the corner with Sebastian, holding him very tightly, but gazing all the time at Ned.

Ned took the kerchief Pat had offered him and wiped some of the blood from his forehead where Lovett's knife had caught him. Then he turned to Kate. "Is Sebastian all right?"

"He is unhurt," said Kate quietly. "But he was so frightened. And he saw what happened to Francis."

Ned bent at Sebastian's knees and took his small hands in his. "Your father," he said, "was a very brave man. He loved you. Thanks to him, you are safe now."

He stood up and said to Kate, "Pat is right. I know too much. Cecil, Northampton, Henry's supporters: they will all want me. I must leave, or I'll endanger you all."

Kate kissed Sebastian and sat him in the corner, on a pile of old canvas. Little Pentinck kneeled down next to the boy and, pulling a length of twine from his pocket, began to show him some sailors' knots. Sebastian rubbed at his eyes with his chubby fists and started to smile through his tears.

Kate said to Ned, "Let me clean the cut on your forehead. We have a little while, I think. There must be some water somewhere I can bathe it with." She went out to look. Pat was waiting, close by; he said to Ned, "There is a ship anchored at Gravesend. It leaves for France tonight. There is room for you, and your lady and the little one, on board."

Then Kate was back, with a basin of water, and her clean handkerchief. While Pat and his men went outside to watch for any sign of pursuit, and Pentinck followed, holding Sebastian's hand, Kate began to bathe Ned's wound. She said, "Ralegh will never be freed now, will he?"

Ned shook his head. "At least he has not been implicated in all this. He would have been proud of you, for the part you played back there. Lazarus—the fireworks—Arbella. You saved your son. And me."

She smiled, though her clear green eyes sparkled with tears. "I couldn't let you take everything upon yourself, could I? I wasn't sure—I didn't know exactly what was going to happen. But my father used to say, when he talked of warfare, that a timely distraction was worth fifty soldiers, so I thought of Arbella and her friends. I told her there was to be a spectacle there which everyone would be talking of. I also told her that her presence would annoy Cecil, whom she hates."

Ned laughed aloud, and took her hand and kissed it.

"When I found Lazarus," Kate went on, "wandering along the wharves, looking for you for some obscure reason, I explained to him what had happened, how you were in danger, because crazy as it sounds, I guessed he might know what to do. Where to get what he needed."

"As one would." He smiled wonderingly. "You were caught up in a desperate plot to kill the King and put his son on the throne; there were hostile soldiers everywhere, people dying, and you thought Lazarus might help. Why was he looking for me? He knows I should have killed him long ago."

"I don't know. He was muttering some story about making gold."

"In that case I don't want to hear it."

"But he saved your life—"

"No. You did," he said.

She turned her attention to his wound again. "Ned, why did you do all this?"

"For you," he said quietly. "And for Sebastian."

She looked at him quickly.

"Kate, Kate, why didn't you tell me earlier about our child? I would have come back to England for you, even though my life was in danger. You could both have come away with me."

She shook her head, closed her eyes briefly. "I would never have forced you into anything. Never."

He was still holding her hand. "You should have trusted me. You should have known that I would have gladly taken you both anywhere with me."

She said, "Ned—"

"What is it? You can tell me everything. You know that."

"Ned." She drew her hand away and pressed her palms to her temples. "Sebastian is not yours. He is Pelham's child."

He felt as if Lazarus's gunpowder were exploding inside his brain. He said at last, "No. He cannot be."

"He is Pelham's." She looked up at him. "He was born ten

months after you left. I would have told you, but by the time
we had the chance to talk, properly, you had already guessed,
already *assumed* he was yours. So I said nothing, although I
kept meaning to. The time was never right. Ned? Ned, please
say something to me."

He said quietly, "There's nothing really to say, is there?"

The door crashed open, and Lazarus stood there, cackling, drunk. Pat stood behind him, shrugging his shoulders in
apology.

"I have it, Master Warriner!" the Scotsman cried out.
"Didn't I tell you I'd find it?"

Kate stood up. She was very pale. "What have you got,
Lazarus?"

"Why, the Philosopher's Stone, of course." He staggered a
little, then pulled a phial of dull, reddish-gray powder out of
his pocket and held it up. His breath stank of wine.

Ned said wearily, "Lazarus, your fireworks were spectacu-
lar. I am duly grateful. But the Philosopher's Stone? I don't
think so. Leave us alone, will you?"

"But I really have got it! It was all thanks to something
your lad Robin found in that letter of Dr. Dee's. He explained
it to me, the poor, clever boy. *'Now increase your fire in the
vessel of orichalcum until it shows a redness like blood...'*
Orichalcum, you see, that's the alchemists' word for brass.
Robin told me to try using a brass crucible. Then he showed
me the rest of what he'd copied from your letter. He told me I
had to heat it again and again, and recite the names of the
seven angels—*'by the names of the Seven are the impurities
purged away—'"*

"Not angels," said Ned wearily, "not angels, but cannon.
Go away, Lazarus."

"Cannon?" Lazarus looked quickly at Kate. "Is he all
right?" She nodded, and Lazarus turned back to Ned with enthusiasm. "Hear me out awhile, my lad. You'll be glad you listened. So, you see, I said the names over and over, while I
heated the mixture in the brass crucible, like Robin told me.
Sabathiel, I said, and Madimiel, and Zedekiel, and the rest—
and it worked, you see? I did it! I have the Stone—I can
change anything into gold!"

Ned said, "It's nonsense, Lazarus." He went to the door to look out. Pat waited just outside. The others were posted around the building, watching the bleak marshes and the distant line of the river.

Then Kate called out to him from inside the room. "Ned, Ned, I think you'd better look at this."

He looked round. Lazarus, grinning insanely, was holding out something that gleamed in the candlelight. It was Robin's tiny vase of silver, the vase with the crooked handles. Only now it was not silver, but gold.

Ned took it and put it down on the table. "Listen. Don't you think I've had enough of all your nonsense?" Lazarus's face fell. Ned went on, "Have you got your notes? The ones you copied from the Auriel letter?"

"Of course I have! I take them everywhere with me. Man, d'ye think I'd ever part with Dr. Dee's recipe for gold?"

He pulled a sheaf of papers out of his pocket, still smiling happily. Ned took the sheets of paper, looked at them, then walked over to the grate and threw them one by one on the fire.

Lazarus shrieked, "What the devil do you think you're doing, laddie?" He ran to the grate, moaning.

"I'm destroying something crazy and false." Ned pulled out his Auriel letter from inside his jerkin and looked at it one last time. *"To Auriel, I will give the gift of gold..."* He dropped it also onto the flames.

Lazarus snatched at it as it blazed up, but he was too late. "You've gone mad," he exclaimed, blowing on his scorched fingers, "quite mad."

"No," said Ned, "but I would have been mad, I think, to believe you."

Lazarus turned and ran out, wailing and tearing his hair. He had left behind Robin's little vase. Kate picked it up and turned it slowly. It gleamed softly in her hands. "Ned ... ?"

"It's a trick," he said, taking it from her, "known by all silversmiths. Robin told me about it. You soak a linen rag in a solution of chloride of gold and burn the rag to ashes, then rub the ashes on the surface of a silver dish until it becomes gilded. Lazarus was mad to think he could fool me like that."

She put it down reluctantly. "At any rate he saved you with his fireworks." She had moved close to him and said very quietly, "Ned, I hope you know that I wish with all my heart that Sebastian were yours."

He took her hands. "I still want him," he said. "I still want both of you."

"Oh, Ned..."

He held out his arms to her. "Pat has told me," he said, "that there's a ship to France, leaving tonight. There are berths for us. We can make a new life for ourselves."

"Oh," she breathed, clinging to him, "it is such a beautiful dream."

"Not a dream," he said, but he knew then what she was going to say.

"Dear Ned," she said, lifting her hands to take his face between her palms, "I shall love you till I die. But I cannot take Sebastian on such a journey. Not yet. He needs comfort, good food, and warmth; he becomes ill so often. You and I, we would tramp the highways together. You would play your lute and we would sleep beneath the stars. But Sebastian is not strong enough for such a life. Not yet."

The door opened. Pat said, "The wherry is waiting to take you to Gravesend, Ned. You must leave here very soon." He left and shut the door.

Ned took Kate in his arms. He said, "What if Cecil and his men learn of your part in all this? In helping me?"

She shook her head. "I don't think he will. Arbella will say nothing because she hates him. And anyway, my relatives will defend me. My uncle Shrewsbury is on good terms with the great men in the Privy Council, and he is feared, not just a little, by them. Cecil would not lightly choose to lift his finger against him."

"Or against those whom he chose to protect."

"Yes." Kate was crying now. "Yes...Ned, when I saw him yesterday, he told me that I could go with Sebastian anytime to stay at his home in the country. I think Sebastian would grow well again, far from London, far from our enemies. Come with me, Ned. There will be room for you there."

"I cannot come with you." He knew that he would be

hunted down, even there. Too many powerful men needed his silence. He smiled. "I'll go abroad and be a lute player again. And someday I will come back to you."

"Or someday," she said, "someday, we will come and join you, Sebastian and I, when you are one of the most famous musicians in Europe. You must write to me. We will be together again." She kissed him.

There was another, more urgent knock at the door, and Pat came in. "You will miss the tide for sure if you don't go now."

Pat was holding out his lute to him. Someone must have brought it from Bride's Fields. Ned picked it up, and his bundle, and Robin's little gilded pot.

He went outside. He kissed Kate, and Sebastian, and shook the hands of his friends.

He left, and he did not look back.

A T THE DEAD OF NIGHT NED WAS ROWED DOWNRIVER to Gravesend, past the unlaunched ships, past the gallows where the pirates' bodies had hung, past Greenwich, where Northampton's palace was. Northampton, who had colluded with his old enemy Cecil, to save the realm from treachery. To save the King from his son.

Ned sat in the bow of the small boat, wrapped in his cloak against the cold wind. The lantern swinging from a pole on the stern gleamed on the little vase, which he held in his hands, as he thought of Robin, and of Master Jebb, and the stories Robin had told him. They reached Gravesend, where the ship was waiting to set sail for Calais. Ned paid the boatman and scrambled up the side onto the deck, where he found himself a corner in the lee of some spare sails. It was cold, but not as cold as his heart. He leaned back and gazed at the stars, and breathed in the scent of far-off oceans. He thought how Kate would have loved all this, the open sea and the sky. He drew out his lute and started to play an old song.

"So he hoisted his sail and away went he,
Away, away to some far countrie . . ."

As the sailors cast off he put away his lute and pulled out Robin's little vase again. It gleamed like fire beneath the light of the moon. Because he did not want to think of the past, or of the future, he idly got out his knife and began to scrape at it.

The golden coating was thicker than he had expected. He tried again, using the point of his knife in a different place. As he worked he remembered Lazarus's anguished cry as he tossed the Auriel letter onto the flames: *"What the devil do you think you're doing, laddie?"*

He turned the pot over and tried to scrape away the coating inside the dish, but he made no impression. As deep as his knife went, he found gold.

"Now increase your fire in the vessel of orichalcum until it shows a redness like blood taken from a sound person..."

Blood. Robin's blood.

He scraped again, weighing it in his hand; he remembered Lazarus shouting out, "I have it, Master Warriner, I have it!"

The little pot was of solid gold.

And he had burned the Auriel letter.

He leaned back against the mast and there, as the deck rolled gently beneath him, he laughed. Other travelers, and two or three sailors, came toward him curiously; they gathered round, watching him. "Are you going to share the joke?"

"Yes. Yes, if you like. I've thrown away the secret of gold. I won it in a dice game, and I've thrown it away. I've also lost the woman I love..."

He sank his head in his hands. Someone brought out a flask of strong wine and pushed it toward him; it was the only remedy for life, they said. They drank to his health; they all got drunk, there beneath the stars, and talked of the places they were going to, the places they'd been: all the hells on this earth.

At last he slept where he lay. In the cold light of dawn he dowsed his face in the rain that had started to sweep across the sea, and got out the stub of pencil and paper which he used to write down his songs. He set his face to the gray horizon where France lay, and began to write what he could remember.

"To Auriel, I will give the gift of gold..." What came next?

And the shores of England, shrouded in mist and rain, receded as he struggled to remember all he'd learned of crucibles, of calcinations, and cohobations. He thought he would go to Prague. They would help him there, the mad alchemists like Lazarus who dwelt in the shadow of the castle. In the Street of Gold.

He saw that his fellow travelers were watching him from a distance now, nudging one another, laughing at him. He bent his head lower over the paper.

F AR AWAY, AS THE WINTER SUN DAWNED OVER LONdon, the tide rose and fell again. By mid-morning King James, with his son at his side, was able to watch with pride as the two ships were successfully launched. And Ralegh, John Dee's Auriel, paced the Tower walls, dreaming his forlorn dreams of gold, and far-off lands, and freedom.

POSTSCRIPT

Auriel Rising is a work of fiction, but the following historical notes might be of interest.

IN OCTOBER 1612, PRINCE HENRY, AGED EIGHTEEN, was suddenly taken ill. Desperate remedies were suggested by his doctors, and there were rumors that the Prince had been poisoned, though his sickness was most probably typhoid fever. When he died, on 6th November, both court and country were plunged into grief. The Earl of Dorset wrote that "our rising sun is set ere scarce he has shone."

Henry's younger brother Charles, a sickly child who had not been expected to survive infancy, came to the throne as King Charles I in 1625. King Charles's conflicts with Parliament led to the English Civil War, and he was beheaded in 1649.

SIR WALTER RALEGH—ONCE QUEEN ELIZABETH'S FA-vorite, a vice admiral of the Fleet, poet, historian, and explorer—remained a prisoner in the Tower until 1616, when he was released in order to sail to Guiana, to renew his search for a gold mine. With him sailed his young son, Wat. Ralegh's men, on landing at the mouth of the Orinoco, clashed with the

Spanish settlers there, and Ralegh's son was killed in the fighting. Ralegh had to abandon the expedition, and returned home in ignominy.

The Spaniards complained to King James about the attack by Ralegh's men on their settlement. James, eager to appease Spain, with whom he was seeking an alliance, revived the old sentence of treason passed on Ralegh in 1603 and ordered his execution.

"A period brainteaser reminiscent of
Caleb Carr's *The Alienist.*"
—*People*

THE MUSIC OF THE SPHERES
by
ELIZABETH REDFERN

In 18th-century London, a strangler walks the teeming streets. His victims are prostitutes with red hair. Before they die, they hear whispers that speak of stars—and of a woman named Selene.

"AS IF *SILENCE OF THE LAMBS* HAS BEEN RESET IN THE NAPOLEONIC ERA." —*BOOKLIST*

"RICHLY ATMOSPHERIC...QUITE WONDERFUL." —*USA TODAY*

"UNPUTDOWNABLE." —*THE GUARDIAN* (LONDON)

0-515-13239-X

Available wherever books are sold or at
www.penguin.com

J664

Penguin Group (USA) Inc. Online

What will you be reading tomorrow?

Tom Clancy, Patricia Cornwell, W.E.B. Griffin,
Nora Roberts, William Gibson, Robin Cook,
Brian Jacques, Catherine Coulter, Stephen King,
Dean Koontz, Ken Follett, Clive Cussler,
Eric Jerome Dickey, John Sandford,
Terry McMillan…

You'll find them all at
http://www.penguin.com

*Read excerpts and newsletters, find tour
schedules, and enter contest.*

Subscribe to Penguin Group (USA) Inc. Newsletters
and get an exclusive inside look
at exciting new titles and the authors you love
long before everyone else does.

PENGUIN GROUP (USA) INC. NEWS
http://www.penguin.com/news